Society Stronghold
A Sovereign Magi Society novel
Book 2

T.J. Vensarn

ISBN-10: 0-692-72955-0
ISBN-13: 978-0-692-72955-7

Cover design by T.J. Vensarn. Artwork by: Nadica Boshkovska
Check out author T.J. Vensarn online at www.vensarn.com
Check out the artist's gallery online at
http://theswanmaiden.deviantart.com/gallery/

Acknowledgments:

I can't even begin to properly thank everyone who has helped or given support to this book, but of course I must first and foremost thank my wife and children who have been a blessing throughout this journey.

I also want to send a big thank you to my friend and fraternal brother Bill who has been a huge source of encouragement and who consistently goes out of his way to support and promote my books. Without Bill, the lands of Menelia would never have found their way to paper.

The Sovereign Magi Society Series

Book 1: Society Dawning

Book 2: Society Stronghold

Book 3: Society Inciting (1st quarter 2017)

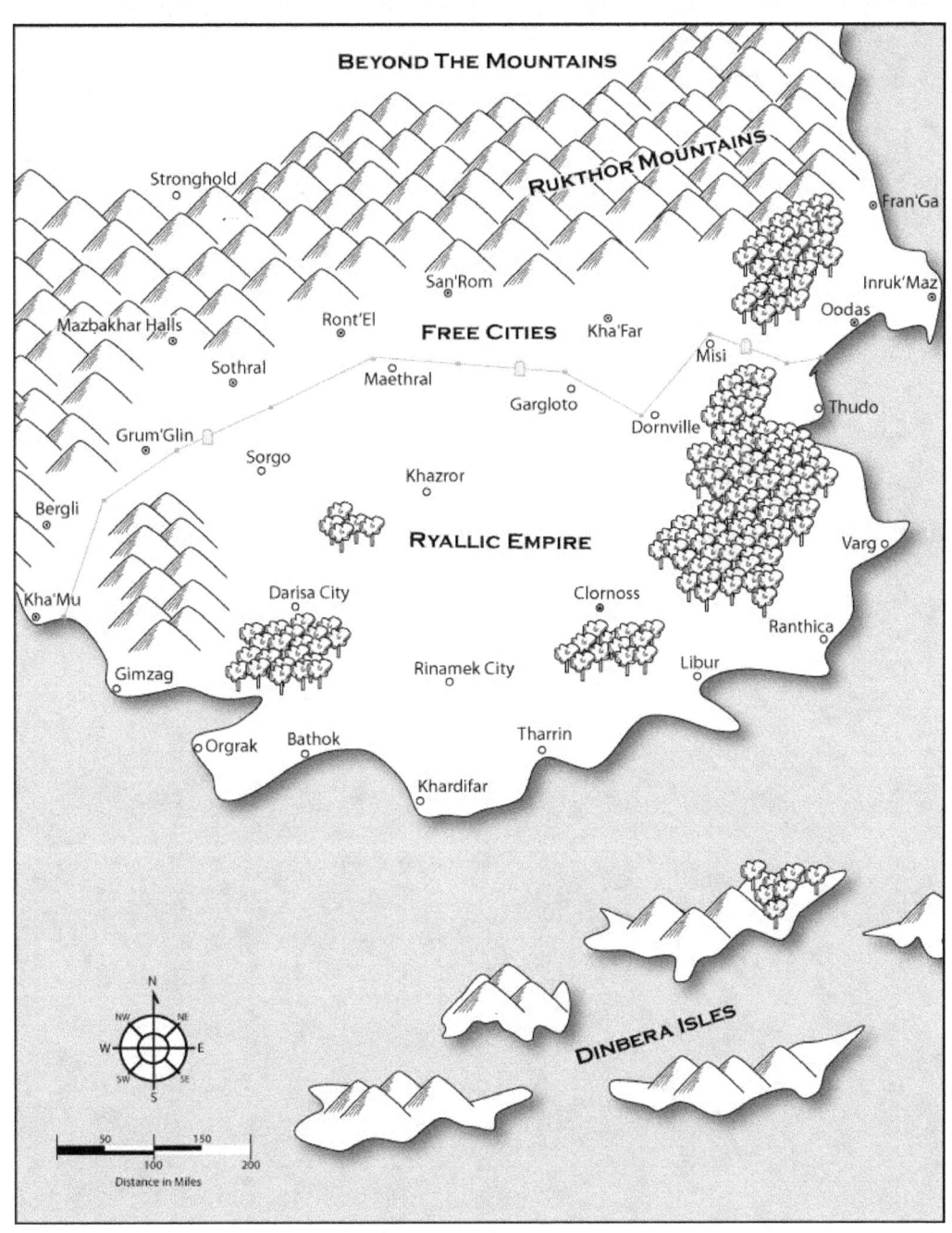

CHAPTER 1

Rissyl

Each time he knocked on a door he grew more impatient. After twelve months, and thousands of homes visited, the search for Bisangar's Signet Ring was beginning to seem hopeless.

Rissyl paused and looked to Aruk, who flashed a goofy grin.

He smiled slightly and knocked on the door.

After a short wait, an old man opened his door and looked at the two Magi. "What do you want?"

"Well met, sir. I am Rissyl and this is my friend Aruk." Both Magi smiled and nodded at the old man at the door. They wore elaborate cloaks that were red on the top and hood, and white on the bottom. The cloaks had intricate runes sewn into the edges down the front, and they were made from very thin fabric that seemed to flow like smoke in the slight breeze.

Rissyl was a young man in his late teens, almost twenty. He was average height and slightly more than average girth. He thought of himself as a fairly decent looking guy. His curly light-brown hair was recently trimmed, so it wasn't as wild as it could sometimes get. He had neither beard nor mustache, but his rough stubble was overdue for a shave.

Aruk was a middle aged Magi of average height and small stature. His bushy brown hair was pushed back away from his face. He was clean shaven and Rissyl thought he usually sported a naturally trustworthy look.

The man at the door frowned and didn't reply.

Rissyl continued, "We're Magi and we had hoped to chat with you a bit."

"You're not coming in my house, get away from the door." Rissyl thought the old man was dismissing them, but the man walked out of his house as the Magi backed away from the door. He shut the door behind himself and walked slowly to a rocking chair on the front porch. He sat down gently and pointed at a bench.

The two Magi sat down on the bench.

Rissyl said, "My friend and I are looking for an old ring that used to belong to the Magi, it might have been in the possession of a Magi named Rifin long ago. It would have a small bird engraved on each side, and symbols like these." He pointed at the runes on the front trim of his cloak.

Rissyl and Aruk were searching for Bisangar's Signet Ring. After a difficult trek beneath the mountains, they found their long-lost Stronghold and it was guarded by Rolimi. The guardians demanded the signet ring before the Magi would be allowed to take possession of their magical fortress. A century ago, after the Betrayal, the Magi Society entrusted the Stronghold into the Rolimi's care and protection to keep it out of the hands of the empire.

Now Rissyl and his companions wanted to reclaim the Stronghold in their efforts to rebuild the Sovereign Magi Society. It used to be the headquarters of the Magi Society and it housed libraries, schools, martial training halls, and other facilities. Supposedly, the Stronghold contained a wealth of knowledge on the ways of magic, and it held an arsenal of magical artifacts and equipment.

For the last several months Aruk, Rissyl, and several other Magi had been visiting with farmers, ranchers, and people from many of the small villages around the Rukthor Mountains looking for the signet ring or some clue to its whereabouts.

They were focused on the area just south of the mountains thanks to evidence that Sarasa had found. Shortly after the raid of the Motlite breeding camp she began searching through Randol's extensive library looking for any leads about the whereabouts of the ring, and she found a clue in an old book. The book said a Magi named Rifin had taken the ring for safe keeping when the Magi Society sealed the Stronghold. The book said that Rifin kept the ring and settled down on a farm south of the mountains.

It was a solid clue, but unfortunately the mountains stretched for over a thousand miles and Rifin could have settled a hundred miles or more south of the mountains. That left an area almost one hundred thousand square miles, with countless farms, ranches, and hamlets scattered about.

Therefore, the Magi had been tirelessly searching the area south of the mountains for any clue about the ring or about the Magi named Rifin. They weren't the only ones looking for the ring. The Magi were in a race against the necromancers who wanted to gain control of the Stronghold for their own nefarious reasons.

After a moment the old man said, "Why would someone give you an old valuable ring, if they did have it?"

"I'm offering a raptor for this ring."

Rissyl could tell that the old man was surprised, because his eyebrows raised noticeably. A platinum raptor coin was a fortune to common folks, and

Rissyl guessed that the old man probably paid a raptor or less for his house.

"Why would you pay so much for an old ring?" The old man looked skeptical.

With a shrug Rissyl said, "Magi business. Let's just say that the ring is very important to us."

The old man was quiet for several long minutes as he stared at the young Magi. Rissyl was starting to think that the man simply wasn't going to answer at all. Finally the man said, "My grandfather was a Magi, you can look through his things."

He stood up slowly and led the Magi into the house to a cluttered room in the back.

He pointed at a large trunk along the far wall. "All of his things are in there. Pull it out and look for the ring, if you want."

Rissyl and Aruk pulled the trunk away from the wall and opened the lid. Inside they found several old articles of clothing, shoes, gloves and the like. Further down were some hand painted portraits in frames. Rissyl carefully took these things out of the trunk and placed them aside.

Towards the bottom of the trunk he found an old green and white Diviner's cloak, and a small stack of books. Rissyl looked through them and found that some of them were old spell books. He placed them and the cloak aside. On the bottom of the trunk was a leather pouch.

He opened the pouch anxiously, desperately hoping to find Bisangar's Signet Ring among the items inside. He poured the contents of the pouch into his lap but a quick search through the pendants, cuff links, snuff cases, watches, and other various trinkets didn't reveal the ring that they sought.

He was disappointed as he returned the items back into the pouch. Rissyl sighed, "Well, no luck. But, thank you for letting us look through your grandfather's things." He began putting items back into the trunk.

Once all of the items, other than the cloak and spell books, were back in the trunk, he and Aruk pushed it back where they found it.

He looked at the old man and said, "There is a conflict brewing between the Magi and the necromancers, and probably the empire." He held up the cloak and spell books. "These items would help us in these troubled times. Could we buy them from you?"

The old man took the items from Rissyl and looked at them. He flipped through some of the pages of the books, and then handed the items back to him. "Take them, I don't need them."

The Magi stood up and Rissyl handed the old man some coins. He said,

"Thank you for your generosity."

They walked out of the old man's house, and made their way down the road a short distance.

Aruk turned to Rissyl and said, "It's getting late, and I told Tobilyn that I would meet her for dinner tonight."

He smiled at Aruk in surprise. "Aruk, you've got a new girl?"

Aruk smiled back with a wide grin. "I do! She is the daughter of a farmer that I met near Fran'Ga a few months ago. This will be our third dinner, and afterwards will be our first walk along the creek." He said the last part with a wink and the two men laughed.

Rissyl put his hand on Aruk's shoulder. "Good luck, my friend. I hope it is a fun night!"

The Magi gave a slight bow and then stepped back. He said, "Kur'Gezbar." One moment Aruk was standing on the street next to Rissyl, and the next moment he was gone.

Watching Aruk teleport reminded Rissyl how truly remarkable magic was and what a powerful gift he'd been given by Nalria, the goddess of magic. Just over a year ago his life had been much different. It was easy to get caught up in the troubles and challenges, and not appreciate the wonders of his magical powers.

Still mostly lost in thought, he continued down the road. He and Aruk had stopped at most of the homes in this little village south of Kha'Mu, and he wanted to visit a few more before he called it a night.

As he walked down the road to the next house, he heard someone approaching from behind. Without much conscious thought he summoned his Magi staff. It had been weeks since he'd last used it, so the staff was resting somewhere in the plane of magic where he stored it with the spell taught to him by his Rolimi teacher. It was a handy spell that allowed him to have quick access to his weapon when he needed it, without having to carry the large weapon all of the time. As he turned around, his red and white Magi Cloak spun and flowed in the slight breeze. Before him was a skinny little man who was almost entirely bald and had a pointy nose and narrow cheeks. The man walked towards him quickly, wearing rumpled old clothes and relying heavily on a walking cane.

He didn't hesitate when Rissyl turned to face him. Instead he walked directly up to the Magi. He stopped next to him and held out his hand to feel the fabric of Rissyl's cloak. He said, "You've been going around asking about a ring owned by Rifin."

Rissyl nodded, "I have. Do know something about it?"

"For a price."

He dug through his coin purse, pulled out a gold cardinal coin, and held it up.

The man took the coin quickly and said, "I know where Rifin lived, and I know his great granddaughter."

Rissyl's eyes went wide in surprise. "You do?"

He smiled and nodded, "Rifin built a farm east of Grum'Glin along the road between the city and the empire. It's along the road on the south side near the empire's wall. His great granddaughter lives there today with her husband and their kids. Her name is Nassani."

"How do you know this?"

The man studied his new golden coin. "I used to work on a farm just east of Grum'Glin. Nassani's husband was frequently at the pub and when he got drunk he loved to brag about his wife's powerful family, including a renowned Magi named Rifin."

Rissyl smiled broadly and patted the man on the shoulder. "Friend, thank you much for this news. It should be a great help."

The man held up the coin to inspect, and then put it into his pouch. He said, "I would've told you for a few copper falcons."

Rissyl reached into his purse and pulled out another cardinal. He handed it to the man and said, "And I would have paid you many cardinals."

They both laughed together as the man accepted the additional coin. As the man turned to leave, Rissyl said, "Safe travels, friend."

With just a wave the man walked away.

Rissyl grabbed his nexus gem and summoned enough magic to activate the communications gem. He prepared the magical artifact to deliver his verbal message to all other nexus gems. He said, "Found a clue. Rifin lived near Grum'Glin. Checking tomorrow." The stone glowed red briefly, and then the color faded.

Messages sent through the nexus gems needed to be short, and a gem couldn't receive a second message until its owner summoned the existing message and emptied the gem. However, he was happy to at least have a way to communicate some information to all of the other Magi.

A few moments later the gem glowed green softly. He held it up near his ear and summoned the magic to activate the gem. He heard Sarasa's voice saying, "I found something you need to see."

He smiled when he heard the gorgeous red-head's voice. It had been too long since he had heard it, and the message made him smile. As he considered his response to her, the gem began to glow green once again.

When he activated the gem it was Kimly's voice, saying, "Congrats Riz, I'm happy for you! Hope you find the ring!"

He was surprised. Kimly had vanished shortly after the Magi rescued her from the emperor's Motlite breeding camp. She spent a few weeks at Randol's as Sarge healed. Then one night she was just gone, and no one had heard anything from her since that night. Rissyl was half afraid that she had run off to join the necromancers. Until receiving her message, he didn't even know that she even had one of the nexus gems. Now that he knew that she had one, he could contact her at some point.

However, he would not be contacting her tonight. There was too much to do. He needed to send a message to Aruk to see if he wanted to join him for a visit with Nassani in the morning and most of all he needed to get home.

The feeling of excitement and vertigo was always present when he teleported, no matter how many times he had done it. As Rissyl arrived back home, he looked around and smiled. He was in the lower foothills south of the Taros Mountains, a small spur of low mountains in the western section of the Ryallic Empire. The area was sparsely wooded and hilly, with lush grasslands stretching out far and wide. Off to the north, the green foothills gave way to the grey rocky Taros Mountains. A mile or so to the west, the grasslands turned to the sandy shores of the sea. The city of Gimzag was several miles to the south, and it was the closest thing to civilization anywhere near his new home.

The strong summer winds blew in the smells of the sea, and he breathed them in happily. It was good to be back. He looked to the east and saw the buildings of his home. Up on the hill was the large cabin-style home and further off to the east was the smaller guest house. He had a large barn, beyond the guest house, down the road to the east. When he came home he always teleported to this spot, a hundred yards or so from the main cabin, to give himself time to enjoy the sights and smells of home as he walked there.

He had taken a good portion of the money his father gave him and bought this land almost a year ago. It was too dangerous to stay in his family's home in Sorgo. After Burga's death it would only be a matter of time before the empire linked the two of them and started asking questions. This land was far away from Sorgo, and it was within about an hour walk of the Gimzag portal stone.

Several months earlier, many Magi set out to find and activate all of the portal stones around the known-lands. Rissyl suspected that portal stones might exist that still sat inactive, but he was pleased with the progress that they had made in reestablishing the transportation network of days gone by.

As he walked towards his cabin, he looked off to his left and saw Cynia working in her large garden. His heart filled with joy at the sight of her and he couldn't resist the urge to teleport over behind her. He was very happy to find her at home.

In the blink of an eye his surroundings changed. He was behind her, his knees were weak with the vertigo of porting again so soon, and she still didn't know he was there. He stepped forward and engulfed her in a big hug that was as much to keep himself from falling over as it was to show her affection.

She gasped in surprise, and then squealed when she saw him. "Dammit Riz! You know I hate it when you do that!" Her words were sharp, but they were said with a giggle as she turned to embrace him.

"Your melons are looking good."

She giggled again and pressed her chest against him, "Thanks, I'm glad you still like my diddies! They've missed you."

He kissed her passionately, "I've missed you, and your diddies. But, I was referring to the melons in the garden. It is starting to look good."

Off in the distance a baby cried. He looked over to see Livia, Cynia's grandmother, carrying a small baby. It still seemed odd to look at the tiny person and believe that it was his son. They named him Chardron after Cynia's great grandfather, the Magi.

Cynia held out her arms as Livia walked over and handed the baby to her. She said, "Chardy is probably hungry. I'm gonna take him over to the gazebo and nurse him." She put her hand on Rissyl's shoulder to drag his attention away from the baby. Then she pointed towards the cabin. "You should go up to the house. There is a surprise for you there."

He groaned, "I don't know if I can handle more surprises tonight. I'd rather sit with you and Chardy while he eats."

She shook her head no. "Rasa is up there, she found something that you need to see."

His jaw dropped open. "Sarasa is here? Now? Why?"

Cynia rolled her eyes. "Aye, she's been here for hours. You should go see her."

He didn't answer. He wasn't sure that he was ready to face her. The last time they spoke was over a year ago when he told her that he chose to be with Cynia. That conversation had gone worse than he expected, and they hadn't seen each other since.

"Dammit Riz. We've got enough problems ahead of us. We don't need things weird between you two. Go talk to her. I'll be at the gazebo." She turned and walked away.

With a sigh he started walking slowly to the cabin. They called it a cabin because of how it was constructed, but it was actually a large house. It was three floors with several bedrooms, a library, den, and various other rooms that one would expect to find in the nicest homes.

He paused as he reached the front door. With a deep breath, and then a long exhale, he readied himself for an uncomfortable encounter.

As he opened the door he saw her sitting in the foyer reading a book. When she saw him she dropped the book on the bench next to her and rushed over to embrace him. She squeezed him tightly for a long time, and he was acutely aware of her scent. He had forgotten the subtle sweet smell of jasmine, but the aroma brought back many feelings and memories that he'd been suppressing for a long time.

She held the embrace much longer than he expected, with her head rested against his chest. He put his cheek against the top of her head for a moment. The smell of her hair was almost too much to take. He realized that this was the most affection she had ever shown him, and suddenly he began to feel that he was approaching a line that shouldn't be crossed. When he finally put his hands on her shoulders and gently disengaged the embrace he could see that she was crying.

He frowned and said, "I'm sorry Rasa. I didn't mean to hurt you. I didn't think-"

She cut him off with a poke in the chest. She said, "Stop Riz. I didn't come here to make you feel bad, or to rehash things from the past. But, I have missed you terribly. We shouldn't be apart so long." She paused and then added, "Because there is so much to do."

He pointed at the book she had been reading. He said, "Let's go to the gazebo so Cynia can hear what you've found."

She picked up the book and followed him outside.

As they walked, he said, "How are things? What's Dalen up to these days?" He hadn't seen her brother Dalen in over a year. Rissyl and Dalen had always had a rocky relationship, and that grew more unpleasant the last time they were together.

"While you, Aruk, and the others have been searching for the signet ring, Dalen has been busy also. He's been focused on patrolling and recruiting new people into the Society. Sarge, Eleyne, Thon, and a few others have been helping him. They've really made a lot of progress. We have small Coteries in four cities now. He is spending a lot of time with Firana these days."

"That's great, Rasa! I know that Cynia's been working on recruitment too, but I didn't realize that we have four Coteries already. I've been so focused on hunting for that ring. Well, that and moving away from Sorgo, and then Cynia having the baby. I can't believe it's already been over a year since we last talked. Where has the time gone?"

She nodded, "I know, it's crazy." She held up the book and pointed to it. "While you all have been busy with your tasks, Randol and I have been doing research in his old books. I stumbled onto something that you need to hear."

When they reached the gazebo, Rissyl sat down next to Cynia. She was naked from the waist up and Chardy was nursing. She held the baby in a large shawl and had one end of it tossed over her shoulder to mostly cover herself. Rissyl was a bit surprised at her uncharacteristic display of modesty. She typically liked to nurse Chardy without having to worry about blankets and clothing getting in her way. He assumed she was being a bit more modest since Sarasa was visiting.

Sarasa sat down on the bench across from them. She opened the book to a marked page and cleared her throat. She said, "I guess I should start with some background info. This book is called *Two Millennia of Magic: An Exploration of the History of Magic from 922 Until Today*. It was written by Mallianitha Bollix in 2920 MC. Most of it is pretty dull reading, even for a history lover like me. But there is some interesting information in here."

Rissyl stopped her, "I'm sorry, Rasa. Help me with the timing. I'm still foggy on the Menelian calendar."

"We are in the year 109 according to the Ryallic calendar. It would be the year 3511 according to the Menelian calendar. The book was written in 2920, almost 600 years ago."

"Wow, that's an old book."

She nodded, "And it is written in Menelian, so reading it is a slow process. There is one part in particular that I wanted to tell you about."

She scanned the page for a moment. Then she read, "During the Cleric Insurrection of 1294 several sects of clerics were armed with new weapons to battle the wizard armies. Garroliron pendants made the wearer impervious to magical attack and garroliron manacles completely blocked a wizard's ability to cast spells. Some accounts from the time claimed that wizards could die by wearing the garroliron manacles for too long. The artifacts were created by artificers working for the clerics, using rare ore from deep in the mountains. The rare ore, this garroliron, had natural properties that absorb magical energy."

Rissyl stopped her again. "I have some questions before you get too far."

Sarasa smiled at him. She said, "Of course you do."

Cynia laughed and added, "Of course he does. Gods forbid that you actually complete a thought."

"You girls are hilarious. Okay, so aren't clerics the bookkeepers at temples? Why were they attacking people?"

"Long ago, many of the gods had followers with special powers. These followers were called clerics. Some clerics were healers, others worshiped evil gods and did evil things. The necromancers that we face these days are clerics of Viator."

He nodded, "Oh! That makes sense. And what about wiz... what was that word? Wizor something?"

"Wizard. It is an archaic term for Magi. Before the Magi Society was formed, all magic users were called wizards. When the Society was created, the founders picked a different name for those who wield magic, because the word wizard was tainted in the minds of the people. When people of the time heard the word wizard they thought of armies of magic users laying waste to each other, and destroying most anything and anyone in their way."

"Okay, that makes sense. So, the book hasn't told us anything about garroliron that we don't already know. Back then they just used garroliron for pendants and such. They didn't have monsters made out of the stuff. This doesn't help us much."

Cynia elbowed him. "If you'd shut up and let her talk, maybe she'd get to the useful part?"

Sarasa smiled and continued reading, "The wizards consulted with their elven allies to devise a way to deal with the garroliron artifacts. After years of testing and research it was found that wands made from Dinberian oak trees could be used as focus objects to cast spells that could affect someone wearing a garroliron pendant. The wands could even be used as focus objects to cast spells that could destroy garroliron manacles. The Dinberian oak was extremely rare and very expensive to acquire, so throughout the course of the war only a few dozen Dinberian oak wands existed. These were wielded by a group that became known as the Wizard Knights of Tharrin."

He looked at Cynia in amazement. He said, "This is remarkable news!"

Cynia turned to Sarasa said, "Do any of these wands still exist?"

"Not that I know of. I talked to Randol and he has never heard of them. We're talking about wands made over 2,000 years ago. Even if they still exist it's unlikely that the owner knows what they're called or what they're made of."

He asked her, "Does Randol think there might be some at the Stronghold?"

"I asked him that, and he said it's possible. But he said there are probably hundreds of different wands on display and in cupboards throughout the Stronghold, and knowing which ones are the Dinberian oak wands would be next to impossible unless they just so happen to be labeled."

"And knowing how things go for us, it's unlikely. So we're out of luck?"

Sarasa raised an eyebrow and said, "Unless..."

They both looked at her in anticipation.

"Unless we go to the Dinbera Isles and get some Dinberian oak on our own."

"You're not serious, are you? The Dinbera Isles are the home of the elves." Rissyl stared at Sarasa in disbelief.

"Of course I'm serious, why?" She closed the book and sat it on the bench beside her.

Rissyl rubbed his temples with one hand. He was starting to get a headache and he strongly hoped that Sarasa was not being serious. "Rasa, the elves are pirates! They plunder merchant vessels and harass the coastal cities all along the southern edge of the empire. They've been a foe of the empire and the Six Kingdoms before that! We have no idea where these trees might be, or how the elves might react if they find us there chopping them down."

"They were once allied with the wizards. Maybe they'll work with us?"

"Or, maybe they'll eat us and throw our carcass to the sharks?"

Sarasa laughed, "Don't you think the pirate stories are a bit exaggerated? I think it's worth trying."

Cynia repositioned the baby, and then said, "Dammit, Rasa. Don't we have enough obstacles without adding another unachievable goal to our list? We still have to reclaim the Stronghold. Maybe we'll get lucky and find some of these wands there?"

"Maybe. But if we don't, we should at least consider a mission to the Dinbera Islands to find some of this wood. We can avoid the elves if you insist."

He brushed a flying bug from his arm. "We'd need more than just the wood, the wands would need enchanted too."

"Of course, but Dalen can do that. That's always been one of the duties of the Order of Champions. He's been practicing on some swords that he's crafted. They turned out pretty good, for his first attempts."

Rissyl shrugged. "Fine, we'll add it to the list. What does Dalen think of this plan?"

Sarasa nodded, "He likes it. One other thing, Randol says that the four of us need to take on the roles of Grand Coterie until we can setup a vote and make it all official. He says that with multiple coteries and a growing number of Magi, the society needs centralized leadership. Dalen wants us to meet in a few days to open our first Grand Coterie meeting so we can chat with the leaders of the Coteries in the other cities."

"I think that sounds like a good idea." As soon as she finished her statement, Cynia gasped. "Dammit kiddo, don't bite! Those are sensitive!" She pulled her nipple from the baby's mouth briefly, and then she let him latch back on.

Rissyl giggled, "I bet that hurt!"

She elbowed him in the side. "I could show you if you want."

"No, that's okay." He looked back to Sarasa and said, "That is fine with me, Rasa. Let me know when they want to do the meeting and I'll be there."

Cynia's Rolimi pup appeared and jumped onto the bench next to her. It was now a full grown medium sized dog with short ears, a thick body, and a short snout. Its coat appeared thick and fuzzy, but each hair looked like a single strand of green sunlight. Even though the dog was made of pure light, it didn't glow brightly, and it wasn't completely transparent. The light seemed to draw the outlines of its features

Cynia said, "Well hello, Skamp. Come on up."

"You named your Rolimi pup?" Sarasa sounded surprised.

Rissyl nodded, "We got tired of calling them Green Pup and Red Pup."

"They're not exactly pups anymore." Cynia reached out and started petting Skamp behind the ear.

"Where is Tiberos?" Rissyl summoned a tiny amount of magic and called out to his Rolimi dog. A moment later it appeared, and seemed to crawl out of the wall at the side of the gazebo. Like Skamp, it was made out of pure light. However, Tiberos was red and shaped differently. It was shorter than Cynia's Rolimi dog, and it was also thick and had a long body. It had short legs, long floppy ears, a long snout, big feet, and a long tail. The shorter red Rolimi dog padded up to Rissyl and sat down at his feet. He said, "Rasa, this is Tiberos my trusty Rolimi hound."

Sarasa looked at the two Rolimi dogs. "They're so big. Mine is much smaller and I think he is full grown." A few moments later a little grey Rolimi dog jumped up on the bench next to Sarasa. The creature was half the size of the other Rolimi dogs. If it was a normal dog, Rissyl would assume it was some sort of fuzzy terrier. The light strands of fur on her dog were longer than on the others, and its fuzzy face had a short snout and little ears.

The three of them sat in silence for a while, as everyone looked at the Rolimi dogs. Rissyl found his thoughts wandering to the Rolimi, and the various challenges that the Magi faced.

He said, "You know, recently I've been wondering about something. When we freed Kimly and the Dregs from that Motlite camp, everything happened so quickly I never stopped to wonder why necromancers were working with the emperor. Over the last several months, I've been trying to wrap my head around that. As much as the emperor hates magic, why would he align with a group of evil necromancers? It doesn't make sense."

Cynia shrugged, "Because he is crazy? I dunno, I never really questioned it much. Why did his grandfather murder thousands of innocent people to kill a few hundred Magi? The only explanation that I have is that they're all crazy and they'll do anything to kill Magi."

"That's just it. Shouldn't the emperor view necromancers as evil magic users? I would expect him to hate them as much as he hates us."

Sarasa said, "I think he does hate necromancers as much as he hates Magi. I talked to Kimly about this shortly before she took off. She said that she got the impression that the emperor didn't know that Jalinox was a necromancer."

"Oh, that's intriguing. So, we don't really know what we're up against or whether our enemies are separate or working together?"

"Exactly. From what Kimly said, Jalinox has very ambitious plans and we shouldn't underestimate him."

He nodded, "Good point. However, all we can do is take on one impossible task at a time."

They all laughed.

Sarasa said, "Speaking of impossible tasks, congratulations on the marriage. If you would have invited us, Dalen and I would have come to share the day with you."

Rissyl and Cynia looked at each other, and then he said, "Well, Rasa, we just got married with a magistrate. We thought we'd do a fancy ceremony

13

once things calm down with the Magi Society and all."

The three of them sat in awkward silence for a few minutes, listening to Chardy aggressively eat his dinner.

After a bit, Sarasa said, "Well, I should get started back to the portal stone. It's a long walk and it is already getting dark."

"Nonsense!" Cynia repositioned Chardy to try to burp him again. "You gotta have dinner with us and spend the night. We've got plenty of room. You can go back to Randol's in the morning."

- = - = -

Rissyl pushed himself away from the table. He was beyond full and regretted having the last biscuit.

Cynia and Sarasa sat and talked with their grandparents as they all finished eating. Grandma Livia and Grandpa Alluster had been living with them for several months, and Rissyl didn't mind having them around. They helped with the baby, and Grandma Livia cooked many of the meals.

After a few minutes Grandpa Alluster said, "We should be getting home, Livia." They stood up and said goodbyes, and then walked out of the dining room heading to the guest house.

Once they were gone, Cynia said, "I told grandpa I'd come over tonight and finish prepping his herbs for sale. He gathered lots of great herbs from the foothills and they gotta be trimmed and packaged. Some should be laid out to dry and others gotta be crushed into a paste. He is making a trip to town tomorrow, and I wanna get it done before he leaves. So I'll probably be working through most of the night down at the barn."

She stood up and kissed Rissyl.

He asked, "Do you need my help?"

She shook her head. "Nope, have a good sleep." Then she looked to Gwen, who had started to clean up the dinnerware. She said, "Please look in on Chardy before you head to bed."

Gwen was a young lady in her early twenties. She was one of Cynia's distant cousins who needed work and a place to stay. They hired her to live with them and work as a maid and a nanny. She was a plump girl with brown hair and a friendly demeanor. She said, "Of course, was planning to."

Rissyl sat at the table and let Sarasa finish her meal in silence. When she was done, he said, "I'll show you to your room." He led her to the third floor, passed his rooms, and took her to the far guest bedroom down at the end of the hallway.

He stopped at the door and she walked right in. As she closed the door she gave him a little smile. She said, "G'night, Riz."

The door closed and he stood next to it for a while. He wished there was something he could say that would make things better between them. After lingering a bit, he made his way to his own room.

The room was larger than his bedroom back home. Cynia had spent a lot of time, and many coins, making the room attractive. The light brown drapes over the windows were large and extended almost to the floor. The furniture was hand crafted and elaborate, and she had accented the room and furniture with a variety of sculptures and nick-knacks that were scattered all about. Most of the house was decorated with more moderate, and less expensive, furniture and décor. However, it was important to her to have nice things in the bedroom.

Overall it didn't matter to him one way or the other. The bed was soft, the pillows were softer, and the blankets were warm. Those were the only things that mattered to him. The little treasures scattered around the room, the paintings on the walls, and all of the live plants in their vases were just things that he tried to avoid touching so he didn't end up breaking them.

He stripped off his traveling clothes and pulled on a pair of sleeping shorts. The cool sheets of his bed, and the soft duck down feathers of his mattress, felt good as he crawled into bed.

After at least an hour or more he still hadn't fallen asleep. His mind was still racing over all of the news of the day. He rolled over onto his side and adjusted his pillow.

The door to his bedroom opened quietly, and closed just as quietly. He smiled as he opened his eyes. He had been disappointed when Cynia said she would be gone all night, so he was pleasantly surprised that she was coming to bed already.

When he looked over he realized in shock and disbelief that it wasn't Cynia after all. Sarasa walked across the bedroom slowly, and held a finger up to her lips to tell him to be silent.

He sat up in bed, looking at her incredulously. She walked to his side of the bed and sat down next to him, facing him, with one leg folded before her and the other foot still on the floor. From what he could tell, she was just wearing a loose fitting pink shirt that barely extended passed her butt.

He scooted away from her a bit, towards the headboard of the bed. In a soft voice he said, "Rasa, by all the gods, what are you doing?"

She didn't say anything, but she leaned forward and started to crawl towards him across the bed. When she got her face almost close enough to kiss him, she started to slide one leg over his legs to straddle him. The expression on her face showed a need and a longing that he never dreamed that she might feel.

He wanted her with every fiber of his being. He had wanted her from the moment he first saw her, but now he wanted her more than ever. Yet, he knew that he could not do it. As she tried to straddle him, he caught her leg and gently sat it on the bed. He scooted a little further away from her.

She reached out and gently grabbed his wrist, and tried to pull his hand to her breasts.

He said, "Please stop, Rasa. You know we can't do this!" He hated those words. He didn't know what he could say to her to make her realize that this was a bad idea, without hurting her and making things worse between them. Part of him cried out that Cynia probably wouldn't even care if he bedded Sarasa. However, the logical side of himself forced him to scoot himself a little further from her.

She reached up, cupped her own breasts with both hands, and squeezed. From her facial expression, he got the feeling that she really loved how it felt. She continued to squeeze them and play with them for a few seconds and he felt his resolve slipping.

Then she opened her eyes and looked at him. She said, "Fiery Khalius, Riz! Her little diddies are so much more sensitive than mine!"

Her statement didn't make any sense. He looked at her in confusion as she started to squeeze them again. Then he realized that it wasn't really Sarasa's voice that said those words, it sounded more like Cynia. He continued to stare at her in confusion for another moment. Why would Sarasa come to his bed and sound like Cynia?

Then realization hit him like a ton of bricks. He jumped backwards and crawled out of bed. He said, "By the gods, Cynia! What are you doing?"

When they rescued the Dregs from the emperor's Motlite breeding camp, Rissyl saw Zahr transform into a gorilla, and he knew that Diviners had the power to transform into other shapes. He never dreamed that Cynia would transform herself to look like Sarasa! Was she trying to trap him to see if he would remain true to her? He felt shocked and betrayed, and more than a little creeped-out.

She crawled closer to him and sat down on her knees and feet. She said quietly, "You don't like it? I've worked for months to learn how to do this for

16

you."

He could tell by the tone of her voice that she was hurt. He was more confused and his head was starting to hurt. He said, "Why would you do this? Are you trying to test my faithfulness?" There was more anger in his voice than he intended.

She responded with anger of her own. "No! Dammit Riz! I've already said I wouldn't make you choose. You want her and you try to hide it, and it's getting in the way of our goals! Besides, I thought maybe if you had her once you would be less curious about what it'd be like and things could get back to normal." She paused and he started to respond. She added, "And I thought you'd enjoy it."

He sat down on the bed, facing mostly away from her. She slid over so she was near him and mostly in front of him.

He said, "That's got to be the craziest, most insane, thing I've ever heard! You would have gone through with it, in her body?"

"Of course I would have! It's not really her body. It just looks like her. What would it hurt?"

Rissyl rubbed his palms across his face in frustration.

She said, "It would be like playing Naughty Wife and the Milkman. It is fantasy playing, lots of couples do it."

"But in Naughty Wife and the Milkman, the wife doesn't actually think she's sarding the milkman! She knows it's a fantasy."

Cynia, who still looked exactly like Sarasa, sighed. She said, "Fine, then let's play Naughty Husband and the Redhead Magi?" Sarasa, who was actually Cynia, winked at him.

He stood up again, "I don't know, Cynia. It seems wrong."

She said, "If you won't sard me like this, you should at least feel these diddies. I worked hard on these for you."

He took both of her hands in his hands gently. He looked into her eyes, Sarasa's eyes, and shook his head no.

CHAPTER 2

Kimly

Kimly was seated on an expensive chair in the beautiful reading room of her opulent mansion, staring at a nexus gem, and thinking about her life. The last year had been a whirlwind of change for her. The nexus gem in her hand brought back memories of the past several months.

A little over a year ago she had been a waif, sleeping in abandoned buildings or in a cemetery mausoleum. Her newly acquired magical powers enabled her to amass a small fortune, pilfered from many unsuspecting Gentry. As a Denizen, one of the commoners of the empire, she grew up poor and hungry. She didn't feel bad taking a little from the Gentry, the wealthy folks.

After being rescued from the Motlite breeding camp she spent about a fortnight at Randol's place. She helped care for Sarge, a Magi from the Barbarian Lands who was badly injured during her rescue. Once she was sure that he would recover she decided that she needed a fresh start. Being a Magi was exciting and it had its benefits. However, her time as a prisoner of Jalinox, and watching other Magi die around her, taught her that being a Magi was a dangerous occupation. If she was going to enjoy her newfound wealth she would need to be alive. She also wasn't too fond of all of the rules and expectations placed on members of the Magi Society.

She left Randol's without saying many goodbyes. They were suspicious of her anyway, because of the necromancer magic that Jalinox had taught. So she made her way back to Sorgo to retrieve most of her ill-gotten treasure that she had been hiding in her great grandparent's mausoleum. She bought some nice clothes, some expensive luggage, a few expensive baubles, and booked passage on a caravan to the far south of the empire.

The city of Khardifar was built on the shore of the sea. It was one of the largest and most affluent cities in the empire. Most importantly, it was far from Sorgo and the Magi, and that was exactly what she wanted.

When the caravan arrived in Khardifar she booked a suite in the nicest inn in the Garden District and introduced herself as Mrs. Kimly VanSlate, a wealthy widow. She made frequent visits to the nicest museums and galleries in the city, and invited herself to afternoon tea with the influential women of the district. Before long she was being invited to lavish parties and dances. In a few short months Mrs. Kimly VanSlate became an accepted member of the Khardifar Gentry community.

The most surprising aspect of this chapter of her life was that she actually made some friends. She had always viewed the Gentry as terrible people, but as she got to know some of the women in the Khardifar Garden District she genuinely liked many of them. Sure, some of the women were superficial and fake, but some of them were good people.

It was at one of these parties that she met Mr. Cletis Watters, a fabulously rich and powerful Gentry widower. He was several years older than her, but he was handsome and sweet. Their courtship had been short and intense. When she was with him she didn't feel like a street urchin playing dress-up, she felt like a real Gentry lady.

They were married in Early-Fall 108 RY, and her dream of life as a rich woman became a reality. When she moved into his mansion it was like moving into a palace. His home, their home, was the nicest mansion in all of Khardifar. Sure there were villas outside of the city where the richest class, the Aristocrats, lived. However, among the Gentry of the city it didn't get any nicer or more lavish than the Watters Mansion. It was situated in the far eastern section of the city and the windows facing south looked out at the sea. She often walked out to their private beach and drank fruity drinks while basking in the sun.

As she sat there looking at the nexus gem, something bugged her. She was starting to see that having all of her dreams come true and living the life of luxury had its down-side. She had everything she could ever want, could buy anything she wanted to buy, and had found a wonderful man who treated her well. However, more and more she found herself craving excitement. What good was fabulous wealth if you just sat around all day being rich?

She stood up and put the nexus gem in her pocket. It was time for an adventure. Her husband was traveling and wouldn't be home until morning, so she hurried to her closets. She removed her nightgown and put on black leather breeches, a tight black tunic, and her new favorite black floppy hat. As she passed a mirror she paused to look at herself. She thought she looked sneaky and maybe even a bit sexy. Her long black hair spilled over her shoulders and added to the overall mysterious profile.

Avoiding the servants' areas she slipped out of the house and out into the yard. She felt a thrill as she summoned a little magic and dropped a *Shadow*

Shroud spell around her. Now, as long as she stayed out of very bright areas, she would be effectively invisible.

She didn't know where she was going, but she would figure that out on the way. It had been dark for several hours and the streets near her home were empty. At first she thought she'd sneak around and steal something. However, she didn't really need any more coin, and the thought of stealing more didn't bring on that excitement that she was looking for.

Before long she found herself at the gates to the Commons District. Getting by the guards wasn't too tricky, thanks to her shroud spell. The sentinels at the gate wouldn't question her anyway, but the excitement was in trying not to be caught. Therefore, she snuck past them and made her way into the part of the city for the Denizens, the common folk of the city.

After more than an hour of wandering around the Commons she started to get bored. The streets were mostly deserted other than a few working girls and the occasional drunken sailor staggering down the road. She was about to head back home for the night when movement caught her eye.

She wasn't certain, but it almost looked like someone started to walk out of an alleyway and was pulled back into it. With just a small hesitation, she hurried over to the alley. Sure enough, several men were leading another man down the dark passage. She followed them quietly for several blocks.

The men stopped at the far side of a dead-end alley. The place was dark and very secluded.

One man stood in the middle. He was clearly about to be the victim of whatever was happening. The man was not very tall, but he had broad shoulders and he was fit and muscular. He didn't look like a man who was easily bullied.

Standing all around him were six young men, they carried themselves like young cocky thugs. Kimly was quite familiar with their type, growing up on the streets of Sorgo she had encountered many young men like them. One of the thugs was taller than the rest and he seemed to be the leader.

The tall man stepped towards the victim and looked down at him. With a quick punch he slugged the victim in the gut. The thug said, "What'ya doing out here, Favin? Out walking the streets, all alone? You know Guild Master Hisaro was very disappointed to hear that you turned down his generous offer to merge your guild with ours. Here's your chance to change your mind."

The victim, Favin, leaned forward slightly and coughed. He took several deep breaths, looking at the tall thug the whole time. He said softly, "Tell Hisaro that my people ain't about to become his lackeys."

Two of the thugs grabbed Favin's arms from behind and held him while the tall thug punched him in the gut several more times. He said, "That ain't how it works, Favin, and you know it. There ain't room for two thieves' guilds in this city."

Several thugs started punching Favin in the sides, back, stomach, and head.

Kimly stopped paying attention to the thugs and their victim as she thought about home. The streets of Khardifar weren't that much different than Sorgo. There was always one thieves' guild or another vying for more power or influence over the others.

A loud grunt from the victim drew her attention back to the situation in the alleyway. She felt bad for the guy, but this was the reality of the street. Surely the man knew what he was risking when he turned down Hisaro's offer.

Favin coughed again and he sounded like the wind was knocked out of him. In a quiet voice he said, "Listen guys, I don't want no trouble. There's still time for you to leave without getting hurt." He spit out a mouthful of blood.

She raised an eyebrow. Favin certainly had nerve.

The tall man stepped in to punch Favin in the stomach again and suddenly the victim became a flurry of movement. In the blink of an eye Favin shifted his hips causing the stomach punch to miss him. With that same movement he jerked his right arm free. He pulled it forward and then slammed the elbow into the face of the thug behind him who had been holding it.

The whole area burst into action as six slow and unskilled fighters unsuccessfully tried to defend themselves against one very angry warrior. Favin fought like a deranged man, and Kimly had never seen anything like it. He easily dealt with three men at once, and moved quickly to keep the others away from him long enough to deal with the threat at hand.

In a couple of seconds five men were sprawled out on the ground. Some of them were knocked out, and some of them might be dead, Kimly wasn't sure. Favin and the tall thug squared off with each other. The thug pulled out a dagger and brandished it before him.

From behind and slightly above her, Kimly heard the unmistakable sound of a crossbow as it loosed its bolt. This was immediately followed by a zipping sound as the large bolt sliced through the air over her head, and it quickly ended in a dull thud as the heavy bolt sunk deep in the side of Favin's chest.

He let out a brief scream and turned to look for the new attacker. Above and behind her, she could hear that crossbow shooter reloading his weapon.

However, Favin's immediate threat came from the tall thug. As Favin turned to look for the crossbow shooter, the tall thug lunged in for a knife attack.

Kimly groaned to herself. She really didn't want to get involved in a local matter, and the last thing she needed was to anger the ruling crime guild in her new home city. She had fully intended to watch the events to liven up an otherwise boring evening. The decision to help the man named Favin was made in a split second and even as she made it she figured she'd probably end up regretting it. However, there was something about the man and it didn't seem right to let him be killed by thugs.

Over the last year she had been studying her spell books frequently. She wasn't actively working with the Magi any longer, but she still wanted to hone her magical powers as much as possible. She was only a Society Magi, one of the entry-level Magi who wore the brown and white cloaks. She wasn't a member of one of the four magical Orders, so she didn't have access to the most powerful spells. However, she was still able to wield some impressive magic and recently she had perfected some fun new powers.

She grabbed a dagger from her belt and tossed it at the tall thug. As it flew she summoned a small amount of magical power, molded it briefly, and slammed it at the dagger. The enchanted dagger streaked towards its target with impossible speed and accuracy, and it struck against the side of the thug's neck with such force that it ripped entirely through his neck and erupted out the other side. Blood showered the area as the thug fell to the ground lifelessly.

Her attack forced her to lose focus on her *Shadow Shroud* and as she threw the dagger she became fully visible. Favin's eyes grew wide as he saw her appear from the shroud spell.

Without even waiting to see the body of the tall thug hit the ground, she summoned magic once again. This time she whispered the magical phrase, "Kur'Lu Sonti." The spell was called *Slow Falling* and it was designed to allow a Magi to float gently to the ground if she was falling. Through trial and practice she found that if she cast the spell when she was already on the ground, it would allow her to jump unusually high and then float in place for a moment before she gently floated to the ground.

She jumped straight up, and the spell allowed her to reach at least fifteen feet in the air. As she felt her upward momentum slowing she grabbed another dagger from her belt and spun to see the crossbow attacker. She saw him standing on a balcony drawing the firing mechanism of the crossbow to a cocked position.

The *Slow Falling* spell caused her to levitate for a moment as she threw the dagger side-arm at the crossbow-wielding thug. She summoned a tiny amount of magic and slammed it into the dagger as it flew, causing it to accelerate at the crossbowman with incredible power. The dagger hit the thug in the chest with such force that it tore through the man's leather armor and embedded itself entirely in the man's chest as it slammed him backwards into the building behind him.

Kimly gently floated to the ground and turned her attention to Favin. He stared at her as if she was a demon, or possibly an angel. He staggered briefly and then fell to one knee.

She rushed over to him and helped him up. "Come on, big guy. Let's get you some help."

In a weak voice he said, "Who are you? Are you a Magi?" The words were soft and his breaths gurgled. Speaking drove him into a coughing fit.

She continued to half carry and half guide him through the alley towards the street. She said, "Don't try to talk."

Once they reached a street, she headed towards the bazaar. After a few blocks her legs were burning and she struggled under his weight. Up ahead she saw a couple of working girls standing near a streetlamp. As quickly as she could manage she led Favin over to the girls.

She said, "Where's an apothecary or healer?"

The street girls both turned their backs to her. In frustration she summoned some magic and used it to grab a nearby rock. Using her magic, she tossed the rock at the back of one of the girls. It hit her solidly and the woman cried out in surprise.

The working girl turned around and said, "What's your sarding problem?"

Kimly growled, "Dammit, he needs a healer!"

The other girl, who hadn't been hit by a rock, turned and pointed down the street in the direction they were already walking. She said, "Doc Algurith has a shop two blocks that way."

The women walked across the street to get away from Kimly and Favin, and they complained loudly about the nerve of some people as they walked off.

Kimly resituated Favin, and then started walking in the direction the prostitutes indicated. She said, "I don't know who would pay good money to sard such ugly chippies anyway."

She didn't look back to see if the women heard her, but they weren't yelling at her so she assumed they did not.

23

Two blocks later, Kimly struggled to get Favin to the door of the doctor's building. She sat him gently on the ground and pounded on the door. An old sign near the door swung on a rusty chain in the breeze, it said, "Doc Algurith – Barbers & Surgeons Guild."

She continued to pound loudly on the door until she finally heard someone working the locks from the other side. A portly old man answered the door. He was wearing an evening robe and slippers. His grey hair, what was left of it, was messy and shoved off to one side as if the man had been asleep a few moments earlier.

He looked at Kimly and then down at Favin. Without saying a word he hurried outside and the two of them carried the warrior into Algurith's building. They pulled him through an open room with several benches and into a separate room in back. The room had a bed and a bench with several unusual tools lying about. She helped the healer lift Favin onto the bed.

The man, whom Kimly assumed to be Doc Algurith, looked at the crossbow sticking out of Favin's side. He looked at her and asked, "What happened to him?"

"He was attacked by thugs in an alley."

He hurried over to a cabinet and pulled out a couple of vials. Then he hurried back to Favin. Without looking at Kimly, he asked, "What's your name?"

"I'm pretty sure his name is Favin."

The doctor began removing Favin's clothing so he could get a better look at the crossbow bolt. He said, "I know Favin. What's your name?"

She stepped away from the bed. The last thing that she wanted was to get caught in the middle of Favin's mess. She certainly couldn't tell the doctor that she was Kimly Watters, Gentry lady. That would lead to all sorts of uncomfortable questions.

Kimly said, "I gotta go. I'll check on him tomorrow." She pulled out her coin purse and starting looking through the coins for a golden cardinal. She figured that would be enough to cover the doctor's services, and discretion.

As she held out the coin, the doctor said, "On the counter, please."

She put the cardinal on the counter and left the building. It was getting late and she was more than ready to be home. She dropped a *Shadow Shroud* spell around herself and headed back home.

CHAPTER 3

Konrad

"Need another ale, Love?"

Konrad glanced at the bar wench and nodded. He pushed his tankard towards her, and she hurried off to get him more drink.

She knew him as Simean Poad, a local warehouse worker and a frequent patron in the tavern. In his guise as Simean he wore simple laborer clothing and work boots. Konrad was tall, fit, and muscular. However, his loose fitting laborer's clothing helped to hide most of his bulk to ensure that he didn't stand out too much. He wore an expensive wig of dark brown hair that went down to around his shoulders.

He had many aliases and had used many different guises over the last few years. These days he was frequently Simean because it served as a good cover for sitting casually in a tavern observing the Denizens.

A pair of sentinels stood up from their table in the back of the tavern and slowly made their way towards the door. They glanced at him but continued walking without even recognizing him.

The sentinels knew him as Major Jon Quiggle, a high ranking officer within the Khazror sentinels. If he was dressed in his formal sentinel uniform with his natural red hair pulled back in a small military tail, as was customary for officers, the men would have immediately snapped to attention. Every sentinel in the city was quite familiar with Major Quiggle because he was the officer responsible for catching and punishing sentinels who abused their power or acted in a manner unbecoming of a city official.

Quite often Konrad sat in random taverns such as this one, in his Simean guise, looking for sentinels who might be taking bribes or stepping out of line.

However, on this night Konrad was not doing work for his Major Quiggle guise.

The bar wench returned with his drink and he handed her a copper falcon. For several minutes he sat alone at his table, staring at the fire, slowly drinking his ale, and listening to the conversations that were happening at the tables near him.

Konrad had always wanted to be a painter. He loved drawing and putting his ideas down on canvas. Unfortunately he wasn't very good at painting. He also couldn't play any musical instruments and he was a dreadful singer. All of these facts annoyed him greatly, because each of those skills sounded like they would make enjoyable careers.

Konrad was skilled in other areas. His most notable skills revolved around memory. He remembered every conversation he participated in or listened to since his childhood and could tell you the date and time of when the conversation took place. He also had a perfect memory when it came to faces, voices, and the written word. If it had anything to do with memory or learning facts, he was a master.

While these skills did nothing for his artistic aspirations, they did tend to be quite useful in his line of work. As he sat in the tavern and listened to the conversations around him, he built a catalog in his mind. There were three conversations happening nearby that he could hear.

One of the conversations was among three locals who were regulars at the tavern. He'd observed them many times and they rarely discussed anything more interesting than general bellyaching about life.

The second conversation was between two people he hadn't seen before, both of whom seemed to be from the capital city of Clornoss. The conversation lingered on gossip about a Clornoss magistrate and his late-night trysts.

Konrad had some contacts in the Clornoss thieves' guilds who knew him as Lamar Limmer, an information broker from Tharrin. He filed away the information from the second conversation for use in his Lamar guise the next time he was in Clornoss.

However, it was the third conversation that was the most interesting to Konrad. Two men sitting at a table to his left briefly mentioned a Magi in Khazror. The men referred to each other as Clide and Waltur. They didn't give any details about the Magi, and Clide seemed uncomfortable even discussing it. However, now Konrad had a new target for further examination. He needed to find more information about Waltur.

Of course he couldn't approach Waltur in his Simean guise that would completely blow the Simean cover. He continued to listen a while longer, just in case they brought up any other details about the Magi. When he was sure they were unlikely to discuss anything else that interested him, he stood up and made his way casually to the door.

When he got outside he slipped around to the back. He quickly pulled off his laborer's clothes, boots, and wig and stuffed them into a bag. That left him in tight dark-grey leggings and a dark grey undershirt. He grabbed a dark grey tunic, a dark grey cap, and some soft black shoes from the bag. He carefully shoved his hair into the cap and pulled it low over his ears. Finally he shoved the bag back in its hiding place.

The night was annoyingly bright, which would make it more difficult to track the man without being seen. Konrad walked quietly to a shadowy area between buildings where he could keep an eye on the tavern door.

Eventually Waltur left the tavern. Konrad was pleasantly surprised that Clide didn't leave the tavern with him. He waited until Waltur was a good distance down the street and then he carefully began tracking him.

The streets were mostly deserted and Konrad had no trouble following Waltur home. Before long, Konrad watched the man enter a small home in the northeast section of the Commons in Khazror. He noted the house address and then made his way back to the tavern to retrieve his bag. His work for the night was done.

Overall it had been a successful night. In the morning he would put on his Major Quiggle guise and find out everything he could about Waltur. Soon Waltur and Konrad were going to have a little chat. He didn't know which guise he would use yet. Deciding that was half of the fun. He was excited to see how things would shake out.

With any luck Waltur would lead him to a Magi, or better yet a whole nest of Magi.

Konrad established a reputation for himself about a year ago in Sorgo. It was a turning point in his life.

He smiled at the thought of his mission in Sorgo. During that mission he had come face to face with his first Magi, and had even allowed the Magi to gaze into his eyes. It was the first time he had conducted a mission using his real name. It was a huge gamble, but he didn't feel he had any other option. If the rumors about the Magi were true, when the Magi gazed into his eyes he would likely be able to read his real name. Konrad had used every technique he knew to blank his mind and block his thoughts from the Magi. It seemed to have worked, the Magi had acted annoyed and surprised at his inability to read his mind.

That night he was unable to infiltrate the Magi group, but he was able to follow one of them home. Patient observations lead to more discoveries, and within a few days Konrad led a group of agents and a squad of soldiers on a raid that brought the capture of two Magi and the deaths of two more in Sorgo.

The emperor rewarded him handsomely for that successful mission. It was in his Imperial Agent Luigey guise where he held the most power, and found his real glory. However he wasn't satisfied enjoying past accomplishments. He was determined that his future actions would far surpass what he did last year.

He knew of two other agents working in Khazror, and both of them already had at least one Magi kill in the last few months. If he was going to uphold his reputation, and stay in the good graces of the emperor, he needed some Magi kills quickly.

Being an assassin for the empire had many benefits, but it was a competitive career with very little job security. Actually, labeling his career as assassin wasn't entirely accurate. As a private agent of the emperor his missions and duties varied wildly and frequently didn't involve needing to kill someone. However, his favorite missions typically involved the untimely death of some miscreant or traitor.

CHAPTER 4

Rissyl

When Rissyl teleported to the wayside inn east of Grum'Glin he found Aruk already there and waiting for him. Aruk gave him a moment to let the vertigo fade and then they started the long walk to the farm.

"So, how was your evening with the farmer's daughter?" Rissyl flashed a grin at Aruk as he asked.

He shrugged, "Her name is Tobilyn and I don't know, to be sure. We had a fine time, and after dinner we did go for our long walk. However, it ended up being a time of deep conversation. She don't understand why I have to be gone so much. She's from a long line of farmers and her family thinks that any man who isn't a farmer must be too lazy to farm."

"Did you tell her about the Magi Society, and the threat from the empire?"

Aruk nodded, "Yes, I did and I also talked to her about the threat from the necromancers. She is from Fran'Ga, a Free City on the far northeast edge of the known-lands. It is a fiercely independent and isolationist region. The people there have very little to worry about when it comes to the empire, and they are entirely focused on themselves and their own immediate needs. If I decide to leave behind my life as a Magi I could get a large swath of farmland and live out my life as a quiet farmer with Tobilyn at my side. We'd probably have a whole gaggle of little ones running around. But, that just isn't an option right now. Maybe after we defeat the 'mancers, and the empire. Perhaps someday I could live that life. By the time that happens, Tobilyn will have settled down with some other local farmer I'm sure."

"By the gods, Aruk. That's pretty deep. I just thought you wanted to sard her." Rissyl kicked a rock down the road.

"Yep, me too. But eventually I'll wanna settle down."

They walked quietly for a while and Rissyl let his mind wander to other things. Over a year ago the emperor ordered his troops to capture Grum'Glin, and they were routed by a necromancer and her swarm of Awakened. He found himself wondering if that battle took place near where they were walking. He knew it happened between the border wall and the city, so they might be close to it.

The walk ended up taking much longer than Rissyl originally expected. The two Magi stopped at several farms along the way, but none of them was Nassani's farm. It was approaching evening when they arrived at the next farmhouse that might be the one they wanted.

As the two Magi walked up to the door, Rissyl tried to straighten his hair. The wind had messed it up. He looked at the other Magi and he noticed that they must make a pretty impressive duo. Two red and white cloaked Magi traveling together would make for an intimidating sight, he assumed.

He knocked on the door and before long it opened up. A young man stood inside the farmhouse. At first Rissyl thought it was a child, because the man was short and scrawny. However, his face looked mature, so Rissyl guessed that the man was probably in his early twenties.

The man said, "What do you want?"

Rissyl asked, "Is Nassani home?"

The man looked from one Magi to the other. Finally he said, "Who wants to know?"

"I'm Rissyl and this is Aruk. We're Magi from the Sovereign Magi Society and we have important business to discuss with Nassani."

By this time another man walked up behind the first. The two looked very similar, but the newly arrived man was a little taller. He said, "What's up, Lyro?"

Lyro said, "Dunno, Lindin. Two Magi asking for Nassani."

After a slight pause, Lindin said, "You oughta invite them in, don't you think?"

Rissyl was getting nervous; there was something odd about the two men. He readied a spell just in case. After a short pause, the two men stepped out of the way and invited the Magi into the farmhouse.

As they walked through the home, Rissyl could tell that the place had been completely ransacked at some point recently. Almost everything looked like it had been broken and then repaired, or it was still slightly broken. The paintings on the wall all had some sort of damage, all of the decorations and nick-knacks around the house showed some damage. Even the major furniture had clearly been repaired poorly.

Lyro led the Magi to the dining room and they sat down at the table.

Lindin said, "I'll fetch Nassani, she's out back."

Before long he returned with a pretty woman with auburn hair and a belly heavy with a child who seemed ready to emerge at any moment. Judging from the size of her belly, Rissyl thought perhaps she might be expecting several children at once.

Rissyl said, "Greetings, my lady. I am Rissyl and this is my friend Aruk. We're Magi with the Sovereign Magi Society."

The woman looked at the Magi gathered in the room, and then looked to Lyro and Lindin. She said, "Would one of you bring our guests something to drink?"

Both men hurried off to do what she asked.

Nassani looked to Rissyl and said, "What brings Magi to my home?"

He replied, "Bisangar's Signet Ring, the ring that your great grandfather Rifin had in his possession."

She said, "That sounds valuable." She looked at the Magi for a moment. "Out of curiosity, if I did have that ring how much would the Magi pay me for it?"

Aruk sighed, "Lady, you don't understand how important it is for us to find this ring. There is a growing danger, and that ring is the key to preventing a lot of bloodshed."

Lyro and Lindin returned with mugs of tea for everyone.

Lindin handed her a cup. A small smile emerged on her face, and she took a sip of tea. "So, this valuable ring is vital to the Magi cause? It seems to me that this makes it even more valuable. How much will you pay for it? Twenty raptors? Thirty?"

Lyro and Lindin gasped and looked at each other with huge grins on their faces.

Aruk slammed his fists down on the table and started grumbling.

Rissyl reached out, put a hand on Aruk's shoulder, and encouraged him to calm down. He said, "Nassani, I appreciate your desire to make a profit. But we both know that twenty raptors is quite unrealistic. Let's start with a simple question, do you have the ring?"

She sat back and looked at the Magi around her table. "I might know where it is. For ten raptors, I'll tell you where you might be able to find it."

"With our Magesight we could simply pull the secrets from your mind and pay you nothing." Aruk's face was red and he took a deep breath to calm himself.

Rissyl turned to Aruk and poked him in the shoulder. He said, "Aruk, please calm yourself."

Lyro moved closer to Nassani, and Aruk massaged his temples as if he had a headache.

Rissyl looked back to her. "I apologize for Aruk's impatience. We've

31

searched for this ring for a very long time. However, no one will be pulling any secrets from anyone's minds. So, here is my offer. I will pay you one raptor, from my own coin purse, when I am holding the ring in my hand. Not a falcon more, and not until I have the ring in my hand."

She sat her mug down and stood up. She said, "Please follow me."

They walked out of the house and into a field behind it. A few hundred yards to the south was a small section of land with a low fence around it. When the group reached the low fence Rissyl could see that the area contained a number of gravestones.

Pointing to one of the gravestones, she said, "My great grandfather Rifin is buried there."

The Magi moved a little closer and knelt down to get a closer look at the headstone. Rissyl couldn't read the inscription because it had been weathered away long ago.

She continued, "My family's stories say that he was buried with the ring to keep it safe. My grandfather always claimed that when the Magi came for the ring, we'd all be rich. Many times my father wanted to dig up the grave to get the ring, to sell it and make the family rich, but my uncle would never let him."

"Can we dig it up?" Rissyl stood up and looked to her.

She shook her head. "No, not for one raptor. I'm sorry it's not enough. I will talk to my uncle and see if he will allow it for any price. But I know that I won't settle for less than ten raptors."

Aruk stood up. "Ten? No chance!"

Rissyl looked at the gravestones, and then looked back to her. "I understand that it's a family legacy, and your family has been looking forward to the day when the Magi would show up and make you rich. I'm sorry I can't offer you more. The war of the Betrayal decimated the Magi Society and we no longer have unlimited resources. But, I'll see what I can do to come up with some more coin to offer you. Perhaps I could come back in three days and we can discuss this further?"

She nodded, "Yes, that would work out fine."

CHAPTER 5

Vendino

"If you run, you will die!" Thorli paced back and forth in front of the gathered force of about two hundred foot soldiers. He was dressed in full combat armor and had a large broadsword at his side, but his helm was sitting on a nearby wagon. His deep blue tabard was trimmed with intricate designs in gold around the edges and it had three golden triangles on the left breast area.

Vendino, the Minister of Affairs and highest ranking official in the emperor's Council of Ministers, looked around and saw that every soldier in the company had his full attention on the general.

They were in a huge field a few miles west of Maethral. Minister of War Thorli, who was once again acknowledged with his previous title of General Thorli, had assembled a huge military force to carry out the emperor's orders of capturing the barbarian city of Ront'El. The army consisted of Wolf Pack, Raptor, and Griffin Regiments. It had well over five thousand soldiers and at least seven hundred support troops such as squires, cooks, smiths, stable masters, and more.

Vendino had heard this speech over a dozen times in the past two days, and each time he could see in the eyes of the soldiers that the point was well received.

Thorli turned quickly and pointed to a group of soldiers. He repeated, "If YOU run, you WILL die!" Each time he emphasized the word 'you' he pointed at a soldier.

He turned back to the other side of the group and repeated himself again, this time even more forcefully. "If you run... You. Will. Die!" He paused and looked at the gathered company of foot soldiers. "Say it with me!"

In a thunderous mob, the gathered troops said together, "If I run, I will die!"

"I can't hear you!"

Even louder, the soldiers shouted, "IF I RUN, I WILL DIE!"

He turned to a soldier sitting in the front and shouted, "Tell me, warrior, if you are ambushed by necromancers or their spawn of Awakened monsters, what is the first reason that you will die if you run from them?"

The grunt shouted his reply, "Because you'll kill me, general?"

"Wrong, warrior! The first reason you'll die if you run from those monsters is because they will eat you! If you run from them they will chase you down, they will catch you, and then they will eat you alive!" He looked around to ensure that the men were being attentive. Everyone one of them was paying complete attention. He continued, "I haven't seen it, but I have heard firsthand accounts that it looks horrible! Just imagine, an Awakened monster ripping at your innards and tearing your flesh with its teeth while you watch in unbelievable agony! That is the death that you have to look forward to if you run!" He paused for dramatic effect, and then he said, "This isn't make-believe! I'm not trying to scare you. This happened to Wolverine Regiment a few short months ago. Your fellow soldiers ran from the Awakened, and many of them were eaten alive. And then when they were dead, the necromancer raised many of the soldiers and made them Awakened monsters and sent them off to chase down and eat their friends!"

As Vendino looked around at the soldiers, their expressions were a mixture of terror and repulsion.

Thorli pointed at another soldier and shouted, "Tell me, warrior, if you run from the Awakened and you happen to escape the monsters what is the second way you will die?"

The soldier shrugged his shoulders. He shouted, "You'll kill me, general?"

Thorli shouted, "Wrong, warrior! If you run from the Awakened and happen to avoid being eaten alive, the second way you will die is by our archers!" Thorli pointed behind the company of soldiers, to a long line of several companies of archers arranged at the far back of the army over a hundred yards to the south. "Do you see those archers? They have been given strict orders to kill any enemy that runs towards them. If you flee the field of battle, if you abandon your fellow soldiers and run for your cowardly life, you become the enemy! Any soldier who would flee in the face of an adversary is my enemy! I swear to all of the gods that our archers will shoot you dead if they see you fleeing the enemy!"

The gathered soldiers all glanced back towards the archers, as if seeing them as a threat for the first time.

Thorli wasn't done. He walked over to the far end of the company and pointed to another soldier in the front line. He shouted, "Warrior! Tell me the third way you will die if you run from battle! If you're not eaten alive, if the archers somehow miss your cowardly arse, how will you end up getting your worthless life extinguished?"

The warrior looked around quickly, but no one offered him any help. He shouted, "You'll kill me, general?"

"You're right, warrior! If you run from the field of battle and somehow the Awakened don't eat you and our archers don't skewer you, then I will personally punch you in the brain!" He resumed his pacing, and looked at the gathered troops. "Yes, I will punch you in the sarding face so hard that my gods blessed fist will land right in the middle of your worthless brain!"

He looked around and the entire company was quiet. He added, "Someone tell me what happened to Wolverine Regiment because they fled the field of battle."

One soldier shouted, "They were hanged!"

Another soldier shouted, "They were made into Dregs."

Thorli nodded. He loudly said, "Yes! The officers were hanged immediately, and all of the rest of the regiment were made into Dregs for life!" As he paced he looked several warriors in the eyes and paused for a moment. Then he said, "Gentlemen, I have no interest in being hanged! Let there be no mistaking. If we fail in our mission to capture this barbarian city, if you flee before a handful of Awakened monsters, we WILL meet the same fate as Wolverine Regiment! Except, I guarantee before I am hanged I will personally find each and every one of you sarding wenches who ran from battle, and I will personally beat you stupid!"

The entire company sat in stunned silence and stared at their general. He paced back and forth in front of them, and he looked fired-up. His cheeks were red and he looked like he wanted to punch someone in the brain at that very moment.

After a short pause, he shouted, "But if you stand and fight, you might live!"

He turned and faced the other direction, and looked directly at another group. He repeated himself, "If you stand and fight, you might live!"

Thorli let his words sink in. Then he shouted, "The Awakened have a weakness! If you drive a blade or a shaft through their heart, they will be dead completely! That's the one thing we learned from Wolverine Regiment's failures. The Awakened can be killed! So I tell you again. If you stand and fight, you might live!"

A cheer went up from the gathered soldiers, just as Vendino had seen with so many other companies in the gathered army.

The general stopped in the middle of the group and looked out over the entire company. He shouted, "Who here is the meanest and toughest bastard in this company?"

The whole company erupted with shouts of "Me!" and "I am!"

Thorli continued, "I know that the meanest and toughest bastard in this company could kill a mindless Awakened with just a knitting needle! So how much more death should you be able to bring with a sword or an ax?"

The company stood and shouted with their fists in the air.

Thorli yelled, "If you run, you will die!"

"IF I RUN, I WILL DIE!"

"If you fight, you may live!"

"IF I FIGHT, I MAY LIVE!"

- = - = -

An hour later the two ministers walked through the encampment together. It had already been a long day for Vendino, having listened to yet another 'motivational' speech by General Thorli to yet another company, and he was tired, sore and ready to return to his tent for a little relaxation.

Vendino despised being stuck out in the field with the soldiers. He was a rich and powerful man, one of the senior ministers within the empire, and he was no longer a young man. He should be sipping a fruity drink while being fanned by Dregs on his lake-side villa. Instead he was traipsing through a military encampment surrounded by thugs and vagabonds.

Being stuck out in the field did have its perks; it kept him out of the emperor's council chambers. From the latest reports, the emperor was growing increasingly frustrated with his inability to deal with the Magi. Vendino worried that if the emperor continued to act irrationally that it could lead to more bloodshed and unrest through the empire. The recent reports of the Magi setting Dregs free were the final straw. From what he'd seen, the emperor held only a tenuous grasp on sanity at the moment, and further setbacks could be catastrophic.

As he walked through the camp he longed for quiet and a soft cot to rest upon. However, Thorli wanted to check in on Lord Jalinox and he asked Vendino to join him. The two ministers had been at the army encampment for almost a month, and Vendino had been able to avoid Jalinox the entire time up until then. Yet, he knew it was just a matter of time before he had to deal with the man.

The gruff old general kicked a discarded gauntlet out of his way as they walked. "Why is that creepy alchemist even with us, and what are those beasts that he brought along?"

They paused as a platoon of soldiers passed in front of them quickly, marching off to their left. The platoon leader called out cadence as they walked, "Left. Right o'er left. Right o'er left, right, left. Left. Right o'er left..." The two ministers stood for a few moments as the line of soldiers passed by. Vendino didn't know much about military things, but he was impressed at how sharp the platoon's lines looked and how all of the soldiers stepped in time together.

When the platoon was no longer in their way, the two ministers resumed their walk. Vendino answered, "I don't know what the beasts are. Something highly secretive, I'm sure. He is here because he insisted and the emperor typically gives into his demands."

The general shook his head and made a disgusted facial expression, but didn't respond.

Vendino looked around the encampment as they walked. He was amazed at how orderly the whole operation was, especially since the entire thing seemed like it was in a perpetual state of chaos. At all times there was someone yelling about something. Someone was always running one way or another, and he had no idea where most of the people were headed or why they needed to run. Spread out across a vast swath of land was a sea of tents, camp fires, banners, and flags. Far off to one side was a large collection of siege machines. In the other direction was a huge corral of war horses. There were campfires every dozen yards, and a low haze filled the sky from all of the smoke. Everywhere he looked he saw people practicing sword combat, cleaning their weapons, throwing around a ball, or doing any of a thousand other things that people do with nervous energy as they wait for the command to go and kill.

Eventually they arrived at a large tent with a wide berth between it and all of the other tents. Next to the tent were several wagons, including many with cages built into them. Inside the cages were the largest, meanest looking, wolves that Vendino had ever seen. They began to growl and howl when the two ministers came near.

Not far from the tent was a campfire, and not far from the campfire Vendino saw two youngsters playing a dice game in the dirt. One was a boy of about ten years of age. He had well-groomed blond hair and wore an expensive and trendy outfit. The other child was a little girl who was about eight years old. She was a skinny little thing with long brown hair and dressed all in black.

Vendino gasped in surprise when he saw that the boy was Prince Edal, the emperor's only son. He changed his path and walked over to the two children. He said, "Prince Edal, why are you away from your tent? Where are your nursemaids?"

Lord Jalinox walked confidently out of his tent, with his assistant Jarla right next to him. He wore his traditional black and red tunic with a black cape flowing behind him. Jarla was dressed similarly, but her black cape had red trim around it. He said, "The prince is visiting Tali. I sent the nursemaids away, they're not needed here."

Vendino groaned on the inside. He took a deep breath to keep his voice sounding patient. "Lord Jalinox, the prince is only ten. I don't think he should be in the middle of an army encampment in the first place. But, if he is going to be here, he really needs to be in the care of his nursemaids. Besides, why is he playing with some stray waif? The prince has plenty of well-mannered playmates of respectable lineage to play with back in Clornoss."

He noticed Jalinox's assistant, Jarla, put her hands on her hips as if she was going to make some comment.

Jalinox put his hand on her shoulder without looking at her. He said, "Minister, our emperor feels that it is best that his heir experience what war is like. If he is to lead the empire someday, he needs to understand the true nature of war. And, as for his choice of playmates, who are we to judge? The prince and Tali have become close friends over the past month. They're about the same age, and it's almost as if they're made for each other."

"I don't care. Going forward I expect his nursemaids to remain at his side at all times. Is that clear?"

Jalinox smiled but did not answer.

After a moment, Thorli pointed at one of the wagons, "Can you at least tell us why there are wolves in cages on those wagons?"

"Yes, General. These are some of my newest creations, and a bit of a secret weapon if I do say so myself." He paused and then said, "Behold, Garrolwolves! Quite possibly the perfect defense against Magi attacks."

The two ministers looked at each other. General Thorli said, "Lord Jalinox, I would prefer that you leave the Magi to my men. Right now I'm more worried about necromancer attacks than the Magi. Letting wolves loose in camp will surely be more harm than help. Do not open those cages without my explicit directions, is that clear?"

Jalinox smirked and then bowed his head slightly, "As you wish, General.

And I have a hunch that you won't have to worry about the necromancers any time soon."

CHAPTER 6

Kimly

"You haven't said anything about your trip. How'd it go?"

Cletis groaned, "I don't want to trouble you with business problems, dearest."

Kimly was leaning back in his lap on a massive luxurious couch in the Pink Room. She rarely came into this room without him, because the whole room was dripping with romance and happiness and if she wasn't careful it made her want to gag. However, he loved the room and it was his favorite place for sexual games. Therefore, she kept her opinion of the room to herself so he could enjoy it when they were together.

The room was dominated by two large comfortable couches, both of which were bigger than most beds. She imagined hundreds of naked ducks roaming the countryside while she lounged around on their feathers in the pillows of the couches.

Other than a few end tables and other miscellaneous hutches, the couches were the only furnishings in the spacious room. The walls were covered with several ancient tapestries featuring angels and humans in various states of undress and captured in intimate situations. As much as she didn't care for the Pink Room, she did get a giggle out of the tapestries.

She closed her eyes when he started caressing her hair. It was a silly thing, but she loved how it felt when he rubbed her hair. In some ways it was like she was a dog being petted by her master, but she tried not to think of it that way or it would start to annoy her.

She said, "I wouldn't have asked if I wasn't curious."

"The Chancellor has banned all wheat and grain imports indefinitely."

She sighed. The whole purpose of his latest trip was to bring a large shipment of wheat and grain from Tharrin. She asked, "Why would he do that? I thought you said that Khardifar doesn't produce nearly as much wheat and grain as it needs and that's why it's so profitable for merchants like you?"

"Oh, it doesn't. Not nearly enough, that's the saddest part. The poorest people of the city will suffer the most. The Chancellor wants to drive up the prices by lowering the supply. The profits from the sale of local wheat and grain go to the Chancellor's coffers. The prices are going to jump, and people will have no choice. They'll have to pay it if they want to eat."

"What about the alms for the poorest Denizens? Lots of people in the Commons only have food when the alms wagon comes around."

He shrugged, "You know how it is, Dearest. The alms are taken around with whatever is left over. When there is a shortage it's the alms that suffer first."

For the most part she didn't care too much about wheat and grain import rules. If the poorest Denizens were that hungry they'd find a way to make their life better. She found a way out of the Commons, and she didn't feel sorry for those who still lived there. No one felt sorry for her when she was hungry and poor. However, the Chancellor's ban would cost her husband a business deal. He'd probably lose some money, and he was obviously stressed and that irritated her.

"What happened to your shipment?"

"It's still in a warehouse in the Tharrin docks. Word of the ban reached Tharrin shortly before I arrived, and the captain wouldn't even load the ship. If this ban isn't lifted soon then I'm going to have to find another buyer in some other city, or the supplies will simply rot in the warehouse while we wait."

"The whole thing seems dumb to me. The Chancellor's people need food, and he makes it harder for them to get it?"

He sighed, "Political games, dearest. It shouldn't last long. Now, how about you give some alms to this unfortunate husband who hungers for his beautiful raven haired wife?"

- = - = -

Several hours later, Kimly was on her way to Doc Algurith's office. Yesterday she promised the doctor that she would check on Favin. Her husband had fallen asleep an hour ago, after a marathon session of naughty games and she was confident that he'd sleep soundly until morning. He hadn't noticed her slip away and she didn't expect it to be a problem to slip back unnoticed in a few hours.

The evening air was uncomfortably warm, and even without the glare of the sun she was still sweating like a troll. Once again she was wearing all black and her favorite black floppy hat. She started her trip into the Commons with her *Shadow Shroud* spell around her, but she dropped it when she was almost at the doctor's place.

She entered the building without knocking, since the door was unlocked. She found Favin laying in the bed where she left him. The man was alone in the room and seemed to be sleeping. When Kimly quietly entered the room he opened his eyes and let his head roll to the side so he could see her.

"It's you. You saved my life."

She shrugged, "How you feeling?"

"Like I was run over by a horde of stampeding ogres." He began coughing and that caused him to wince in pain and grab his side. When he regained his composure he said, "But I'd be dead if it weren't for you."

She shrugged again, "I just pulled you outta there." She didn't feel comfortable with all of the gratitude. She never did like being in the spotlight, she preferred to observe things from afar so she could ridicule those people in the spotlight.

He looked at her for a long while, and then asked, "You're a Magi?"

She cursed profanely on the inside. The very last thing she wanted was to have the Magi problems follow her to her new home. However, she couldn't deny that the things he had seen had been magic. She nodded slightly, "Perhaps."

"I've heard rumors the Magi Society was back"

She raised an eyebrow. Suddenly she had an idea. She said, "Slow down, Orc-Brains. I said I'm a Magi, I didn't say anything about the Magi Society."

"There are magic users who ain't in the Society?"

She leaned a little closer and looked into the man's eyes. She opened her magesight and focused for a moment. After a second she saw the double-vision that happened when she used her regular sight and her magesight together. The magical sight allowed her to look through his eyes and view his soul, or at least her magical interpretation of his soul. She assumed that Order Magi could do much more with the magesight. For her, the main use was to see if someone possessed a magewel, the magical reservoir needed for a Magi to access and manipulate the magical essence within their body. It took only moments for her to see the glow of his magewel.

She closed off the magesight and blinked a couple of times to clear her vision. Favin possessed a magewel, so he had the potential to become a Magi. Her devious mind was reeling with the possibilities. Could she train him? The thought of having a Magi ally, who ran a thieves guild and owed her his life, filled her with excitement. The possibilities were staggering.

Kimly smiled devilishly, and said, "Of course there are magic users who ain't in the Magi Society. I'm one of the Shrouded, it's a secret guild. We're Magi, but we got our own rules." Yes, it was completely false, but she had always been quick at coming up with convincing lies. She assumed he would respect her more if he thought she was a part of a large group instead of a single rogue Magi.

He looked skeptical, "I ain't heard of them."

She smirked at him, "Secret guilds are like that. And we don't usually work in Khardifar."

He got a surprised look on his face, and then the pain took over his attention once again. After a few minutes of quiet, he said, "What kind of guild is it, what do you do?"

She wasn't sure how to answer him, so she gave him a stern look and said, "A secret one. Our missions and goals are our own." She hoped that would satisfy him.

He wasn't satisfied. He asked, "Are you assassins?"

She shrugged, "Maybe. Our missions are different all the time. We're trained to be ready for any mission that we're assigned. Sometimes someone ends up hurt or dead, but not always. Sometimes the mission is just delivering packages from one place to another. The missions usually need some sneakiness. They always need secrecy."

"Were you on a mission in that alley? Was I your target, or was it Hisaro's men?" He tried to adjust so he was sitting up more, and then grunted in pain. He seemed to give up on getting comfortable and settled for being still.

"You really struggle with the whole 'secret guild' thing, don't you? Besides, if we wanted you dead, you'd be cold by now."

"So, Hisaro's men were your target? Is there a larger guild war brewing? Are the Shrouded going to take on Hisaro? Perhaps you need allies?"

She smiled on the inside. "Well, if you want to help the Shrouded, I might have a way you can get involved. I hear that you have a thieves' guild of your own. We may contact you soon."

"What services do you need? Most importantly, how much do I get paid?"

"There would be no pay for this mission. It is a test."

He laughed sarcastically, and then groaned in pain. After a few moments he said, "You want to hire my guild, but you don't want to pay us? You're joking, right?"

"What I'm offering can't be bought, it is a gift much rarer than platinum."

He looked skeptical. "And it is?"

"Have you ever wanted to be a Magi? To know power like most people can only dream about?"

Favin was quiet for a long time. He didn't move, he just looked into her eyes. She assumed he was trying to decide if she was swindling him somehow. He said, "Yes."

"Then this is a test. If you pass our test, we will train you as a Magi."

He was quiet for a few moments again. "Will I become a member of the Shrouded?"

"If you pass the test, you'll become an agent of the Shrouded."

"My guild is small. After two brutal months of pressure from Hisaro's men, I've lost over two-thirds of my people. We don't got much to offer."

She pulled out a coin pouch and counted out four platinum raptors. She held them out and dumped them in his hand.

Favin was so shocked that he tried to sit up quickly. The pain made him whimper and he closed his eyes and stopped moving briefly until the pain subsided. Then he said, "By the gods, woman! Where'd you get all this? Why are you giving it to me, I thought the job was unpaid?"

"That's not payment. It's a little something to get your guild back to full strength. You're gonna need to recruit cutpurses, sneak thieves, and several body guards. You'll probably need equipment and some hush money."

He didn't respond, he just stared at the coins in his hand.

She added, "Once you are a Magi you'll see how easy it is for Magi to get coins beyond anyone's wildest dreams. By this time next year the idea of being paid for a job will be comical, because you'll have more coin than you could possibly spend."

She could tell that he wanted to tell her that she's delusional. Then he looked down at the fortune in his hand once again.

He said, "If I accept this money, then we become your lackeys. I don't like that much."

"You told the thugs that you ain't no one's lackey. I ain't no one's lackey either. The Shrouded offers missions and contracts. I accept the ones that interest me, I refuse the others. If you join, you'll have the same freedom. Shrouded Magi have only one pledge, that they will not harm or hinder other Shrouded. Beyond that, no one cares what you do. Make a fortune, or don't make a fortune, that's all up to you."

"It sounds like a child's fantasy tale."

"The best things in life usually do. Will you take the test?"

"What is the mission?"

She smiled, "Let your wounds heal, and start rebuilding your guild. We'll talk about the details of your test later."

Before he could reply, Doc Algurith walked into the room. He walked over to the bed and placed the back of his hand against Favin's forehead. Then he looked at the wound, poking it gently, and causing the guild leader to shout a long series of colorful curses.

Kimly sat quietly while the Doc looked at his patient. After a few minutes Doc Algurith left the room without saying a word to either of them.

CHAPTER 7

Jessa

"Come on, willya? We're never gonna get outta here if you girls can't keep up!" Flat-Nose Idiot laughed as he looked back at the stragglers.

Red-Hair Idiot looked back at them and laughed as well, "Shoulda known better than to take women out on a man's mission."

Jessa swore loudly as she struggled to walk through the wet and slippery mud. Each step she took caused her foot to sink almost to her knee in the thick muck. Her leg muscles burned and she was completely worn out. On top of that she was wet, cold, dirty, exhausted, and angry. The woman beside her began to slip and fall, and reached out to grab Jessa's arm. She snatched it away quickly before the woman could capture it.

The woman fell in the muck and struggled briefly to stand back up. Jessa ignored her and kept walking. It was difficult enough to get herself through the terrible mud, the last thing she needed was someone else making it worse.

They had been traveling through the underground nightmare for a fortnight, and Jessa was losing patience with the mission. The first several days had been mostly traveling through caves of solid stone. Eventually they got to some old abandoned mines or something similar. Once they moved out of the abandoned mines they made their way through more natural caves. The hardships thus far included attacks from many different types of creatures, walking across narrow ledges, scaling rock walls, dealing with an endless array of bugs, and a long list of other annoyances. The muddy floor began yesterday, and had steadily grown worse since then.

Part of her wished that she had never gotten involved with the Magi or the necromancers. It seemed like just the other day when her and her brother Burga had discussed becoming Magi with Rissyl and Cynia. Her life had been much simpler back then. Now her brother was dead, and she was covered in mud on a stupid quest for a demented necromancer. However, that weak side of Jessa seldom surfaced these days. The vengeful and power-hungry side typically won out. She believed that Jalinox could help her bring her brother back to life, and she was certain that through the power she gained as his apostle that she could get vengeance on the emperor who brought about Burga's death.

First she would need to find a way out of the dreadful mud and muck.

She had brought the whole mess on herself a couple of months ago when she was discussing the Stronghold with Lord Jalinox. While she listened to him rant about how important it was for the necromancers to find the ring so they could capture the Stronghold from the magical beings, she asked the fateful question. "Couldn't the Motlites defeat the magical creatures?"

Jalinox had looked at her with an astonished expression, and then he hugged her. The next fortnight had been a whirlwind of preparations, and a team was put together to travel to the Stronghold.

The team was being led by Flat-Nose Idiot, and his band of brutish thugs. Jalinox referred to them as combat specialists, and the six of them were there to escort Jessa, another Dark Apostle wench, and the three Motlites to the Stronghold.

Jessa wished that she could say that they didn't need the six idiots to accompany them, but that would be a lie. The two Dark Apostle women could use their necromancer skills to raise Awakened servants and to battle most foes, but some of the challenges they'd faced in their travels under the mountains had required great strength and agility. She knew that she and the wench wouldn't have been able to make it this far without a group of strong warriors. She just wished Jalinox could have found some strong warrior women instead of sticking them with six cocky men.

She looked back and saw that her swarm of Awakened servants was having even more trouble in the mud than she was. She wasn't worried about them, they would catch up eventually or she would replace them.

"Aw, sweetheart! Did you fall down? If you need me to come back there and carry you, just ask. But I will expect special payment when we reach camp."

Jessa looked up and saw that it was Crater-Face Idiot who made the comment. As soon as he said it, all six idiots began laughing and whispering to each other.

She really hated each of the six idiots and she desperately wanted to use her new powers to drain the life out of them. Many times she fantasized about making them all Awakened and watching them amble along behind her, mindlessly doing her bidding. Unfortunately Lord Jalinox had very strict rules about such things. If she broke his favorite idiots, he would be furious. So, she ignored them as best as she could.

Her legs burned with fatigue and she tried not to breathe heavily so the idiots wouldn't see that she was tired. She turned her attention inward, and tried to let herself get lost in thoughts of being anywhere else. That only worked for a few steps, because she needed to keep her full attention on moving through the muck or she would end up face first in it like the wench behind her.

After what seemed like hours of one step after the next, she heard the idiots up ahead of her begin to complain. She looked up to see what their trouble was and she saw that the level tunnel they had been trudging through was turning into a steep slope up. Eventually she caught up with the Motlites and then the idiots, as they each struggled to climb up the muddy tunnel.

It felt good to stand still for a while, and it gave her a chance to catch her breath. After a few minutes the other Dark Apostle wench caught up to her, and after that the Awakened started to catch up as well. She leaned slightly on the stone wall. She thought about sitting down, but she wasn't entirely certain that she'd be able to coax herself into standing back up any time soon.

The idiots were laughing at each other, as they would make a little progress and then slide back down into one another as they tried to make their way up the slope.

Wart-Chin Idiot grabbed a backpack from Red-Hair Idiot and opened it. He said, "Ok, you're all a bunch of girls! Stay down here with the ladies and I'll climb up with a rope. I'll find somewhere to tie it off, and then I'll holler down to you. Try not to get your pretty lacy dresses dirty while I'm gone." He laughed at the others as he pushed his way past them and began crawling up the slippery slope.

The others made a variety of crude remarks to him as he began crawling up the slope, but they all squatted down so they could watch his progress.

After several minutes, Jessa heard yelling and swearing coming from the tunnel. Wart-Chin Idiot was screaming something about large bugs.

Quite a while later, she could hear Wart-Chin Idiot yelling again. This time he was yelling that he was outdoors. They had finally made it through the freaking mountain to the other side!

She pushed herself away from the wall and looked towards the tunnel in excitement. The other idiots started crawling up the tunnel, and she stood impatiently waiting for her turn. Eventually the last idiot disappeared up the steep slippery tunnel and then the Motlites began the climb.

The other Dark Apostle wench moved like she was going to climb up the tunnel behind the Motlites, and Jessa moved over to cut her off. The woman had been lagging behind all day. She could just wait her turn.

The wench said, "We'll all make it up eventually, there is no need to be rude."

Jessa turned to the wench and gave her an insincere smile.

Once the Motlites had made some progress up the tunnel, Jessa climbed in after them. The ground was cold and wet, and in some places her knees sank so deep that her belly was in the mud. She had to hold onto the rope with both hands, so she had to support her weight on her knees and elbows as she pulled herself up the slippery slope. The Motlites above her were constantly kicking mud and gunk down onto her head.

She wanted to cry. She wanted to scream. More than anything she wanted to blast things with Khalius Fire, the purple magical fire that was the main weapon of the necromancers. Instead she continued to slowly pull herself up the slope.

One of the idiots yelled. Soon several of the idiots were yelling about bugs. The shouts almost sounded panicked, and she was certain the idiots were in a great deal of pain.

A short time later she saw the first bug, it was walking across the mud and coming for her. It was at least as long as her finger, as thick as two fingers, and it had large pincers and creepy eyes. She let go of the rope with one hand to swat at the bug, splattering the mud with its green innards.

As soon as she dealt with the first bug, she saw several more of them. They were coming from the walls, and they seemed to be coming after her. Within seconds she was covered in awful bugs. They crawled all over her and some of them were biting her, hard!

She screamed and tried to pull herself up the rope faster. The screams from above her hinted that things weren't much better up there.

The biting was getting worse, and she was afraid to look at her body because she knew that she was covered with the huge bugs! She could feel them on her arms and legs, and all along her back. They were under her clothes, and they were biting her all over.

There was nothing she could do but pull herself up the rope faster. She tried brushing them off, but more crawled onto her faster than she could push them off. The bugs were everywhere, and the tunnel was crawling with them.

She started blasting some of them with Khalius Fire, but it was no use. She was more likely to kill herself or someone else in their party before she made any significant impact on the mass of giant bugs.

With another scream of frustration, she kicked forward and tried to crawl

49

and climb faster to get away from the bugs. Something hit her left elbow, and she realized that she was climbing past a motionless body. As she climbed passed it she saw that it was Red-Hair Idiot. The bugs had already eaten out his eyeballs and were scurrying out of his mouth and eye sockets when she crawled past.

She could feel them biting deeper on her back, legs, and top of her head. She rolled around in the mud, pushing her sides and back up against the walls of the tunnel as much as possible. She hoped that she squished some of the horrible bugs in the process.

Screaming again, she pushed several bugs off her face and away from her ears and then pulled herself up the rope as fast as she could. She didn't know if pulling the bugs off was Red-Hair Idiot's downfall, or if he died because he didn't pull any of the bugs off.

She tried to ignore them, and focused on climbing. With each reach of a hand higher up the rope, she slammed her elbow down in the mud killing more bugs. They were in her hair, and crawling up her pants. It tickled and hurt at the same time. She thought that she just might go insane before the terrible things finished eating her alive.

Screeching at the top of her lungs, Jessa threw a fit. She slapped at her arms and legs, killing as many bugs as she could. She smashed her knees and elbows into many of the bugs. Then she summoned more Khalius Fire to her right and left. The purple magic hit the walls next to her, and fanned out to both sides.

It didn't help, but it made her feel like she was at least doing something. All the while she continued to climb as best as she could. She was beginning to doubt that she could make it out alive. With all of her new necromancer powers, it would be tragically humorous to be killed by bugs.

She smashed a bug on her face, with much more force than necessary. Its gooey insides splattered her cheek and ran into her lips.

She continued to climb until she finally felt her fingers catch the ledge of the slope. She looked up and saw the open sky! As quickly as she could, she scrambled out of the cave and started brushing bugs from her face and head. She brushed off her arms and legs, and then started stripping off clothes to get at the bugs under them. As they scurried away she stomped on them with all of her might.

Normally Jessa was extremely modest, especially around the idiots. At this point she simply didn't care. If the sex-obsessed trolls wanted to ogle her diddies, she couldn't care any less. Her clothes went flying, piece by piece.

She slapped, swatted, brushed, and squashed bugs one at a time. Some of them were trying to burrow into her skin and those she had to pluck out of her flesh.

Before long the panic began to subside and she looked around the area. The five remaining idiots, and the wench, were all standing around her and they were all naked. The wench was still screaming and crying while two of the idiots helped her smack bugs from her skin.

She grabbed Flat-Nose Idiot by the shoulder. When he turned to her, she said, "If you check me for diggers, I'll check you."

She expected some sort of sexual innuendo or sarcastic comment, but he just nodded. He quickly looked around her body for burrowing bugs. She yelled in pain as he squeezed a tender place on her inner thigh, and she felt him pull one of the bugs from deep in her flesh.

He said, "I got that one, but I think its head is still inside you. I'll need to dig that out with a knife."

Jessa nodded, "Ok, but let me check you first."

- = - = -

The next morning, Jessa woke up with the sunrise. She hurt everywhere and as soon as she tried to move, her body felt like it was going to explode in pain. However, she was relatively warm and dry. That was better than she had been in days.

Next to her was the wench. The woman was curled into a ball, and had snuggled up against Jessa at some point in the night.

Moaning in pain, Jessa sat up and scooted over to the tent flap. She let herself out of the tent and looked around.

Last night, after searching each other for bugs, the group had moved away from the cave opening and then set up camp. Red-Hair Idiot was dead, but the other idiots all seemed fine. They were working around camp getting breakfast prepared. Given the events of the last fortnight, the mood around the camp was surprisingly happy. Some of the idiots laughed and joked with each other as they worked.

The Motlites were fine, for whatever reason the bugs didn't bother them at all. All three Motlites were sitting next to a tent.

None of the Awakened made it out of the tunnel. Jessa didn't know if they simply couldn't make the climb, or if the bugs had eaten them. She didn't really care.

She walked a short distance away from camp to take care of morning needs. Off to the east the sun was just beginning to rise over the tops of the mountains. She took a moment to look around her surroundings. They were in the lower foothills, presumably on the north side of the Rukthor Mountains.

Off to the northwest she could see the Stronghold, or what she assumed was the Stronghold. There were dozens, maybe even a hundred or more, towers and buildings of all shapes and sizes. Around it all was a large wall. Something glowing red stretched around the base of the entire wall, Jessa assumed that was something added by the magical guardians.

When she walked back into the camp she said, to no one in particular, "I'm going to activate the talisman."

Immediately the mood around the camp changed. The idiots stopped joking around. She smiled to herself and breathed a sigh of relief. She knew that when Lord Jalinox arrived, things would be better. The idiots wouldn't dare treat her poorly with Jalinox around.

Jessa pulled her backpack out of the tent, and reached inside for the talisman. Several of the huge bugs scurried out of her pack and she blasted them with Khalius Fire. It was overkill, but she felt good watching the bugs fall over dead. She wondered briefly if she could turn dead bugs into Awakened, and then pushed that thought aside to focus on the task at hand.

She pulled the talisman from the pack and walked over to an open area away from the tents and the idiots. The talisman was made of sticks, beads, feathers, and wax. It had a short bone spike sticking out of the back. After looking at it for a moment, she shoved the bone spike into the ground. A few moments later the beads began to glow softly and the wax melted and flowed around the talisman and onto the ground.

For a few minutes Jessa stood there watching the talisman. She knew that it could be a long time before Lord Jalinox even noticed that the paired talisman that he possessed had started to glow. Once he noticed it, he would need to prepare his things. It could be hours before he arrived.

She walked over to the camp and helped herself to a bowl of breakfast goop. It might be poddidge or oatmeal, but she wasn't sure. She didn't really care. It tasted terrible, but it was warm and filling.

As she finished the tasteless goop she heard someone walking up behind her.

Lord Jalinox said, "It took you longer than I expected. If you're done lounging around, let's go claim my new Stronghold." He didn't even pause as he walked past them.

Jessa grabbed her bag and followed Jalinox as he walked towards the Stronghold. The idiots scurried around packing up the camp and putting away their things. She assumed the wench would pack up their tent.

She said, "How was your fortnight, My Lord? Has the army taken the barbarian city yet?"

"It was wonderful, my dear. The emperor's cub is taking nicely to little Tali, and everything is coming together as I've planned. The army hasn't moved against Ront'El yet, but I expect that to happen at any time. Once we take the Stronghold there will be much cause for celebration, indeed!"

"That's great!" She wanted to tell him about everything they had endured on their trek to this place, so he would appreciate all that she had gone through for him. However, she knew he didn't want to hear the details. Everything she wanted to say would just sound like whining, and that wouldn't make her look good in his eyes. Therefore, she kept quiet.

Before long the wench, the idiots, and the Motlites all caught up with them.

Wart-Chin Idiot said, "Lord Jalinox, it's good to see you. I hope you've been well."

"Wallie, if I was any more wonderful I'd be giggling. I see Ronde isn't here, apparently you encountered difficulties in your journey?"

"Yes, we did. It was awful! For most of the beginning-"

Jalinox cut him off in mid-sentence, "I see that my Dark Apostles and the Motlites made it through. You all did your job commendably. We have more work to do." He looked towards Flat-Nose Idiot as he walked. He said, "Fowlar, prepare your men and the Motlites. When we get closer I will stop, as will my Dark Apostles. You'll take the Motlites and assault the Stronghold. The vile guardian should appear when you get close. Let the Motlites do the attacking, your job is to keep anything from getting to us. Are we clear?"

Flat-Nose Idiot nodded, "Yes, Lord Jalinox!"

They walked quickly through the long grass for several minutes. When they were about fifty yards from the wall, Jalinox stopped. Jessa stopped next to him, and she noticed that the wench stopped beside her. The idiots and the Motlites continued walking towards the wall.

When the Motlites got near the glowing red magical barrier near the fence, they all lunged at it together. As the malformed humanoid Motlites grabbed the magical fence it began to glow brighter in the section near them. After a few moments Jessa noticed the fence starting to disappear. It started furthest away from the Motlites, and then it was as if the fence was being sucked into the Motlites. Within moments the entire fence was gone.

Suddenly a huge magical creature appeared before the idiots. It was made entirely from light outlining all of its features in a deep red color. It was taller than the Motlites and was shaped like someone with massive muscles. The magical creature was semitransparent, but it had a deep red glow inside of it, like some sort of power or aura was pulsating within its chest. In one hand, it had a large halberd, made from the same magic as the creature.

The creature had the halberd planted in the ground, blade side up. In a deep booming voice, which resonated throughout the area, the creature said, "Humans, present Bisangar's Signet Ring to claim the Magi Stronghold!" It was looking at the idiots and didn't even seem to notice the Motlites at all.

Then it was too late. One of the Motlites rushed over to the magical creature and grabbed it by the neck. The creature simply faded from view, until it was completely gone.

Jessa wanted to rush down, but Jalinox held out his hand before her.

Everyone just stood still for several long moments, and then a dozen more magical creatures appeared. It was as if they walked right through the large stone wall that surrounded the Stronghold.

The largest creature said, in a booming voice, "Who dares to attack the Rolimi?"

The Motlites all rushed at the Rolimi creatures. As the carnage carried on, it was clear that the Rolimi creatures couldn't even see the Motlites. Jessa tried to suppress a laugh, but it came out quietly. Within moments half of the magical creatures were extinguished without even putting up any sort of resistance. The remaining creatures looked as though they were about to panic. Another Motlite grabbed an unsuspecting Rolimi creature and it was quickly extinguished as well.

The largest Rolimi creature shouted, "Flee!"

The remaining five creatures jumped back into the wall of the Stronghold from where they had emerged, and the field got quiet once again.

After several long minutes the magical creatures did not return, and Jalinox began walking towards the Stronghold. He said, "Fowlar, get your men onto the wall. If the Rolimi are not around, open that gate. Let's enter our new Stronghold!"

The idiots all rushed towards the wall and formed a human ladder. Soon several of them were on the wall, and they jumped down onto the other side. After a short while, the gate opened from the inside.

Jessa followed Jalinox into the Stronghold. The Rolimi creatures were nowhere to be seen.

Jalinox said, "Fowlar, set up patrols around the walls. Keep those creatures and any Magi from entering. I want one Motlite with me, one should search the Stronghold grounds for stray magic creatures. The other one can patrol the walls with your men." He stopped and looked around the courtyard with a huge grin. "Ladies, let's go find our destiny!"

CHAPTER 8

Rissyl

Looking around the room, Rissyl felt a little overwhelmed. They were at Randol's home in the basement, in a large ceremonial room. The room had four large chairs along the east wall, arranged side by side. The middle of the room was filled with benches stretching from the north to the south wall. The benches were all facing the east and could accommodate several dozen people. The room was sparsely decorated, featuring only a few candles and a single banner on the south wall. However, the furnishings and items in the room were all extremely well made and valuable.

Rissyl, Cynia, Sarasa, and Dalen sat in the four large chairs in the east. Randol and Firana sat in the benches facing the four large chairs. All six of them wore their cloaks, but none of them was armed.

Rissyl opened a large tome and flipped to the page that explained the process for starting a meeting of the Grand Coterie, and it detailed the spells used during the beginning of the meeting. He quickly read the first paragraph and then sighed heavily. Even though he had been practicing this part, he was still nervous.

He looked at the book one last time and then he closed it and looked around the room. He said, "We are gathered today to join with our fellow Coteries in peace and prosperity. All Coteries from the calm seas of the east to the stormy shores of the west, from the barrier mountains in the north to the rocky shores in the south shall answer the call and join us now." He let out a sigh of relief that he was able to remember the whole paragraph and say it without stumbling over anything.

Randol motioned for him to stand up. He stood up and placed the tome on the chair behind him. He said, "All Magi will rise!"

Everyone in the room stood up.

Rissyl said, "Grand officers, summon your implements of power." He summoned his staff. He assumed that Cynia summoned her staff, Dalen summoned his magic sword, and Sarasa summoned a magic dagger. He resisted the urge to look at them to make sure.

Then he quietly performed the first spell of the night. It was a complicated spell, and he wasn't entirely sure that he understood how it worked. He knew it was a ritual spell and he was only responsible for part of it. The other grand officers would be casting their own portions of the spell along with him, and if they worked their magic properly then the ritual would be complete soon. He summoned the magic and molded it into the intricate pattern as described in to tome. Once the magic was ready he released it into his staff as he said, "*Vaelth.*"

The runes along his staff glowed bright red. He held the staff horizontally in both hands and placed the top end straight out in front of himself. He said, "The first principle of the Society is truth. We will be true and loyal to ourselves, our fellow Magi, and to the Society."

Cynia said, "*Salven'Tik.*" The runes along her staff began to glow green. She held the staff horizontal and crossed the tip of her staff on the tip of his staff. Then she said, "The second principle of the Society is morality. We will always strive to preserve the sanctity of human life."

Dalen said, "*Kolpassil.*" The runes along the blade of his sword began to glow blue. He placed the tip of his sword at the point where the two staffs were crossed. The runes on all three weapons continued to glow brightly. He said, "The third principle of the Society is compassion. We will strive to help those less fortunate who are worthy of such consideration."

Sarasa said, "*Zoventia.*" The runes along the blade of her dagger began to glow a greyish white color. She took a step closer to Rissyl and sat the tip of her dagger on the other three crossed weapons. She said, "The fourth principle of the Society is sovereignty. We will strive to ensure that our Covenant to the Society extends beyond the petty and ever shifting political boundaries set forth by nations."

Rissyl could feel his heart pounding inside his chest. He was nervous and excited. He wasn't really sure what to expect next, but the decisive moment was upon them. With a deep breath and a pause he tried to calm himself. Then he said, "The fifth principle of the Society is justice. We will strive to defend the fundamental right of all people to be treated equally and judged on their own actions and merit."

He paused to remember the exact details of the spell that he needed to cast. He summoned magical essence from his magewel and began to mold and shape it carefully. When it was ready he released it into the four crossed weapons before him. As he did so, he said, "*Justivik*"

A wave of bright light sprang out from all four glowing weapons, and it gradually engulfed the entire room. When the bright light reached the walls, ceiling, and floor it seemed to stick to those surfaces. Soon all of the walls, as well as the floor and ceiling, shimmered in a magical glow.

Rissyl placed his staff in the special holder on the right arm of his chair, with the top pointing at the ceiling. Its runes still glowed red. He sat down in his chair he looked out across the room.

He smiled in awe as he watched the magical semi-transparent images of other Magi appear around the room. Most of the Magi were positioned throughout the middle of the room where the benches sat, but a few of the Magi were seated along the outside walls of the room. The ritual merged the meeting of the six Magi in Randol's home with similar meetings being conducted by Magi throughout the lands. Now all of the participating Magi could be seen around the room, although most of them looked ghost-like and mostly transparent.

Randol stood up and said, "Greetings Magi! Normally you will be greeted by the acting Grand Evoker, Rissyl Sokigo. But since this is our first assembly, this is all very new to everyone so I should probably speak first. For those who don't know me, I was the Grand Diviner of the Grand Coterie of Sovereign Magi of Menelia. Yes, I did hold that office before the Betrayal, and yes that does mean that I am well over one hundred years old."

The partially transparent Magi in the crowd sat quietly, for the most part. A few people whispered to each other. As Rissyl counted all of the Magi in attendance, he was shocked to see thirty-four Magi present. Additionally, there were a number of Magi not present. He could think of at least twenty Magi who were not here in person, or magically. He didn't see Sarge, Aruk, Zahr, or most of the other Free Cities Magi. He also didn't see Kimly.

The vast majority of Magi present were the Society Magi, those Magi who were not a part of one of the four Orders and wore a brown and white cloak. Most of the Order Magi present were seated along the walls and represented the leadership of the various Coteries in attendance.

Randol continued without pausing, "I'm glad to see so many of you were able to join us. I hope you were able to perform the rituals that we sent you without too much trouble. The plan is to establish a regular schedule of assembling once a month, like this." He paused and turned to Rissyl. "Would you like to conclude the opening ritual?"

Rissyl cleared his throat, and then said, "Esteemed Grand Diviner Cynia, you will lead us in reciting the Magi Covenant."

Cynia stood up and said, "Magi, join me in reciting the Magi Covenant. I swear, to the goddess Nalria, that I will always remain loyal to the Society and all of its fellow members, and that I will always strive for the preservation of life and the freedom of all people. I will use my magical gifts for the enrichment of mankind, and never for evil or nefarious motives. I will not allow the secrets of magic use, nor any of the spells, rituals, or powers that I learn as a Magi to be revealed or taught to anyone who is not a worthy member of the Society."

When she sat down Rissyl stood up and said, "I proclaim this assembly of the Grand Coterie of Sovereign Magi of Menelia officially open."

He looked around the room, and he was surprised at how many faces he didn't recognize. A lot had changed over the last year as he devoted most of his time to finding the ring. He said, "Thank you all for coming to the assembly tonight. I know this is new and it seems kind of weird and archaic, but this is how our Magi forefathers did it. Let's do some introductions, and then we'll get started. My name is Rissyl. I am a member of the Order of Evokers."

He looked over at Cynia and the others and all three of them introduced themselves one at a time.

Rissyl said, "You've already met the Exalted Grand Diviner, Randol. In addition we have one other Evoker, Firana, present with us here."

He looked over to Thon, who was once Sarasa's fighting guild teacher. The semi-transparent image of Thon was seated along the wall and he wore a blue and white cloak, indicating that he was a member of the Order of Champions. Rissyl said, "Champion Thon, who is with you?"

"Our Coterie is in Sorgo, and there are nine of us including myself."

Rissyl then looked to Eleyne. She was the only candidate that he chose from those who responded to Burga's flyer, over a year ago back in Sorgo. That seemed like a long time ago. He was happy to see that she was doing well; she seemed very shy and unsure of herself at the time. He was surprised to see her in a green and white cloak, indicating that she was a member of the Order of Diviners.

He said, "Diviner Eleyne, who is with you?"

"My Coterie is in Libur, and there are eleven of us."

Next he looked to a red and white cloaked Magi sitting along the wall. He was one of the other Magi who was recruited in Sorgo along with Eleyne, but Rissyl couldn't remember the man's name. He looked over to Cynia, but he couldn't catch her eye.

Finally he said, "I'm sorry, Evoker, I've forgotten your name. Please introduce yourself and tell us who is with you."

The semi-transparent image of the Magi stood up and looked at the other

Magi gathered around the room. He said, "I am Evoker Ferth, leader of the Maethral Coterie. There are only three of us. It is good to see so many Magi gathered. It would be nice if some of you would come to Maethral and help us recruit and grow."

Rissyl raised his hand and motioned for Ferth to sit. "Yes, Ferth, thank you. We'll discuss needs and grievances soon."

He looked to the final Order Magi around the perimeter of the room. She was a blue and white cloaked Magi, and another of the Magi recruited in Sorgo when Eleyne and Ferth joined. Unfortunately, he couldn't remember her name either.

He said, "Champion, please introduce yourself, and tell us who is with you."

The semi-transparent image sat casually in her chair. She waved at the gathered Magi, and said, "I'm Keta, and I'm here with three other Magi from Khazror."

Rissyl nodded an introduction to them all. He said, "It is great to see so many Magi gathered for this meeting. Thank you all for joining us! Hopefully at our next meeting we'll also have the other Magi who weren't able to merge with this meeting."

He paused for a minute and Ferth stood up to start talking. Rissyl motioned him back down, and then held up a finger to encourage him to wait. He said, "First let me update everyone on what your acting Grand Coterie Magi have been doing lately. Cynia and I, along with a few other Magi from the Free Cities, have been hunting for the signet ring that will allow us to claim the Stronghold. We have information that it is buried with its last owner, and we're working with the landowner to get permission to dig up the body. Hopefully we'll have that ring very soon!"

He motioned to Dalen, who stood up and straightened his cloak.

Dalen said, "Over the last year I've spent a good amount of time helping Champion Thon in Sorgo. We've gone on many missions to free Dregs, and we've also done some good recruiting in Sorgo. When I'm not out freeing Dregs I'm back here improving my *Abjuration* and *Artificing* skills."

Rissyl couldn't help but cringe on the inside. Dreg was the term used for those wicked or unfortunate souls who were forced into slavery by the empire. The emperor and the chancellors of the various cities didn't house criminals in dungeons, they were forced to work in the fields, build roads, work in quarries, and do many other menial tasks. Some of the Dregs were sold to individuals to serve as servants, or worse. Cynia had once been a Dreg owned by Rissyl's father. The topic of freeing Dregs had been a point of contention between Rissyl and Dalen since they first met.

Sarasa stood up and said, "I've been working with Randol, doing painstaking translations of ancient Magi texts and tomes looking for clues to the whereabouts of the signet ring. We've also been searching for anything in the old books that will assist us as we rebuilt the Magi Society."

As she sat down, Rissyl noticed that Ferth looked like he was about to burst from his chair. Clearly he had something to say. Rissyl said, "Evoker Ferth, you'd like to go next?"

"Yes I would!" He jumped up and started pacing around in front of his chair while he talked. His semi-transparent image merged with the images of other Magi who appeared to be seated near him as he walked, although they were actually in cities far from each other. "While you all were messing around trying to find a lost ring, we're already fighting a battle against the emperor in Maethral! We need more Magi, and we need your help! We've lost six Magi already, in the last five months. The city has been crawling with imperial soldiers, and the emperor's agents are everywhere. Maethral isn't a safe city for Magi, and most of the population that we're supposed to help doesn't seem to even want us around. More often than not it's some random Denizen who turns us in to the sentinels. It's extremely difficult to recruit new Magi when we're being killed faster than we're growing."

Rissyl motioned for him to sit down, and said, "Thank you Ferth. I'm sure it's been a difficult time. We'll see about getting some help in Maethral soon."

Ferth didn't sit down. He placed his hands on his hips and looked directly at Rissyl. "That don't fill me with confidence. If we don't get assistance soon, we're going to abandon Maethral. We'll meet up with a Coterie in a different city or something. You're running out of time."

"Thank you, Ferth. Champion Thon, how are things in Sorgo?"

Thon stood up and his semi-transparent image looked over to Ferth's image. When Ferth finally sat down, Thon said, "Grand Evoker, things have been pretty good in Sorgo. With the help of Grand Champion Dalen we have grown some-"

Ferth stood up and cut him off. "This is exactly what I'm talking about! If we got this sort of assistance in Maethral, several of our Magi might be alive today!"

Randol, Cynia, and Dalen all stood up, but Rissyl was up first. He was angry, and as he grabbed his staff by instinct he let some of his anger flow through him to his staff. Bright flames erupted briefly from the gem of his staff, and all of the Magi near him moved quickly away from the intense heat. Even some of the Magi who weren't present at Randol's moved back, out of reflex.

In a commanding voice he said, "That is enough! You will sit, now! You need assistance, we hear that. Now, let Thon speak in peace."

The others, including Ferth, sat back down. Rissyl remained standing, and he motioned for Thon to continue.

Thon stood back up, and said, "With Dalen's help we have grown some. We've also successfully freed dozens of Dregs. Each night we go on patrols, and we've been able to help countless people around the city. The people of Sorgo have embraced us, and we often hear people on the street talking about the Magi Society in a positive way. There have been rumors of imperial agents looking to capture or kill Magi, but that has not yet been a problem."

"Thank you Thon. Eleyne, would you like to go next?" Rissyl looked at Ferth to make sure he remained seated, and then he sat down as well.

The image of Eleyne stood up. "Things have been pretty good in Libur. Several of our Magi are people who were freed from the Motlite camp last year. We've also managed to recruit a few others in the last several months. We're practicing our magic and trying to grow stronger. We patrol when we can, and so far there haven't been any attacks by the emperor's agents."

"Very good, thanks Eleyne. Keta, you're up."

The image of the Keta stood up and she looked around the room. "In Khazror we're dealing with some of the same struggles that Maethral has faced. There have been many soldiers passing through the area, and imperial agents are actively hunting us. Over the last several months we've had three Magi ambushed and killed by the emperor's men. The people of Khazror seem to be too afraid of the sentinels to openly support us, but most of them don't act like they're against us. I'm afraid I must echo Evoker Ferth's plea for some assistance from the Grand Coterie. We have one Magi who joined us yesterday, other than that recruiting has been slow. If we're going to stand a chance against the emperor's men we must grow in numbers and power, and it must be done quickly."

"Thank you Keta. There are some Magi in the Free Cities who might be able to help Khazror and Maethral right away. The Grand Coterie will also be assisting you as soon as we can as well. Next, let's turn our focus to Magi Education. For our first meeting we wanted to discuss some important defensive spells that all Magi should master as quickly as possible. For that discussion, I'll turn things over to acting Grand Champion, Dalen."

Rissyl breathed a sigh of relief, and sat slightly more comfortably in his chair. Dalen's spell lessons would take quite a while, and he hoped that would give Ferth a chance to calm down a little. With any luck they'd be able to get through the rest of this first meeting without any further problems.

CHAPTER 9

Sarge

Sarge was in some sort of chapel. There were four guards, two of them near the door, and two of them pointing swords at two women. There was a third woman in the room, off by herself. There was also an overweight man in priest's robes wearing a stole with a black leaf on both ends; he was standing on a dais on the far side of the room.

Rissyl called out, "Jessa!"

Somehow Sarge knew that he was dreaming, reliving the events back in the Motlite breeding camp. He was, once again, seeing the events that ended with him unconscious and near death. However, the knowledge that he was dreaming couldn't keep the dream from happening again.

In his dream he watched himself thrust his sword at the first guard. It was just a distraction, and he withdrew the attack and redirected it into a circular strike. The feint worked perfectly, he completely avoided the guard's defensive parry and cleaved his sword deep into the shoulder and neck of the guard. Once again he could feel the blade hesitate slightly as it hit a bone and then bounce slightly as it hit another bone, until it came to a sudden stop against one of the guard's ribs.

Time seemed to be going in slow motion, and for a long time he stood there locked in the death blow and staring into the lifeless eyes of the guard that had not yet even fallen to the ground.

He watched himself yank the sword free of the corpse as it slowly dropped to the floor. Before it hit, Sarge turned to engage the next enemy. He was vaguely aware of thunder and bright lights of magic streaking off to his left, but he paid it no attention. The taste of blood was intoxicating; he could even feel the effects a bit in his dream-like visit to this battle.

Sarge turned the motion of his steps towards the next guard into his powerful downward vertical strike with his sword. He watched himself, in slow motion, drive the attack directly at the guard's head. The beads of nervous sweat were already forming on his enemy's forehead and from within the dream Sarge could see the panic and fear in his enemy's eyes. The guard was able to bring his sword up to block the vicious attack, barely getting it there in time.

He watched himself step forward, reposition his sword for another attack, and unleash one ferocious vertical strike after another. Each attack was harder than the last, and each time the guard struggled more to block in time. Sarge almost felt bad for the young guard. When the fifth savage attack slammed down, the guard was not able to block, and the sword cut the guard's head from the crown to the chin.

Sleeping Sarge almost felt sick to his stomach seeing it all over yet again. However, he had no choice but to keep watching. There was nothing he could do to stop the dream.

When the guard fell to the ground, Sarge watched himself look to the rest of the room for his next target. He saw that in the dream Rissyl had taken out the other two guards. Up on the dais, on the far side of the room, he could see the large priest with his hands up in submission.

Sarge screamed at himself through the dream to tell himself not to trust the priest.

The Sarge in the dream didn't hear him, and said "Don't worry, ladies, you're safe now." He watched himself point his sword, worthlessly, at the priest.

The girl with the dark hair, who he now recognized as Kimly, said, "Wait, you can't trust-"

From his right he saw the first purple magic orb fly towards him. It hit his cloak and spread out around it. The cloak protected him from most of the evil purple fire, and the attack hadn't hurt very much. The first one was followed by a steady stream of purple magic orbs speeding at him, in slow motion.

He heard the other girl yell, "Get out of here, Rissyl! I don't wanna hurt you, but you're not taking me from him!"

Sarge rushed over to the woman who was attacking him with necromancer magic. In his dream-like blur, the rush to the woman felt like running through tar.

Suddenly he was surrounded by the purple necromancer magic. It erupted from the floor, and he watched it in slow motion, towering out of the floor and engulfing him.

The first sensations of pain came from his feet. It felt as if someone was taking a large knife and dicing his toes and feet into tiny little toe-sized chunks. Even in his dream-like state, the sensation was horrifying and unbelievably painful.

When the pain eventually moved to his legs it was a different kind of pain.

It felt like a dozen people with thin iron spikes were jamming the spikes, one after the other, completely through his legs.

One would think that the two pains together would be enough to knock him unconscious, but he was awake and well aware of both types of pains.

Next his fingers, hands, and arms felt like they caught fire. It started on the pads of his fingers and quickly spread up his arms. He couldn't see flames, and the skin didn't blacken. However, the sensation felt as real as if he were really on fire.

He tried to scream out, however he was reliving but a moment and hadn't yet got to the screaming part.

When the pain reached his torso it felt as if his innards were being pulled from his body, through the skin. Intense pressure built until he felt all of his life's energy rushing from his body.

Finally the Sarge in his dream cried out in pain as he flailed around in the maelstrom of purple necromancer magical energy. From within the dream he watched as his body gyrated and the life force spilled from it. He could still feel each individual pain as it consumed his body.

The pain seemed to last for an eternity, and every time he got to this portion of the dream he felt like maybe he would die in his sleep from the pain and despair that he experienced all over again.

Just as the pain seemed unbearable, Sarge saw a mountain of a man kneel beside his body. Even viewing the impressive man through the foggy slow-motion blur of his dream still filled him with an overpowering wave of reverence and adoration. Sarge was certain that he was looking upon a god, and the god was kneeling next to his body.

Sarge watched as the hulking man placed his hand on the chest of Sarge's body. The purple magic violently swirled and raged around him, but it no longer touched his body.

The divine man appeared to have a slight glow. He wore ornate armor and a closed helm with ram horns. Strapped to the god's back was a majestic battleax. Engraved in the chest piece of the armor was an unusual symbol that Sarge had never seen elsewhere.

He watched the god look down at him and say, "You've not yet fulfilled your destiny. It is not yet your time."

Suddenly it felt like the ground was shaking. There was a voice, far away, calling to him. He ignored the voice and stared at the god kneeling beside his body within the dream.

The shaking became more severe. Gradually Sarge woke up to find Zahr shaking him violently.

"Sarge! Wake up! You're having a nightmare, wake up!"

He growled and pushed Zahr away roughly.

"That was quite the dream, are you alright?"

Sarge nodded, "Yes, yes, dammit! I'm fine. Leave me be."

He looked to the bedroom door and saw two little girls peeking in the crack of the mostly shut door. He stuck his tongue out at the girls. They giggled and scurried away from the door.

With a big stretch and a groan, Sarge repositioned in the bed and looked around the room. It was a small room, but furnished with nice things and attractive paintings. He was in Zahr's home in the Free City of Ront'El. He had stopped by to visit last night, and Zahr's wife Shella insisted that he have dinner and spend the night instead of getting a room at an inn. Sarge should have turned down the offered hospitality because of the nightmares. However, Shella had been quite insistent.

"How often do you have nightmares like that?"

Sarge felt very uncomfortable talking about the dream, because he didn't want to burden others with his problems. He said, "Go away. Really."

"Sarge, you were screeching as if you were being killed horribly. It was the most intense yelling I've ever heard from a man who wasn't actually dying. So, you can't sit there and tell me that it was nothing."

He rested his head on his palms, and then massaged his temples. After a moment he said, "Dammit Zahr. I didn't mean to wake your family. I should go."

"Nonsense! I wasn't complaining. Please, tell me about this nightmare."

He laughed an incredulous chuckle and flashed Zahr an expression of disbelief. "Clearly you have me confused with someone else. Do I look like the sharing type?"

"You look like a friend who needs to talk. Spill it. Don't make me turn into a gorilla and knock it out of you." Zahr smirked.

For a long time Sarge just sat there. Eventually he said, "It's a nightmare I've been having since I awoke from the battle at the Motlite breeding camp. I dream about the battle that knocked me out of commission."

Zahr shook his head slowly, "That sucks. From the sounds of your screams, it must be a pretty intense dream. How often does it happen?"

His first instinct was to say it didn't happen much, or just to tell him to mind his own business. Instead he decided to talk about it for the first time. "Too much. Sometimes several times a week. Sometimes every night. I rarely go more than a day without it."

"I've heard of warriors going through that after extreme trauma or intense battles. It usually gets better over time, or so I hear."

"The craziest thing is that I see a god, in the dream."

"What?" Zahr's face showed his surprise.

Sarge kicked himself mentally. He shouldn't have said anything about it, but it was too late to back away from it now. "After the attack that knocked me out, in my dream I see a god kneeling next to my body. Almost like he is protecting me or keeping me alive."

After a long pause, Zahr said, "That's amazing. Could you tell which god came to your rescue?"

He shook his head, "It was not one of the Pantheon of Nine."

Zahr looked aghast, "But... what god could it be other than the Pantheon of Nine? There are no other gods."

Sarge shook his head, disgusted. He was annoyed at himself for even bringing it up. "Move, so I can get up."

"No, I'm sorry. Please continue. Why do you think it wasn't one of the Pantheon of Nine?

He sighed in irritation. "The god was wearing fancy armor, and had a ram horn helm on his head. The chest piece of his armor had a symbol that I had never seen before. It was like two ovals side by side with a triangle in the middle."

"Are you sure it was a god, and not just a vision of some powerful warrior that your mind created to comfort you?"

He ignored Zahr's question. "I've been talking to prelates and religious scholars all over for the last several months. Of course I never told them about my dream, but I did ask about the symbol and the ram horn helmed god. None of them knew what I was talking about."

"I'm not surprised, I've never heard of any such thing."

Sarge looked Zahr in the eyes and debated whether to tell him the rest. He'd already gone this far. "Until a fortnight ago."

"What happened a fortnight ago?"

"I visited a temple in the foothills north of San'Rom. There I met a cleric who knew of the symbol I described. He said the symbol belonged to Kelegar."

"Kelegar? One of the Ancients? Kelegar, the father of Nalria? The father of five of the gods of the Pantheon of Nine?"

Sarge nodded, "According to a cleric."

"That can't be. The Ancients died eons ago, long before written history. When our ancestors still lived in caves and hunted with rocks and passed down the histories through stories."

"I know! I'm as confused about all of this as you are. I don't think it was real, but I don't know what it means. I can't help but think that I have to find out more about this Kelegar if I'm ever going to get a normal night's sleep again."

"Well, be careful. If people think you're worshiping a god other than one of the Pantheon of Nine, they're likely to brand you a heathen."

"Zahr, I've never been a religious man. It wouldn't be the first time I've been called a heathen."

"In the empire it is a crime to worship someone other than the Pantheon of Nine. Just be careful."

"I will. Keep your mouth shut, I don't need other people meddling in my business."

Zahr nodded, "Of course."

Sarge decided to change the subject. "So, how does the family like the new house?"

"It's much bigger than our old house in Sothral, but there are a bunch of things that need fixed."

"Why'd you move to Ront'El?"

"Shella has family here. I'm away from home a lot these days for the Magi Society, and she wants to be close to family in those times when I'm gone."

"That makes good sense."

Zahr asked, "Do you think Dalen and the others will be mad that we didn't join that meeting thing last night? They sounded like it was important."

"Zahr, we went back and forth about this last night. We're Free Cities Magi, we're not in any of their imperial coteries. Besides, I have no interest in ancient Magi ceremonies and traditions."

"I know, I just-" Sarge held up his hand to stop Zahr in mid-sentence.

Sarge listened for a second and then said, "What's that yelling about outside?"

They were both quiet for a moment. He could hear some sort of ruckus outside.

Zahr said, "Let's go see."

Sarge followed him down the stairs and they hurried outside.

Someone was running down the street yelling. "Get up! Get up! The imperial army is nearby! They're going to destroy Ront'El! Get up!" The man was running door to door, beating on the doors and shouting.

Further down the road, in the direction the man had come from, people were already out of their homes.

Sarge looked at Zahr and said, "You need to get your family out of this sarding city, now!"

Zahr tried to push past Sarge to go outside. He said, "We need to fight them!"

"Have you lost your sarding mind? You need to flee!" Sarge grabbed him by the collar and pulled him close until they were face to face. "I fought the empire in Misil'Kayl, I know what this is going to be like! Pack up a few vital things and get your family back to Sothral."

"But, we're Magi, we can-"

Sarge cut him off. "No! Within a few hours the entire city will be surrounded, and then escape will be impossible. Get your family out, now!"

Without responding, Zahr turned and ran up the stairs.

He watched the Magi run up the stairs to gather his family, and shook his head in despair. It was such a nice home. He pulled the nexus gem from his pocket and used a small amount of magic to activate it. He said, "Imperial army about to invade Ront'El. Need help evacuating the city. Portal twelve."

CHAPTER 10

Rissyl

"This must be the most peaceful place in the world."

Rissyl smiled and caressed Cynia's hair as she snuggled up next to him. He was lounging next to her on a blanket in the field to the south of their house. The sun was just starting to rise over the foothills in the east, casting a gorgeous orange glow across the landscape. The summer breeze was soft and warm and he was more relaxed than he'd felt in ages.

He said, "And the only thing more breathtaking than the sunrise is the amazing woman in my arms."

She giggled, "You're so full of it. You know that you don't need to flatter me to get in my nightgown, right?"

"It helps, doesn't it?" He reached down and pulled her night dress over her head, and let his hands wander.

She moaned softly, "Maybe, just a little bit." She rolled over to face him, and they kissed passionately.

Then he heard some sort of noise from the north. He stopped kissing her and looked around.

He heard Gwen's voice say, "Don't look, Chardy. Mommy and Daddy are once again trying to make a little brother or sister for you."

He sat up and adjusted his clothes.

Cynia sat up, but made no effort to cover herself. She said, "By the gods, Gwen. Don't you ever knock?"

"Knock on what? You're outside!"

"How do you always know when I'm about to have sex?"

Gwen laughed, "That's your boy's fault! He's the one who thinks he needs to eat all the time."

Rissyl said, "That's it, kid. You're getting punished. Ten lashes!"

The ladies both giggled, and Gwen handed Chardy to Cynia.

Gwen said, "I'll bet if you look around the house you'd find a room or two that'd be perfect for love making."

Cynia winked at her, and said, "Yeah, but we've done it in all those rooms."

Rissyl nodded, "Even your room."

They all laughed and Gwen said, "Well, you've done it here too. Just a few days ago."

"No, that was over there." Cynia pointed a few feet to the east. "The view is different over there."

Gwen made a face, pretending to be disgusted. She said, "I'll be back in a while to take Chardy when you're done feeding him, so you can get back to business."

Grabbing his boots, Rissyl said, "Thanks, but it'll be too late by then. I've got to travel to Grum'Glin this morning to get the signet ring."

They watched as Gwen headed back to the house. Cynia positioned Chardy so he could begin nursing, then she said, "So, what do you think of Ferth?"

"I'm worried about him. He doesn't respect us and I don't think he supports our overall goals."

"He don't seem to respect us, but I think he'll support our goals once his people stop dying. It'll help a lot when he starts seeing some growth. Sarasa and Dalen have both said really good things about him."

"When did he become an Evoker? How was I not involved?"

"Over the last six months Dalen and Sarasa have made several new Order Magi, including Eleyne, Thon, and Keta. They wanted to have at least one Order Magi in each Coterie, so they could join us magically for the meetings."

He nodded, "That makes sense. I just wish I would have been involved."

"You could have been, but you were always searching for that ring. Speaking of not respecting us, why didn't any of the Free Cities Magi join our meeting? I know they received instructions."

Rissyl shrugged, "I don't know. I didn't see Kimly either. We'll have to find out."

They sat quietly for a while. After several minutes, Cynia asked, "If you find the signet ring today, how soon do we want to take possession of the Stronghold?"

"Oh, right away! Maybe later today?"

"That'd be great! Who all should we bring along?"

"I've been thinking about that. We should probably move the Grand Coterie to the Stronghold. Randol will want to come with us, I'm sure. Once we've got things situated, then we'll probably want to bring all new Magi to the Stronghold so we can do their training and such there. It will be nice to have a place to train new Magi without fear of an imperial ambush."

"I can't wait! It seems like ages since we started the quest to claim the Stronghold. It is a bit hard to believe that we may finally be about to finish that task. I'm so excited."

He held up his hands, "Well don't jinx us! I don't have the ring yet." He leaned over and kissed her. "With that, I should be on my way. Wish me luck."

"Wish daddy luck." She took Chardy's hand and made him wave bye.

Rissyl smiled and then stood up. He summoned his cloak and staff, and then began the spell to teleport himself to Nassani's home.

- = - = -

He stood still for a few moments to let the vertigo of teleporting subside. He looked around, expecting to see Aruk nearby waiting for him. Over the last several months the two Magi had traveled together on countless occasions and Aruk always arrived early. Rissyl couldn't remember a time when Aruk wasn't at the appointed meeting spot before him.

There was talking coming from Nassani's house, but Rissyl was sure that Aruk wouldn't go to the house without him. He decided to send Aruk a message on the nexus gem to see if he was held up. However, when he reached into his pocket he discovered that he left the nexus gem at home on his dresser. He'd been so anxious to follow Cynia out to the field to watch the sunrise that he hadn't even grabbed it.

He was already at Nassani's; there was no reason to delay any longer. He'd have to figure out why Aruk didn't join him at another time.

Rissyl walked down the path towards the front door of the house. Before he even knocked, the door opened for him.

One of the men he'd met before, Rissyl was pretty sure the man's name was Lyro, held the door open. When he walked inside, Lyro said, "We can wait here at the table. Nassani will be here soon."

The two men sat at the table in uncomfortable silence for a few minutes.

Rissyl asked, "Are you and Linden brothers of Nassani?"

The man looked nervous and seemed like he didn't want to answer the question. He kept looking for someone to walk through the door, but finally he said, "No, she ain't our sister. We…" He struggled for words. "That is, she was kinda captured by imperials when the army came through." He looked again for someone to save him from the question. After several moments he added, "After the necromancer attacked the army, we rescued her."

He regretted asking the question. With two men living with a very pregnant woman that they saved from an invading army over a year ago, it didn't take him long to decide that he probably didn't want to ask many more questions about their situation.

Nassani walked down the stairs with the man named Linden, and Rissyl was happy with the opportunity to change the subject.

She walked directly to the table and sat down. "You've come back for the ring."

He nodded, "I said I would. Did your family decide if we can dig up the grave to look for the ring?"

The two men grinned at each other, but Nassani remained straight-faced. She said, "We've already dug up Rifin's grave."

Rissyl felt his excitement building. He'd been looking for the ring for so long. He tried to calm his anticipation, for fear of experiencing yet another let down. He exhaled a deep breath slowly, and then said, "Did you find the ring?"

She didn't answer one way or the other. She said, "How much coin did you bring?"

He looked at her for a long moment and sighed. He was beginning to get frustrated. She must have found the ring, and now she wanted to play games. He had no intention of playing her games, so he sat there and looked at her waiting for her to answer his question.

For almost a minute she sat there looking at him. Finally she reached into a pouch and pulled something out. With a loud thud she sat the ring onto the table.

Rissyl's eyes grew wide and he could feel his heart pounding in his chest. He reached out slowly to take the ring.

In one quick motion Linden drew a dagger and slammed it into the table very near Rissyl's outstretched hand. Linden said, "No so fast, Magi."

Nassani raised an eyebrow. "How much coin did you bring?"

He didn't remove his hand. He looked her in the eyes for moment and then said, "I'll offer three raptors, and that's it."

Linden let go of the dagger and left it in the table. He and Lyro looked at each other and grinned widely.

Nassani said, "That's not nearly enough."

"It's all I'm offering."

"What else can you offer to sweeten the deal?"

He was about to lose patience. "The ring belongs to the Sovereign Magi

Society, and I would be well within my rights to take it, by force if necessary, and give you only a few golden cardinals for the value of the gold. Take the three raptors, it is more than generous."

She made him wait for several seconds. Then she said, "Three raptors, and you must make me a Magi."

Lyro and Linden both gasped and then started hooting and hollering, cheering her on.

Rissyl shook his head no. "It doesn't work like that. Becoming a Magi is not something that can be bought, and it's certainly not something that can be demanded. It is a gift from the goddess Nalria."

"My grandfather was a powerful Magi. The gift is in our bloodline. Surely I can become a Magi."

He wished that Cynia was there. She was much better at this sort of thing than he was. He opened his magesight and gazed into Nassani's eyes. His magesight gave him a glimpse at her soul. Buzzing around on the outskirts of her soul, from his perception, were thousands of random thoughts flying all around. Hers was the busiest soul that he had read, and it was difficult to focus on looking for her magewel because of the constant movement and buzzing from the other thoughts. After a bit, he caught a glimpse of what he sought. Glowing in the far side of her mind was a smallish magewel.

As soon as he saw what he was looking for he closed off his magesight. He shivered with a dark sense of foreboding, but he didn't know why. When he refocused his regular sight, Nassani looked at him as if he had done something offensive.

She said, "What was that about? Were you inside my head?"

"You said you wanted to be a Magi. I was looking to see if you have the potential."

"Do I?"

He was unsure what to say. They needed to grow the number of Magi, and they needed her ring. However, he was not convinced that she was the kind of person they wanted as a Magi. On top of that, he certainly didn't have time to train a new Magi. What he needed was for a Diviner to gaze at her soul to better tell if she would be a good fit. That thought gave him an idea.

He said, "It is hard to tell. We will need a Diviner to examine you to know for sure. I will arrange for one to visit you soon."

"How do I know you'll do what you say?"

He pushed the coins towards her and held out his hand for the ring.

She hesitated before finally placing it in his hand.

He said, "The Magi need new members, we would be foolish to turn away the granddaughter of a powerful Magi. Trust me, a Diviner will be by to visit you soon."

Rissyl stood up. "I should be on my way."

Without any further fanfare, he began the spell to teleport home.

- = - = -

The excitement of finally finding the ring, and the relief of being home was completely spoiled when he teleported to his normal spot near his house and found Gwen sitting in the grass waiting for him. The expression on her face told him that something was terribly wrong. Chardy was playing in the grass next to her, but he didn't see Cynia around anywhere.

"What's wrong?" A sense of dread quickly filled him.

Gwen stood up; she started crying as soon as she opened her mouth. "I tried to make her stay! I begged her, but she insisted on going!"

Rissyl grabbed her shoulders and shook her softly to get her attention. "Gwen, what in Khalius is going on? Where is she? What happened?"

She took a deep breath, and let it out slow. "I'm sorry, I'm just so scared. The empire has attacked one of the barbarian cities! The Magi are meeting there to help the city evacuate. I begged her to stay, but Cynia insisted on going! She is going to battle the Imperial Army! I have such a bad feeling that I'm never gonna see her again!"

He let her go, as he felt his heart sink to the pit of his stomach. "Don't talk like that, she can take care of herself." He believed the words, but he hated not being with her to help keep her safe.

Gwen picked up the baby.

He said, "I've got to go to her. What city?"

"I don't know! I'm sorry, she didn't say."

"No problem, my nexus gem can tell me." He started to run towards the house, but she stopped him.

"Here, she told me you'd need this." She handed him his nexus gem.

It was glowing when she handed it to him, so it had a message waiting for him to hear. He summoned a tiny amount of magic to activate the gem.

He heard Sarge's voice say, "Imperial army about to invade Ront'El. Need help evacuating the city. Portal twelve."

Rissyl wondered how long ago Sarge had sent the message. He hadn't even looked at the stone since before he went to sleep last night. The whole battle might already have been fought and finished by now. He put the stone in his coin pouch, and put the signet ring on his finger.

CHAPTER 11

Sarasa

The soldiers were all around her. Sarasa was leaning against a tree in the middle of the army encampment, on the southwest side of Ront'El. There were about a dozen trees close together, and the army was sprawled out in every direction around the trees. She was three hundred yards or more away from the city's walls, in a section of the encampment set aside for siege equipment and the soldiers responsible for it.

About thirty minutes earlier she had been with Dalen, Cynia, and several other Magi at the north gate of the city. The Magi were trying to keep the evacuation as orderly as possible so it could happen quickly. However, getting tens of thousands of people out of a city, while carrying all of their most cherished possessions, and while they're panicked because of a blood-thirsty invading army was nearly an impossible task.

To make matters worse, they could see the army approaching the south end of the city. They needed a way to keep the army from surrounding the city and cutting off the evacuation, or at least to slow it down significantly. A handful of Magi bravely volunteered to harass the army on the east and west sides of the city to slow them down.

Against Dalen and Cynia's pleas, Sarasa summoned a veil of invisibility around herself and rushed towards the heart of the army to see what kind of chaos she could cause.

Now, standing all alone in the middle of a massive army, she was starting to doubt the wisdom of her actions. Countless times she had rushed headlong into a fight with her invisibility veil to protect her until she was ready to strike. However, this was different. Once she dropped her veil, she could be overwhelmed by an impossible number of foes.

Far off to the north she could hear the sounds of battle. She had no idea if that was the army battling Magi, or if the army was battling militia from the city. She looked at the city walls and didn't see any ladders or attempt to scale the walls yet. Therefore, she assumed that the army had not yet begun a full assault on the city.

Two imperial soldiers walked towards her, but they didn't seem to be looking at her. They were having a discussion as they approached.

"Why'd he do that?"

"Who knows? Guess he just wanted me to have his coins!"

Both men laughed and they stopped by a tree near her. They moved their tabard to one side and started unbuckling a piece of armor covering their crotch.

"Is the unit gathering for a card game tonight? I'd like some of your coins"

"Dunno? We gonna starve the barbarians out? If we ain't attacking yet then I'm sure someone will get a game going."

She felt a little embarrassed for watching the men as they began to relieve themselves, but she couldn't look away. She rolled her eyes at the unfairness of nature. If she was in full armor it would be much more difficult for her to pee on a tree. Just when she decided to look away, because she was not the kind of lady to stare at strangers while they relieved themselves, she saw both men began to shake themselves vigorously for a couple of seconds. She placed her hand over her mouth to keep from laughing aloud. It was the goofiest thing she'd ever seen, watching two soldiers flopping their manhood this way and that with droplets flying every which way.

Sarasa pushed herself from the tree and started walking quickly and quietly to the south. She was still invisible, so she wasn't too worried about anyone seeing her. She passed several catapults and battering rams. After walking a bit further, weaving around different groups of soldiers, she stopped next to a large ballista mounted to a wagon. Looking to the south of the ballista she saw the section of the encampment for archers. Stretching far to the south was a field filled with archers. They were setting up camp, building fire pits, pitching tents, emptying wagons, and scurrying around in an endless array of other tasks.

Not far from the large ballista, she found several siege machines sitting close together. There was a large siege tower, two catapults, a battering ram, and a few large devices that she didn't recognize. They were all made out of wood, and none of them was being guarded at the moment. Sitting beside the tower were several opened barrels of a sticky goo with a very strong odor. Stacked on a separate wagon nearby were hundreds of large rocks with burlap wrapped around them. The burlap was soaked in the same smelly sticky goo that was in the barrels.

She was not an expert on siege warfare, but she was pretty sure that the sticky goo would burn well.

She looked around one last time and saw that no one was paying attention, so she cast an *Invisible Helper* spell, which created a magical hand to assist her. She directed the hand to stack the smelly gooey rocks on all of the wooden siege machines. When she had several rocks on each machine, she sent her magical assistant to pick up one of the barrels.

Unfortunately the barrel was too heavy, and she couldn't get the magical assistant to lift the barrel so she had to do it herself. The barrels weren't very large, but they were extremely heavy. She hefted one up onto the wagon of a catapult, and then dumped it to the side. The smelly goo spilled all over the machine. Over the next couple of minutes she placed several more little barrels onto several of the other machines and knocked them down. The manual labor caused her to lose focus on her *Invisibility* spell and before long her actions could be seen by everyone.

From behind her, she heard someone shout. "By the gods, woman! What are you doing?" Several soldiers started running towards her. The commotion drew the attention of several other soldiers who also started moving her way.

She wasn't an Evoker, so fire magic wasn't really her strength. However, all Magi had the ability to summon simple fire orbs. That was one of the first spells that she learned. As the soldiers rushed her, she quickly formed the spell to summon an orb. Then she said, "Krol'Tu."

When the fiery orb hit the siege machine, the large wooden catapult caught fire immediately. The sticky goo was quick to catch fire, and the flames spread in a flash. Within seconds, all of the siege machines were ablaze and the heat near the fire quickly grew unbearable.

Chaos broke out among the soldiers anywhere near the machines. Several of them rushed Sarasa, but others started trying to extinguish the flames.

She lunged away from the flames and quickly cast an *Invisibility* spell. In the blink of an eye she vanished. The advancing soldiers gasped in shock. She rushed away from the fire, careful not to crash into any of the panicked soldiers as they hurried around trying to do anything to put out the fire.

The entire area began swarming with soldiers, and she carefully made her way out of the siege weapon encampment.

The further she got from that section of camp, the more things returned to normal. When she got well into the archer section of camp she was able to pause and catch her breath. She didn't see any targets in this section that really stood out as something she could do to make a large impact. So, she continued on to the next section of camp, the encampment for the mounted soldiers.

This part of camp was like a city of tents. The parts she had been through earlier had one or two tents every dozen yards. She assumed they were for a leader of the troops, and that the other soldiers would just sleep in the grass. This section of camp had tents all over the place. Some of the larger tents had horses tethered nearby. Most of the tents did not, and a few dozen yards to the southwest was a large fenced area filled with horses.

She headed towards the horse pen. She had to be careful walking through the tent area. Whenever she got close to one of the horses tethered near a tent, the horse would sense her or perhaps smell her and start to get agitated.

Three soldiers stood guard near the entrance to the horse pen. She quietly walked up behind the meanest looking soldier. While still invisible she summoned her daggers and magic cloak.

When she attacked, the soldiers didn't see it coming. She quickly slit the throat of the meanest looking soldier, which caused her to lose concentration on her invisibility spell. The second soldier was so stunned by the sudden spray of blood from the neck of the man he had been chatting with, and the appearance of a woman out of thin air, that he didn't even move as she stepped towards him and drove her dagger up to the hilt in his throat.

The last soldier screamed a battle cry and rushed her as he drew his sword. She stepped to the side, spun around to her right while flipping the dagger in her right hand around to a reverse grip so the blade was coming from the bottom of her fist. She continued that motion and plunged the dagger deep into the soldier's chest as he ran at her. She let her spinning motion carry her into a full circle as she turned to face the soldier. He looked at her with shock as her second dagger rushed at his neck.

As the man fell she jerked her dagger from his chest. All around her she could hear angry shouts. Several soldiers nearby looked out of their tents to see what was going on.

She rushed to the gate and pulled the rope over the post, and then she flung open the large gate. The horses all shied away from her as she hurried to the far end of the pen.

Quickly, she started summoning magic for an *Explosion* spell. It was just an illusion, but she knew from experience that it would startle people. If it could scare nearby people, she was confident that it would scare horses that were already spooked.

The spell worked perfectly. The huge explosion, centered on her, rattled the wooden beams of the fence. All of the horses galloped towards the gate in a panic. Those who couldn't fit through the gate quickly enough, simply jumped over the fence in their terror. She watched as over a hundred war horses galloped off into the open prairie south of the city.

The soldiers, who had been rushing at her, turned towards the horses trying to stop them before they all got away. Some of the horses were already slowing, so they would surely capture some of them, but she hoped many of them would escape and that would be far fewer mounted soldiers that the city would have to deal with.

She dropped another veil of invisibility around herself and then hurried over to the fence and climbed over. After walking quickly and quietly for a while she moved from the section of the camp for the mounted troops and into the foot soldier's section. This section of camp was, by far, the largest and it stretched on for hundreds of yards even wrapping around the southern end of the city.

Foot soldiers were everywhere, and most of them were chatting nervously as they awaited some sort of orders. She heard several groups of men talking about Magi and necromancers. Some of the men seemed anxious to get into the fight, but some of them already looked nervous. She smiled to herself, and hoped that her actions had some small effect on their nervousness.

Not far to the east she saw a fairly short soldier step into a tent, in the middle of a large field filled with foot soldiers. Quietly she hurried towards the tent. Her invisibility was great, but it took magic to maintain and she'd been maintaining it for a long time. She could feel herself running dangerously low on magical essence, and once that was gone there would be no more invisibility. If she drained her magic too far she could end up unconscious, or worse. So, it was time to find a different way to blend in. This short soldier could be just what she needed.

When she was next to the tent she listened outside of it for a few minutes. She didn't hear any conversation going on inside the tent, so she quietly slipped inside.

Sitting on a cot at one side of the tent was an older man in full armor. He wore a blue tabard like most of the other soldiers. His helm was sitting on the floor next to him, and he was pulling off his armor footwear.

She moved to the far side of the tent and watched the man as he rubbed his feet. After a moment he stretched out on the cot and closed his eyes.

Sarasa peeked out of the tent to make sure no one was about to enter, and then she moved to the left side of his cot near his head. She pulled a short length of rope from her hip pouch. She let the invisible rope dangle down to the man's nose.

The soldier sat up quickly and brushed at his face as if he was expecting to see a large spider.

That was all of the opening that she needed. Sarasa hopped onto the cot, behind him. She tossed the rope over the man's head, wrapped it around his neck, and quickly yanked it as tight as she could. As the man struggled, she scooted back and pulled him down onto his back, while shoving his chin towards his chest. The old soldier struggled for several seconds, and then finally went limp.

She kept the rope tight around the man's neck for a couple of minutes to ensure that he was dead before she released it. Then she quickly began removing the man's armor and strapping it to herself.

When she was completely dressed, she looked down at herself. The tabard was a little longer on her than it probably should be, but other than that she thought everything fit much better than she originally expected. She pulled the man's sword from its scabbard and tested its balance. She approved and returned it to the scabbard on her belt.

On the left breast area of the tabard were three stripes that extended to the edge of the tabard. She wasn't sure, but she guessed that those stripes represented the soldier's rank.

Before leaving the tent she decided to shove the soldier's body under his cot. Then she positioned his blanket to fall over the edge of the cot to mostly conceal the body. It wouldn't fool people for long, but she hoped it would give her some time to get away from this section of the encampment.

The breastplate was not designed for a woman, and she found that it was uncomfortably squishing her breasts. For a moment she pushed on the armor and snaked her fingers in through an arm-hole to try to pull her breast into a more comfortable position. However, it was no use, she was just going to be uncomfortable.

The noises outside the tent changed noticeably, and her heart began to race. She wondered if she had somehow been discovered already.

The tent flaps were thrown back as someone rushed into the tent. As the man entered, he said, "Sergeant-"

In the blink of an eye Sarasa summoned a dagger, stepped forward, and pressed it to the man's neck. She pulled him fully into the tent.

The man looked terrified. He said, "By the gods, Sergeant! I'm just passing along orders!"

She removed the dagger from the man's neck and took a step back, turning the dagger to a reverse grip to hide the runes on the blade behind her forearm. She didn't reply to him.

He said, "The General has ordered that Eagle, Firehound, Grizzlybear, and Hyena Companies get ready for deployment. You'll be sent to the north side of the city to secure the north gate. The signal to attack could be given at any time, so get your men ready."

The man didn't wait to be dismissed. He turned and rushed out of the tent.

Sarasa let out a sigh of relief as the man left. After a brief pause to calm herself, she stepped out of the tent.

Several soldiers were gathered outside. She swore to herself. They must have seen the messenger enter the tent and they were awaiting some orders from their sergeant. The men stood there looking at her, as she stood just outside the tent.

After a moment, one of the men at the left side of the line said, "The other platoons are already breaking down camps, did we get orders to move?"

She knew that voice. She took a step towards the man and looked more closely at him. She was right, it was Brandam! It had been almost two years since she'd seen him last. They were both students in Grandmaster Thon's fighting guild together. He had been the top student for years, until he suddenly joined the army and left Sorgo.

He said, "Sergeant Tollis, did we get orders to move out?"

She stopped and nodded her head twice.

Brandam said, "Do you want us to break down camp and get ready for further orders?"

She nodded again.

Brandam looked to the rest of the men. In a loud voice, he said, "You heard the Sergeant! Break camp! Fill your waterskins and ready your weapons!"

The men rushed off to do what they were told. Brandam looked at her and she motioned for him to follow her. She led him into the tent, and took off her helmet.

He looked at her for a moment, and then his eyes widened with recognition. He said, "Rasa, is that you? When did you join? How are you a Sergeant so fast? Wait, where is Sergeant Tollis?"

She needed to know why he had joined the army. In all the years that she knew him, he had never shown any interest in being a soldier. He had been more critical of the emperor and the treatment of Dregs than anyone else she knew, with the possible exception of Dalen. So, it had come as a great shock to everyone when he suddenly gave up everything and enlisted as a soldier.

The voices outside the tent hinted that soldiers already had questions. She was certain that they didn't have much time before someone else barged into the tent to say or ask something.

She put her helmet back on and said, "Why did you join the army?"

He stood up straighter and looked directly forward. He replied, "To serve the emperor, of course, Sergeant!"

Sarasa rolled her eyes, but she knew he couldn't see that through her helm. She stepped closer and whispered, "You and I both know that's a lie. I've known you since you were ten years old. It was just a few years ago that you told me that you thought the emperor was a tyrant and that it was unfathomable that any good leader would allow some of his own people to live as slaves! Now, why did you join the army?"

Brandam looked scared and he fidgeted with his tabard nervously. He said, "Sergeant, I've been a hard working soldier and I haven't violated the terms of my enlistment. Rasa, whatever you think of me, I swear I haven't been causing problems."

"By all the sarding gods, Bran!" She spoke sharply, but quietly. "I'm not really a soldier! Please answer my question!"

He continued to fidget with his tabard nervously, and he glanced at the tent opening quickly. Finally he said, "About two years ago I was visited by sentinels. Someone told them I had been speaking out against the Dreg policies, and the emperor. I was charged with sedition, and given the choice of joining the army or becoming a Dreg. I chose life as a soldier over life as a Dreg."

She looked into his eyes and opened her magesight. She was not at all surprised to see his magewel glowing brightly in her magical vision. It was large and vibrant, and she knew that he had the potential to become a powerful Magi. It wasn't surprising, she had always been drawn to him. Over the years she felt a bond with him that was more than just the infatuation that a younger girl may find in a strong, older, attractive boy. It had hurt her deeply when he suddenly announced that he was joining the army, and then left within days of the announcement.

Now she understood. She said, "You realize that the emperor is about to attack a city filled with innocent victims who simply want to live their lives in peace?"

He didn't answer for a few seconds. Finally he said, "They're barbarians."

"They're people! And the army is going to kill most of them. You are going to kill some of them."

"It's not my choice, Rasa! I'm just doing what I'm ordered!"

She took a step closer to him. "That's a bunch of troll dung and you know it! Those who aren't killed will be made Dregs. You are about to be responsible for hundreds of new Dregs!"

"That's not fair, Rasa! I have no choice!"

She poked him in the chest against his breastplate with a thud. "You always have a choice!"

He looked at her incredulously, "What choice?"

Sarasa summoned a small amount of magic and pulled the veil of invisibility over herself. He gasped in shock and stepped back as he watched her vanish.

She dropped the invisibility and stepped towards him again. She said, "I'm a Magi, Bran. The Magi Society is here, we're helping the people of Ront'El escape before the army kills them all. It's not too late, you can help us!"

"How could I help? I'm no Magi, I'm just a single soldier."

"You could be a Magi! You have the gift, I've seen it. Come with me, help me save some of the people of Ront'El, and we'll make you a Magi!"

"Rasa, I can't leave! It'd be a Dreg sentence for sure!"

She grabbed his tabard and pulled him towards her, while she pointed towards the city. "I know you! How would you live with yourself knowing that you were responsible for helping to make hundreds or thousands of new Dregs? Can you live with the blood of thousands of women and children on your hands? Come with me!"

He was quiet for a long time. Finally he slammed his helmet onto his head. "Sarding Khalius, Rasa! I'm going to regret this. I'm in, what is the plan?"

"I'm still working on the plan."

He groaned, "You haven't changed. Always rushing in for the attack without a solid plan for how to finish the fight."

"At least I'm predictable. I just know that I've been in the middle of the army alone for long enough. My magical essence is running low and I need to rest soon. Let's keep quiet for now. Soon we'll be given orders to march to the north gate. That's where the other Magi are. We'll join up with them then"

He paused for a moment, and then said, "That sounds like a good plan." He was quiet for a few seconds as they both looked at each other. Then he said, "I've missed you."

She smiled behind the helm, even though he couldn't see it. She said, "You're dismissed, soldier."

He didn't leave the tent. "My rank is Corporal. If you don't address me by rank, the men might become suspicious." He pointed to the two bars on his tabard. "These two bars mean I'm a Corporal."

"That's great, Bran. Don't you think my girlish voice will make the men more suspicious than the title I use for you?"

He laughed, "Good point. Stick near me, and I'll issue the orders for you. It isn't uncommon for me to lead the troops anyway."

"Great. You're dismissed, soldier."

He grinned and turned to leave the tent.

CHAPTER 12

Rissyl

A rushing horse whinnied and veered to left, causing the wagon it was pulling to list to one side. The driver shouted, "Get outta the sarding way!"

Rissyl stumbled to his right, only to move into the path of a large man pulling an over-filled trunk. The man shoved him to the side roughly.

He had just teleported to Ront'El, and the vertigo wasn't subsiding quickly enough. He stumbled to his left and smacked into the side of the wagon as it pushed past.

A sea of people was fleeing the city and they were content to trample him underfoot as they shoved past him. He grabbed onto the side of a cart being pulled by a mule as it passed. At least that would get him moving along with the flow of the masses, and give him something to lean on as the vertigo passed.

A man walking behind the cart shouted, "Let go of my cart, you're slowing it down!"

Rissyl ignored the man for several steps, until he was relatively confident that he could walk on his own. Then he pushed away from the cart and gradually made his way through the mass of fleeing people.

After several minutes, and multiple curses and rude gestures, he finally emerged from the west side of the river of people. He moved several feet further west to move out of the way of the stragglers moving along the sides of the main group.

When he finally had a moment to look around he discovered that the scene outside of the river of people fleeing the city was just as chaotic as the craziness that he'd just left. As far as the eye could see there were groups of people engaged in battle. Dozens, if not hundreds, of Imperial Foot Soldiers were scattered around locked in battle with a thousand or more armed citizens who fought to protect the others who were trying to flee.

Scattered around the various battles, Rissyl could see several Magi. He saw a ball of lightning flash to his right, further away he saw someone else throw a fire orb. It was a bit surreal, but it filled him with pride and awe to see the Magi scattered around the battlefield helping these people escape.

He needed to find Cynia. He moved around the battlefield, in the space between the outflow of refugees and the main battle areas to the west. As he scanned the area, he had no idea where to even look to find her. She could be on the other side of the refugee flow and he'd never see her from here, or she might even be inside the city.

He was getting angry, and he cursed to himself. He wished she hadn't run off without him.

Up ahead two imperial soldiers broke away from a skirmish and rushed towards the refugees. One of them grabbed a woman out of the flow of people and pulled her to him.

Rissyl lowered the top end of the staff between the soldier and the woman, and used it to push the woman away from the soldier slightly. Then he pushed the gem on the top of the staff up against the soldier's neck. The man looked at him in fear as he tried to back up. Rissyl didn't let him retreat. He summoned an orb of fire through the staff and sent it directly into the soldier's neck.

The man tried to scream and grabbed his neck. His face and neck caught fire as he crumbled to the ground. The woman screamed and hurried away.

The second soldier lowered his sword and tried to rush Rissyl. Without hesitation Rissyl released the staff with his right hand, and then pointed the palm of that hand towards the advancing soldier. He whispered the vocal component of the spell calmly and watched the orb of electricity streak towards the soldier.

A moment later the soldier screamed briefly as his body shook with violent convulsions. Rissyl didn't even watch the dead soldier fall, as he continued on in his search for Cynia. He turned his search to the west.

He lost track of time as he weaved his way through the multitude of small skirmishes in the field outside of the north wall of the city. Several times a soldier or two tried to impede his progress, and he quickly dispatched them. After a while he got close to a group of militia soldiers fighting alongside an Order of Champions Magi in a blue and white cloak as well as two Society Magi in their brown and white cloaks.

He shouted, "Magi, have you seen Diviner Cynia?"

The Champion turned to him and he saw that it was Keta, the leader of the Khazror Coterie. He was happy to see that some Magi from the empire had come to the assistance of the Free City. She said, "I saw her fighting near the city's north gate not long ago."

He hollered, "Thanks!" He wasn't sure if she even heard him. She had already returned her attention to the battle before her.

He cursed to himself, he'd been moving in the wrong direction. When he turned to head back in the direction he had come from, he saw that he was far enough west to look down the west wall of the city. The skirmishes between the imperial soldiers and city militia, and Magi, stretched on for a good distance to the south along the west wall. Far off in the south, extending up the hill, he could see a massive number of imperial soldiers who had not joined the fight. They were standing near large siege weapons. There was no telling how many soldiers were on the other side of the hill, off towards the south side of the city. On the far side of the hill was a massive fire. He couldn't tell what was burning, but it was much bigger than a campfire and he could see the flames and smoke rising into the air.

One thing was clear. They were all going to be in a great deal of trouble when the main body of the imperial army was unleashed. He guessed that these weren't even the most experienced soldiers. These were probably just skirmishers and expendable foot soldiers sent to test the strength and numbers of the city's resistance.

The sounds of battle were almost overwhelming. He slowly made his way back east, heading towards the city's north gate, and as he carefully picked his way through the chaos he took in the sounds of war. The screams of the dying were the most troubling, and they seemed to come from every direction. He also heard battle cries, shouts of encouragement, screamed curses, and more that were all melding into a maddening rumble. Adding percussion to the battle voices were hundreds of wooden and metal weapons smashing against leather, metal, and bone.

The macabre rhythm of it all was almost hypnotizing. Thud, thud, crash, clank... scream. Thud, thud, clank, scream... crash. He heard a thud from his right and then a scream from his left. Behind him he heard the piercing clank of two metal weapons smashing together at full force. The battle symphony played on as he made his way back through the small battles scattered all around the field.

He saw movement to his right, as he looked that direction he felt something slam into his side hard enough to knock the wind out of him. He staggered to his left and tried to position his staff between him and the attacker. The soldier was right next to him before he even fully caught his balance from the original attack. To make matters worse, he couldn't catch his breath enough to think clearly.

The ground crashed against him, and the soldier jumped on top of him.

Rissyl desperately tried to draw in a full breath, and having the heavy soldier planted on top of him didn't help at all. He saw the man trying to hit him with a large mace, and he wasn't entirely sure that he hadn't already been hit by it a few times since hitting the ground.

He tried to summon enough magic the cook the attacker, but he couldn't focus his mind enough to do anything other than attempt to breathe. He was vaguely aware that his arms were trying to fight with the soldier to control the man's mace. However, the only thought on his mind was finding a way to breathe.

Suddenly the soldier's head jerked forward, and then the soldier fell off Rissyl and landed on the ground beside him.

Rissyl looked up and saw an old man dressed like a farmer standing over him. He was holding a large club in one hand, and reaching out the other hand to help Rissyl stand up.

He took the farmer's outstretched hand and stood up slowly, picking up his staff in the process. Rissyl leaned on the staff and took several deep breaths, thankful to finally be able to get full breaths into is lungs.

As he reached forward to put his hand on the farmer's shoulder to thank him for saving his life, a long sword erupted from the farmer's chest. The man got a shocked look on his face as he looked down at the weapon protruding from his chest. He didn't even scream as he fell to the ground.

Behind the farmer, the imperial soldier who killed him didn't stick around long enough to make sure the farmer was dead. He turned to engage another target. The battle all around Rissyl was intensifying. He was sick to his stomach that the farmer who saved his life was just as quickly killed right in front of him. His first instinct was to murder the soldier who killed the farmer. However, the furious pace of battle had already shifted all around him and his window of time where he had a clear shot at the attacker vanished before he could even raise his staff.

He needed to get to Cynia. The battle was too chaotic and it seemed like it was getting worse. He hurried to the east, pushing his way past people to try to get back to the north gate. His ribs hurt, his head was spinning, and he was already anxious to be away from this nightmare.

The footing continued to get more difficult as the number of dead bodies increased. As he carefully made his way east, he noticed several times where combatants tripped over a body, and then became a corpse themselves as their opponent finished them off as they tried to get up off the ground.

Several vines quickly grew up from the ground a short distance to his right.

The vines began ensnaring everyone nearby, and he saw a bunch of soldiers become trapped in the quickly growing vegetation. He knew that spell well, and he was filled with encouragement as he looked to see if he would find Cynia nearby.

It didn't take long. Far ahead of him, and off to his right, he found a group of city militia near the north wall. Fighting alongside them were several Magi, including Dalen and Cynia.

A series of large fire orbs from his staff quickly cleared a path between him and Cynia's group. He rushed over to her and joined Dalen in battle against a number of lightly armored imperial soldiers.

When Dalen glanced over and saw him nearby, he said, "Nice of you to join us, did we interrupt your nap?"

Rissyl noticed with alarm that Cynia was bloody, but he didn't know if it was her blood or someone else's. She had some blood on her arms and face, and it was smeared on her clothes as well.

He used his staff to deflect an incoming attack from a soldier's long pike, and then launched a fire orb at the man through the gem of his staff. Before the man could scream, Dalen turned and finished him off with a quick slice of his sword.

Rissyl looked back to Cynia, and shouted, "You okay?"

She stepped over to smack a soldier in the side of the face with her staff. The soldier was locked in combat with a militiaman to her right. When her staff hit the soldier in the side of the head, he turned towards her. That was all of the opening that the militiaman needed, and he quickly ran his sword deep into the soldier's chest.

Cynia said, "Never better."

"Nice to see that you dressed for combat." He didn't normally comment on what outfits she chose. Cynia was not a modest woman, she looked good in revealing clothing and she was not shy about flaunting it. However, he was surprised to see her dressed in a skimpy skirt, knee high stockings, and some sort of top that barely contained her breasts while fighting against imperial soldiers.

"You're such a troll! I didn't expect combat today, I was actually dressed to take you into town to celebrate your achievement!" A moment later her voice sounded urgent, and she said, "Riz, lookout!"

He watched her shoot a sonic wave at something behind him. The wave emanated from her outstretched hand and then streaked past him, leaving a rumbling sound buzzing in his ears in its wake. He spun around quickly and saw a soldier crumple to his knees as the sonic wave enveloped his head.

Rissyl lowered his staff to finish the warrior, but Dalen beat him to it.

He asked, "What is our goal here?"

Cynia said, "To stay alive! And to keep the Ront'Elians alive while they escape."

Dalen added, "To keep the imperial army from blocking the north gate and trapping the people inside the city!"

The conversation stopped as all of the Magi focused on the battles at hand. They worked together smoothly, assisting each other and watching each other's back. Rissyl lost track of time, as he continued to burn through the magical essence in his magewel. He started using his staff as a bludgeoning weapon without the use of magic as much as possible to conserve his magewel.

The number of imperial soldiers making it all the way to their location near the north gate continued to increase, and as he glanced off to the west he noticed that the ratio of militia to imperial soldiers was gradually changing to favor the imperial soldiers. It wouldn't be long before they had no choice but to retreat or be overrun.

Off to the east, in the direction of the flood of refugees fleeing the city, Rissyl heard a little girl scream. It was not a scream of pain or fear. It was a scream of fury. The scream caught his attention over all of the other screams and shouts around him, so he turned that way to see what was going on.

A dozen yards or more to the east he saw the little girl. She was a young girl of perhaps nine years, with long black hair and light brown skin. The girl stood with her fists clinched and hands held down at her waist, and she continued to scream. On the ground beside her were several bodies, and two soldiers were walking towards her. She was clearly screaming at the soldiers before her.

The little girl continued to scream. As she did, something climbed out of the dirt. Rissyl gasped in shock as he saw that the creature climbing from the dirt was a large magical creature. The creature was mostly transparent, and its features were outlined in green and brown colored light as if it was some sort of Rolimi creature. As it stood to its full height, Rissyl guessed the creature was at least seven feet tall to the top of its shoulders. It was shaped like a large bear with the head and beak of a hawk.

When the little girl pointed at one of the soldiers, the bear-hawk creature lunged forward and grabbed the soldier in its beak. It easily fit the soldier's upper body in his large beak and it reared its head back and swallowed the soldier whole. The soldier fell through the magical creature's body and landed on the ground with a thud, and didn't move. The little girl pointed at the other soldier, who took off running and screaming. In two large strides the magical bear-hawk creature caught the fleeing soldier and captured him in its deadly beak. The magical creature played with its prey briefly before finally swallowing the soldier's broken body whole, and then it fell through the semi-transparent creature's body and to the ground.

Rissyl started moving towards the little girl. He noticed Cynia moving that way also. The shocked expression on her face as she stared at the magical bear-hawk told him that she also saw what had happened.

The little girl directed the magical creature after several other soldiers before Rissyl and Cynia reached her. As they got close to the girl, she said, "Thank you, Ranmithisar!"

Rissyl looked to the magical creature in time to see it climb into the dirt and vanish, not unlike his Rolimi dog did sometimes.

Everyone had fled the massive magical creature, leaving a large area devoid of people. Rissyl noticed that the sounds of battle had stopped momentarily. That didn't last long, as combatants resumed their fights or found new ones as soon as the threat vanished.

Cynia asked the little girl, "Are you hurt?"

She started crying, and pointed to the two bodies on the ground near her. "The imperials killed my mom and dad!"

"Do you have other family nearby? Grandparents, or aunts and uncles?"

The little girl shook her head. Through her tears she said, "Mom and dad were my only family. I ain't got no one else." She looked at all of the people rushing past her, fleeing the city. She said, "I dunno where to go."

Cynia said, "You'll come with us, we'll keep you safe. What's your name?"

"Ayris."

"That's a very pretty name, Ayris. Can we take you someplace safe? Would you like come with us?"

Ayris looked at the lifeless bodies of her parents for a long moment before answering. Finally, she nodded once.

Rissyl gave Cynia a questioning look, "We can't leave Ront'El now, what are you doing?"

Cynia shoved him forward as she stood up and took Ayris by the hand. "We don't have time to argue, we've got to get this girl someplace safe!"

He started moving along with them. Behind him and to the left he heard a man shout, "There she is, get her!"

He looked back to see several soldiers rushing towards them. He wanted to lob a nice big fireball at them, but there were far too many innocents nearby. Instead he sent a few smaller fire orbs at the soldiers, hitting at least one of them squarely in the chest.

Cynia started running, holding Ayris' hand and leading her away from the soldiers. She lowered her staff as she ran and fired off a few magic orbs.

Rissyl hurried to keep up with them. He said, "Let's try to meld into the flow of refugees to keep the girl from being seen. Maybe the soldiers will forget about her." He pushed his way into the river of refugees, and helped Cynia and Ayris move into the flow as well.

They moved with the flow of refugees for nearly half an hour. Eventually the sounds of battle faded in the distance, and they were replaced with the sounds of crying, complaining, and bickering as the citizens of Ront'El expressed their despair and frustrations more loudly with each passing step.

Eventually Rissyl felt fairly confident that they were no longer being followed, and he led Cynia and Ayris out of the flow of refugees. They began the long walk to the portal stone nearest Ront'El.

As they walked they finally had time to catch their breath and find out more about the surprising child. Rissyl said, "Ayris, what was that creature that helped you back there?"

Ayris had been extremely quiet the entire time they'd been walking; she seemed lost in her own thoughts. She didn't answer his question.

He stopped in front of her and knelt down so he was closer to her level. They were out in the country, a few miles from Ront'El. The city was visible off in the distance, but he couldn't make out details of what was happening there. They certainly weren't safe, but he wanted to get the girl talking.

He said, "You're not in trouble, and we're not mad. We want to help you, and for that we need you to talk to us."

Cynia knelt down in front of the girl as well, and she put her hand on Ayris' shoulder. She said, "You can tell us, what was that creature?"

Ayris shrugged her little shoulders. "I dunno what kind of creature he is, but his name is Ranmithisar."

"Rissyl, look!" Cynia pointed towards the city. Several mounted riders were headed in their general direction.

He stood up and said, "Chat will have to wait. Let's go."

They walked quickly through the tall grasses. As they walked, Rissyl said, "To use the portal stone, she is going to have to be able to summon magic."

Cynia nodded, "I know. She has a magewel, it's actually extremely large for someone so young and untrained."

"Ayris, has someone taught you to use magic? Is that how you summoned that creature?"

The little girl looked confused, "Magic? No, he is my friend. I called out to him and he came to help me."

He followed Cynia across the rolling grasslands as she led them towards the portal stone.

"Oh, Cynia I have great news!" In all of the chaos, he had forgotten to tell her about his great news.

"Did you find the ring?"

"I did!" He held up his hand and showed it to her.

She looked at it for a moment and then hugged him tightly. "That's great news!"

"Very soon the Stronghold and all of her secrets will be ours."

They started walking quicker, as if getting to their destination would make it that much sooner when they could claim the Stronghold.

The riders were still headed in their general direction, but they didn't seem to be coming directly for them. If needed, they would fight the mounted imperial soldiers, but Rissyl hoped to avoid them if possible. They had already seen enough battle for one day, and he preferred to conserve what little magical essence he had remaining in his magewel. Besides, the little girl didn't need any more trauma in her day.

With Cynia's guidance they found the portal stone at the top of a gentle hill, a couple hours walk from the city.

Ayris' eyes grew wide as she watched Cynia cause the stone obelisk to rise out of the ground. It stood almost three feet high when it was fully extended, and it had elaborate runes all around it.

Cynia knelt down beside Ayris and said, "How would you like to learn to cast a magical spell?"

The girl looked skeptical. "Mommy said magic is dangerous. Daddy says all the real Magi died long ago."

"The goddess Nalria is bringing the gift of magic back to the known-lands. She has put the ability to summon magic inside you. I can show you how to use that gift. Would you like that?"

She nodded her head slowly.

"Hold your right hand here, and turn your palm to the sky. Now close your eyes. Picture your right hand in your mind. Can you see it?"

The little girl nodded again.

"Now focus on the energy all around inside your body, you can feel it if you try. It's is almost a tingly buzzing feeling on your insides, but it's oh so soft. There is some energy in your feet, even in your toes. Use your mind to gather up some of that energy from one of your toes. Smoosh it together with the energy from one more toe. Can you feel it? Can you move it up towards your belly?"

Ayris was smiling, and she nodded slightly.

"Very good! Now, slowly bring that energy up towards your hand. Squish it like clay, until the energy is shaped like an egg. Squeeze it tight until it's the smallest egg you can make it, with all the energy from those two little toes. When you're ready, gently move that magical energy egg to your right palm and say the words Mayl'Hok."

After a moment, Ayris said, "*Mayl'Hok*"

A large, egg shaped, glowing orb appeared in her little hand! It was large enough to fill her palm. She pulled her right hand closer to her face to look at the glowing orb. With her left hand she started poking it, and then she rolled it from one hand to the other. She said, "It's sticky, and it glows! Was that magic?"

Rissyl was extremely impressed. He had to admit that the girl had a natural knack for magic. He said, "Yes, great job! You did it!"

Cynia patted the girl on the shoulder. "That was great! You just summoned a magic light orb. Magi use those all the time to bring light to a dark room. You can stick that to a wall or desk and it'll keep the room lit up for hours. I'm very proud of you!"

He looked back to the riders, and saw that they had changed their course. "Cynia, we need to go now. They're headed this way."

"Are you ready to try another spell?"

Ayris shrugged. She looked towards the horsemen, and then back at Cynia with concern in her eyes.

"Don't worry about them, listen to me. First I want you to learn the words. The words for this spell are Foer Tov Ac'Tovik."

With an uncertain expression on her face, Ayris said, "Foer Tor Av Tavlik?"

"Foer Tov Ac'Tovik."

"Foer Tov Ac Tovik?"

"Ac'Tovik. These two words should be said quickly together almost like one word. Foer Tov Ac'Tovik."

"Foer Tov Ac'Tovik?"

"Yes, good. Say it a few more times."

Ayris said them a few more times, each time saying them correctly.

"Good, now for the harder part. Reach out with both hands, and grab onto the stone at the top of the pillar. Close your eyes. Picture your body in your mind, and picture all of that buzzing energy in your body. Can you see it?"

"My two little toes are still empty."

"Yes, that magic energy will come back over time, probably a few hours. Next, take a little energy from your left hand and wrap it around your left wrist. Make sure that it is wrapped tightly with energy. Then do the same thing with your right wrist, and both of your ankles. Gather little strings of energy together throughout your body, and link all of those bindings around your ankles and wrists. Each ankle and each wrist should be connected by a tiny thread of magical energy. Do you still feel the stone in your real hands? Wrap one end of that magical thread around that stone. Tie it tightly! If it's tight, your hands should feel like they're bound to the portal stone and your feet should feel like they're planted in the ground. Do you feel that?"

The girl nodded quickly.

"Great, keep that magical thread tied to that stone. Rissyl is going to say the word Ty and then all together we're going to say the words for the spell. Are you ready? Keep that magical thread wrapped tightly around your ankles and wrist, and the other end around that portal stone!"

Ayris nodded again. Her eyes were closed tightly in concentration.

Cynia and Rissyl both grabbed onto the portal stone.

He looked at the horsemen and his heart pounded heavily. The mounted soldiers were getting much closer.

He said, "Ty."

Together Rissyl and Cynia said, "*Foer Tov Ac'Tovik!*"

The view changed instantly, and like always the unnerving vertigo of teleporting gripped his stomach. He looked around and only Cynia was with him. Little Ayris was not there.

"Dammit!"

"We've got to go back!"

He shook his head, "No, you've got to stay right here. I'll be right back!" He didn't wait for her reply. He summoned some of his rapidly dwindling reserves of magic essence and quickly formed it for a teleporting spell. He could use the portal stone to teleport back, but Evokers had the ability to teleport without needing the portal stones and he'd use less of his magic essence that way. He quickly said, "*Kur'Gezbar.*"

A blink of an eye later he was standing back in the field near Ront'El. His head spun terribly and his knees felt weak. It was unwise to teleport so soon after already having teleported, and he felt happy that he was able to remain standing long enough to reach out for the portal stone to steady himself.

That happiness faded when he saw how close the mounted soldiers had gotten.

He looked over at Ayris. She was standing with her eyes closed and tears streaming down her face.

She said, *"Foer Tov Ac'Tovik!"*

Just like that she was gone. He smiled and reached out for the portal stone. He summoned a tiny bit of magic and caused the portal stone to sink back into the ground, hiding it from view. Then he teleported back to Randol's to rejoin Cynia.

He hoped to find Ayris there when he arrived.

When he returned to Randol's place, his head felt like it might explode. His legs were jelly and they refused to support him. He fell to the ground in a heap.

After a few seconds his head cleared enough that he felt safe to open his eyes.

Sprawled out on the ground next to him was Ayris. She was groaning and holding her head. She said, "I feel icky." Then she vomited in the grass next to her.

Rissyl sat up and patted her on the foot. "I feel icky too."

CHAPTER 13

Jessa

"Dammit!" Jessa threw the book to the ground, next to the countless other books she had thrown over the past several hours. She'd been looking through books, tomes, scrolls, and endless other written works for days and so far she hadn't found a single useful page. Everything was written in some language that she didn't even understand. She was losing patience quickly. If she had her way she'd burn down the entire place, building by building.

It had been many hours since she'd last seen Jalinox, so she decided to look for him. They were both in the same building, but she had gone up stairs while he went to search the basement level.

It was a bit unusual for him to spend so much time in one building; they had been spending only a few hours searching each building. She wondered if perhaps he had found something. As she walked down the stairs towards the basement, she hoped that their efforts had finally paid off.

The basement was like the basements of all the other buildings in the Stronghold. It was smoothly carved stone, with a single long dark hallway extending to the far end of the basement and a few doors scattered around both sides of the hall.

She passed several open doorways and peeked in to see the rooms tossed and disorderly. The last door on the left was different from the others. It wasn't a simple wooden door, it was a metal door and it looked like it had once been locked. The locking mechanism was on the floor in pieces, and she saw Lord Jalinox sitting in the small room beyond the door. He was at a desk reading a large tome, with several very old looking tomes piled on the desk next to him.

She walked in and said, "What'd you find? Anything worthwhile?"

He hissed, "Hush, child! I'm reading!"

She pulled up a stool and sat next to him. Obviously he had found something interesting. In the days they'd been in the Stronghold, this was the first time she had seen him sitting and reading something.

Several long minutes later, Jessa started growing restless. She had abandoned her friends and what was left of her family to gain power and seek revenge. For too long they'd made no progress and she was anxious to start seeing some kind of results.

"My dear. Kindly ask Wallie to join us. I have something I'd like to try."

She was happy for any excuse to move around. "Right away, My Lord." She ran down the hall and up the stairs.

Once she was outside she looked around for any of the idiots. Before long she found Flat-Nose Idiot walking around as if he was on patrol. She hurried over to him. She said, "Lord Jalinox wants Wallie. Right away."

He pointed up towards the east wall. "He is up there."

"I don't sarding care where he is at! Run along and fetch him. We're working in that building over there." She pointed to the building, and then turned and walked away without waiting for him to reply.

In a sadistic way, she hoped that Flat-Nose Idiot chose to ignore her orders. She'd love to see Lord Jalinox kill the man slowly.

She walked back into the building she'd been in most of the day, and right away she ran into the wench. Since Lord Jalinox arrived, the wench had been trying to act as if the two Dark Apostles were best friends. The very thought turned Jessa's stomach. Jessa was a Gentry, and thus she was much better than all of these low-life scum that she'd been stuck associating with since she decided to follow Lord Jalinox. It was worth it, of course. She had to tolerate the miserable morons, but she certainly didn't have to like it.

The wench started following her across the room. She said, "We've been in this building a long time. Has our lord found what he's looking for?"

Jessa looked at her with distain, and did not answer her.

A few minutes later the wench said, "Why are we waiting in the foyer? Maybe Lord Jalinox needs our help with something?"

"You're a parasite, why do you insist on speaking to me?"

The wench slapped her hand down onto a desk. She said, "You think you're so much better than the rest of us."

The door opened and Wart-Chin Idiot walked in. Jessa said, "It's about time, Wallie. Lord Jalinox is not in a patient mood. Follow me." She turned to walk out of the room. When she got near the wench she said, quietly, "That's because I am better than you."

Wart-Chin Idiot followed her to the stairs and down into the basement.

When they entered the last room on the left, Lord Jalinox stood. He said, "Wallie! I was beginning to think you weren't going to join us! Please, come stand over here by me. I want to try a little experiment."

Wart-Chin Idiot walked over and stood by Jalinox. Jessa watched excitedly to see what would happen.

Jalinox began reading out of the open tome before him. His words were strange, and she was almost certain that he was speaking a completely different language.   Judging from the cadence and vocal inflections, it sounded like he was reading some sort of prayer. The impassioned reading went on for well over a minute, and Jessa had no clue what he said.

At the end, Jalinox reached over and touched the Wart-Chin Idiot on the side of the face.

Instantly the idiot's facial expression went blank, and Jessa was certain that she watched the life leave his eyes before Jalinox pulled his hand away. Before the idiot's lifeless body started its drop to the floor, his skin began to turn to dust leaving his muscle and bone exposed.

As the body hit the floor, most of its muscular structure and internal organs had turned to dust.

Jessa watched in fascination as the remaining bits of flesh and innards turned to dust before her eyes, leaving only his skeleton, clothing, and equipment scattered on the floor. The bones were bright white, and there wasn't a drop of blood or shred of skin in the pile.

Jalinox shouted, "Whoa, that was exhilarating! Did you see that?" He smiled the broad smile of a kid with a new toy.

The wench muttered, "By all the gods."

Jessa nudged one of the bones with her foot. "Lord Jalinox, you have no idea how long I've wanted to do something like that to him! What was that spell?"

"It was a ritual called *Disintegration Curse*, and it worked so far beyond my wildest expectations! But wait, there is more."

Jalinox turned several pages in the tome. Then he grabbed the idiot's skull from the ground and held it out to his left. Eventually he began reading from the tome again. Once again he spoke words that Jessa didn't understand.

The rhythmic chanting was much shorter than his previous spell. When Jalinox finished his ritual, the bones on the ground quickly began to reassemble to the skull. Once the skeleton was fully assembled, Jalinox released the skull and the skeleton continued to stand on its own. Its eye sockets glowed with an eerie bright green light.

It stood there quietly. Jalinox looked to the wench and said, "Ezmorelda, please hand Wallie his sword."

She picked up the sword and placed the hilt in the free standing skeleton's hand. The bones of the hand closed around the hilt.

"My dear, I think you're going to need to remove the scabbard from the sword or it won't do him much good. Going forward, poor Wallie will not be doing much deductive reasoning." He waited for the wench to pull the scabbard from the sword, and then he said, "Very good. Please step over here so I can try something."

The wench hesitated, looking terrified.

Jalinox paused, "Oh come now, Ezmorelda! I'm not going to disintegrate one of my Dark Apostles! Now be a good girl and step over here so I can try this."

Slowly the wench walked over to him. He placed his hand on her shoulder, and began chanting in the strange language. Jessa looked at the wench, who made a pleading expression. Jessa just laughed at her quietly.

When the chanting was over, Jessa was disappointed to see that the wench was still alive. She seemed unharmed, and she looked relieved as she stepped back towards the wall.

Jalinox said, "Alright Jessa, dear. It's your turn."

She felt like her stomach dropped to the floor. She did her best to look calm as she stepped over to him, but on the inside she was about ready to run away in fear.

He placed his hand on her shoulder and began the ritual chanting. Jessa did her best not to tremble visibly the entire time she stood next to him. When his ritual chanting was finished she didn't feel any different.

She was greatly relieved to still be alive, and she was mildly surprised to feel like nothing had happened to her. She couldn't help but wonder if his spell had failed.

"Very good!" Lord Jalinox clapped his hands together. "I think that worked wonderfully. Let's test it out, shall we? Wallie here is now an unwitting participant of the *Adherent Drudge* ritual. If I'm understanding the notes of the ritual properly, Drudges will be much more useful than the Awakened."

Jessa was shocked. The Awakened, the undead zombies that necromancers animated, were the primary weapon of their sect. If these Drudges were more useful than Awakened, it could be a very important discovery. She said, "They don't look all that dangerous, what makes them more useful than Awakened?"

"Great question, my dear. An extremely good question indeed, and we're about to find out. Please step out into the hallway."

Jessa followed the wench out into the hallway.

Once there, she heard Jalinox say, "Drudge, guard this room."

Jalinox walked out of the room and stood next to the women in the hallway. He looked at the wench and said, "Kindly go into the room and fetch the tome from the desk, and bring it to me."

With only a brief hesitation, the wench walked into the room. She returned a few moments later holding the large tome that had been open upon the desk.

He smiled and said, "Fantastic, you made it out alive! Now we know that my mark worked! I placed my mark upon you, so the Drudges will ignore you."

The wench looked down at her arms and clothing, looking for some sort of mark.

"Not that kind of mark, it's a magical mark. It can't been seen. But, all Drudges will know it's there until I remove it. Now, Jessa, kindly return the tome to the desk in that room."

She took the book from the wench's hand and walked slowly into the room. The skeleton stood in the same spot where it had been, the sword was still firmly in its hand, and its eye sockets still had the eerie green glow. It did not make any movements as she carefully walked into the room. Once the tome was back on the table, she hurried back out to the hallway.

"Ah yes, another successful test. Ezmorelda, please be a dear and run out and fetch one of the guards and ask him to come join us."

The wench hurried off to do his bidding.

Several minutes later she returned with Big-Ear Idiot. Jessa tried, unsuccessfully, to suppress a smile. She was very confident that Big-Ear Idiot was about to die, and the moron had no clue. She would have paid a mountain of coin to see this, and now she got to watch it for free.

Jalinox said, "Broede, thank you for coming so quickly! I have need of my tome that I left in this room over here. Would you run in and grab it for me, please?"

The idiot replied, "Yes, Lord Jalinox!" He hurried into the room.

Jessa stepped a few steps to her left so she could see into the room. As soon as the idiot got into the room, she saw the Drudge lunge forward and drive the sword directly into the idiot's abdomen.

The idiot drew his own sword as the Drudge pulled the sword from his body, and it prepared for another strike. The idiot thrust his sword at the Drudge but it slid right through the spaces between its bones. As the idiot tried to regain his balance from his strike, the Drudge brought its sword down at an angle with a surprising amount of force and drove the blade deep into the idiot's shoulder at the base of his neck.

The idiot dropped his sword as he slumped to the ground dead.

Jessa had hoped to feel great joy watching the idiot get killed, unfortunately she didn't enjoy it as much as she'd hoped. In the end he was just one more pawn to give his life at someone else's whim, and she almost felt bad for him.

Jalinox laughed. "Yet another successful test! This Drudge ritual is truly remarkable. Let's test it further. Jessa, please make Broede an Awakened and direct him to attack the Drudge. Let's see what happens."

She stepped closer to the idiot's corpse and began her dark prayer to Viator, the god of death. A few moments later, the idiot stood up. His eyes glowed with a dull red light as he moved to obey Jessa's command to attack the Drudge.

The Skeleton rushed over, and drove its sword completely through Awakened Idiot before Jessa's minion had even finished standing. The attack had no effect on the Awakened since it completely missed its heart.

Awakened Idiot howled an unholy scream as it reached out and grabbed the Drudge. It ripped bones completely from the animated skeleton and threw them across the room. Over and over the Awakened attacked. Each attack saw more bones flying in all directions.

Within moments the Drudge was missing both arms, and several rib bones. The Awakened screeched in fury as it relentlessly continued its attack.

Jessa felt an odd sense of pride as she watched her Awakened rip apart Jalinox's Drudge.

The skeleton's right arm flew back across the room and reattached itself to the Drudge. Other bones started flying back as well. The animated skeleton attacked again with the sword, striking the Awakened against the side of the head.

Before long the room was filled with flying bones, some being thrown from the cursed creature and others flying back to rejoin it. The Awakened continued to howl and scream as the two undead creatures circled each other and battled with frightening ferocity. Neither creature cared for its own wellbeing; it was solely dedicated to the destruction of its foe.

The battle continued for several minutes, which seemed like an eternity. Jessa was starting to get annoyed. She wished that Jalinox would just admit that it was a stalemate. She knew that wasn't entirely true, because at some point she would need to dismiss the Awakened. Controlling them used her life force so eventually, albeit many hours from now, she would have to concede. She was starting to think that Jalinox would let the battle continue that long.

Even when the Awakened smashed and broke the bones of the Drudge, they simply reassembled and flew back to the skeleton a few seconds later.

Then, without warning, the Drudge thrust its sword through the torso of the Awakened and Jessa's undead servant fell to the ground. The Drudge's strike happened to pierce the Awakened's heart, and suddenly Jessa's creature was defeated. The skeleton walked slowly back to the corner of the room and resumed its guard duty. For several seconds random bones flew across the room, returning to their rightful spot on the skeleton.

She looked at Jalinox, and he looked like he was about to break out into a giggling fit.

He grabbed her shoulders and held her at an arm's length. He said, "Did you see that? Wasn't it incredible?"

She nodded slowly. "I did. The Drudge won, congratulations."

"Don't you see how important this is?"

"The Drudges can beat the Awakened in combat. That is impressive. They also seem impossible to beat. Clearly that will come in handy in our impending quest for domination."

"My dear, you're missing the most important point!"

She stared at him for a moment. She wasn't sure what else was so important about what they just watched.

"I was no longer controlling the Drudge. Once I assign a Drudge to a task, it doesn't take any of my life force to control it. It continues to follow my instruction, forever. Wallie will stand here for years, centuries even, faithfully carrying out my simple instruction."

She nodded, "Oh, that is handy." She wasn't exactly sure that a skeleton guarding a room for all eternity was something that would turn the tide of the impending war, but it was certainly useful.

He sighed, "You still don't see? This means there is no limit to how many Drudges I can control! We can only control a dozen or so Awakened at once or we risk draining our life force too fast. However, I could create dozens of Drudges a day, and eventually I'll have an army of thousands of undead soldiers! All of them content to follow my every simple command!"

Jalinox laughed maniacally, it was loud and it carried on for a long time.

The insane laughter brought a chill to Jessa's spine. She was starting to see the long term impact of such a wonderful weapon.

He walked into the room and opened the tome. After flipping through a few pages to find his place, he turned to the skeleton in the corner. He said, "Drudge, bring that corpse to me."

The Drudge walked over, picked up the idiot's bloody corpse, and held it out to Jalinox.

Jalinox placed his hand on the corpse's head. Once again he chanted the long and rhythmic prayer of the *Adherent Drudge* ritual. When he completed the ritual, the corpse of the Big-Eared Idiot stood up on its own, with a bright green glow emanating from its eyes.

Jessa said, "So apparently Drudges don't have to be skeletons?"

"Oh no! That's the beauty of them! We can use fresh corpses or the skeleton of those who have been dead for a millennium. These mindless minions will continue to follow our simple instructions, no matter how much damage is done to their bodies. They'll rebuild themselves, even if they're disassembled and broken to bits of bone."

Ezmorelda shook her head, and said, "That's incredible."

Jessa asked, "Does it have to be a complete corpse? What if bones are missing?"

He said, "No, the ritual just needs an intact skull. The skull is the key."

CHAPTER 14

Rissyl

Randol took a sip from his cup, and then said, "Is she awake yet?"

Cynia walked into the dining room and sat down at the table next to Rissyl. She shook her head no. "She is still asleep."

"This is really good, Randol. What is it?" Rissyl held the spoon close to his mouth and blew on it, to cool off the yellowish green mush.

"I call it Marmot Stuff. It's good for any meal, although my favorite is to have it left-over for breakfast like this. It's made from a secret recipe of herbs mixed with milk, eggs, and wheat. And, of course, with fresh chunks of Marmot tossed in."

Cynia tasted a spoonful from her bowl. "By the gods!" She blew vigorously into her hands trying to cool off her mouth.

Randol laughed, "Be careful, it might be warm."

"Some might have seen me blowing carefully on mine, and realized that theirs might be Khalius hot too." Rissyl stuck out his tongue at her.

She made a rude gesture at him. "You can both go sard yourselves. That crap could melt someone's face."

"Maybe, but they'd die happy and full."

Rissyl said, "So how long should we let the girl sleep? It's been almost twelve hours, do you want us to wake her?"

He shook his head, "No, it sounds like she has been through a lot. Just let her sleep."

Ayris walked into the room slowly, rubbing her eyes as she walked. She'd been crying and her eyes were red. Without a word she climbed onto a chair and put her head down on the table.

Cynia asked, "Would you like some breakfast?"

She shook her head. "No, I'm not hungry."

The three Magi looked at each other, and then Randol said, "It's really yummy."

"And it'll burn off your face." Rissyl gave Cynia a goofy grin.

"Still no, thank you." Ayris sat up, and leaned back against the chair. She was still crying some. She put both feet on the seat of the chair and pulled her knees back to her chest, wrapped her arms around her legs, and rested her chin on her knees.

The adults ate their breakfast silently and let Ayris sit quietly and start to process all the things she had been through.

After a short while Ayris asked, "Am I in trouble?"

"No! Why would you think you'd be in trouble?" Cynia ran her fingers through the little girl's hair and gave her a little smile.

"Because I asked Ranmithisar to eat those imperials"

Cynia continued to stroke the girl's hair. "You didn't make that creature eat the soldiers."

She shrugged, "I asked him to come to our land."

Before Cynia could reply, Randol said, "How did you bring the creature here? Where did it come from?"

There was a long pause before she answered. Then she said, "My mommy and daddy said I should not talk about it, people will think I'm crazy."

"We won't think you're crazy, sweetheart. Please tell us."

"When I close my real eyes and open my inside eyes I can see another place. It's a pretty place. Ranmithisar lives there."

Rissyl looked over to Cynia and then to Randol. They were both looking at him, and he knew they were thinking the same thing he was. This little girl somehow knew how to use magesight.

Randol asked, "Do you talk to the creatures there?"

"Some of them. Some of the creatures are nice, but some are mean."

Rissyl asked, "Do you ever talk to Rolimi that look like people?"

"Rolimi?"

"Yes, people who are kind of see through and look like they're traced in light. Like Ranmithisar was."

She shook her head. "He doesn't look like that in his land, silly! He is only see-thru and glowy when he is in our land." She paused for a second and Rissyl was about to ask her another question. Then she added, "I'm see-thru and glowy when I'm in their land."

The three Magi looked at each other. Randol said, "Wait, Ayris. Do you mean that you're transparent and traced in strands of light when you're seeing yourself in that creature's realm?"

She nodded, "Yep."

Rissyl asked, "Then, what does the creature look like in his realm?"

"He is shaped the same, but he's not see-thru! He's brown and green, and his belly is white. He's got a furry body and feathers on his head."

109

"Have you brought the creature to our lands before? How'd you learn to do that?"

"No." She shook her head. "I dunno how I did it. Ranmithisar is my friend, I talk to him in his lands a lot. When the imperials killed mommy and daddy I cried out to him, and he came to save me."

The three Magi looked at each other again quickly. Randol said, "So maybe the girl didn't summon the creature with her own power? Perhaps she has the power to communicate with this other place, and the creature somehow came here on its own? The Rolimi come here on their own."

Cynia nodded her agreement. "Our Rolimi Pups don't seem to have trouble coming here. Maybe the creature is from the same place where the Rolimi live?"

"The plane of magic?" Randol looked thoughtful. "If the girl can communicate with creatures in the plane of magic, that would be a remarkable situation."

Rissyl looked to Randol and asked, "Is it possible for Magi to communicate with beings in the plane of magic?"

He nodded slowly, "Back in my day, some very powerful Diviners could use their magesight to communicate with beings in the plane of magic. I was a powerful Diviner, and I've never done it."

"Have you heard of it being done by a novice, or someone who is not training in magic use?"

"If you would have asked me that yesterday, I would have told you that it was impossible."

Cynia looked to Ayris, "How did you learn to do that? To close your eyes and see the other land?"

"Armothulos showed me."

She nodded to the girl. "Who is Armothulos?"

The little girl closed her eyes for a moment. A little transparent kitten crawled out of the floor and climbed up Ayris' body. The kitten curled up on the girl's shoulder and nuzzled its nose into the base of her neck. The kitten looked much like the Magi's Rolimi Pups but it was white.

"Well, look at that, the girl's got a Rolimi Pup." Rissyl looked at the girl in surprise.

"Actually it's a Rolimi Kitten." Cynia said, without taking her eyes off the girl.

Rissyl asked, "Does Armothus talk to you?"

"Her name is Armothulos. Yes, sometimes I can hear her in my mind."

"Are you hungry yet, do you want breakfast?"

"No"

"Would you mind playing outside or upstairs in your room so the grown-ups can talk for a bit?"

Ayris hopped down from her chair and headed slowly towards the stairs. She was crying as she walked.

Rissyl put his hand on Cynia's arm as she started to get up to follow the little girl. He said, "She's gone through an awful thing. She needs to cry, and she needs to have some alone time to start to deal with things. You spent hours with her last night, giving her comfort and trying to encourage her that things will be all right. You did a great job, and now she needs time to let the healing start a little."

"Poor little thing watched her parents get killed. She has no one now. What an awful thing to happen to someone so little!" Cynia wiped a tear from her eye.

Randol asked, "Are you sure she has no other family that she can stay with?"

"When I was talking to her last night, she said that she knows of no grandparents, aunts, or cousins. She said her father's name was Edwold Carroy Esquire and her mother was Lady Edeth Carroy. It's odd that her parents have different last names."

Randol shook his head, "No, esquire is not a last name, it is a title. Before the formation of the empire, we didn't have Gentry we had nobles, and esquire was a title between commoner and the nobles. It makes sense that the people of the Free Cities still use the old titles and such."

"So, little Ayris Carroy came from a family with a little money but not much political importance?"

"Yes, it seems like it."

Cynia looked to Rissyl, "So, what are we going to do with her?"

"I want to meet up with the others anyway, to see how everyone is doing. We can ask around while we're there to see if any of our Free Cities Magi know of the Carroy's. If we took her to the other people who fled the city, she would be an orphan in a sea of refugees. The best thing for her is probably to stay with us."

Randol added, "We need to better understand her natural magical abilities. The best thing for all of us is if she stays with us, regardless of what distant relatives she might have among the refugees."

A couple hours later Rissyl and Cynia walked up to Uli's Ranch. The place brought back many memories for Rissyl. The last time he was here, Sarasa told him that she had feelings for him and that he'd have to choose between her and Cynia. He reached over and squeezed Cynia's hand, he was happy with his choice.

The ranch was not too far to the south of Sothral, and there was a portal stone within a few miles. The ranch had already been a central meeting place for the Magi in the Free Cities area, and the discovery of a portal stone not far from the ranch made the place even more popular for the northern Magi.

As they walked up to ranch, he saw several Magi sitting at tables around a large bon fire. Many of them waved or said greetings to the pair as they walked up. Rissyl didn't recognize most of them.

Sarge stood up and walked towards them. He didn't greet them and he didn't pause as he passed them. He just said, "We need to talk."

Cynia raised an eyebrow at Rissyl, and they turned to follow Sarge. He led them to the far side of the barn.

He threw a small backpack up onto a bale of hay, and then he leaned against the hay and looked at the other two Magi. After a moment he said, "I've got to leave for a while, probably a long time."

Rissyl looked confused, "Where do you need to go?"

"I don't know."

"How long will you be gone?"

There was a haunted look in Sarge's eyes, and it looked like he hadn't slept in a week. The old warrior shrugged, "No clue." He paused as if he was going to say something else, and then he reached up and grabbed his pack.

Cynia put her hand on Sarge's shoulder. "What's wrong, why do you have to leave?"

For a moment, Rissyl thought the old warrior would push past them and leave. Instead, he paused for a second and then dropped his pack back onto the hay. "I haven't been sleeping well since recovering from the Motlite camp battle. I keep having nightmares about that battle."

Rissyl nodded. Before he could say anything, Sarge started talking again.

"In the nightmare I see a god save my life. Now, I feel myself being drawn somewhere to learn about this god. I don't know. I've got to heed the call. I know it sounds crazy, but the need gets stronger every single day. There is some place I need to go, and I can't put it off any longer. I'm sorry."

Cynia asked, "Which god saved you? Was it Nalria?"

He shook his head. "You wouldn't believe me if I told you. I'm not even entirely certain that I believe it myself, and I see him each night in my dreams."

"Which god?"

"Nalria's father, Kelegar."

Rissyl looked to Cynia to see if she was as confused as he was.

She looked thoughtful, "I can see why you thought we wouldn't believe you. People haven't worshiped the Ancients in modern times. I know very little about them."

"Ask Sarasa." Sarge pointed at the barn. "Not surprisingly, she is quite knowledgeable about them. All I know is that he's calling me south."

"Do you want someone to travel with you? I'm sure we can spare someone."

"No need, I'm a big boy."

Cynia grabbed him and hugged him tightly.

Rissyl clasped him on the shoulder, "Stay safe. I hope you find what you're looking for."

Without another word the old warrior grabbed his pack and walked away.

They watched him for a few steps. Then Cynia said, "Let's go see how the others are doing."

They walked around the large barn to the entrance. Inside they found several Magi lying on cots and crates with linen bandages binding one part of their body or another.

Sarasa jumped up from a stool next to one of the cots. She had a large blood-drenched linen wrapped around her left arm and another on the side of her cheek. She ran over and hugged Rissyl and Cynia, and said, "I'm so glad you're both alright. I was worried about you."

He smiled, "We were worried about you too. Are you okay?"

Cynia gave her a stern look. "It was foolish to go running off by yourself like that. You are more valuable to the Magi Society if you're not dead. We need you!"

She looked at her cousin and grinned, "Yes I'm fine. You've got no faith in me, Cynia. But, enough of that. Dalen has been asking for you two."

She turned and walked back to the cot, the other two Magi followed her.

Dalen looked up at them from the cot. He had blood soaked linens tied around both arms, his ribs, one of his legs, and his left hand. Sitting up carefully, he said, "You both missed all the fun."

"We were there, we just didn't throw ourselves on every sharp object we saw." Rissyl grabbed a stool and sat down next to the cot.

Cynia sat on the cot next to Dalen's feet. She asked, "Are you hurt badly?"

"No, I'll be fine. I just needed Uli to make me stop leaking."

"Were there any swords on the battlefield that you didn't bleed on?"

Dalen gave him a rude gesture and then said, "Where'd you go? After that Rolimi bird-bear creature showed up, I didn't see either of you any more."

Cynia explained to Sarasa and Dalen about little Ayris and her remarkable natural magical abilities.

After listening to Cynia's descriptions, Sarasa said, "That's amazing. I can't wait to meet this little girl. I've read about a few people, long ago, who had innate spell abilities and didn't need spell books. Historically, the Magi Society has not been kind to magic users it couldn't control."

Everyone was quiet for quite a while as the implications of Sarasa's comments sunk in.

Eventually Dalen said, "Did you hear that Sarge is leaving for a while?"

Rissyl nodded, "Yes, we saw him." He held out his hand and showed them the signet ring.

Sarasa squealed! "You found it? That's great, Riz!"

Dalen smiled broadly, "When will we claim it?"

"Do you think you'll feel up to it in the morning?"

Dalen nodded, "I'm fine. Let's do it as soon as you're ready."

"Well, there is one thing I want to do first." Sarasa pointed out towards the group of people by the fire. "When I was in the imperial camp, I found my friend Brandam. We were students together at Thon's fighting guild."

Rissyl said, "He's an imperial soldier? You brought him here?"

"I trust him completely, but you can have Cynia read his soul with her magesight if you want. He has nothing to hide."

Cynia shook her head, "No, I'm sure that won't be necessary. If you trust him, I trust him too."

Rissyl was more skeptical, but he kept his concerns to himself. Both of the women fully understood what was at stake, and how dangerous it could be to bring an imperial soldier into the society and risk having a spy for the emperor.

"If we're going to wait until morning to claim the Stronghold, then I would like to get Bran obligated and let his Magi training begin."

Cynia nodded, "That's a great idea. You should go and get him, I'll get a Rolimi box from Uli, and we can go over to the other side of the barn and get him started."

Rissyl watched as both women ran off to get things ready. He looked to Dalen and said, "Did you want to come over and watch, or are you happy here?"

"I'd like to watch. I can make it over there on my own. Would you bring my cot so I can I don't have to stand the whole time?"

"Sure thing."

As Rissyl moved the cot to the other side of the barn, Sarasa and the man she pointed out earlier walked over to them. Cynia walked back with a small wooden crate and joined them.

Sarasa said, "This is Brandam. Bran this is Rissyl and Cynia, you've already met Dalen."

They exchanged greetings and then Cynia sat the box on the ground.

She placed her hand on the box, and said, "Sovereign Magi Society. Class is in session."

The box was just a foot wide, two feet long, and a foot tall. It was much too small for someone to climb out from inside. However, when the lid opened up, a Rolimi squeezed his way out of it with no problem. He stepped to the side and then pointed a long thin arm at the box. A large arched doorway popped up from the center of the box. Several other Rolimi started coming through the doorway. They carried a desk, a chair, and a chalkboard with them.

The Rolimi said, "I am Mr. Silnosticust. You may call me Mr. Silno." He wrote his name in the top left corner of the chalkboard. He was about four feet tall, but he was extremely skinny and even his head was elongated. He had long narrow arms and legs, and a long narrow body. His hair was long and flowing, and each hair looked like a single strand of sunlight. Even though the man was made of light he didn't glow brightly, and he wasn't completely transparent. The light seemed to draw the outlines of his features.

"If you don't know, I am a Rolimi. We are a race of gods-blessed beings from another plane. The Magi Society of old was a friend to the Rolimi and over the centuries we agreed to teach new Magi the basics of magic use. When Nalria asked us to help you rebuild the Society, we were happy to comply. We have agreed to assist you, as we served your forefathers, for now. If you want to earn the respect we once held for your society, you must earn it on your own merit as your forefathers did before you."

It had been several months since Rissyl had heard the Rolimi speaking. He had forgot how fast they talked. At times it was difficult to understand what the Rolimi was saying. In addition, the Rolimi also spoke with no voice inflections what-so-ever. The entire statement was at the same pace, tone, and inflection. To make it worse, the little man rarely paused as he spoke, so one sentence blended directly into the next. He had forgot entirely about the almost inaudible buzzing sound to the Rolimis' voices.

Mr. Silno said, "Before we begin, you must take the Magi Covenant. This is a binding agreement between you and our beloved Nalria. Taking this Covenant makes you a member of the Sovereign Magi Society, and by taking this-"

In the middle of the Rolimi's speech, everyone's attention was drawn to the box as another Rolimi stepped out of the archway above the box. It was Mr. Pyllis, the Rolimi who had done most of Rissyl's initial teaching.

Mr. Pyllis said, "Silnosticust, I apologize for the interruption. Magi, we must have a private discussion."

Rissyl was shocked to see his Rolimi instructor emerge from the arch. He said, "All of us?"

"No, the new student can resume his lesson, but the rest of you should join me over here."

They followed the Rolimi to a spot a few feet from the lessons. Rissyl said, "We found the signet ring, so we can claim the Stronghold now."

"That's what I need to talk to you about. It is too late, someone else has already captured the Stronghold."

Rissyl's stomach dropped to the floor. As hard as they had worked to find the signet ring and someone else had beaten them to the Stronghold anyway. It was almost more than he could take.

Everyone began talking at once.

Finally Mr. Pyllis put up his hands, "I have been there myself. I think it's controlled by necromancers now."

Dalen and Cynia cursed at the same time. Sarasa leaned against the wall, placed her fingers on her forehead, and began rubbing her temples with her thumbs.

Rissyl asked, "How? I thought the Rolimi were guarding it?"

"They were attacked by invisible creatures, something capable of sucking the magic from Rolimi. Some of our guardians were killed, the others fled. It must have been a horrendous death. Rolimi should not be able to die in your realm, because we are not fully there we just project a portion of ourselves there with magic. These invisible creatures were able to completely suck the magic from our guardians, leaving their physical bodies in our realm as just a lifeless corpse."

Cynia muttered, "It must have been Motlites, the magic-draining monsters that the necromancers created."

"This is horrendous news." Sarasa sat down onto the floor.

Mr. Pyllis said, "That's not the worst news."

Everyone looked to him in surprise.

Sarasa asked, "How could it get worse?"

"The Rolimi Elders have called for an emergency Synodus, to discuss the unprovoked human attack on the Rolimi. Some of the castes are calling for a war against all humans."

"What?" Sarasa jumped to her feet.

Dalen smashed his elbow into the wall, in a display of his rage. He then roared in pain. "Are you sarding crazy? A war against the humans?"

Rissyl held out his hands, pleading, "Mr. Pyllis, this is insane. We can't let this happen, what can we do to stop it?"

"That's why I'm here. According to our laws, the humans are permitted to send ambassadors to the Synodus to speak on your behalf. If these ambassadors can convince the Elders to reject war, much bloodshed could be avoided. I'll warn you, most of the castes believe war is the best option."

Sarasa looked at the others, and then asked, "How do we decide who speaks on behalf of all humans?"

"Your choices are limited. The Ambassadors would need to be at our Synodus in person, and that will be a very difficult task on its own. Only strong conjurers are capable of travelling to our plane. Since your evokers study the magic schools of evocation and conjuration, it will need to be someone from your Order of Evokers who serves as an ambassador."

Everyone turned to look at Rissyl. He felt a growing sense of dread. He never asked to be a leader of anything. When he was growing up he envisioned a quiet life in a nice home with a wife, a couple of kids, and a few Dregs to call his own. His dreams of a quiet life crashed to a halt when Nalria appeared to him and implored him to take up the banner and help in this insane, and perhaps impossible, endeavor to bring the Magi Society back into existence.

Unfortunately, his dreams of a quiet life were built around a flawed outlook on the world. He understood now that it was wrong for the empire to inflict servitude on people by making them Dregs. As much as he didn't feel qualified or capable, he grudgingly accepted that he was one of the leaders of the new society of magic users.

He looked over at Cynia. She smiled at him reassuringly and she squeezed his hand. His heart swelled with pride. For some unknown reason this amazing woman believed in him, even when he didn't believe in himself.

Then his gaze turned over to Sarasa. She was standing on the other side of the Rolimi. It was clear that she was angry, because her cheeks were red and her body posture looked like she was about to pounce on someone. Even in the middle of terrible news, and facing yet another difficult task, he couldn't help but notice how beautiful she was. Seeing her on the verge of feral anger triggered a surprisingly powerful attraction in him. The woman affected him at such a primal level, that he wasn't certain that he'd ever get over it.

"Looks like it's up to you, Riz." Dalen backhanded Rissyl in the arm.

Rissyl realized that he was probably openly staring at Sarasa, and that always annoyed Dalen. When he looked over at the blue cloaked Magi he expected to see a dirty look, or at least an annoyed expression. However, the expression on Dalen's face was almost friendly. It might have even been supportive and encouraging.

"The lives of countless humans could rest on your shoulders and your ability to negotiate with a magical race of people that we barely understand. That sucks a lot." Dalen paused and placed his hand on Rissyl's shoulder. "I give you a lot of grief, but we've all got faith in you. You can do this, and you don't have to do it alone. You could take Firana, Aruk, and Ferth with you."

Rissyl slapped Dalen lightly on the shoulder. "Thanks Dalen, I appreciate that. I'll talk with Firana and Aruk to see if either of them wants to join me. I'm not sure that I trust Ferth that much, yet." Then he looked to Mr. Pyllis, and said, "How long do we have?"

"I'll meet you back here at this time two nights from now and we'll discuss details about your journey. Once you get here, it will take time to travel to the Synodus. Time is a bit different in our plane, but you will still be away from your friends here for several days or fortnights." He paused and looked over to Mr. Silno who was still instructing Bran. "I should also inform you that this pupil will be the last Magi trained by the Rolimi until these matters are settled. Our agreement to assist the Magi is formally frozen at the completion of that Magi's introductory lessons."

Sarasa took a step towards the Rolimi, and for a moment Rissyl feared that she would strike him. Her anger had grown to fury, and he had never seen her so upset. She said, "I trusted you! I viewed the Rolimi as mentors and allies, and you're willing to cast that aside and wage war against us

118

because of the actions of our enemies? It's a disgrace! You can take your teachings and toss them in the middens, because I'm through with you. Even when you change your mind, we don't want your help. We'll teach our own new Magi!"

Cynia held up her hand to try to calm her, but it was no use.

Sarasa stepped back and placed both hands on her daggers that appeared at her sides. She said, "I, for one, am not afraid of war with the Rolimi. If you want a war we'll give you a war!"

"Rasa, enough!" Dalen stepped over towards her. "I'm as angry as you are, but this won't help!"

Mr. Pyllis placed his hands on his semi-transparent glowing hips. He said, "My caste is on your side. It will not help your cause by turning us against you as well."

With no warning, the Rolimi took a step forward and fell through the floor.

Everyone stood in silence, wondering if he had returned to his plane or if he was coming right back.

After several moments, Dalen said, "So, what do we do now?"

Without hesitation, Sarasa replied, "We prepare for war."

Rissyl thought about saying something to try to calm Sarasa, but her anger was infectious. She was right, this was the last straw. He had spent a great deal of time and effort trying to please people or trying to do the right thing without offending anyone. More often than not it just ended up offending them anyway. He agreed to Nalria's terms, and he was sure that she wouldn't have chosen him if she didn't see something in him worth choosing. If they were all expecting him to be a leader, it was time for him to stop thinking of himself as a follower.

Cynia said, "Sarasa, war is the last thing we need. We need time to build and learn, time to grow and mature as a society."

She replied, "Sorry, Cynia, but war is already here. In two cities our Coteries are under intense threat from the empire, and we are in serious danger of losing them both. Now the necromancers have captured the Stronghold, and we must take it back! Every day they control the Stronghold, is another day that they grow in power. If they have Motlites with them it's going to be difficult, but we are going to have to deal with it immediately." Sarasa crossed her arms, almost daring anyone to speak against her.

Rissyl cleared his throat and spoke loudly. "We need to get to Randol's immediately. I want to hold an emergency Grand Coterie meeting." He looked to Dalen, "We'll get a wagon, so you can ride to the portal stone. Send a nexus gem message to all Magi, tell them we're having an emergency meeting in six hours and all Magi are expected to participate even those from outside of the empire." He looked to Sarasa, "Rasa, talk to every Magi here at the ranch. I want each and every one of them to travel to Randol's with us, no exceptions. Yes, even the fossils who just want to sit around and complain. They can ride the weenie wagon with Dalen."

Dalen punched him in the arm, and Rissyl flashed him a quick grin. Then he looked at Cynia and said, "Please arrange for a couple of wagons to take to the portal stone. Then help Rasa spread the word and get people organized to head out within the hour."

Cynia squeezed his hand again, and he realized that he'd been holding it since the discussion with Mr. Pyllis had begun. He squeezed her hand back. He knew he was lucky to have such a wonderful and supportive partner at his side. She said, "Many of the northern Magi are going to want to stay here so they can get back to helping the Ront'El refugees."

Dalen added, "And there are many injured Magi here. The battle against at Ront'El was brutal, and many of these people are going to need time to heal and rest."

Rissyl shook his head. "I don't care what they want. It's time that everyone starts working together. This nonsense of everyone doing what they want has got to stop. If traveling to Randol's will kill them, they can stay here. Otherwise I expect them on that sarding wagon."

He walked away and Cynia walked with him. Over his shoulder he said, "I'm going to talk to Firana and Aruk. Plan on leaving in one hour."

Cynia said, "I like the assertive side! It's quite the turn on. Maybe we could find a secluded hay bale somewhere?"

She smiled at him slyly, and he winked back.

- = - = -

The room used for Grand Coterie meetings was much fuller than during the first meeting. Over twenty Magi were in the room, and at least that many more had joined magically.

Rissyl had just finished explaining the new Rolimi threat, and the capture of the Stronghold by the necromancers, to the assembled Magi. The room was in chaos as a dozen Magi tried to talk over each other to get their point across.

He stood up and shouted, "Shut up!" He waved his hands once on front of his body, ending with them spread out to the sides. Then he held his hands up, palm out, pleading for quiet. "Listen, please! We're not going to accomplish anything by talking on top of each other." He pointed to Ferth, the leader of Maethral Coterie. The always vocal evoker was the loudest in the room again, and Rissyl figured that if he didn't let the man talk first he would be obnoxious until it was his turn.

The image of Ferth placed his hands on his hips, and he said, "The Magi from Maethral Coterie won't be able to assist in whatever plans you're going to make. It's all we can do deal with imperial problems here at home!"

There was a low murmur around the room as several Magi began muttering to each other. Rissyl knew that he needed to deal with Ferth assertively. If it looked like Ferth could dictate the direction of his Coterie, they would lose control of the entire thing. He paced back and forth in front of his chair and looked at Ferth for almost a full minute.

He desperately wanted to chat with Cynia, Sarasa, and Dalen to get their suggestions and guidance. However, historically it was the evoker who presided at these meetings and it was the evoker who made final decisions for the coteries and the Grand Coterie. The other three had made it clear on several occasions that they wanted him to take more of a leadership role. If he was going to establish himself as the man who should be in charge, this was the time to start.

He stopped pacing and looked to Ferth. "The Maethral Coterie and the Khazror Coterie are under constant attack from the imperials, and you can no longer function as independent groups. This is interfering with the overall needs of the Sovereign Magi Society. It has become disruptive, and I need to address this problem. So, effective immediately those two coteries no longer exist. All Magi from both of those groups will be relocated here to Randol's place as your base of operations until the Grand Coterie decides how to proceed."

The image of Keta, the leader of Khazror stood up to speak, but Ferth's image stepped forward and spoke over top of her.

He said, "This is an outrage, and I refuse to submit! Maethral Coterie has gone through a lot together, and we're going to rebuild! We've given our blood for this coterie, and we'll not abandon our city." The three other Magi from Maethral stood up to show support to their leader.

Rissyl said, "In our last meeting you were threatening to pull the coterie from Maethral, and now it's an outrage? Refusing to submit is your choice, Evoker Ferth. However, if you refuse to submit to the lawful directions of the

Grand Coterie, I will bring you up on charges of violating society law. I will demand the most severe punishment, and I am confident that you will be found in violation of our laws. You will be stripped of all rights as a Magi, you'll be made Magic-Barren, and you'll be exiled from the society." He paused for a minute and the brown and white cloaked Society Magi from Maethral sat back down. He added, "That goes for everyone here. Ladies and gentlemen, make no mistake we are at war. We need to rally to one banner and work together for a common goal or we will surely be killed one at a time by our various enemies. If you can't put the needs and directions from the Grand Coterie ahead of your own desires then you are just another part of the problem, and I'm sick and tired of problems."

Ferth didn't appear ready to concede yet, however he did back up and he lowered his voice. "You're not even really the Grand Evoker; you're just the interim person until the rightfully elected Grand Evoker can be chosen. Why do we have to follow you?"

Rissyl heard Sarasa stand up. Without looking at her, he held his hand up to encourage Sarasa to sit back down. Rissyl said, "Cynia, Dalen, Sarasa, and I were chosen by the goddess of magic herself to rebuild this society. In her name we serve as the interim leaders of the Grand Coterie until such time as the society is strong and stable enough to do things such as hold elections. For now, we need to focus on survival. In due time, you'll have a chance to vote for new leaders, but for now we're in charge. So, will you submit to the authority of the Grand Coterie, or shall we have an inquiry?"

The evoker from Maethral stood for a few seconds and then nodded his head slightly. "I submit to the authority of the Grand Coterie. Please excuse my outburst." He sat down.

Rissyl noticed Randol looking at him and smiling. He felt relieved to see the old diviner's approval. He then looked to Keta, the leader of the Khazror Coterie, who was still standing.

She said, "Grand Evoker, I would just like to say that I support your decision. It is wise. Thank you." She sat down as well.

"Great, thank you. Now that those things are out of the way, let's move on to more productive things. We need to come up with a unified solution. We have three problems to deal with. First, we must convince the Rolimi that humans are not their enemies, just the necromancers. I will be dealing with this, along with Aruk and Firana."

Both of those evokers stood up and bowed slightly, and Rissyl returned the bow.

Then he said, "Second, we must carefully avoid confrontations with the imperials. Recruiting, patrols, missions to free Dregs, actively battling imperials during their invasions, and anything else that will antagonize the emperor must stop immediately."

That drew angry comments and outbursts from several Magi, especially those from the Free Cities. The main objections included comments about defending their homes.

Rissyl raised his hands again, palm out. He said, "Magi, calm down. If past examples are any gauge, the emperor is going to want to assimilate Ront'El before turning his attention to other cities. I would guess that we'll have years before we have to worry about another invasion. If the people of Ront'El want to reclaim their home they must do it without Magi assistance! I'm glad we were able to assist in the evacuation. But now we must focus on our goals. Yes it's important to free Dregs and go on patrol, but right now we have other priorities."

He paused to let the side-conversations calm down. Then he said, "Third, and probably most difficult, we must recapture the Stronghold from the necromancers."

Eleyne stood up. Once Rissyl nodded to her, she said, "Rissyl, some of our newer Magi may not know why the Stronghold is so important or why it's catastrophic that the necromancers control it. Would you explaining that to them?"

"Yes, Eleyne, that's a good idea. The Stronghold is a massive fortress built ages ago by our Magi predecessors. It is said to contain vast libraries of spell books, magical artifacts, weapons, relics from ages gone-by, and the gods only know what else. The spell books alone could be a priceless treasure. Just imagine what wondrous new spells could be waiting for us there! Not to mention armories filled with enchanted weapons and other magical artifacts. The Stronghold also offers us a refuge where we can train and grow, far from the reaches of the emperor. Unfortunately it is now controlled by the necromancers. Every passing day is another day where they could be destroying our priceless artifacts! Most of these things are useless to them because their magic is different from ours, but denying us these things is a huge blow. However, that is not the only threat. We have information that suggests that hundreds of years ago the Magi also stored necromancer tomes in the Stronghold. If that information is accurate, then the necromancers could gain access to new and more powerful magics to use against us. That could make this situation even worse."

As he looked out at the Magi, especially the newer brown and white cloaked Magi, he could see the full weight of the situation starting to dawn on them. Even Ferth looked like he was starting to see how important the Stronghold was.

He continued, "We have no clue how many necromancers might be there, or how many of their Awakened spawn they might have with them. We know that there is at least one of the magic-draining Motlite monsters there, and there is no way of knowing how many of those we'll have to deal with. This place is a magical fortress designed to help whoever possesses it to defend it from attackers. Even without the Motlites this would be a terrible fight. One thing that might help is a discovery that Sarasa made. There is a type of wood called Dinberian oak that can be used to craft wands or staffs. When those Dinberian oak weapons are enchanted they'll be able to be used as focus objects to summon magic that should be able to kill Motlites. We would need to send people to the Dinbera Isles to gather some of that wood."

"It should be able to kill Motlites. But we're not sure?" Keta stood up. "Why do we think this wood can help any?"

Rissyl replied, "Great question, Keta. The Motlites are tainted by a greenish ore with magic draining properties. This ore is called garroliron. Sarasa found an old book that discussed this in great detail. She is convinced that Dinberian oak is the key to defeating the Motlites, and I trust her assessment. If we can get some Dinberian oak, that would be a great weapon against the Motlites and it would make assaulting the Stronghold much more manageable."

"Before we get too far in the planning, I should throw out there that I plan to sneak into the Stronghold and assess the situation." Sarasa stood as she talked.

Rissyl jerked his head around to look at her. "Absolutely not! You can't wander around the Stronghold alone, it would be a suicide mission! Kimly said the Motlites could see through magical shrouds and invisibility."

Dalen stood up slowly. When Rissyl turned to look at him, he noticed that the linen bandages around his chest were completely soaked with blood and he guessed that the wagon ride and teleporting didn't help his healing progress any.

He said, "Riz, I've got to say that it's been good seeing the assertive side of you. It's nice to see you've finally grown a pair, and you just might be the leader we need you to be after all. Just keep in mind that all four of us have a voice in Sarasa's suggestion."

Feeling adequately chided, Rissyl nodded to Sarasa, "Esteemed Grand Shadow, please state your case for this course of action."

She gave him a quick pat on the shoulder, "I appreciate your concern. However, this is exactly the type of mission that is the specialty of the Order of Shadows. We must know what we're up against. I can find out. You're right, I'll need to avoid the Motlites and it will be dangerous. Everything we do is dangerous, and nothing will compare with the danger we'll all be under when we assault the Stronghold. You can't deny that advanced knowledge of what we're facing could be vital to our success."

As she sat down Uli stood up. He said, "Esteemed Grand Shadow, I would like to go with you."

Rissyl smiled and nodded to Uli. As the only other Order of Shadows Magi that they currently had, Uli was the perfect choice to accompany Sarasa. "Noted, thank you Uli." He turned to Cynia, and said, "Esteemed Grand Diviner, what is your opinion of this idea?"

She stood up. "I hate it, but Rasa is right. It needs to be done."

As she sat back down, Rissyl turned to Dalen. "Esteemed Grand Champion, your opinion?"

"I like it less than any of you. Rasa is my sister and I want to keep her safe. But she is a skilled warrior, and a talented Shadow Magi. I trust that she can do this, and I feel better knowing that Uli will go with her. No one should have to face that alone." When he finished talking, he sat down.

Rissyl sat back down as well. He said, "For the record, I am still adamantly opposed to this. I agree that Rasa is the perfect Magi for the job, and that it is good that Uli will go with her. I would be opposed to it if it was any two Magi among us, because the mission is just too uncertain and too dangerous. However, I defer to the opinion of the group. If that is what you think is best, then we should do it."

"Excellent." Dalen tried to stand up, and then winced in pain. He said, "I think I'll keep sitting if you don't mind. I will be leading the group who'll be obtaining some Dinberian oak. Who wants to join me?"

Keta and Ferth both stood up at the same time. Thon, Eleyne, and several brown cloaked Magi also stood up.

Keta said, "Since Khazror Coterie doesn't exist any longer anyway, we will all join you on your journey. Besides, I've always wanted to see the Isles."

"Maethral Coterie will travel with you as well. It will give us something productive to do, so we're not sitting around wishing for revenge on the emperor." Ferth nodded slightly to the four interim grand officers.

Several other Magi started to speak, but Dalen held up his hand. "That is plenty. If we have too many volunteers it'll be too much. When the formal meeting is complete, let's get together to discuss the details."

"Thank you for stepping up." Rissyl stood up and gave a thumbs-up sign to Keta and Ferth. Then he said, "Cynia will be working with the evokers as we travel to the Rolimi's homeland. Everyone else should meet at Uli's ranch, just northeast of Portal Stone number eight. Thon, would you make sure that everyone there is as proficient as possible with some sort of melee weapon?"

Thon stood up, "I'd be happy to."

Rissyl smiled at the old fighting guild master. Then he said, "Eleyne and Ranik, please make sure that all Magi know what's going on."

They both stood up. Rissyl hadn't seen Firana's brother, Ranik, much since the day they'd met. He had, however, heard some good things about the Order of Champions Magi and he was confident that he and Eleyne could rally the other Magi.

Rissyl continued, "Travel to the absent Magi if you need to, and get them to the ranch to start preparing. I believe that Zahr is with his family, trying to find somewhere for them to live after fleeing Ront'El. If necessary, bring the family to the ranch. Also, try to find Kimly and get her to the ranch as well. Every Magi should be ready to join us in our assault on the Stronghold once these other two missions, the journey to the isles and the ambassador meeting with the Rolimi, are accomplished."

Randol stood up and asked, "What about us old fossils who can no longer fight?"

He looked at Cynia and Sarasa for suggestions.

Sarasa stood up and said, "Obviously we don't expect our elderly Magi to learn combat or travel the Stronghold. If you want to help, there is plenty of research to be done here. Randol has an extensive library that might hold very valuable information."

CHAPTER 15

Konrad

Keta stood up and pulled her sword from its holder beside her chair. The runes on the blade quit glowing and all of the ghostly images of Magi around the room disappeared.

She said, "This meeting of the Khazror Coterie is now closed." She slid the sword back into the scabbard on her belt. She looked around the room and then frowned. "I'm sorry that we have to leave our homes. Please get your affairs in order and plan on meeting back here the day after tomorrow at first light. We'll travel together to Randol's and then it's off to the isles to find some wood."

The other Magi gathered their things and Konrad watched Keta walk over and start talking to one of the other brown and white cloaked Society Magi. It was an interesting title for the lower class of Magi who hadn't yet been chosen for an order. He found the entire thing fascinating.

He stood there watching her for quite a while. The woman was alluring and he couldn't help but imagine all of the things he wanted to do to her. He took a deep breath and let it out slowly. This was not the time to let physical needs get in the way of his mission.

He straightened his magical cloak and smiled at Waltur who waved and walked out the door. He had been shocked the other day when he approached the man and asked about the Magi, and Waltur confessed to being a one himself. Konrad had been half tempted to kill Waltur on the spot, earning himself a Magi kill and a big bonus from the emperor. Before Konrad could kill the Magi, Waltur asked if Konrad was interested in joining them.

Konrad felt like a kid with candy as he looked around the room at the remaining Magi. In seconds he could kill them all, and that would easily elevate him to the top of the emperor's list of private agents. That, however, would be stupid because he had just witnessed a meeting of all of the Magi. He now knew the names and faces of each of the group's leaders. This was an incredible discovery, and if he acted carefully he could single-handedly destroy the entire society. In his wildest dreams he couldn't even begin to imagine how fantastically the emperor would reward him. Surely there would be a disturbing amount of coin, homes, women, and the gods only knew what else.

He couldn't act hastily, or he'd blow his one chance. The Magi weren't ignorant, and they were growing in power. If he acted rashly, he'd end up getting himself caught or killed.

Besides, the Magi had actually taught him how to utilize a source of power within himself that he never knew that he possessed. In the past day he had learned some truly amazing things and had actually summoned magic himself. The feeling was exhilarating and the possible advantages to his life and career were staggering.

He would bide his time, learn, and plan. It looked like he'd be stuck traveling to the isles to help the Magi gather the wood they wanted. After that he assumed that his coterie would meet up with all of the other Magi at a place they called the ranch. That sounded like the perfect place to ambush the Magi and kill all of the leaders at once.

Keta noticed him staring at her and she walked over to him. As she got close, he could smell the scent of her hair and just a hint of some sort of perfume. He liked the smell a great deal. It took all of his self-control to keep from confessing his strong attraction to her.

She said, "Konrad, I'm sorry to drag you away from your home so soon after joining us. I hope this isn't too much of an imposition on you."

His heart skipped a beat when she said his real name. He decided his Magi guise would include the use of his real name, for the same reasons he gave his real name to Rissyl a year ago when he sat in the little room with the Magi to let him gaze into his eyes. It was risky, but it seemed prudent. However, he would probably never get used to having someone call him by his real name while he was on a mission.

"No, it is not a problem at all. I joined to help the Magi in any manner possible. I'm happy to accompany you to the isles."

She smiled at him and placed her hand on his shoulder. "That's great. We're happy you've joined us. We'll continue your basic lessons during the journey, so your learning and growing shouldn't suffer."

The touch of her hand on his shoulder was almost more than he could handle. He placed his hand on top of hers and smiled back. "I am looking forward to it. Good night, Keta. I'll see you the day after tomorrow."

He turned quickly, while he still had a few shreds of control. He was a powerful man and he'd been with countless women, but few stoked his fires like this woman had. He picked up his pack and headed out the door. He almost forgot to use the spell to send his cloak to the place the Magi called the plane of magic.

The warm summer breeze hit his face, and it felt good after being cooped up in the hot storage building for so long. As he walked down the street he thought about the Magi woman. He wondered if perhaps she had ensorcelled him. That would explain the powerful physical attraction he felt towards her. It seemed unlikely, she was a beautiful woman with an impressive body and he was certain she didn't need magic to attract men.

When he killed all of the Magi he would have to find a way to keep her alive, so he could claim her for himself when things were done. After single handedly destroying the new Magi Society, he had no doubt that the emperor would let him keep one Magi woman alive as a trophy. At least, he hoped the emperor would allow it. He'd prefer not to have to keep her a secret from him.

The emperor didn't need to know that he was now a Magi.

The thought sent chills down his spine. Things had happened so quickly over the past couple of days, he still hadn't had a chance to meditate on the events to get a deeper understanding of them.

Just for fun he summoned magic and dropped a *Shadow Shroud* around himself. This spell alone would be an incredibly powerful tool for his career. Before he killed them all, he needed to learn as much magic as he could.

CHAPTER 16

Kimly

"Are you sure that you're up for this? How are you feeling?"

Favin whispered, "I feel pretty good. I'm surprised that my test from the Shrouded is to attack Hisaro directly."

Kimly shrugged and then quietly said, "Seems like a logical test to me. If the Shrouded is going to operate in Khardifar it needs a powerful ally. If you take out Hisaro it'll send his guild into disarray, and it'll set up your guild as a powerful force in the city. They'll rebuild eventually, but the power struggle will weaken them and in that time your guild will surely grow. Are you sure the mercenaries you hired are reliable?"

They were sitting inside of a large shrub, across the road from the building being used as headquarters for Hisaro's guild. At one time it was a large inn, but it had been converted to a heavily guarded compound.

He said, "As reliable as coins can buy, I suppose. Let's go over the plan."

"Just like we practiced it back at that warehouse. You give the signal to your mercenaries to attack. Once they get the guard's attention, we'll both drop a *Shadow Shroud* spell and sneak over to that corner over there." She pointed to the southeast corner of the building. "Then we'll cast a *Monkey Climb* spell so we can climb the south wall, up to that window on the third floor."

"That spell is fun."

She smiled at him, "Yeah, it really is!" It was another spell that she had discovered in her spell book a few months ago. There were so many handy spells in that book. She knew she could continue to learn fun and exciting things from it for years to come. In a way she regretted leaving the Magi Society before being selected for one of the magic orders. She could only imagine what kinds of amazing spells she would have learned then.

He whispered, "The hardest part is keeping my concentration on the shroud spell while climbing the building with the monkey spell."

"Yes, but you were doing pretty good during practice. Just remember to keep focused, don't let your mind wander. Once we get up to that window, I'll use an *Invisible Helper* spell to reach through the window and unlock it. I'll go in and guard the door to the hallway, while you go to the bed and finish off Hisaro."

"How do you know he is in that room?"

She gave him a mischievous smile. "Magic! Okay, really I've been staking out this building for a few days. I've seen Hisaro through that window. I've climbed the wall, and I've seen him sleeping in a bed in that room. There are two doors in there, one goes to the hallway and the other goes to a private office with no other exits."

He seemed nervous and he didn't return her smile. He said, "After he's dead we go back to the window and use a *Slow Falling* spell, and then we jump out the window and escape?"

"No, after he's dead you go through the valuables in that office. You take as many coins, jewels, and other goodies as you can quickly gather. Then we use a *Slow Falling* spell, and jump out the window to escape. How long will your mercenaries keep attacking?"

"They've been told that they get to keep any valuables they capture, so I image that they'll be ruthless in their attack and thorough in their search through the building. We should have plenty of time, as long as Hisaro is where we expect him to be. Most of his men should be scattered around the city on their own missions or at their own homes, only a small fraction of his men should be at the headquarters at any given time."

He looked like he wanted to say more. After a taking a deep breath, he aimed his little crossbow and fired. The bolt flew true, and quickly drove deep into the skull of one of the guards. As the man slumped to the ground, the sound of several more crossbows echoed around the building. Over a dozen bolts soared through the air at the remaining guards.

Pandemonium broke out as guards rushed for cover, or cried out in agony as bolts slammed into them. A dozen or more mercenaries darted across the street, rushing to overtake the remaining guards before they could start to recover from the shock of the surprise attack.

Kimly dropped a *Shadow Shroud* spell on herself and watched as Favin set the crossbow on the ground and shrouded himself. She said, "Let's go!"

She raced across the road, hopped over the small fence, and stopped next to the wall of the building. She was directly under the window that they wanted to enter.

Without waiting to make sure that he had made it, she began summoning the magic for her *Monkey Climb* spell. She whispered, "Col'Ze." Then she faced the wall and quickly started climbing. She used edges of the window frame, the small cracks between bricks, vines growing up the side of the building, and anything else that she noticed at the time as she easily scaled the outside wall of the building.

The feeling was exhilarating, and too soon she was at the window and was no longer able to enjoy the fun of climbing the building. She positioned her feet on the window ledge, and held on to the top of the window frame as she summoned an *Invisible Helper* to unlock the window.

When she looked inside she discovered that the window wasn't even locked. She thought that was odd and looked into the room. Everything seemed quiet, so she pushed the window open.

She looked down and saw that Favin was almost up to the window. Unfortunately he had lost focus on his *Shadow Shroud* spell, so he was visible as he climbed the final few feet up to the window.

He didn't even hesitate when he got to the window; he climbed directly into the room and rushed over to the bed.

Kimly moved into the room also, and headed over to the door that led out to the hallway. She would have liked to have been able to shove a dagger under the door to jam it closed, so they wouldn't have any surprise visitors while Favin looked for goodies. That wasn't possible since the door would open out into the hallway, not into the room, so she just took up position beside the door.

When she looked over at Favin, he was standing over the sleeping figure. Hisaro was completely covered by blankets, and Favin held this dagger poised to strike the man dead in his sleep.

As he raised his dagger to strike, Kimly noticed a little hand and wrist tied to the frame of the bed. She gasped softly in realization and then whispered, "Favin, wait!"

He stopped the downward motion of his death blow just as it began, and he looked over towards her, but she was still shrouded.

Kimly reached forward and grabbed the blankets, and jerked them down some.

Hisaro was not in the bed. Instead there was a young lady in her mid-teens. Her arms were spread wide, she was tied to the bedposts, and she had a gag tied around her mouth.

The blanket being removed woke the girl and she looked up to see Favin standing over her. She began screaming into her gag, and she thrashed against her ties. Judging from the motions of her legs under the covers, her ankles were tied to the bedposts as well.

Both doors to the room burst open and several guards rushed in with weapons drawn. Hisaro walked in behind his guards and stood next to Kimly, who was still hidden in the shadows of the room.

Hisaro laughed, "This was a very bold move, Favin! Very bold indeed. I must admit, when one of my men told me that you were planning an assassination attempt I didn't think you had the nerve."

One of the guards took the dagger from Favin who stepped away from the bed and placed his hands in the air, palms forward to show he was unarmed. Two guards stood next to him with swords pointed at his chest.

Hisaro continued to laugh, "We brought the Chancellor's daughter to enjoy the comforts of my bed tonight. I'm a little disappointed that you didn't kill her yourself. I was hoping to let you escape after you killed her, then I could drop her little body on your boat or something. I would have enjoyed watching the Chancellor deal with you. In his sorrow, I'm sure his punishment would have been much worse than anything I could come up with. Sadly, you didn't kill the little brat."

He made a motion to his guards. Then he added, "Take him and the girl to his boat, and kill them both." Looking back to Favin, he said, "With tears in my eyes, I'll apologize to the Chancellor that I wasn't able to save his daughter before you killed her. However, I'm sure I'll be rewarded handsomely for killing his beautiful daughter's murderer. Don't you think-"

His sentence was cut short as Kimly drove her dagger deep into the base of his neck.

She grabbed the hair of the guard in front of her, pulled his head back, and slit his throat before he knew that his guild master was falling to the ground dead beside him. The attacks caused her to lose focus on the shroud spell, and she faced the other guard fully visible to him.

He reached out to grab her, and she sliced his arm with her dagger. Then she brought the weapon overhead and stabbed down at his neck.

The guard blocked her attack and punched her in the face, hard.

The force of the blow caused her to stagger and take several steps back. She felt the wall behind her stop her backwards motion. She blinked twice, but her eyes were flooded with tears and it was almost impossible to see through them. She furiously wiped the tears from her eyes so she could see.

She felt the soldier grab the front of her tunic and pull her forward. The man had the tip of his sword pointed at her throat and she could hear that he was laughing at her.

Kimly again wiped the tears from her eyes just in time to see the flash of a blade slice cleanly through the neck of the man before her. His head popped in the air slightly and spun in a circle as it dropped to the floor. Blood shot wildly from the man's neck as his body slumped against her. The whole thing would have been almost comical, if it wasn't such a gory mess all over her clothes and face.

She pushed the body away from her and looked up to see Favin standing before her. He reached out his hand to guide her through the gore. All of the guards in the room were dead. In the bed, the girl continued to scream into her gag.

Kimly said, "Cut the girl free and let's get out of here!"

He quickly cut the four ropes holding the girl's arms and legs. She heard him say, "It's going to be alright, we're not going to hurt you. But I need you to be quiet so we can get out of here safely." He took the gag out of the girl's mouth.

The girl stopped screaming, but she continued to sob.

Kimly looked down the hallway, it was clear but she could hear the sounds of battle echoing through the halls. She looked to Favin, and said, "We can't float down with the girl. Let's go this way."

She made her way out into the hall, and then let Favin take the lead. The girl looked at her and shied away. Kimly assumed that she must look frightening, covered in blood. She would have probably shied away from herself too, if she could.

They found the stairs down to the second floor quickly enough. Once there, they encountered two guards who were running away from three mercenaries. Favin held them at bay briefly until the mercenaries caught up and quickly finished their quarry.

Favin said, "Men, I need you to lead me and the ladies out of here, then you can return to plunder."

The mercenaries were clearly annoyed, but they turned and quickly ushered Favin, Kimly, and the girl down to the first floor and out of the building. Along the way they passed a few battles between guards and mercenaries, but the compound was fairly large and most of the fighting sounded like it was off in the other wings of the building. Without waiting to be dismissed, the mercenaries rushed back into the building to claim their spoils.

Kimly said, "That didn't go exactly as planned."

"No, and most of Hisaro's men are elsewhere. When they learn of the assault on their headquarters and the death of their guild leader, they're going to be enraged."

She put her hand on his shoulder, "And you are the hero who rescued the chancellor's daughter from Hisaro's men. You killed their guild leader, and walked out unharmed. People are going to be begging to join your guild."

"I hope that is so. How is your nose, does it feel okay? It looks broken."

Kimly shrugged. It wasn't the first time she'd had her nose broken, "I'm fine. Do you think you can get the girl to the sentinels without me? I'd like to go clean up."

"Yes, of course. Are you sure you are alright? I could have someone accompany you."

She shook her head no and walked away. She dropped a shroud around herself as she moved away from the sounds of battle. With a growl she kicked the foot of a dead guard out of her way as she walked. She was annoyed that Favin saw her vulnerable. She was more annoyed that he had to save her. Getting punched in the face, and getting her nose broken, didn't help her reputation as a powerful Magi of the Shrouded.

She was in a foul mood by the time she made it back to the mansion. Since she was covered in blood, she couldn't just walk into the house and change. So she walked around to the southern part of her yard and went down to the beach. It was fairly dark with only a partial moon and most of the stars blocked by clouds, so she waded into the sea.

The sticky blood covered her, and had started to dry in several places. She knew that her clothes were ruined, including her favorite floppy hat. As she washed herself in the warm waters of the sea, she discarded her clothes to be carried away by the tides.

Up upon the shore, her house was an impressive sight from this angle. All of the windows were dark, except one. There was a soft light glowing in the master bedroom, and she could see a silhouette standing in the window, looking out at the sea. She was surprised to see Cletis awake at this time of night. Then she realized that during the struggle to get the blood from her body and hair, she had lost focus on her shroud spell. She was fully visible standing naked, waist-deep, in the sea.

She cursed softly. She was fairly far from the house, but she assumed that he could see her in the water because of the partial moon. If he could see her, he must know that it was her. She wondered how long he had been awake, and if he knew how long she'd been gone. Even without being covered in blood, a broken nose, and naked in the sea it would be tricky to explain where she'd gone so late at night. At the very least it would look like she was being unfaithful.

Her foul mood turned even darker as she walked naked and wet towards her home. The warm breeze blew on her wet and naked body, and made her chilly very quickly. She shivered as she mentally braced herself for her first fight with her new husband. During the walk to the house she fabricated plausible lies to counter whatever accusations he threw at her. By the time she got to the house she was ready for a verbal battle. Overall it had been a crappy night and she was fully prepared for it to get even worse.

The walk through the house was dark and quiet. She made her way to the washroom to comb out her hair and look in the mirror to make sure she got all of the blood off. Her nose was obviously broken, and she almost screamed as she pushed the bridge of her nose back into shape. That got it bleeding again, and she shoved small strips of linen in her nostrils to get the bleeding to stop. Looking in the mirror, she was fairly pleased with how the nose looked. She was able to get it relatively straight on the first try.

For a few minutes she just stood there, looking at herself in the mirror. The image flickered in the candle light. This was not how she expected to end her evening. She picked up a cloth and dried off, dried her hair as much as possible, and grabbed a robe from a hook in the corner of the room.

She half expected her husband to be in her bedroom when she walked in. However, the room was mostly dark when she entered. A single candle burned on her dresser. She could tell that it had only recently been lit. On her bed, someone had laid out a clean night-dress and undergarments. On top of them was a single red rose.

She was flabbergasted, and didn't know what to think. Was this his way of saying that he knew that she had snuck out? She slipped on the clothes that had been laid out for her. Then she walked over to the door that connected her bedroom with her husband's. She opened it quietly, expecting to find the room still candle-lit and him waiting for her in anger. However, the room was completely dark and he was in bed.

Closing the door quietly, Kimly walked over to her dresser. She put the rose on the dresser and blew out the candle.

At least he was going to let her get some sleep before the fighting began. That was a bit of a relief. It would give her ample time to come up with a believable lie to explain why she'd been out.

- = - = -

Kimly awoke feeling worse than when she went to bed. Her face and nose hurt, and she was pretty sure that she was going to have at least one black eye from where Hisaro's guard punched her in the face.

She had spent several hours tossing and turning, unable to fall asleep. She thought about her early teen years, and the many times she had been caught sneaking out. Her mom had beaten her severely every single time. After a while it became like a game to see if she could get back without getting caught, without yet another severe beating.

Kimly was certain that her vile mother enjoyed beating her. The woman would take great pleasure in standing over her young daughter, hitting her over and over with whatever was nearby. The woman enjoyed telling her that she should appreciate the fact that she was willing to beat Kimly gently, and assured her that when she grew up her husband would certainly beat her much worse if he caught her sneaking around.

For years Kimly heard how awful it would be to endure the beating of a wrathful husband, and she realized that she was about to find out how correct her mother had been.

Cletis seemed like such a sweet and gentle man. However, surely even a gentle man could not stand by and let his wife get away with sneaking out in the middle of the night without some kind of beating, could he? Could she still care for the man if he beat her?

She was a Magi, and she knew that she could defend herself. She just wasn't certain that she should. She could hear her mother in her ear, laughing at her and telling her to get out of bed and face her beating like a proper wench.

The anger started to come back slowly. She cursed her mother for her beatings, and again for trying to make her weak.

When she heard a soft knock on the door, she groaned aloud. She wasn't ready for the fight.

The door opened and one of the Dregs said, "I'm sorry to bother you, my lady. Lunch is served, and Lord Cletis wishes for you to join him."

Kimly snaked an arm from under the covers and flashed a rude gesture at the Dreg. After a moment she heard the door close softly.

She was half tempted to go back to sleep, but then decided that she might as well get things over with. She crawled out of bed, tossed off the night-dress, and pulled on a pair of trousers and a tunic.

When she got down stairs she expected to see Cletis waiting to confront her in the foyer or the common room. However, she didn't even see him until she got to the dining room. He was seated at the table, about ready to start eating a bowl of soup. There was a place setting for her.

She sat down next to her husband, and tasted her soup. It was warm and delicious, and she found that she was starving. They both ate in silence for several long minutes. He looked at her several times, and she saw his eyebrows raise in alarm when he saw her black eye and linen-packed nose.

When she finished her soup she sat there quietly, waiting for him to confront her. He continued to slowly eat his soup, without saying a word.

Eventually she said, "I guess you're wondering where I was last night."

He took another bite of soup, and shook his head no. After a moment he said, "Did Favin give you the black eye?"

She dropped her spoon in surprise, and looked at him. She said, "Wait, how do you know about Favin?"

"Dearest, I'm one of the most powerful and well-connected men in the city. You don't really expect to wander around the city and not have anyone report it back to me?"

She sighed, "Doc Algurith?"

He nodded. "He sent someone to me the night that you dragged Favin into his apothecary shop."

"It's not what it looks like. I'm not sleeping with him. I'm... he's... it's complicated." She was at a loss for what to say. She'd planned a hundred different lies, but she hadn't even considered what to say if her husband already knew half of the truth.

"I didn't accuse you of that. Did Favin give you the black eye?" He sounded angry, and she didn't really blame him.

She wasn't sure if he was angry at her, or angry because he thought that Favin had given her a black eye. She shook her head no. "Favin didn't do this."

"Tell me who did it, and I'll have them dealt with."

Kimly felt a shiver crawl down her spine. As long as she'd known Cletis, she'd never heard him sound so angry. She said, "The person who did it has been dealt with already."

He looked at her for a moment. "Are you in danger?"

She shook her head, and said, "No."

Cletis pushed the bowl away from himself, and wiped his mouth on a cloth. He said, "Have a nice afternoon, Dearest. If you'll excuse me, I have some business to attend to."

She stood up as he did. She said, "Wait, Cletis. Please don't leave while you're angry at me. Aren't you even going to ask me what I was doing last night?"

He looked at her, and his expression softened. "Would you answer me honestly if I asked?" He didn't wait for her to respond. As she started to nod, he said, "Please don't answer that. We both know that you've been less than honest with me since the day we met. If I wanted an honest and demure wife, I would have chosen one of many other suitors long ago."

Once again she was shocked, and she didn't know how to respond. Quietly she said, "Do you think I'm a liar?"

"Dearest, I know you to be a skillful liar. But, I also know you to be a loving and faithful wife, and that is all I ask. I have to work a bit harder to ensure that you're safe, but I'll not ask you to reveal things that you wish to keep to yourself. I knew you to be a woman with deep secrets long before I asked your hand in marriage, I wouldn't expect you to change that now." He paused for a second, and then added, "Besides, you're not the only one here with secrets. A man doesn't become one of the richest men in the city simply by selling wheat and grain."

He smiled at her sweetly, and she stood in stunned silence. Her head was reeling and she wasn't sure which to be most shocked about. She walked over and leaned against him. He held her in a strong hug for a long time before taking her head gently in both hands and turning it to look up at him. He kissed her tenderly and released her.

She sat down at the table and watched him walk out of the room.

CHAPTER 17

Rissyl

"Is this really all there is to it?" Rissyl sat the spell book down on a crate and looked to Mr. Pyllis.

The Rolimi nodded. "Yes, that's it. First I need to create the portal and then you walk through it, using the spell outlined in the book."

Rissyl looked at the Rolimi and then looked at Cynia. He said, "This spell is almost identical to the spell I use to send my staff away when I don't want to carry it any more."

"Precisely! When you send your staff away, as you put it, you're sending it to A'Etharus, which you call the plane of magic. The runes on the staff are tied to a certain place within A'Etharus and that is where it goes when you send it away. It sits there until you call it back to your realm. This spell is the same thing, you're sending yourself to A'Etharus. But you don't have magic runes on your body tying you to a location so you need the portal to act as a conduit between your realm and mine."

Cynia asked, "How long will you be gone?"

Mr. Pyllis bobbed his head back and forth. He said, "There's no telling. Like I mentioned before, time is different in A'Etharus. An hour in my realm is like ten hours here, and a year in my realm is like ten years here. Our negotiations may last a few hours, or they may go on for days."

She looked shocked, "So he'll be gone anywhere from a day to a month?"

"Perhaps longer, it all depends. Some Synodus have carried on for months."

"He could be gone for years?" She was practically yelling.

Rissyl placed his hand on her shoulder to try to calm her.

The Rolimi said, "He'll be able to come back here occasionally to give you updates. He won't simply vanish for years."

"Mr. Pyllis, is there anything we need to bring with us?" Firana sounded nervous.

He shook his head, "There is nothing you can bring with you. If you're about ready, place your clothes and possessions aside and meet me by the box."

All three of them undressed in silence. It made sense when he considered it, but he hadn't realized that they'd all be getting naked for their journey.

As she walked over to the Rolimi, Firana said, "If I knew I was going to get naked in front of everyone, I would have shaved my legs." She giggled as she said it, but from the way she crossed her arms in front of her chest Rissyl guessed that she was very uncomfortable being naked in front of them.

Cynia said, "Don't worry, dear. No one is looking at your legs."

Rissyl giggled at her joke, and Aruk turned to look the other way. Rissyl could see that Aruk was blushing.

"That don't help, Cynia. Thanks." Firana blushed furiously as she looked to Cynia and stuck out her tongue.

Mr. Pyllis pointed at the box that the Rolimi had crawled from to teach Bran a couple of days ago. An archway raised up from the box. "There you go. Walk toward the archway. When you get to it, cast your spell with the archway as the target."

Rissyl walked forward, and summoned a small amount of magic. He formed it almost exactly as if he was about to send his staff or cloak away. Instead of sending the magic to the staff, he sent it to the portal.

For a brief moment he felt the familiar vertigo as if he had teleported, but it wasn't nearly as severe.

When he looked around, he thought the spell had failed.

Nothing looked any different.

He was still inside the barn. The crates looked the same; the dirty floor was the same. Even the box with the portal archway was the same.

However, when he looked at Mr. Pyllis, the Rolimi looked completely different. He was whole and solid; he wasn't mostly transparent or traced in magical light. The Rolimi was the same size and shape, but he was as real as the crates and walls. He was wearing remarkably ornate robes with a variety of frescos embroidered across the entire garment.

The Rolimi motioned Rissyl forward and he moved just as Firana stepped through the portal. She looked around in confusion.

When he looked at Cynia and Aruk, he found that they were mostly transparent, and traced in magical light! He was seeing Cynia how he normally viewed the Rolimi, and it was a creepy sight.

Aruk stepped through the portal, and he suddenly looked whole once again. He looked as confused as Rissyl felt.

As he watched Cynia, her movements looked extremely slow. It was as if she was moving through water or thick molasses. He looked to Mr. Pyllis and said, "I expected the plane of magic to look different."

The Rolimi smiled and said, "Like this?"

All of a sudden the barn, all of its contents, and even the ground itself vanished. He felt as if he was falling!

At first everything went black, and there was nothing but darkness and falling.

It wasn't a feeling of falling, like falling off a cliff. It was more like falling through water. As he moved his arms, he was able to direct his movements like he was in water. When he started kicking his feet, he was even able to stop his falling motion all together.

He paused, kicking his feet slightly and waving his arms side to side as if treading water. He was suspended, swimming in nothing.

As he looked around, he saw that it wasn't nothing. There was a slight current of orange flowing all around him. Below him he saw Firana, Aruk, and Mr. Pyllis. They were all treading water, without the water, and they were looking around.

When he turned his attention to his surroundings, he was astonished to see that the blackness seemed to go on forever. Snaking through the blackness were long rivers of the orange stuff that he was floating in. It was as if he was within some magical stream and he could see that his stream connected to endless other magical streams that meandered around the darkness, interconnecting occasionally.

He imagined that this might be how an ant felt, in the middle of a massive wadded-up bundle of fishing net with the ropes of the net intersecting sometimes in a heap of ropes and knots. However, instead of walking on the outside of the ropes like an ant would, he was swimming inside the magical ropes.

Beside him, he saw Mr. Pyllis swim past him, moving back up towards the place where the barn had been.

He said, "Follow me." His voice sounded slightly muffled, but not as muffled as if he were talking under water. More like he was talking through a thick scarf.

Rissyl kicked his feet faster and paddled his arms like he was trying to swim out of the deep part of a lake. He watched the Rolimi continue to rise and move toward what looked like the black bottom of some large surface. Then he just vanished through the blackness.

As Rissyl swam up through the orange magic stream, he felt like his head would smack against the black surface he was swimming towards. Suddenly he burst through the surface and found himself in a large meadow. He literally crawled out of the ground, just like he'd seen his Rolimi Pup do so many times. He stood up and walked over to Mr. Pyllis. A few moments later Firana and Aruk climbed out of the solid ground also.

The grass felt cool and soft under his naked feet. When he looked around, at first it seemed like they were in any field back home. The meadow continued for a hundred yards or more in each direction, and then it just seemed to drop off to black nothingness. He looked to the sky, and everywhere he looked the sky was streaked with orange magical rivers. The rivers crisscrossed throughout the sky, forming a random latticework of orange netting. Looking to all four compass directions the sky looked the same, it was endless orange magical rivers in every direction. When he looked straight up he noticed the sun, or at least what he assumed was the sun. It was much smaller than his sun back home, but it was bright in the sky. Back home, his entire night sky was filled with endless white dots. Here the sky was filled with thin streams of orange rivers, interwoven throughout the sky with a small sun straight overhead.

When he looked back to the others, he saw that Firana was clothed in a thick wool jerkin, leggings, and tall boots.

He said, "How did she get clothes, and where do we get some?"

The Rolimi pointed towards her. He said, "She wanted to be dressed, so she became dressed. If you want clothes, then will some into existence."

Rissyl noticed that the Rolimi didn't sound unusual now that they were in both in A'Etharus. Instead of sounding like he was talking really quickly, the Rolimi actually seemed to talk rather slowly.

He closed his eyes and imagined himself dressed in a loincloth made of leaves and feathers like the ancient barbarians of his homelands wore. When he opened his eyes and looked down, he was wearing exactly what he pictured.

He laughed excitedly and looked to Aruk. The man was wearing the long colorful outfit of a court jester; he even wore the goofy hat with bells on the ends.

Firana laughed loudly at both of them, and even Mr. Pyllis smiled.

The Rolimi said, "Clever, both of you. So, what do you think of A'Etharus thus far?"

Aruk asked, "What happened to the barn? It was just here a moment ago. Then we fell through the floor, and when we swam back up the barn was completely gone."

"That is a great observation, Aruk. Let me explain. Look to the sky and you see the orange rivers of A'Ethar. That orange that you see flowing is pure magic energy, which we call A'Ethar. It flows in rivers and streams throughout our realm, which you call the plane of magic. There is no world as you know it. There are no endless stretches of land that lead to oceans of water, or giant mountain ranges. Here, there is only an endless maze of A'Ethar streams that flow on forever."

Firana said, "So, your people live your whole lives swimming around in the orange streams of magic?"

"Yes, some do. Much like fish in your realm, many creatures in A'Etharus spend their entire lives within the A'Ethar streams and rivers. Even some of the Rolimi live out their entire lives in the A'Ethar flows, but most live on creations such as this meadow. Look to the sky again. Each of the places where the orange streams intersect is called a nexus. A nexus is a powerful confluence of magical energies, and at any nexus we can build a mesa like this one. A mesa is surface area that acts like a plot of land in your realm."

The Rolimi looked at each Magi to make sure that they were following along.

He continued, "When we were swimming in the A'Ethar, I created this mesa to be like an open meadow from your land. It isn't tied to any certain place; it is simply a replica of a meadow that I've seen while I visited your realm. I thought it would be a nice place to explain some things about A'Etharus to you. I wanted you to feel more at home. When we are done with this mesa, I will cause it to vanish and this will once again be simply another nexus within the A'Ethar. While it's an empty nexus, any Rolimi could travel here and build a new mesa."

Rissyl was pretty sure he was following along. It was so much to take in, but he was fascinated about the place. He said, "So, before you created a mesa here with a nice meadow on it, you created a mesa that was like the barn on Uli's ranch?"

"Yes, but that was a little different. This mesa is just a small square mesa that looks like a meadow in your realm. There is nothing special about it." The Rolimi closed his eyes for a moment and suddenly a barn appeared all around them. It looked much like the barn on Uli's ranch. He said, "Now I've added a large barn to the mesa. We are inside the barn. If we walk over here, we can exit the barn and look at the outside just like if we were in your realm. However, there is nothing special about this barn. It's just a wooden structure, created with magic and designed to look like a structure in your realm."

The three Magi followed him out of the barn.

He continued, "The mesa that we were on when you first traveled to A'Etharus, was a special kind of mesa that was actually tied to a location in your realm. That kind of mesa is much harder to create, and it usually takes some sort of focus object in your realm to connect with."

Aruk said, "Such as the Rolimi boxes that we have, so your instructors can visit us?"

"Yes, exactly! So then, I can go to any nexus and create a mesa that ties with that box and its surroundings. The mesa will be created and when I look around the mesa it will look like the place where that box resides in your realm. I'll see any nearby humans, but they'll look transparent and traced in light, much as we look to you in your land. Since there is such a difference in time between our realms, I have to talk extremely slowly so that humans can even understand me."

Firana nodded, "And even though you're talking really slowly here, it still sounds like you speak really quickly when we hear you."

"That's correct, Firana. Additionally, we've gotten used to moving slowly when appearing to humans, so our movements don't look like we're zipping around from place to place."

Rissyl asked, "Are all mesas so temporary like these?"

"Oh no! There are many mesas that have been around for eons. Many of them are home to various creatures that are native to A'Etharus. Some nomadic animals travel the A'Ethar streams and create mesas at nexus points when they want to. Some of the mesas created by the animals are quite remarkable to behold!"

"So, do you ever just wander around and visit random mesas to see what's there? Sort of like explorers in our realms who yearn to see what's over the next hill." Firana looked intrigued, and Rissyl thought she asked a great question. He was very curious to hear the answer.

"Yes, and no." The Rolimi caused a large pillow to appear, and he sat down on it. "Do you remember when you were swimming towards the bottom of this mesa, and it looked black? All mesas created by an individual, whether it's a Rolimi, or another A'Etharus creature, will have a bottom that looks black like that. If you're traveling through the A'Ethar streams and you come across a nexus with a black mesa, you shouldn't enter it uninvited. It would be like walking into someone's home in your realm. Somebody created that mesa for their own reason, so it would be rude to just climb into it. It can

145

also be quite dangerous. The creator of the mesa could be a pack of vicious creatures, and they will view the mesa as their territory. Many A'Etharus creatures are extremely protective of their mesa."

Rissyl caused a large fluffy feather bed to appear and he crawled onto it and relaxed. He asked, "So the bottoms of all mesas are not black?"

"No, there are a variety of colors. The purple ones are created by Rolimi and designed to be public. All Rolimi are invited to visit them. They are the various sections of what you would probably consider to be a Rolimi city. The dark brown mesas have existed since before recorded memory and they are the A'Etharus equivalent to landmarks and natural wonders. I've only been to a few of those, but they are truly amazing to behold."

Aruk seemed awestruck. He said, "That's amazing! What are some of the other colors?"

Mr. Pyllis stood up. "Sadly we don't have time to sit around chatting for too long. We have a Synodus to attend, and it's about time to move on. When I cause this mesa to vanish, you'll once again find yourself drifting in the A'Ethar. Remember that you can use magic to change yourself, so it's easier to navigate through the flow. Some Rolimi change their shape to that of a shark or fish from your realm. Others choose creatures from other realms that they've visited. I usually just give my feet some big flippers. It's all up to you. Just be careful not to swim out of the A'Ethar flow."

That caught Rissyl's attention. He sat up and said, "Wait, what happens if we swim out of the stream?"

"Well, imagine that you're back in your realm and you're in a boat in the middle of the sea. Okay, now assume that being in the A'Ethar flow is like being in the boat, and the sea is the vast expanse of blackness outside of the magical stream. If you jump out of the boat, you'll float out into the sea and drown or be eaten by a shark. If you swim out of the flow into the open blackness, you will likely perish."

The Magi looked at each other, and Rissyl was relieved to see that the others looked as uneasy as he felt.

The mesa disappeared, and Rissyl felt himself falling once again. This time he didn't fall very far. He caused himself to grow flippers on his hands and feet, and then he could easily navigate the orange flow of A'Ethar. Below him he saw the other two Magi following Mr. Pyllis. Aruk and the Rolimi had flippers on their feet. Firana had turned her legs into a tail and she looked like a mermaid.

He followed them through the steam of magic, and he was surprised at how quickly they were traveling. The Rolimi looked back a few times to make sure the Magi were keeping up, and then each time he increased the pace a little bit.

As they swam they turned occasionally when they reached nexus points. Rissyl noticed that the A'Ethar stream was getting wider. A few times they passed other creatures swimming in the opposite direction. The A'Ethar stream was easily large enough for a dozen or more people to swim side by side comfortably, so it was no problem staying to the side while others passed in the other direction.

After a while he saw a whole pack of animals native to A'Etharus swim past them in the opposite direction. The creatures were almost catlike, and their sharp teeth were visible as they passed. There were at least a dozen larger creatures and about half that many that were much smaller. He was more than a little nervous that the creatures would turn around and attack him while he swam through the magic stream. However, he looked backwards several times and the creatures never slowed.

He continued to swim quickly through the flow, following Mr. Pyllis for a long time. He had no way to tell the time, but he guessed that they'd been swimming through the flow for an hour or more.

Without warning, Mr. Pyllis stopped at a nexus point. Above them Rissyl saw the bottom of a mesa, and it was a light blue color. He asked, "What does light blue mean?"

The Rolimi swam up towards the mesa and out of the main flow of the A'Ethar. Then he said, "This mesa is for my caste. You are our guests, as ambassadors for the humans. You'll want to get rid of the flippers and change to more formal clothing to meet my people."

Rissyl closed his eyes and imagined himself in a formal looking tunic and trousers, with a red and white cloak on his back. When Aruk and Firana saw him in his Magi cloak, they caused themselves to be wearing a red and white Magi cloak as well.

Mr. Pyllis nodded once, "I approve." He swam upwards and climbed through the bottom of the mesa. Looking up, Rissyl noticed that this mesa was much bigger than the other ones he had seen.

When Rissyl climbed through the bottom of the mesa he found himself in what looked like a small city with wild and fabulous buildings that could have come from his dreams. They were spiral shaped with tall columns and pillars all around them. Everything was white, or very light shades of primary colors, and looked immaculately clean. The roads were paved with white marble, and they were lined with large fountains and statues.

If he was going to build a city of splendor and wonder with the power of his own mind and magic, it would probably look much like this. He walked a few steps, looking around in awe. The entire thing was even more majestic and fantastic with the A'Ethar rivers throughout the sky wherever it showed through between the tall buildings.

Mr. Pyllis said, "The elder's building isn't far, let's go meet him."

As they started to walk up the road, Rissyl heard a deep barking sound behind him. A large dog with short legs, a thick body, floppy ears, and a long snout was running towards them. It barked happily as it got closer. It was dark brown and black on its body with lighter fur on its legs and belly.

Rissyl shouted, "Tiberos!" He knelt down and the big dog jumped into his arms, knocking him backwards on to the ground. The dog licked his face as it ran in circles around him. Then it flopped down next to Rissyl and tried to bury its nose under his neck. Rissyl petted the dog's head and chest aggressively and then rolled over a bit to give it a big hug. "I never expected to see you in all of your non-glowing furriness! You're much slobberier in person!"

He petted the dog for a bit more, before standing up and introducing Tiberos to everyone.

The dog barked and sat down close to Rissyl's feet.

Mr. Pyllis said, "We've met. Come along, let's not keep the elder waiting any longer."

- = - = -

The elder wore elaborate robes of the same light blue color as the bottom of the caste's mesa. As Rissyl looked around the simple office where they stood, he saw that most of the room was decorated with items of that color.

Mr. Pyllis gestured towards the Magi, and said, "Respected elder, permit me to introduce the three human Magi who will serve as ambassadors. This is Rissyl Sokigo, that is Aruk Arugelo, and that is Firana Aestelya."

Each of the Magi stepped forward and bowed their head slightly as their name was called, as Mr. Pyllis had previously explained that they should.

He then gestured at the elder, and said, "Magi, this is Meligoricko, the elder of our caste."

The elder moved slowly, but it didn't seem to be slowness caused by infirmity or age. He just didn't seem to be in a hurry. In a slow and soft voice the elder said, "You're late, Pyllistacaillian. We'll be needed in the council hall soon."

Mr. Pyllis didn't respond and the elder turned his gaze to the Magi. For several moments he simply looked at the humans.

Rissyl wanted to say something, but nothing seemed appropriate so he stood in silence.

When the elder finally spoke, it was in the same slow and soft voice he used earlier. "Unfortunate situation, this. War is not the answer. What will you offer to persuade the council against war?"

Rissyl wasn't sure how to answer. That was the question he'd been struggling with since the whole mess started. He looked to Aruk and Firana for guidance. Firana made a facial expression and hand gesture indicating that she would speak, and Rissyl motioned her forward.

She stepped up and said, "Respected elder, we-"

Meligoricko held up his hand to stop her in mid-sentence. He said, "You respect nothing, most especially not the Rolimi elders. Do not use titles you do not mean, it is offensive."

She frowned, "My apologies. Mr. Meligo... ri..." She paused, and Rissyl groaned on the inside. He knew he wouldn't have remembered the elder's complicated name any better than she had. He placed his hand on her shoulder and she stepped back.

Mr. Pyllis said, "Meligoricko. It is important that you remember Rolimi names. It is disrespectful to hear, and promptly discard, someone's name. If you discard someone's name it is as though you discard that person's importance as well. Meli-go-ricko." The second time he said the elder's name, he emphasized the syllables as if he was pronouncing it for a child.

Rissyl sighed. This was going to be even harder than he feared. It was as if these people were looking for excuses to be offended. He stepped forward, "Elder Meligoricko, I intend to explain that the Rolimi were attacked by necromancers. Humans are not your enemy; the necromancers are your enemy and our enemy."

The elder held up his hand once again. He spoke slowly, but raised his voice slightly. "Magi, I am on your side. Yet, even I find your argument weak. If your lambs were slaughtered by wolves, would you care that the wolves were brown or black? Or would you hunt down any wolves you could find just to thin the numbers? Your response to the wolves isn't necessarily about bringing justice to the specific wolves who murdered your lambs it's about lowering the chances that wolves will attack your lambs tomorrow. Am I right? Then how is this different? Humans have attacked the Rolimi, there are many among the Rolimi who think that the human numbers need to be thinned to instill proper reverence towards the Rolimi and ensure that humans do not presume to attack us again."

Aruk stepped forward, "We are not animals! You can't just –"

Rissyl grabbed the scruff of his neck and tugged backwards. Aruk stopped talking and looked towards him with an angry glare. His expression quickly softened, and he stepped back.

Meligoricko leaned forward in his chair. His eyes grew wide, and he smiled slightly as if amused. "You're not animals, you say? To the Rolimi you are like animals. Your species propagates like rats, overrunning an area with your countless offspring in just a few generations. The vast majority of your species is violent and uncivilized, inflicting as much horror and carnage on each other as they do to the lands and creatures that they come in contact with. Your lives are remarkably short and for the vast majority of your species your lives are pointless, leaving little to no positive impact on the lands or the other creatures in them. To be blunt, the reason that our caste has been so generous with your Magi Society over the decades is because it has been one of the few bright lights in an otherwise dark and twisted species of creatures."

He felt his heart sink further with each additional statement. If these were the opinions of the Rolimi who were on their side, then Rissyl was sure that he was faced with certain failure. There was so much wrong with the things the elder had said, and yet most of the statements were not entirely inaccurate. The only thing he could grasp on that was completely false was the assertion that human lives were remarkably short.

Rissyl stepped forward and stood up straighter. He said, "How can you say that human lives are short? Many of us live well into our sixtieth year, and some even live more than a century! Most animals live a fraction of that."

The elder smiled gently, and held up a hand slightly as if to appease the Magi. He said, "To you, that must seem like a long time. Even the turtles of your realm live as long as you. The dwarven and elven folk of your lands live for many human lifetimes. Yet, to me those things are but a season. I have trinkets that were made before your great grandfather's great grandfather was born. To you, the death of the original Magi Society seems like ages ago. To me, it seems like a short time ago. Time passes differently here than in your realm. Yet, even so, we are much longer-lived than humans. It is uncommon for a Rolimi to live less than three hundred years, which is three thousand years in your realm."

Meligoricko paused as if to give the humans time to process what he had just said. "The Rolimi that were killed by your necromancers were young by our standards. Yet, they were all born more than a thousand of your years before your lifetime. They were born before your original Magi Society was even conceived, during the time of the Six Kingdoms in your lands. Had they not been murdered by humans, they would have lived beyond your lifetime for another two thousands of your years."

The elder paused once again. Rissyl was about to respond when the elder spoke once again. He said, "Imagine a creature whose entire lifetime was only three of your years. Compared to your one hundred, the lifespan of a creature who only lives for three years seems extremely short, does it not? How important is the life of one of those creatures, compared to your life? Now consider your brief life compared to the life of a Rolimi who generally live about thirty times longer than humans. Do you now see why we consider your lives so brief?"

Rissyl wanted to shout that he understood the elder Rolimi's point. The elder might have thousands of years to dwell on the subject, but Rissyl was sorry he even brought it up. It was becoming clear that these creatures had very low regard for humans, and it was unlikely that Rissyl would be able to say much to change that.

The elder stood up, and when he did Rissyl saw that Mr. Pyllis bowed deeply. Aruk and Firana reactively began to bow as well, but Rissyl motioned for them to remain standing. If the elder didn't want the humans to use reverential titles that they didn't mean, it was unlikely that he wanted the humans to bow. Meligoricko said, "I need to go to the council hall now. Pyllistacaillian will lead you there shortly. You'll be given the opportunity to address the Synodus individually."

With alarm in his voice, Aruk said, "We'll not speak at the Synodus together?"

"Of course not, you are individuals. You'll each represent your people individually."

Rissyl wanted to respond, but with a small gesture of his hand the elder simply vanished. The Magi looked to Mr. Pyllis.

The Rolimi said, "That went better than I feared it might. If you'll follow me, we'll make our way to the council hall."

CHAPTER 18

Sarasa

The dizziness from teleporting always gave Sarasa a thrill, similar to the thrill she got while sledding down the hills outside of Sorgo when she was a young girl. It was a feeling that she enjoyed, so she closed her eyes for a moment as she held onto the portal stone.

While her eyes were closed, she heard Uli say, "Baeldin? What are you doing here?"

She knew that name and recalled that he was a Magi, but she couldn't remember who he was. She and Uli had just teleported to the Stronghold; she didn't expect to see any Magi there. So, she was as surprised as Uli sounded that they met another Magi there.

When she opened her eyes and saw him, she instantly remembered him. Baeldin was a large man, both in height and weight. His large head was almost completely bald, and he sported a big bushy brown beard. He wore the brown and white cloak of a Society Magi, and at his side was a long sword.

Sarasa remembered him as the loud mouthed Magi that she met last year at Uli's ranch. She and Baeldin had engaged in an argument, and later that day he stormed away from the ranch in anger after not being selected for one of the four Orders.

She had heard nothing about the man since then, and for the most part she had forgotten about him.

Baeldin stepped towards them and put his hand on Uli's shoulder. "I'm glad to see you too, old friend. It's been too long."

She let go of the portal and said, "What are you doing here, Baeldin?"

"I'm here to help! I want to prove that I'm worthy of one of those grey cloaks."

She shook her head, "Please go back. You don't have access to Order of the Shadows magic; you'll only hinder our progress."

"Oh, how I've missed you, young lady. You really know how to make a guy feel welcome! I went through a lot of trouble to make it here to help you two. You'd think you would show some gratitude. I'm not an Order Magi, but I'm not a cripple either! I can use *Shadow Shroud*, and I'm skilled in a great many other ways. I won't hinder you, as long as we avoid open areas in broad daylight."

Sarasa looked at Uli, and he shrugged. He was no help. If he would have been vocal about Baeldin not joining them, she would feel more justified in turning the man away. With Uli being non-committal she started to wonder if she was refusing Baeldin's offer to help unfairly. She didn't like the man, but felt that she should give him a chance to prove himself.

She sighed, "Fine. The Stronghold is right over there. Let's get invisible. Everyone stay close enough to see my outline."

She dropped an *Invisibility* spell on herself and waited for Uli to do the same, and for Baeldin to get shrouded by his spell. Then she reached out and grabbed Uli's shoulder. She summoned the magic and cast a spell called *Limited Outline* which would enable him to see her outline, even though she was invisible, as long as he stayed fairly close to her. When that was done she repeated the spell for Baeldin so he could see her outline as well.

She said, "Can you see my outline?"

Uli said, "I sure can."

Baeldin said, "Yes."

"Great, let's go."

She led them away from the portal stone and towards the Stronghold. She could see it off in the distance; the Stronghold was a sprawling complex of buildings and defenses. There were many towers and buildings of all shapes and sizes. Around it all was a massive wall.

As they got closer she could see a few figures moving around on the tops of the walls. She chose their approach carefully to ensure that they didn't make any more noise than necessary.

She swore quietly to herself. Up ahead, standing next to the outside of the Stronghold walls, spread out every five yards or so, were a dozen or more Awakened. They were unlike any Awakened that she'd ever seen.

When Uli moved next to her, he whispered, "By the gods. Awakened, with no skin or muscle? If they don't have hearts, how are they killed?"

She said, "Have you ever seen them with green glowing eyes?"

"No."

About half of the undead creatures were entirely skeletal; the others were in various stages of decomposition. None of them looked complete enough to be Awakened.

Baeldin said, "I've been here a few hours waiting for you. I've done some scouting. If we move to that side of the Stronghold there are no Awakened or guards."

She watched the motionless macabre guards for a few more moments, and then she said, "Fine, we'll go there."

They made their way around the Stronghold, keeping a wide berth between themselves and the green-glowing eyes of the new Awakened. Once on the other side they found the section of wall that Baeldin had mentioned.

She waited until she could hear Uli and Baeldin's footsteps right next to her and then she whispered, "Do you think we could jump onto that wall with a *Frog Leaping* spell?"

"You two might be able to, I know I couldn't. My poor old knees would hardly handle the run, let alone the jump. I've read about a *Monkey Climb* spell in my spellbook. I haven't tried it, but maybe we could use that?"

"No, some of these rocks are sharp. If you cut yourself, you might end up breaking the spell and then you'd fall. Let's do it the old fashioned way." She took her backpack off and untied the length of rope and grappling hook from it.

She moved closer to the wall and started swinging the rope, with the grappling hook on the end, in a wide circle. Then she released it and looked up as the invisible grappling hook soared into the air. She heard a clanking sound and then felt the rope go slack.

She sprinted away from the wall, since the grappling hook was falling and it was invisible. It landed with a dull thud on the ground not far from the wall. Walking back over to the wall, she curled the rope for another toss.

When it was in position she started circling the grappling hook once again. She released it, and a few seconds later she heard a satisfying clank as the metal hook latched against the top edge of the wall. She just hoped it wasn't so noisy that it drew unwanted attention.

She tested it a few times, and then handed the bottom end of the rope to Uli, and said, "Keep hold of this, you'll need it. When the rope stops wiggling, I'm probably at the top. Then you two can climb up."

He said, "I'll do my best. It's been ages."

She climbed the rope quickly and moved to the other side of the wall. The Stronghold was breathtaking. There were so many buildings spread out across the huge fortress. She only saw a few guards on the tops of the walls. For a moment she thought that the three Magi together could take out the guards, and maybe take back the Stronghold on their own. Then she noticed that at least one of the guards on the walls was misshapen and walking oddly. Most likely it was a Motlite, she wasn't sure that the three of them could take

155

out a Motlite.   Additionally there were the crazy green-glowing eyed Awakened, and whatever else awaited them inside, that she needed to consider. She decided it would be much smarter to stay hidden so she could accomplish her primary mission without alerting the necromancers to their presence.

Behind her, she heard Uli breathing heavily and struggling to pull himself over the edge. She hurried over and helped him onto the top of the wall.

He said, "Sarding Khalius, I'm getting too old for this."

Baeldin said, "You're not much older than me. I made the climb with no problem. Maybe you should spend more time patrolling and less time sitting by the campfire with the elderly Magi?"

Sarasa ignored the mouthy Magi's rude comments, and hoped that Uli would also. She said, "Look at this view!"

Uli was still breathing heavily from his climb. He exhaled a deep breath and said, "It's very impressive. Let's take a nap."

She laughed at him as she felt around for her grappling hook. She pulled the rope up, and curled it neatly. Then she dropped it down the other side, and attached the grappling hook to the top of the wall.

She said, "Go ahead and make your way down the rope. I'll make sure the hook stays in place."

There was a thump sound next to her, and then she heard Uli screaming as he fell from the top of the wall. She looked down into the stone courtyard inside the Stronghold wall, and heard Uli hit the ground with a sickening crunching sound. The Magi had landed head and shoulders first and she was certain he couldn't have survived such a horrible landing on the stone below. When he died he naturally became visible once again.

She looked back towards Baeldin and said, "What sarding happened? Did you push him?" She couldn't see him, but she could hear him moving around near her.

He sounded incredulous, "Of course not! We've got to get down to him, hurry up!"

The man was up to something, and she didn't trust him. She wanted to believe that he wouldn't kill someone he had known for so long, but she wasn't going to let her guard down. She had a mission to accomplish, and that required her to climb down into the stronghold. She put a leg over the wall and started climbing down the rope.

Before she'd taken three hand strides down the rope, she heard the sound of metal scraping stone above her. Suddenly the rope gave way and she was falling towards the stone courtyard below.

She had hoped she was wrong about the man, but she was prepared for his treachery. As she started to fall she quickly summoned the magic for a simple *Slow Falling* spell.

Almost immediately her motion slowed drastically. As she softly stepped onto the ground, she heard the grappling hook hit the stone beside her with a loud clank.

Up on the wall she heard Baeldin say, "They're here! Go now! They're in the spot you selected! Get them, there are two of them a man and a woman! The man might be dead."

She looked up to the top of the wall in horror. She was in disbelief that one of their own would betray them.

When she looked back to the buildings around her, a number of the green glowing-eyed Awakened stepped from behind several buildings and started walking towards her. Off to the left were two soldiers, including one that looked like a malformed Motlite, and two black robed necromancers.

One of the necromancers started shooting purple orbs of necromancer magic at Uli's body.

The male necromancer hissed, "Forget the male, I'll raise him soon enough. I want the female alive!"

The necromancer woman said, "Where is she, I can't see her!"

"Watch the Drudges and the Motlite, they can see her!"

Sarasa cursed to herself. She was trapped. A group of at least ten of the green glowing-eyed Awakened, which the necromancers referred to as Drudges, had her trapped from her right. Another group of about ten Drudges, as well as the necromancers and the Motlite had her trapped from the left. There was a large building in front of her and a wall behind.

As soon as she began attacking she'd lose her invisibility, and then things would get ugly quickly. Her only option was to try to break through the Drudges to her right. The moment she started moving in that direction she heard Baeldin shouting from up on the wall.

He said, "She is moving north along the wall towards the rear of the Stronghold!"

She started running towards the undead creatures. As she ran she screamed, "I'll get you one day, you sarding traitor! You'll die by my blades!" She summoned her daggers and drew them both.

She heard him yell back, "You ain't going to live that long, wench!"

The Drudges saw her, as the necromancer predicted. As she got close to them, they all closed towards her and they started slashing and thrusting their weapons mindlessly in her general direction.

For a moment she thought she might get through them, until she felt the first blade slip past her protective cloak and slice deep in her upper right thigh.

She bit back the pain and refused to scream out. Behind her, she vaguely heard the male necromancer shout, "Get her now! Don't let her get away!"

Purple spheres of necromancer magic started slamming into the Drudges near her. One of them hit her in the back, but her cloak protected her from most of the effect.

She plunged her long dagger directly into the heart of the Drudge right in front of her, hoping to drop it and create a little room to sneak through the line of monsters. The strike was a perfect hit, sliding through the ribs and she was certain that it slid straight into the Drudge's heart.

The monster didn't even slow down. Its short sword thrust up at her, she lunged to the side but another Drudge was right next to her and she couldn't fully move out of the way. The tip of the short sword found her flesh and sliced deep up her right side, clear up to her armpit.

She screamed and started shoving the Drudges away, desperately trying to break through their quickly closing line. Several more purple orbs exploded near her, and the shouts from behind told her that the other line of enemies was almost on top of her.

Another blade found its mark into her stomach on the left side, but it didn't seem very deep. She slammed a dagger into the temple-area of the skull of one of the Drudge with such force that she heard the skull shatter. The creature fell to the ground, opening a small hole for her to squeeze through.

The deep wound on her leg, and the long cut up her right side, made it difficult to run. She ran as fast as she could. The combat with the creatures made her Invisibility spell fail, and the necromancers were sprinting towards her. With every step even more purple fire exploded near her.

She darted between buildings, sprinting as quickly as her injured leg would carry her. Then she started a zigzag pattern of running, turning left at one building, and then right at the next. As soon as she felt she had a slight lead between them, she stopped to drop another Invisibility spell on herself. She opened the door on the building next to her and left it slightly ajar, but did not go inside.

She resumed running, hoping they would see the open door and assume that she ran into the building to hide. The invisibility spell should hide her blood trail, at least for a while. She needed to find a place to hide and bandage her wounds soon or it would be too late.

She'd lost a lot of blood already, and she could feel light headedness coming on.

A building off to her left caught her eye, and she moved in that direction. It was a tower, and a tree next to it would give her easy access to a second story balcony.

Climbing the tree sucked much worse than she thought it might. Once on the balcony she pushed open the door and rushed into the room. She found a bed in the room, and a bed sheet would make fine bandages.

She stabbed the bed violently, and cut the sheet into a few strips. The wound on her leg bled freely, and she tied the strip across it tightly. Not enough to cut off the blood to her leg, but hopefully enough to stop the blood from oozing out of the cut. Then she turned her attention to the long gash on her right side. It was much longer than she hoped, but it didn't seem nearly as deep as the leg cut.

The dizziness and light-headedness was getting worse. For the most part she had stopped the bleeding, but she wasn't sure how much longer she could stay conscious. She wanted nothing more than to just curl up on the bed and sleep.

She knew she couldn't do that. Eventually her blood trail would lose the effects of her invisibility spell, and she needed to move somewhere else or it would lead them right to her. She grabbed a large square of cloth from the bed sheet and then headed through the door and down the stairs to the first floor of the tower.

She opened the door slowly and looked around. She could hear the necromancers talking loudly, looking for her nearby. Without further hesitation she opened the door and ran, which was more like a quick hobble, across the road. As quickly as she could, she moved to the far side of the Stronghold, and found the least noticeable building she could find. It was a little one story building; she guessed it was someone's home at one point.

The door was not locked and she rushed into home, slamming the door behind her. She noticed stairs to the left, and hurried down them. There was a large trunk in the corner of the basement, surrounded by barrels and crates. It was mostly empty and she climbed inside and closed the lid. With one of her daggers she punched a few holes in the back side of the trunk to give herself some air.

Then she closed her eyes. She welcomed the darkness when it insistently called for her. It was going to win anyway, she was thankful for the trunk to hide in before the darkness caught up with her.

Her last thought before giving in to the darkness completely was a quick prayer to any god that would listen. "Please let me live, so I can hunt down Baeldin and kill him slowly! Amen."

CHAPTER 19

Sarge

"One more." He held up his empty ale mug.

The wench stopped next to Sarge's table and looked at him for a moment. "You look half dead, maybe you should get a room and sleep a while."

"Believe me darling, I feel much worse than I look. Bring me another ale."

He rested his forehead in both palms and closed his eyes while he waited for the ale to arrive. In his lifetime he had experienced many battle injuries and suffered his share of sickness and pain, but nothing he'd ever experienced compared to the crippling weakness of not being able to sleep. He felt stupid and helpless for letting something as silly as sleepiness cripple him so severely.

For months his sleep had been frequently disturbed by dreams of the necromancer attack at the Motlite camp and the ancient god who saved him. However, it had grown increasingly worse over the last several fortnights. He was fairly certain that he hadn't slept more than a few minutes a night in a few days. Perhaps it had been many days.

The days were all starting to run together, and he was having a very difficult time thinking clearly. The ale didn't help, and he knew it. However, it did dull the body aches and seemed to take the edge off of the all-consuming weariness.

Two days ago, or possibly four or five, he said goodbye to Rissyl and Cynia and he took a portal stone to the imperial city of Khardifar. Something deep in his soul was calling him south, and Khardifar was as far south as he could go in the mainland. Now that he was in the southernmost reaches of the empire, he didn't know what to do next.

He'd traveled from one side of the city to the other, frequently visiting taverns and inns. He'd even stopped in a variety of temples to see if any of them felt like the place where he was being called. No matter what he did, he still felt himself being called south.

Sarge stood up gently as the wench finally arrived with his ale. He placed a coin on the table and walked slowly out of the tavern. He knew that something was seriously wrong with him because he wasn't even vaguely interested in getting into the comely bar wench's dress, and comely bar wenches were his guilty pleasure.

The bright light of the mid-day sun hurt his eyes, and he covered them with one hand as he walked across the street.

Walking down the street without his Magi Cloak and his sword made him feel naked and vulnerable. He lived his whole life in the Free Cities, and in those lands those few Magi who survived would always wear their Magi cloaks proudly. He didn't even know the spell to send his weapon and cloak away to the plane of magic until Rissyl taught it to him recently.

As vulnerable as he felt without them, he had to admit that it was an extremely useful spell. Especially, now that he was wandering around an imperial city. Being seen in a Magi cloak in an imperial city would invite all sorts of problems.

He walked down the street towards the docks. He had no idea where he was going, but he had not had any luck with any of his other plans. So, it was time to walk south until he couldn't go any further. He figured he'd either find what he was looking for, or he'd die trying. At this point, either would be fine.

The docks area was much larger than he expected, or he was somehow traveling in circles. He had a sneaking suspicion that he had passed the fishmonger store with the large smiling fish sign at least three times already. As much as he was trying to focus on travelling south, his mind kept wondering to other things and before long he found himself passing the smiling fish sign once again.

When he saw the smiling fish sign for the sixth time, or possibly the seventh, he started to get annoyed. He felt like he was walking through fog, and he wasn't entirely sure if he was awake or dreaming. Part of him hoped that he was in fact asleep and dreaming of something other than ancient gods and necromancers.

A different sign caught his eye, it said "East Gate" and it had an arrow. The east gate sounded like a fantastic route; at this point he was happy with any route that did not include a smiling fish sign.

Before long the dock gave way to a part of the city dominated by shabby homes and warehouses. He continued along slowly, avoiding anyone who looked like they might want to talk or ask him directions. He didn't know where anything was at, and he wouldn't give anyone directions even if he did know where it was.

The east gate was a large wooden door set in the stone walls of the city.

It was guarded by a couple of city sentinels who were busy inspecting a line of wagons waiting to enter the city. He was able to walk out of the city without being bothered by anyone. He considered that a win.

He smiled slightly to himself. He almost felt like celebrating with a little woot or possibly a fist wave in the air, but both of those seemed like way too much work. Besides, celebrating that something went right was the perfect way to tempt fate into dropping something awful on him. He wasn't in the mood to deal with awful things at the moment.

The road followed the south shoreline, and he was happy to be out of the city and on the open road. He was sweating like a troll in a stew pot. Being from the Free Cities in the north, he was accustomed to hot summer days. However, hot summer days in the southern section of the empire were hot and wet. Even though it wasn't raining he felt like he was walking through a damp mist. His exhaustion, combined with the draining effects of the summer heat and humidity, was almost more than he could bear.

As he moved further from the city, the breeze picked up and felt great. It blew against his damp skin and clothes, and it brought a great deal of relief. Sarge started to think that he might make it through the day after all.

The day dragged on and eventually the sun sunk low in the western sky and Sarge followed his shadow down the road. Off in the distance he noticed four riders approaching. He moved to the side of the road to stay out of their way.

When they got close, he could see that they were sentinels and he assumed they were from Khardifar. They were probably patrolling the outlying roads looking for bandits or other ruffians.

The lead horse stopped abruptly as they neared Sarge, and the others followed suit. The four sentinels dismounted and walked up to him.

He was tired and in a dreadful mood. The very last thing he wanted was trouble with imperial soldiers, but he was unwilling to stop.

The lead sentinel reached out his hand and grabbed Sarge by the chest. He tried to slow the old warrior, but Sarge refused to stop.

"Where you going in such a hurry that you can't stop and talk to us?"

The other sentinels blocked his path and forced him to stop.

The lead sentinel said, "You know, boys, I think I recognize this one. Ain't he the sneak-thief that stole the jewels from the Andresen manor in the Garden District the other night?"

The shortest sentinel said, "What do you mean? We have no idea what that thief looked like, no one saw him."

A sentinel with a long scar under his left eye elbowed the short sentinel in the ribs, hard. Then he said, "Yep this is him, I'm sure that on the way back to the city he will confess."

Sarge knew that he needed to handle this with care. He had plenty of coins; he could probably buy his way out things if he didn't do anything foolish first.

He grabbed the wrist of the lead sentinel, who was still holding him by the chest. He looked at the man and said, "Go sard yourself."

He reached up quickly with his other hand and grabbed the lead sentinel's forearm. With a quick jerking motion he twisted the sentinel's wrist in one direction and twisted the man's forearm in the opposite direction. The wrist snapped with a sickening popping sound, and the man yanked his arm away with a scream.

Sarge quickly cast the spell to bring his blue and white Magi cloak, and his sword, back from the plane of magic.

When the cloak and weapon appeared, one of the sentinels shouted, "Magi!"

Sarge drew the sword in an upward arc that sliced up the scar-faced sentinel's armor. It was merely a distraction. Once the sword was at full extension above his head he spun the sword into a reverse grip and slammed it with both hand down into the chest of the scar-faced sentinel, entering right at the neckline of the man's armor.

As quickly as the sword penetrated that sentinel's chest cavity, Sarge yanked the blade back out in the same path it had entered. Two of the remaining sentinels had their weapons drawn and were about to become a threat. He stepped to his right, spun three-quarters of a turn, and shoved the blade into the abdomen of the sentinel who was now behind him.

He leaped forward, landing on his hands and falling into a forward roll. He was well-practiced at rolling with his sword still in hand, and positioned it horizontally before him, laying it against the ground away from his body as he rolled over it. It was a maneuver designed to quickly put some space between him and the people behind him, and it worked perfectly. As he stood up from his roll, he turned and faced the remaining two sentinels. Only one of them had a sword drawn.

The lead sentinel edged closer with his sword held out in front of him in his left hand. He held his right hand close to his chest, and Sarge could tell by the unnatural angle of the hand that the wrist was badly broken. The lead sentinel said, "Kill the Magi! Don't let him get away!" He shouted as he rushed Sarge.

As the sentinel rushed forward, Sarge said, "Mayl'Hok." He summoned a sticky light orb and threw it at the sentinel's face as he advanced.

The distraction worked better than Sarge hoped. The sentinel screamed and raised both hands to guard his head. With his injured right hand he tried to knock the sticky ball of light from his face.

Sarge stepped forward and executed a strong diagonal attack with his sword, and it slammed hard against the sentinel's sword causing the man to drop the weapon.

The honorable and merciful warrior within him urged Sarge to offer the disarmed foe a chance to surrender.

Sarge didn't listen to the wiser warrior within. He followed the motion of the disarming strike with a horizontal strike in the other direction, perfectly at neck level. The decapitated sentinel dropped to the ground in two distinct thuds, and Sarge turned his attention to the shortest sentinel who still hadn't drawn his weapon.

The man held up his hands. He said, "Please don't kill me, Magi! I'm sorry we even stopped to bother you! Please let me live! I have a wife and a tiny baby girl at home who need me!"

Sarge spun his sword in a single Butterfly movement as he advanced on the young sentinel. He wanted to finish the job and make sure this one didn't bring an army of sentinels after him later. However, as he approached and looked into the man's eyes he just couldn't do it.

The lead sentinel had been intent on killing Sarge, and even disarmed the man would surely have still been a threat. This man surrendered, begged for mercy, and hadn't been a threat at all. Sarge wiped the blood from his sword and slammed it back into its scabbard.

He said, "Hand me that rope from your horse, kid."

"You're going to let me live?" The young sentinel turned and retrieved the rope from the side of his saddle bags.

Sarge took the rope and said, "Now give me your sword."

"What?"

"Dammit, you heard me!"

The young sentinel drew the sword slowly and handed it to the Magi.

Sarge reached down and grabbed the bloody tabard from the decapitated sentinel. He used it to smear blood all over the young sentinel's face, hair, armor, and tabard.

The young man jumped back in surprise. He gasped, "What are you doing? Freakish Magi!"

Sarge stepped towards him, still holding the young man's sword. He said, "Shut up and stand still."

"By the gods! Is this some creepy Magi ritual? Are you going to kill me with magic?"

The Magi smashed the flat side of the sentinel's sword up against the side of the young man's face. The blow hit the man hard enough to knock him to the ground.

He screamed and quickly brought his hands to his face to stop the bleeding that he assumed would be there. He seemed very surprised to see that he didn't have a large cut on his face, and he wasn't bleeding.

Sarge said, "Stand up!"

The sentinel stood up slowly. He was still rubbing the side of his head, and Sarge could see that a large bruise was already starting to form on the side of the young man's face.

The sentinel shouted, "Do you want me to fight? Is that what this is about? Are you going to let me go or are you going to kill me?"

The old Magi sighed, "Zortha's diddies! Shut up and kneel on the ground so I can tie you up."

The young man hesitated, "Are you going to tie me up and blast me with magic?"

"Dammit kid! If they find you unscratched and looking pretty while the rest of your squad is dead in pools of their own blood then you're going to look like a wuss or a traitor. Now, you look like you fought like a soldier. Kneel down so I can tie you up."

"You're going to leave me tied on the side of the road with these bodies?" The sentinel knelt down and looked up at Sarge.

Sarge growled, "For the love of all the sarding gods, shut up! I can't have you running back to town right away. Someone will find you eventually, and I expect you to forget that you ever saw me. Tell them a band of rogues attacked you. I swear to the gods that if you even think about coming after me I will turn you into a sarding lizard and eat you for dinner!"

The young man didn't say a word as Sarge tied him tightly.

Sarge knew it was only a matter of time before someone found the young man. He had to assume the sentinel would tell his commanders what really happened and they would send a large force to look for him.

He continued east along the road until the sentinel was out of sight and then he turned south. The road had separated from the shoreline slightly, and he travelled south to follow the shore.

An hour or more later, as the last rays of the sun cast an orange glow in the western sky, he came across a small cabin. He assumed it belonged to a local hermit or trapper. The place was dark and quiet, and he was tempted to see if it had a warm bed. However, he knew he wasn't going to sleep anyway so there was no sense laying down.

Further down the shore he noticed a campfire near a small boat. There were people standing around the campfire, but he was too far away to hear what was being said.

Once he got closer he saw five people around the campfire. Four of them were wearing simple grey robes tied with a crude rope. The four men were not wearing shoes, and their hoods were pulled up to mostly conceal their faces. The fifth man was a short man dressed like an average rural hermit, and Sarge assumed he lived in the nearby cabin.

The hermit said, "You've been here over a fortnight! You're scaring off my critters, you've got to move along! Go somewhere else!"

The four men just ignored the hermit. They stood around the fire with their hands slightly extended, their heads bowed. They were each mumbling something that Sarge couldn't understand.

The hermit shouted, "Stop ignoring me!" He lunged forward and shoved one of the four men. The old hermit might as well have tried to shove a stone wall. The robed-man didn't budge an inch and didn't even stop mumbling."

Sarge said, "What's going on here?"

The old man turned, and his eyebrows shot up in surprise. "A Magi?" After a short pause, he continued, "Maybe you can help me? These interlopers have been camped out on my land for a fortnight. I want them gone."

The four men looked up from the fire and saw Sarge. They instantly dropped to one knee and crossed their fists over their heart, with their faces looking directly at the ground. One of the men said, "The Azure Paladin has arrived as prophesized!"

Sarge laughed humorlessly, "Sorry, Bub. You've got the wrong guy. I'm just passing through."

The four men continued to stare at the ground from their kneeling position. The same robed man who spoke before said, "Kelegar's seraphim announced your impending arrival. We travelled far to wait for you here."

He held up his hand preparing to dismiss the robed men and walk off, and then he stopped in shock. He questioned whether he really heard what he thought he heard. He said, "Did you say Kelegar?"

"Of course, Lord Paladin! Kelegar sent his seraphim to us, so we could prepare for your arrival."

Sarge pinched his own arm to make sure he was awake. He said, "By all the gods! Could this be real?"

The robed man who had been talking stood up and the others stood up also. They all continued to look at the ground, and they carefully avoided looking Sarge in the eyes. The man said, "Not all of the gods, just Kelegar. The divine-sire."

Sarge noticed that the robed man who had being doing all of the talking had extremely dark skin, almost black as the night. The other robed men were also dark skinned, but not nearly as dark as the only one who had spoken.

It was common to see people of all different skin tones, but Sarge rarely saw people with skin as black as the night.

The black man motioned towards the boat. He said, "Shall we go?"

Sarge stared at the little boat, wide-eyed. Then he looked out at the vast sea. "In that? To where?"

"Back to the island, of course. Will you permit us to take you there?"

The Magi had never been on a boat, and the little boat they wanted him to enter barely looked like it would keep the water out. The sea looked rough and dangerous, and he wasn't ashamed to admit that he was frightened.

The four robed men stood there waiting for him to enter the boat. The hermit stood there in disbelief, watching the whole thing.

Finally Sarge took a few tentative steps towards the boat. The men held it for him as he stepped into it. They urged him into the front of the boat, and then each took up a station at one of the four oars.

When he was inside the boat it seemed a little bigger than he originally thought. There was plenty of room for all five men to walk around the boat, and there were also a few baskets and bags of supplies at the back end.

Before he knew it, they were at sea. The black man moved to a bench in the front of the boat near Sarge. Two of the men continued to row and the other bowed his head, assumedly to pray.

The black man said, "I am called Hrangolis, and all four of us are Kelegarian monks. We are his faithful servants, in a world that has forgotten him."

Sarge nodded. He didn't know what to say. The monk was correct; clearly the world had forgotten Kelegar. However, for some reason the god chose to save him from death. Once again he asked himself, why. What did the god want from him? He said, "Do you know why I was drawn here?"

Hrangolis nodded. The monk still hadn't looked him in the eyes; instead he looked out to sea. He said, "Of course. You're to become the Azure Paladin. You're to be rewarded with fourteen wives, and your many babies will become the priests and priestesses of our temple. Once the ascension is complete, we're to bring you back to the mainland to fight evil and right wrongs in the name of Kelegar as the Azure Paladin. It has been prophesized for several millenniums, and the time of the ascension is finally upon us. My people have lived in seclusion on the islands awaiting this day for countless generations. We are so very blessed to live during the time of your arrival!"

His head was spinning. The exhaustion battled with the motion of the sea to garble his thoughts. He wasn't entirely sure that he understood correctly what the monk was trying to tell him. It was all so very overwhelming. He closed his eyes and rubbed his temples.

"Lord Paladin, we have a long voyage ahead of us and you look very tired. Please rest."

Sarge wanted to avoid the dreams, but he couldn't stay awake forever. He closed his eyes, and he was asleep almost instantly."

CHAPTER 20

Rissyl

The antechamber outside of the council hall was small and completely quiet. Rissyl sat there as he waited for Firana to finish her talk to the Synodus. Aruk had gone first, and eventually the door opened and Firana was beckoned out of the antechamber. That had been quite a while ago, but he wasn't sure how long.

He sat in silence and thought about what he would say to a group of magical creatures who viewed humans as little more than violent animals. His stomach was tied in knots as he considered that a war with the Rolimi would bring widespread death and destruction to his people, and for some terrible reason it was up to him to try to prevent it.

When the door to the council hall opened, he jumped a little. He took a deep breath to calm himself, and then stood up and walked into the room.

The council hall was every bit as impressive as Rissyl figured it'd be. The room was large and spacious with short walls that ended in a roofless view of the strange plane of magic sky, with A'Ethar rivers of orange crisscrossing the vista like an eerie celestial net. In the center of the room was a large hexagonal table with ten large chairs positioned around five of the sides. The sixth side of the table was open, and that's where the guard motioned for Rissyl to stand.

Each chair was overly large, and the backs of the chairs towered above the heads of the Rolimi who sat in them. The chair backs were made in the shape of intimidating creatures, all of which moved on its own and they all seemed to be watching him as he stood before the table.

The chairs were all different colors, and Rissyl saw Meligoricko in his light blue robes sitting in a light blue chair. The chair next to his was dark blue. As he looked around the table he noticed that the colors of the chairs formed a pattern. Each side of the table had two chairs of similar color, one lighter and one darker.

He then turned his attention to the individual Rolimi in each of the chairs. He was surprised at the vastly different appearance of each one. Meligoricko was shaped much like Mr. Pyllis and the other Rolimi who had taught the Magi. He figured that they must all belong to the light blue caste. However, each caste had a very different and unique shape. The elder in the dark red chair was large and muscular like the guardian Rolimi that the Magi had met outside of the Stronghold. The elder in the light green chair had a large body, short legs, and four arms.

The elder in the light yellow chair spoke. Her voice was strong and loud, but she spoke slowly. "Human, you are to be the last to speak on behalf of your people. Make the most of this opportunity. We shall vote as soon as you finish."

Rissyl cleared his throat. He wanted to sound confident but friendly. He said, "Rolimi elders, thank you for the chance to address this Synodus. First let me give my heartfelt condolences for the loss of your people at the Stronghold. The deplorable act of violence against you by a small group of humans is inexcusable and you have every right to be angry."

Several of the elders began murmuring to each other, and he was afraid that he might be making his position worse.

He quickly continued, "I give you my word, in the name of Nalria, I swear that the Magi will bring the necromancers who attacked you to justice! When we have dealt with them, they will no longer be a threat to you."

The elder in the dark red chair slammed his large hand down onto the arm of his chair with a loud banging sound. He said, "Human! How dare you swear a vow on the name of the goddess of magic! Who are you to invoke an oath on her name?"

Rissyl was beginning to get annoyed. He could swear an oath in the name of any of the pantheon that he wanted. He said, "I am one of Nalria's own chosen, picked by her to bring magic back into our world!"

The large Rolimi in the dark red chair laughed. He said, "I am the grandson of Nalria! My own sire squirted from between her divine legs when your ancestors were still hunting elks with stone hammers! Do not soil my grandmother's name by murmuring it through your human lips in the form of a pathetic oath!"

"I am sorry, I didn't realize." Rissyl felt like an idiot, and he was about out of ideas. It was clear that the Rolimi were going to do whatever they wanted, regardless of anything he said.

There was a commotion behind him, and he turned to see two dogs running towards him. One of them was Tiberos. Both rushed over to him, and they were both barking.

He had never seen Tiberos barking so aggressively. The dog ran straight to him and jumped up shoving both front legs into Rissyl's abdomen. Then the dog stood before him, barking loudly.

Rissyl's heart sunk even further. Even his Rolimi hound had turned against him? He held his hands out in front of him to try to calm the dog.

Suddenly he heard a voice in his head, it said, "Pack female injured!"

He shook his head in confusion. He wasn't sure what was happening. It seemed like Tiberos communicated with him, by speaking in his mind. He looked at the dog, and said, "Pack female? Cynia? Is Cynia injured?"

The dog barked loudly. In his head he heard, "Other pack female!"

Rissyl didn't understand what the dog was trying to tell him, and he wasn't entirely convinced that voice in his head was from the dog.

The other dog started barking, and he looked over at it. His eyes went wide when he realized that it strongly resembled Sarasa's smaller Rolimi dog. He said, "Sarasa? Is she injured?"

In his head he heard Tiberos say, "Badly. Dying."

He didn't know what to do. His heart was racing and he felt a desperate need to get to her. He said, "Where is she now?"

Again the hound's voice appeared in his head. "We will lead to pack female."

The elder in the dark red chair said, "Enough of this. Guards, remove these creatures! Human, you're wasting what little time you have to plead the case for your people!"

Rissyl turned to face the elder who spoke. He said, "Elder, the dog has warned me that my friend is badly injured and I must save her! Could we postpone this meeting for a short time?"

"Absolutely not!"

He was getting even more frustrated, almost becoming desperate. "Time is different here than in my realm. Even if it takes a full day in my lands, it would only be an hour or two here. Surely you could take a short break for an hour or two!"

The Rolimi in the dark green chair said, "No!" She was short and skinny with a pointy, almost birdlike, head. Her lips came to a point in front of her face, and Rissyl couldn't help but think of a parakeet when she spoke. She continued, "This is your chance. Speak and then leave us to vote."

The thought went through his mind that every minute he spent arguing with the elders was another ten minutes closer to Sarasa's death. He struggled to keep his growing anger in check. "My friend is dying! I must help her, I will be back very soon!"

The large Rolimi in the dark red chair waved his hand dismissively. He looked to the other elders and said, "Let him leave. The words of a human aren't going to change anyone's mind anyway. I've said all along that it was useless to waste time with ambassadors!" He turned to Rissyl, "Leave, so we can vote. I suspect we'll be seeing you soon on the battlefield."

With that comment, Rissyl lost the battle with his growing rage.

He took two deep breaths, trying to calm himself, but it was no use. With each passing second his friend was getting closer to death, or may have already died. He felt himself growing larger as he stood before the table. He began to pace from side to side, looking at the elders with distain. In that moment he hated their arrogant attitude and superior stares.

Without knowing it would happen, he caused a large sphere of fire to appear in each of his hands. The spheres did not burn him, even though flames rained down onto the floor and smoldered there.

Several of the elders gasped and held their hands up as if to shield themselves from his fire. The elder in the dark red chair stood up and shouted, "This is an outrage!"

Rissyl shouted, "You can vote however you want." He held one of the flaming spheres before him, pointing it at the elder in the dark red chair. "But let me warn you that your aggression against humans will come with a heavy cost! As Rolimi are fond of pointing out, humans are violent and uncivilized. We fight among ourselves frequently, just imagine the horror and carnage that we'll bring when we have a common enemy. The necromancers aren't the only humans who can create Motlites to invisibly suck the magic from your bodies! We may be short-lived and uncivilized, but few species understand how to bring pain and misery as well as humans do!"

Rissyl looked around the council hall and found every single elder sitting in stunned silence. Even the elder in the dark red chair had sat back down. Rissyl added, "I wanted the Magi Society to be your ally. But if you force our hand, we will be a deadly foe!"

With that, he turned towards the doors. To the left was the door he'd used to enter the council hall. He assumed that the others went out the right door, so he stormed towards that door. As he walked he extinguished the flaming spheres in his hands. When he was almost to the door he reached out with his mind and grabbed the door, slamming it open.

Firana, Aruk, and Mr. Pyllis were in a small room beyond the door. They all stood as the door slammed open.

Rissyl did not pause as he walked past them, saying, "Pyllistacaillian, we need to get back to our realm as quickly as possible. Sarasa is in trouble."

- = - = -

It felt odd to be back in his own realm. Rissyl looked around the large barn on Uli's ranch and it was just like he left it. The air smelled like hay and dust, he hadn't noticed that the realm of magic didn't have many memorable scents.

Cynia ran up to him and gave him a strong hug. She whispered in his ear how much she missed him and how worried she had been. He just hugged her and didn't respond.

When she released him and took a step back, she looked into his eyes for a moment and then asked, "What's wrong? Did the Rolimi decide to bring war against us?"

He shrugged, "Quite possibly. We don't know yet. But Sarasa has been hurt, badly. Her pup told Tiberos, and he warned me. I'm afraid she is dying, if she's not already dead. I'm going after her."

Cynia stared at him in shock. "No, Riz! Please, you can't rush in there alone! You have no idea what you might be facing! Let's put together a force and we'll go together!"

Firana stepped over to them. She said, "I'm going with him."

"Me too." Aruk walked up behind her.

Rissyl shook his head, "No, it's way too dangerous! I need you two here to lead the invasion on the Stronghold if I don't make it out. I'm not waiting for a force, I'm going right now."

Cynia grabbed his shirt and pulled him towards her, demanding his full attention. "I know you care about her. She's my cousin, and I love her too. If you must go, at least take these two with you. You can't help her if you're dead. If I could teleport, I'd go with you."

He looked at her for a moment, and then pulled her to him and kissed her passionately. He could feel her tears running down his cheek to his neck.

When he finally released her, he looked to the two evokers. He said, "Thank you, both. Let's not waste any more time."

He led the two evokers out of the barn, so Cynia wouldn't hear them talking. He would have enough to worry about at the Stronghold without needing to keep her safe as well. The three Evokers would need to use a portal stone, and he didn't want Cynia to know that or she'd want to join them.

Once they were outside, and he was certain that Cynia couldn't hear him, he said, "You two haven't been to the stronghold, so we'll teleport to Uli's portal stone nearby, and take that stone to the Stronghold."

The two Magi nodded, and he said, "Kur'Gezbar."

- = - = -

The events of the day had taken a lot out of Rissyl, and taking the portal stone to the Stronghold immediately after teleporting from the barn to the portal stone near Uli's Ranch affected him much more than usual. All three of them suffered a significant case of vertigo, and they grasped the portal stone briefly to keep from falling.

When the world stopped spinning, and when he was confident that he wouldn't throw up on anyone, he released the portal stone and looked around. It was just starting to get dark for the evening, or perhaps it was beginning to get bright for the day. He wasn't exactly sure, because his time in the Rolimi's realm had completely disoriented his sense of time in his own realm. He looked around and found the western sky glowing orange, indicating that it was almost nighttime.

Far off in the distance was the Stronghold. He couldn't make out too many details because of the twilight haze.

Off ahead he saw Tiberos and Sarasa's Rolimi dog running to the east. He hurried off after them. He could hear Aruk and Firana following behind him.

The dogs were mostly transparent once again, since he was no longer in their realm. They didn't glow brightly, but the illumination of their fur made it fairly easy to follow them in the twilight.

As they walked, he couldn't help but glance over at the Stronghold. They were looking at the south wall of the massive fortress, and he noticed that the glowing fence that had stretched all along the base of the structure was no longer there. He mused that it shouldn't have surprised him, since the Rolimi no longer protected the place, but he hadn't thought about it until then.

The Rolimi dogs were leading the Magi to the far east side of the Stronghold. He had no idea if they were going that way because the dogs were following a scent or if the dogs had some other reason for choosing this path. He hoped that there was some logical reason and that the dogs weren't just running randomly.

For a moment he started to worry that they were wasting valuable time that Sarasa might not have. He took a couple of deep breathes and forced himself to calm down. Becoming irrational was not going to help anything.

He checked behind him to make sure that the others were keeping up. They had lagged behind slightly, but they were still following. The dogs had set a difficult pace and Rissyl was starting to get winded. He'd never been particularly athletic, and the long jog was more exercise than he'd done in a very long time.

He slowed to a fast walk and forced himself to breathe in through his nose and out through his mouth. He didn't know if it would help, but Sarasa had recommended it a few times in their weapons practices.

Those practices seemed like so long ago, and the thought of her laying somewhere possibly dying brought tears to his eyes. He started jogging again with renewed vigor.

After what seemed like an eternity, they finally reached the outer wall of the Stronghold.

Rissyl leaned against the wall and gasped for air.

Aruk arrived shortly after Rissyl and placed his hands on his head, he took several deep breathes and then put both hands on his hips. He said, "Well, how much did that suck?"

Firana jogged up and patted Rissyl on the back. She said, "Let's keep going."

The Rolimi Dogs both barked once, and then walked right through the stone wall.

"How are we going to get over this sarding thing? Teleport up there?" Rissyl pointed up to the top of the wall.

Firana whispered, "Col'Ze." She walked up to the wall and started easily climbing up it. She stopped after a few feet and looked back. "Don't you remember the *Monkey Climb* spell from your basic book of spells?"

Rissyl cursed himself for not thinking of that sooner. He rarely used those types of spells, and he had to think for a moment just to remember how to properly form the magic to cast the spell.

By the time he started up the wall, Firana was almost to the top and Aruk was halfway up.

Like many of the other spells in the basic book of spells, the *Monkey Climb* spell always seemed like a silly spell used to entertain the kids. He didn't consider it to be a practical spell that he might need in an emergency.

He'd never really been good at climbing things, but with this spell he felt like his fingers and forearms were much stronger than normal. He had no trouble pulling himself from one stone to the next, and he confidently began scaling the outer wall fairly quickly.

A sharp stone sliced several fingers on his right hand as he climbed up the wall. The sharp pain broke his concentration, and caused the spell to fail. As soon as the spell failed he felt the fingers on both hands lose grip on the stones he'd been holding. His right foot slipped as he tried to reposition his hands and before he knew it he was falling. The uneven stones of the wall seemed to jump out to smack into his elbows and knees as he desperately tried to grasp onto anything to slow his fall.

Shortly after the fall started, the unforgiving ground suddenly stopped his downward momentum. He hit feet first, and then fell to his left and slammed his rear end onto the ground. He was able to avoid hitting his head on anything, and as he moved his arms and legs he felt relieved to see that nothing seemed broken. If he was going to fall off a large wall, at least he did it before he'd climbed very high.

He looked up to see the other two Magi standing on the top of the wall looking down at him.

He gave them a thumbs-up sign to let them know he wasn't damaged too badly. He cursed his own ineptitudes once again and then stood up.

With a quick summoning of magic and a whisper of the trigger word, he cast the spell once again. This time he climbed extremely carefully, and made it up the wall without further problems.

The climb down the other side was uneventful and before long he found himself breathing a sigh of relief as he stepped onto the ground on the other side of the wall.

"By the gods! Uli!"

Rissyl turned to see what Aruk was talking about. That's when he found Uli's body not far from the wall. It was badly broken and clearly he had fallen a long distance. He was lying in a pool of dried blood and his sightless eyes stared up towards the heavens.

Firana and Aruk rushed over to the body.

He said, "We've got to keep moving or Sarasa is going to be just as dead!"

The two dogs hurried off to the north and Rissyl rushed off to follow them. They led the Magi in a zig-zag pattern through the various buildings of the stronghold.

It didn't take long for Rissyl to get completely lost. It didn't help that more than once the dogs stopped and reversed course and then darted down some other alleyway between buildings. Twice Rissyl stopped so quickly that Aruk ran into him from behind.

When Rissyl was again beginning to fear that the dogs were genuinely just running around randomly, the two dogs ran up to the door of a little building and they ran right through the door.

Just as he was about to dart across the street to follow the dogs into the building, he heard voices off to his right.

He looked back to the other Magi, and whispered, "Someone is talking. It's coming from that way." He pointed to his right.

Firana whispered, "Is it Sarasa?"

He whispered, "I don't think so. The dogs went into that building over there, and the talking is coming from that way."

Aruk said, "I don't see anything. Let's rush over there before it's too late."

Rissyl didn't wait for further encouragement. He rushed across the street to the door. As he opened it, he saw two people down the street to his right. They weren't looking at him, so he hurried into the building. He looked around the room quickly, and then he heard the Rolimi dogs barking from a stairway in the room.

He hurried down the stairs as Aruk and Firana ran into the building. He saw Tiberos sniffing around the room. Sarasa's dog scampered over to a large trunk on the far side of the room. It started clawing at the trunk and sniffing it.

He heard the other two Magi running down the stairs. Aruk said, "Is she down here? Those people down the street saw us; I think they're coming this way! They're probably 'mancers."

Rissyl cursed under his breath and rushed over to the large trunk. He threw open the lid and looked inside. His heart skipped a beat as he found her motionless inside the trunk. He whispered a quick prayer to any god that happened to be listening, "Please gods, let her be alive!"

It felt like his heart was going to beat out of his chest, and time seemed to move in slow motion as he reached down to her. There was so much blood dried on her clothes and on the bottom of the trunk that he was certain that she must be dead.

When his shaking hand finally reached the soft and dirty skin of her neck, he was shocked and relieved to find her that her skin was warm. He could feel a faint blood pulse, and he choked back tears as he lifted her out of the trunk. She felt so light and fragile in his arms that he was afraid of holding her too tightly, for fear that he might squeeze what little life she had left, right out of her body.

Firana shouted, "Here they come!"

Purple necromancer magic slammed into him from behind, and he could feel that his cloak absorbed most of the force. He kept his back to the necromancer to shield his friend from the evil caster. He said, "Cover me, I'm going to teleport her out of here!"

He heard Firana send a lightning orb at the necromancer, and then she said, "Rissyl, no! It's too dangerous! Teleporting a non-evoker is dangerous in good conditions at full strength! Let's fight past the 'mancers and make it to the portal stone!"

Then he heard Aruk finish a spell, and that was immediately followed by a low growl. He quickly peeked over his shoulder and saw a large bear running towards the stairs.

The necromancer on the stairs screamed, "A bear!" Rissyl heard her running up the stairs, and the bear growled viciously as it chased her. Aruk had grown quite adept at summoning animals, and this time it proved extremely useful.

Rissyl turned and carried Sarasa towards the middle of the room. He said, "Keep me upright until the spell finishes. I'm taking her to Randol's. He should be able to help her, meet us there when you can."

Aruk said, "Firana, keep him upright. I'm going to guard the stairs. The bear won't hold them long. Hurry, Riz!"

Rissyl began summoning the magic for the familiar teleportation spell. The variant that would allow him to teleport with a tag-along was not much different in terms of how he formed and shaped the magic, but it drained his magewel significantly more than a typical teleport. He'd never actually attempted it, and he wasn't certain he had enough magical essence in his magewel to even accomplish it. One way or the other, he'd only get one attempt.

He finished forming the spell and then muttered, "Kur'Gezbar Duri."

As the world went dark, he felt himself falling.

CHAPTER 21

Vendino

"Forward, march!" General Thorli spurred his horse forward, and the entire contingent began moving along at his pace.

Vendino was extremely relieved to be moving once again. He'd already been away from home for far too long. The march back from the newly captured city of Ronel, formerly called Ront'El by the barbarians, had been slow and frustrating. Somewhere along the way General Thorli sent a runner ahead to inform the emperor of their success and of their return to Clornoss.

Several hours ago a runner had returned from the capital city of Clornoss with instructions for the contingent to make camp and to time their march so they arrived in Clornoss at the sounding of the mid-day twelve bells.

That meant several hours of sitting around and waiting, so Vendino had to wait that much longer before he could enjoy the comforts of his own home.

Most of the army was still in Ronel, to keep the city secure so the builders could come in and cleanse the city and get it ready for the eventual population by imperial citizens.

The contingent traveling back to Clornoss consisted of General Thorli, Minister Vendino, Prince Edal, and about a hundred elite guards. It also included some of the cooks and other support people as well as Jalinox's assistant and her child.

According to the runner, the delay was caused because the emperor wanted the troops to arrive home to a large parade and festival in their honor. The support people and other non-soldiers would be diverted to a side entrance before they arrived at the city. Of course those people would not be a part of the parade and celebration.

The runner also brought a suit of armor especially made for the emperor's son, so he could return home looking like a small warrior. Vendino looked over to the prince and shook his head in exasperation. The child was dressed in the fancy platemail armor, and he had a small sword sheathed at his side. He wasn't wearing a helm, so he would be clearly visible to the citizens as they passed by.

As Vendino watched the young prince, the boy turned to General Thorli and said, "General, have Miss Tali brought up front. I'd like her to ride with me during our parade."

The general said, "My prince, the parade is for the military, not for the support people who came along to help us. Perhaps it would be best if Tali stayed with her mother for now?"

The boy shook his head, "General, it is my wish for her to see the parade with me."

The general looked like he was going to protest further, but after a moment he motioned to a soldier riding near him. That soldier hurried off to the back of the formation to retrieve the young girl. Several minutes later he returned with the child riding behind him.

The soldier positioned his horse next to the prince's horse as the contingent slowly marched down the road, and the young girl climbed onto the prince's horse as they road. She settled down behind the prince and wrapped her arms around him as the horse plodded down the road.

The girl wore riding breeches and a fancy red tunic, and Vendino had to admit that she looked more like a Gentry child than a denizen even though the style of her clothes was a little behind the times. He made an annoyed expression as he looked away. She may look like a Gentry child, but she certainly didn't look like an Aristocrat or the class of child who should be associating with the prince. Her social class was so far beneath the prince that Vendino was certain that the emperor would be furious to see her riding with his son in the parade.

The gamble was whether the emperor would be more furious if the girl rode with the prince, or if the general denied the prince's request for the girl to ride with him. As princes go, Prince Edal was not normally a very demanding child. He was typically well mannered and easy to get along with. So, Vendino could see how the general would be reluctant to deny the prince's request. To do so was very likely to draw significant rebuking from the emperor.

The contingent rode for an hour before the Clornoss walls came into view. Vendino noticed the back third of the group broke off from the rest of them and they travelled north. The remaining members of the group were the soldiers who would be received by a grand parade, or so the runner had claimed.

Vendino shivered as he remembered the homecoming that the soldiers received after the humiliating defeat at Grum'Glin. If the emperor wasn't satisfied with the results in Ronel, then the upcoming parade might actually be a formal escort to the gallows.

He pushed those thoughts from his head and watched the city walls grow larger as they approached. Before long they arrived at the gates and they were opened for them. He could hear the music playing before he saw the crowd.

Once inside the city walls, Vendino was astonished to see so many people lining the streets. A large band was playing patriotic music and the band began marching out front of the soldiers as they rode proudly into town. There were over a dozen flag bearers holding large flags and banners representing the Ryallic Empire, the City of Clornoss, the emperor's family, as well as Wolf Pack, Raptor, and Griffin Regiments the three units who captured Ronel. The flag bearers spread out among the line of soldiers and joined in the procession.

A loud Decree Caller walked next to the band, and every few minutes he called out, "ALL HAIL THE IMPERIAL CHAMPIONS, THE LIBERATORS OF RONEL! ALL HAIL PRINCE EDAL AFTER HIS FIRST VICTORIOUS CONQUEST AGAINST THE BARBARIANS AND THE MAGI!"

Vendino had to struggle to keep from rolling his eyes when he heard the caller refer to the prince as if he had personally led the troops or had some effect on the outcome of the battle. He glanced at General Thorli, but the grizzled general did not look his way. Instead he rode proudly and looked straight forward as countless citizens on both sides of the street cheered and shouted.

The young prince seemed to be basking in the attention. The boy smiled and waved at the masses of citizens lining the street. Behind him, Tali simply sat leaning against the prince with her arms around him and her head resting against his back. She smiled at the crowd but she did not wave, and Vendino got the impression that she felt uncomfortable in the spotlight. He felt that was fitting, because she had no right to be in that spotlight in the first place.

The band led the imperial heroes up the main road through the capital city. Vendino was shocked, as he saw that the massive crowd was not just near the city gates. They continued to line the streets through the marketplace, and all of the way through the Commons District. The people turned out in droves to witness the triumphant return of the conquering heroes.

When they passed through the gate and into the Garden District the road was still lined with a large crowd of people. These people were better dressed, and they behaved more respectably. They still cheered and clapped for the troops as they passed by, but the crowd wasn't nearly as boisterous as the mass of people in the Commons had been.

The Decree Caller continued to shout out his message, and the prince continued to smile and wave enthusiastically all of the way to the Chancery District. Once they passed the gate into the Chancery District the parade was over. The band and the flag bearers stayed behind in the Garden District and the contingent walked up the immaculate stone path through the Chancery and up to the emperor's palace.

- = - = -

Two hours later, Vendino was in the Royal Hall in the middle of a meeting with the emperor.

General Thorli, who was dressed in his robes more appropriately identifying him as Minister Thorli, member of the Council of Ministers, sat across from Vendino. He had just finished giving a detailed account of the capture of Ronel.

Vendino was impressed at how smoothly the old general embellished the tale when necessary, particularly in the number of Magi killed. The official total was ten dead Magi, although if you listened to the soldiers talk it would seem that at least twenty had been killed. Vendino had his suspicions that the number was closer to zero since he hadn't seen a single body. However, he was happy to let Thorli paint whatever picture he wanted to paint. Whatever made the emperor happy and kept Vendino out of another army encampment.

The general had also glossed over the details that the vast majority of barbarians fled the city and were still alive. The official account was that at least eighty percent of the residents of the city were captured and/or killed. Vendino knew that at least two hundred barbarians had been taken prisoner and would soon be delivered to the various cities as new Dregs. The large number of new Dregs seemed to satisfy the emperor and he didn't question the general's account of the enemy casualties.

The emperor was in the best mood that Vendino had seen in years. He was smiling and joking throughout the entire meeting, and the happy atmosphere of the room seemed to affect all thirteen of the ministers present. Vendino assumed that there must have been some success in the emperor's hunt for Magi, that was the only thing that could bring about such a huge change in the emperor's mood.

Vendino looked to the far end of the table and made eye contact with Lord Jalinox's assistant, Jarla. The other ministers still gave Jarla the cold shoulder during these meetings. The crazy alchemist might have forced his way onto the Council of Ministers, but he didn't make any friends in doing so. Adding to that insult was the fact that he insisted on having his assistant sit in on council meetings in his place. Most of the other ministers refused to speak to or even acknowledge the woman unless the emperor insisted, which had been very rare.

Jarla sat at the table in Jalinox's chair, she wore her typical black outfit with red trim and she couldn't possibly look more out of place if she tried.

He looked away from the woman and tried to hide the disgust that he felt at having her at their table.

The emperor said, "What do you think, Minister Vendino?"

Suddenly he realized that he had grown lost in his own thoughts, and had completely ignored the last few minutes of the meeting. He looked to Thorli, but the old general was no help. Finally, he said, "Forgive me, Majesty. My thoughts were far away on the horrors of the battlefield. I apologize, please repeat the question."

He expected the emperor to rebuke him for his inattention, but instead the emperor smiled genuinely. He said, "No, it is I who should apologize. You've had a long and trying ordeal and I should have given you time to rest and reflect on the events you just experienced. My question was in response to Minister Thorli's comments. He said that Prince Edal had spent a great deal of time with the girl named Tali, and even insisted that the girl ride in the parade on his horse. What are your thoughts?"

Vendino groaned on the inside. He was certain that there was no right answer to this question, so he decided to go with honesty. "With all due respect to Miss Jarla, young Miss Tali is basically a commoner who has been elevated way beyond her rightful station. It is beneath the dignity of the prince to spend his time with the child."

Jarla stood up, "We were Gentry before I accepted the position as Lord Jalinox's assistant. It is rude and offensive to call us commoners, and I insist that you apologize!"

The emperor put up his hand to prevent Vendino's reply. The emperor said, "Miss Jarla, the Minister did not mean offense. I asked his opinion, and I would appreciate if you would have the dignity to refrain from further outbursts."

Several ministers around the table began whispering and murmuring to each other, with several glancing towards Jarla as they did so.

The emperor looked back to Vendino, "My son is very rational for his age, and he has always been extremely picky about who he accepts as a friend. His nursemaids have frequently mentioned that Edal usually prefers to play alone or with his sister instead of playing games with the other children. If he has chosen this Tali girl to be his friend, then so be it. A boy, especially a prince, needs some friends even if they're from a different social class."

Vendino bowed his head slightly. He hid his surprise at the emperor's uncharacteristic pragmatism in the matter. He said, "Yes, Majesty."

"That brings us to the most exciting part of this meeting." The emperor smiled like a cat in the bird-house.

Vendino looked through the notes spread out before him, and there was no mention of whatever other item the emperor might be talking about. He looked to the emperor and awaited the news along with the other ministers.

The emperor looked around the room patiently, letting everyone's anticipation build for several moments. Then he said, "I received word a few minutes before the meeting started that our agents in Libur have captured several Magi in that city, and several others have been killed! After our victories in Sorgo last year, we've gone several months without good news about the Magi problem. I was beginning to get frustrated. However, the great success against the Magi in Ronel as they tried to defend the barbarians and now greater success in Libur has been a huge boost for us! The captured Magi are being brought here as we speak and this time they're going straight to the Dross here in Clornoss."

The room burst into loud cheers and celebration unlike Vendino had seen at a meeting of ministers. He turned to his right, and the minister beside him held up his hand for a celebratory hand-smack. With a large smile, Vendino smacked the hand of the man next to him. The normally somber ministers looked like a group of rowdy teens. It had been a long year, and watching the emperor slip deeper and deeper into depression and anger had put everyone on edge. This news was a huge relief, and the reaction of the ministers pointed that out well.

After a few minutes, the emperor called the room back to order. He said, "The agent who led the successful operation is coming here to tell us what he has learned. It is my hope that we can share this information with other agents and maybe we'll begin to see this level of success in all cities. We're on the right track to eliminate these evil Magi once and for all!"

The room burst into loud cheers once again. The emperor let the celebration carry on for a few minutes. Finally he called for order. The emperor added, "Additionally, I want agents and local sentinels to follow up on every report of magic use, and I want the reported people dealt with mercilessly. We need to make an example of them."

Vendino felt a sick feeling in the pit of his stomach. Dealing with known Magi was one thing, but encouraging people to report their own neighbor was asking for trouble.

The emperor looked to Vendino, and asked, "Is there any further business that we need to attend to?"

Vendino said, "Majesty, there have been increased reports of dwarves being spotted in the hills to the north of Clornoss. I even have isolated reports of dwarves sneaking around within the city."

The emperor waved his hand dismissively. With a smile he said, "Fine, have someone look into these reports."

CHAPTER 22

Ferth

There was a very long list of things that Ferth hated. Over the years he had formalized it into an actual numbered list, ranked in order of his level of hatred. He affectionately called it his Sarding Grubby Chippies list. Not surprisingly, sarding grubby chippies was actually number one on his Sarding Grubby Chippies list. He didn't normally pay for the services of working girls, but when he did he really expected them to be clean and to smell nice. There was literally nothing that he hated worse than sarding grubby chippies.

As he sat on the deck of the *Howling Banshee* he thought about his list, and where on the list he should add boats. Until this trip started he'd never been on a boat, so boats weren't on his list. Shortly after the voyage started, boats had quickly earned a spot on the list.

Ten Magi had been floating towards the islands for several days on the *Howling Banshee*, and each day seemed worse than the last. On day three in the water, the cross winds had picked up and the large waves caused the ship to list from side to side throughout the day and the entire night. The constant rocking was enough to bring frequent vomiting to all of the Magi, and overall it was a miserable day.

The morning of day four the winds changed, or the boat changed course, or something awful happened. Ferth didn't know what specifically caused the change, but the annoying side-to-side listing turned into terrible forward and back tilting. The boat would tilt backwards far enough for items to slide across the deck, and suddenly it felt like they were falling as the front of the boat dropped and the whole thing tilted forward. The boat would sail down the front of a wave as Ferth's stomach shot up into his throat. Eventually the boat would level out and then tilt backwards again, and the whole thing started over.

This continued for a couple of days and nights. For a while it would ease, and then it would get even worse than before. When he wasn't vomiting, he was praying to whichever god might be listening. He hadn't been a saint in his life, but over those first few days of the voyage he made promises to several gods to change his life around and be a better person if they'd just get him back to dry land safely.

Just when he thought that things couldn't get any worse, they got much worse. Sometime during the night, two nights ago, a storm moved in. He knew something dreadful was happening when the horrible forward and back tilting changed. The forward and back tilting got worse, and then came the added excitement of violent side to side listing as well. He didn't understand how the water could be throwing them in every direction at once, but somehow it was happening. That was followed by thunder, lightning, and pounding rain. The ferocious winds threatened to tear the ship to shreds and he grew more and more certain that the boat would be ripped apart.

The storm lasted much of the day, yesterday. By last night he changed his prayers and just begged for the gods to just sink the craft quickly and end the boat nightmare.

A few hours ago things finally started to calm down. He even got a few hours of sleep, which was a refreshing change.

This morning he found himself sitting on the deck of the *Howling Banshee* next to Dalen and Keta. The seven Society Magi were below deck in their cabins, probably sleeping. The waters were calm for a change, and the morning breeze felt pretty good.

He finally decided on number nine. Boats would push imperial sentinels down to number ten on his Sarding Grubby Chippies list, and that would knock his old nemesis Alphanzo Perriz out of the top ten, down to number eleven. These days it wasn't very often that he saw a change in the top ten items on the list. However, boats were genuinely terrible and they would forever hold a special spot on his list.

Keta leaned back against the starboard sidewall of the boat and stared off the port side. She said, "I'm so glad that the sea is calm today! I don't know how many more days of that I could take."

Dalen nodded, "I was able to eat something this morning. If the calm seas keep up, I might even keep it down. I feel so weak, it's not even funny. Hopefully we don't face anything more threatening than bunnies in this forest for a few days. If we ever even find land."

"Dalen, don't say that!" Keta reached out and pushed Dalen softly. "I'm nervous enough without those comments."

Ferth sprawled out on the deck, next to the other Magi, on his back. He folded his arms so his head rested on both hands as he looked up at the clear blue sky. He said, "It's possible that the storm blew us off course. We could have missed the islands entirely. We may never find land; we might just sail along for days until we fall off the edge of the world."

"Ferth! That's awful, why would you say that?" Keta gave him a dirty look.

"He is right. I've heard lots of stories of boats setting sail and never coming back. They can't all sink; surely some of them get lost and drop off the world at its edge."

She groaned, "You don't really think the edge of the world is that nearby do you? Wouldn't you think it would take months to sail there?"

Dalen shrugged, "No one knows. Anyone who gets close enough to see the edge must surely get caught in the current of water falling off the edge? How could they survive that?"

"I've heard that some astronomers claim that the world is a sphere like a massive round boulder."

Both men laughed at her. Dalen said, "You don't really believe that crap, do you? That's the stupidest thing I've ever heard."

Before Ferth could add his own condescending comments, he heard someone above him shout, "Incoming boat, starboard side!"

That comment started a flurry of activity from the seamen. Soon after, a bell began ringing loudly. All three Magi stood up and looked off the starboard side of the boat. Ferth could see a large boat with several masts sailing towards them.

The seaman up in the crow's nest, at the top of the main mast, shouted, "All hands, prepare for boarding! Elf pirates inbound!"

The large boat approached quickly. When it got close, it fired two large flaming bolts from massive crossbows mounted to the front of the boat. The fiery bolts missed the *Howling Banshee* by several feet. Ferth assumed that it was a warning shot. The elven pirate boat was several times larger than the *Howling Banshee*, and a large black and green flag flew above the main mast. He'd never seen such a flag, but he assumed that it did not mean 'we come in peace'.

He watched the large boat navigate quickly until the two boats were side by side, and then the elves tossed grappling hooks onto the deck and tied the two boats together. They dropped several planks onto the deck of the smaller boat and two dozen elves rushed onto the Magi's vessel.

The elves were about as tall as an average man's shoulder, and they were all very lanky. Most of them had long green or bluish hair, and a slight greenish tint to their complexion. The elves all had their hair pulled back into one or two braids that dangled down to their belts. They were armed with

189

thin swords and thin daggers, and they were all lightly armored.

Ferth looked to Dalen to see if it was time to start killing, but the Order of Champions Magi shook his head no, slightly. He resisted the urge to start blasting the creepy greenish humanoids.

If it wasn't such a dangerous situation, the whole thing would be comical. Ferth couldn't help but think of the elves as tall and skinny children, scurrying around their boat with toy weapons, pointy ears, and green or blue dye in their hair. He had grown up thinking of the people from the Free Cities as barbarians, but these elves were the closest things to barbarians that he'd ever seen. They were small and dirty looking, and they scurried over each other like rats as they rushed this way and that, looking in every crate and container of the boat.

The other Magi hurried onto the deck, and rushed over to the Order Magi looking for guidance.

Dalen held his hands out to the sides as they approached. He said, "Don't make any threatening movements or actions. Don't attack unless we have no choice. Those fiery crossbows can easily cause our boat to sink, and there are plenty of elves on that other boat to burn us to dust."

The elves rushed around the ship, dragging crates and barrels to the center of the deck. They all spoke in a sing-song language that Ferth had never heard; he assumed that it was a language unique to the elves. However, it could have been a language of the mermaids and sea nymphs and he'd have no clue.

As the elves gathered supplies from around the ship, they frequently stopped to point their swords and daggers at whatever seamen or passengers happened to be close by. The crew of the boat made no moves to stop the elves, and before long the little pirates began carrying the spoils of their raid over to their boat.

Within a few minutes, Ferth watched the elves release the ropes and then the pirate boat sailed off into the distance. Once he could no longer see them he sat back down and let out a sigh of relief.

- = - = -

A few hours later Ferth was still sitting on the deck near the starboard wall of the boat. Dalen and Keta had gone below deck, along with the four Order Magi from Keta's coterie. He sat there with Cao, Peke, and Asha the three remaining Society Magi of his coterie from Maethral.

Cao usually went by the name Bull. Cao was pronounced like cow, and he was a big fellow, so his friends started calling him Bull. Ferth and Bull had been friends since they were children, and Ferth considered him a brother. The two of them became Magi together, and they were the two most responsible for building a coterie in Maethral. Bull was tall and round, with bushy brown hair and a chubby face.

Peke was the newest Magi in Ferth's coterie, but he was also one of the most enthusiastic. His family had been heavily involved in the Sovereign Magi Society back before the Betrayal, and he was fascinated with the organization. He was raised by a Gentry family in the Garden District of Maethral, and he was a very well educated man. Some people accused him of being a know-it-all, but Ferth had come to rely on the man as a great source of knowledge about things that most people had never even heard of. Peke was fairly average when it came to height and weight; his hair was blonde and cut short. He had strong cheek bones, a narrow face, and narrow shoulders.

Asha was the quiet one from the wilds, and that was about all that Ferth knew about her. The girl was average height, and more muscular than average. She was dark skinned and had black hair, which she had pulled up tight along the sides of her head and bound at the top and down the back so the large tightly curled hair looked almost like a bushy Mohawk across the top and back of her head. She seldom spoke, and she never seemed very comfortable around people. Before she joined the coterie, Ferth had never met her. He didn't know where she came from, and he didn't know anything about her background. She just walked up to him one day in the market place and asked him to help her become a Magi. He wasn't even sure how she knew that he was a Magi.

For several months Ferth didn't trust Asha. The imperial attacks started around the time that she joined, and he knew nothing about her background so it seemed like she might be the problem. However, Ferth and several other Magi had followed her for a long time, and it soon became obvious that the girl didn't have any involvement with the imperials. She seemed to live in the wilderness. She would meet with the others for patrols and things, and then when her duties were done she headed right back to the forest near Maethral and she would stay there in the wilderness all alone.

Bull said, "Dammit, Ferth, are we ever going to get to dry land?"

Peke nodded, "Yeah, Bull, I expect that we'll reach the islands today. I've been monitoring the approximate wind speeds, our bearing, and the amount of time that we've been running on only half-sails. I've also been checking the relative position of the stars compared with how they'd look back home and if my calculations are correct then we should be getting extremely close to the islands."

Asha added, "Been smelling trees for an hour. We're getting close."

The other Magi looked at her. It was unusual to hear her say anything at all, so Ferth was surprised to hear her add to the conversation. He said, "Well, if the two of you agree then I should probably head to my cabin and pack up my things." He stood up.

Ferth hadn't taken more than two steps towards the stairs when he heard the seaman in the crow's nest shout, "Land ahead!"

He turned back to the Order Magi, and he saw Peke smiling smugly. Asha stood and brushed some dust from her clothes.

Bull stood up and charged for the stairs, shoving Ferth out of the way as he passed. He shouted, "Land! I'm coming for you, land!"

Ferth made his way to the cabin that he shared with the other male Magi. The ship was a flurry of activity as the seamen hurried around the boat shouting to each other as they made preparations to drop anchor. Most of the other Magi were already heading to the deck as he entered the cabin.

He grabbed the few things he had left to grab, and then made his way back up to the deck. They would have much less to carry now that the elves had looted the ship. That would make for easier travelling, but now they'd have to live off the land and sleep without blankets or shelter.

When he got to the deck, Dalen and the boat captain were talking.

Dalen said, "But we agreed on five days!"

The captain shook his head, "That was before we were boarded and looted by elves! We don't have the supplies to sit here that long. You have two days, and then we're leaving with or without you."

Dalen stood there quietly for a moment, with his eyes shut. Ferth could see that he was summoning magic. He hoped the young Magi wasn't about to do something rash, but he prepared himself for battle just in case. He looked around quickly to assess the position of the various seamen, in case things went sideways.

After a moment, Dalen looked to the captain and said, "Never mind, captain. You can set sail as soon as you get us to shore. We won't be riding back with you."

Ferth stared at him in astonishment, but he remained quiet.

The captain looked equally surprised, but he didn't argue. Instead he put his crew to work lowering the small boat that would be used to ferry the Magi to the shore.

The ordeal of getting to shore took much longer than Ferth would have liked. After so many days at sea, everyone was anxious to get to dry land. When the little boat finally grew near the shore, Bull didn't even wait for the seamen to quit paddling. He jumped from the little boat and swam the final twenty yards to the beach.

When he got there, Bull rolled around in the sand like a carefree child. The large Magi, in a soaking wet breeches and tunic, rolled in the sand and tossed it in the air. He shouted, "Land! Oh how I love you, land! I'll never leave you again, I promise!"

When the small boat slid into the sand of the beach, Ferth jumped off first. He kicked sand at Bull, "Get up, you big oaf. You look like a fool rolling around like that." His words were sharp, but he said them with a smile. He and Bull may be exact opposites when it came to personality. However, sometimes Ferth was jealous of Bull's carefree and fun-loving personality.

Once the seamen began rowing the boat back to the *Howling Banshee*, Keta looked at Dalen. She said, "You told the captain to leave without us. What's your plan?"

"I was able to detect a portal stone, about a day's walk from here. I doubt they'd build it at the bottom of the sea. So, we should be fine."

Peke said, "Not to be Mr. Negative, but I've read that some inert portal stones can never be activated. Sometimes they're damaged or rendered useless in some other way. If any land is going to be tough on an ancient artifact, it's this place." He pointed at the forest further inland.

As they looked south, off to the east the land was swampy and wet, and off to the west the forest grew thick and dark. The underbrush looked thick and thorny from far away, and Ferth was certain that it wasn't going to be easy going.

Asha added, "We have no idea what lives in these woodlands. The portal stone might be in the middle of a vicious beast's lair."

Dalen repositioned his packs. "Or it might be out in the open with a basket of muffins just waiting for our arrival."

One of the Society Magi from Keta's coterie said, "No way to find out, without getting started. Daylight is wasting." Ferth couldn't remember the Magi's name but he thought it might be Konrad or something like that.

All ten Magi made their way towards the edge of the forest. When they got to the underbrush, Dalen searched around for the easiest path into the forest.

Ferth noticed Asha with her eyes closed, summoning magic. Then she said, "Dalen, the forests have always been my home. Will you let me lead?"

He replied, "Be my guest." He motioned for her to move in front of him. Then he pointed to the southwest, "The portal stone is in that direction."

She nodded, "I know. Do we go straight to the portal stone, or should we look for Dinberian oak trees first?"

"Let's find the portal stone and go from there. Maybe we'll stumble onto the trees along the way? Besides, once we have the stone active, it won't be difficult to get back here to look for these trees."

- = - = -

The next morning, Ferth woke up as the sun was just beginning to rise. He sat up and stretched his arms and back. He felt terrible and he was certain that his body was going to ache all day.

They had traveled through the woods as far as they could before the darkness sat in, and then Asha led them to a small clearing for camp. Dalen assigned pairs to serve as guards in shifts throughout the night. As his luck would have it, Ferth was chosen for the middle of the night guard duty. By the time he fell asleep on the hard ground it was already time to wake up and serve as a guard for about an hour. He sat guard with Peke and the hour went by uneventfully. When his guard duty was done, he had difficulties falling asleep with all of the sticks and roots poking into his back and legs all night long.

As he wiped the sleep from his eyes, he was certain that he only got about an hour or two of sleep total throughout the night. It was going to be a long day.

The others were still asleep, other than Asha and Bull who were the final guards of the night. When he looked to Asha, she put her finger to her lips to tell him to keep quiet.

He walked over and knelt down beside her. Asha whispered, "We're being watched."

Ferth's heart started beating faster as the excitement of a possible battle grew. He looked around, but he couldn't see anyone watching them.

Over the next half hour, each of the other Magi woke up and before long everyone was preparing to break camp.

He stepped over to Dalen and said, "Asha says someone's watching us."

Dalen nodded and looked around, "I've had the same feeling all night, but

I don't see anyone."

After a few minutes everyone was ready to break camp and Asha led the way. She cleared a path through the underbrush with her sword. The going was slow because of the thick underbrush, ever-present thorns, and sharp poking sticks.

Several hours later, Asha motioned for Dalen to come up to her. Ferth and Keta followed him up to the scout. Asha pointed in front of her, she whispered, "Look there, a well-travelled trail. This was either made by large animals or humanoids, and my guess is humanoids. Should we cross it, or follow it?"

Dalen looked to Ferth and Keta, and both of them shrugged. He said, "I dunno, Asha. What do you think?"

"It's hard to say. It could lead to water, or it might lead to certain death."

Keta laughed, and Dalen groaned.

Ferth appreciated the woman's direct approach.

Dalen said, "Keep heading towards the portal stone."

The scout cut through the brush, crossing the well-travelled path in the process.

From high up in the trees to the right, Ferth heard a horn blowing in a long low tone. At first he thought it was some sort of animal. After a moment, several horns answered the first one. Most of them sounded fairly far away, and they came from every direction.

The sounds sent cold chills running down Ferth's back. Whatever was following them, it was intelligent enough to make horns. That ruled out monkeys and tree lizards. He had been really hoping that it was a tree lizard that was watching them.

They travelled slowly for another hour or more before he heard the nearby horn sound once again. It was again answered by several other horns in every direction.

Ferth stepped over to Dalen to ask him a question, but Asha stopped and motioned them forward before he could ask.

He followed Dalen and Keta up to the scout.

Asha pointed up in front of her. He got closer and looked through the thick underbrush and between the closely packed trees. After a few moments of looking, he saw what the scout was referring to. There was a large clearing up ahead.

He moved forward more to get a better view. As he got closer to the clearing he could see just how large it was, and throughout the clearing were dozens of grass huts.

Noises from all around caught his attention and he turned to see several small elves move in around the Magi, surrounding them. The elves were carrying spears and bows, and they ushered all of the Magi up to where Ferth and the others stood.

Dalen held up his hands to show he didn't mean any harm. Ferth would have preferred to fight; surely a large group of Magi could take out a slightly larger group of elves with sticks.

Dalen said, "We mean no harm."

The elves herded the Magi forward and into the large clearing, where several other elves approached. The elves all wore outfits made of animal pelts and various plant life. Several of them wore beads, bird feathers, and a variety of different shells for decorations or perhaps rank distinction on necklaces, ear rings, and head bands. All of them were armed with spears, crude axes, large clubs, or bows with arrows ready.

The Magi were slowly guided towards the middle of a crude village, which was built throughout the clearing. Off to one side, Ferth saw several large cages made from heavy sticks and strips of animal pelts. Some of the cages housed large pig-like animals, but he got the sinking suspicion that at least one of those cages was destined to house the Magi soon if they didn't do something.

Dalen must have made that same assumption, because the Magi stopped walking and he caused his blue and white cloak to appear. Ferth noticed that the champion also caused his swords to return from their storage location in the plane of magic, but Dalen left them sheathed for the time being.

Ferth called his cloak and staff, and each of the other Magi quickly followed their example. Within a moment there were two blue and white cloaked Order of Champion Magi, a red and white cloaked Order of Evokers Magi, and seven brown and white cloaked Society Magi standing in the middle of the primitive elves.

He felt much better, having his cloak on his back and his staff in hand. As badly as he wanted to rain fiery death down upon the foul elves, he held his hand until Dalen gave the order.

The elves began rambling on in their crazy sing-song language, and he had no clue what they were saying. Until, he heard one of the elves say, "Magi."

When the Magi summoned their cloaks, it didn't take long for the elves to change their demeanor. When the first elf said, "Magi" several other elves started saying it as well. Some of the elves started lowering their weapons.

One elf stepped forward. He carried a large thick staff with many feathers and shells tied to the top end. The elf walked up to Dalen and poked the top of the staff into Dalen's chest. He talked for several moments in the primitive elven language, but Ferth had no clue what the elf was saying.

Dalen shook his head, "I'm sorry, I don't understand you."

Peke stepped up to Dalen, and said, "I'm not certain, but I'm pretty sure he introduced himself as Chief Uzlugshur, listed off several accomplishments in his life, and then he asked who you are."

Ferth looked at Peke in amazement. The man really never ceased to astonish him. He'd seen Peke come up with some impressive facts and display some impressive knowledge on obscure topics, but he didn't know that the man also spoke the language of elves.

Dalen looked surprised also, but he said, "Well, tell him I am Dalen of the Sovereign Magi Society."

Peke spoke to the elves. Ferth had no clue if what he was saying was in elven, but he did hear the words Dalen and Magi.

Uzlugshur spoke another long string of questions or statements in his native language.

Peke looked at Dalen and said, "I'm not sure exactly what he is saying, I only know as much elven as I was able to teach myself from an old text many years ago. To make it harder, his version of the language seems more primitive than what was used by the pirates. However, I think he wants you to prove that you're a Magi by making that rock grow tall."

Ferth looked in the direction where Peke pointed. In the center of the village was a shrine of some sort. There was a crude fence built around a stone. The fence was adorned with bones, pelts, beads, shells, and other trinkets.

Keta walked over to the low fence and looked closer at the rock laying in the center of the fence. It was about the size of her fist, and didn't look remarkable in any way. She looked to Dalen, "Is that the portal stone?"

He nodded and walked up to it. He focused briefly, and then summoned the magic to activate the portal stone. The stone rose out of the ground and the intricate runes carved up and down the sides glowed to life. It was a three feet tall stone obelisk. He knelt down next to it and looked at the glowing runes.

He looked to the Magi, and said, "*Fevin Tryz*. It's portal number fifty-three."

Keta asked, "Why would there be a portal stone in the middle of a primitive tribe of island elves? It makes no sense?"

Dalen replied, "We're here because of the text Sarasa found. It documented that before the Betrayal, the Magi were allies with some elves. It's possible that the Magi built the portal stone here so they could more easily travel here, and the elves must have built their village around the stone. Perhaps the Magi traded with the elves more than we realize?"

When Ferth looked around at the elves, he noticed that they had all lowered their weapons.

The chief walked up to Dalen and spoke slowly. When he finished, Dalen looked to Peke to translate.

Peke said, "I think he is saying that they've been waiting for us. I'm pretty sure he asked if we brought spices and fruits."

The chief nodded, and then he said, "Spysez. Frootz. Horr."

Peke and Dalen looked at each other and shook their heads.

Peke looked back to the chief, "Horr?"

Turning around, the chief motioned for them to follow him. He led them to a large hut that looked to be a primitive metal smithy. It had an ancient looking forge, a bellows contraption, a large anvil, and various other blacksmithy tools and equipment. From the dust and neglect, it didn't seem that they had been used in a long time.

The chief pointed towards the forge and repeated, "Horr!"

Dalen smiled, "Oh, ore?"

With a nod, the chief put his right hand on Dalen's left shoulder. "Trate? Magi spysez, frootz, horr!" Then he put his right hand on his own shoulder, and said, "Elvinarin woodz, rootz!"

"I think he said that he wants to trade. He wants the Magi to supply spices, fruits, and ore and in return the elves will supply wood and roots?"

Dalen looked at Peke and smiled. "Yeah, I worked that out. I don't need you to translate when he's trying to speak our language. Does anyone have any clue what kind of root he would be referring to?"

Ferth said, "If the Magi were getting special wood for the wands here, and getting this root, it's likely that the root is useful too."

"I agree. Tell him yes, we will have to travel to our lands to get what they need, and we'll be back very soon. Ferth and Bull, I would like for you to go to a market and get us some fruits and spices. Peke and I will get some ore."

Dalen thought for a moment and added, "Asha, you should come with Peke and I. Then you'll come back here with us, just in case we need your skills. Let's meet at Uli's ranch and then we'll come back here together. Keta, please take your Coterie to Uli's and prepare for the Stronghold assault."

CHAPTER 23

Kimly

"How many merchants have signed-on so far?" Favin opened up a book and grabbed a quill.

He was sitting behind a large desk with a variety of books, papers, and other items scattered around. The room was fairly large but dimly lit. There were two couches and several comfortable chairs spread around the room, as well as some large down-filled pillows on the floor.

Kimly sat on a small balcony, looking down on the room below. She was concealed by a *Shadow Shroud* spell so the thieves below didn't know she was there. Favin knew that she periodically watched from the balcony, but the others had never even met her. That's the way she liked it, she was perfectly happy to guide things from the shadows and let Favin be the face of the operation.

Other than Favin, there were four people in the room below. All four of them were thieves in Favin's guild. They all also possessed a magewel and, with Kimly's guidance, Favin had taught them how to cast *Shadow Shroud* and *Invisible Helper*. As far as the four thieves knew, they were now level one agents of the Shrouded. She was actually sort of disappointed that out of over a hundred members in Favin's growing guild, he only found four that possessed a magewel.

"Fifteen so far." The large man who replied was a thief called Floppy. He was tall and muscular, and he kept his curly black hair cut short. He wasn't the most handsome man Kimly had ever seen, but he was built like a docks worker.

He had been friends with Favin for many years and he had recently been named second in charge of the guild. Kimly didn't pay much attention to the inner workings of the guild, but she thought Favin had made a good choice there. The man seemed ruthless, mean, and competent. He was just the type of person Kimly would want as her right-hand-man if she was running a guild of thieves.

Favin looked up from the book. "Fifteen? There are hundreds of merchants in this city, and we've only found fifteen who are willing to pay for our protection?"

Floppy shifted position on the couch, sitting up a little straighter. He said, "There's been at least a dozen new groups that've popped up since Hisaro's guild died. Ours is growing, but we're not the only guild in the city. Some merchants won't pay any guild for protection, and the others don't wanna pay more than one. It's like everyone is just sorta holding their breath to see how things shake out."

Sprawled out on the floor, with several large pillows below her, was a girl called Skoots. She rolled from her back onto her stomach, and positioned one of the large pillows below her chin. She said, "I'm hearing lotsa new guilds wanna target merchants that won't pay them, especially the ones that're paying their rival guilds for protection."

Skoots was a small woman with long light-blond hair and a youthful appearance. Favin trusted her as valuable source of information about the latest gossip and rumors from the streets. Since learning the *Shadow Shroud* spell, the woman had become an even greater resource for information from around the city.

Favin nodded, "That's good to know, Skoots. Try to find out which guilds are targeting our merchants and we'll need to think about dealing with them."

He looked to the man sitting in a chair to his right. He said, "Rath, I'm planning to put all of our mercs and men-at-arms in your hands. Once I tell the others, I'd like you to make sure that we have a strong presence at every merchant that pays us. There should be no doubt that we're keeping them safe. If any of these weak guilds hit merchants that we're protecting, it's going to make us look stupid. I don't want to look stupid. If you need more men, hire more men."

Rath smiled and nodded his head. He said, "Thanks boss, for making me a Shrouded and for your trust. I won't let you down!"

Kimly didn't know much about the man called Rath. He was a wiry little man, but he always looked like he was angry at the world. The man was covered with little scars, a variety of small faded tattoos, and his brown hair was just starting to get a few streaks of grey. She knew he'd been a soldier and a mercenary for years, but she didn't know how he got involved with Favin's guild.

"I know you won't Rath." Favin looked back to Floppy, and said, "Floppy, now that you're a part of the Shrouded, I'd like to let someone else worry about our merchant protection racket so you're freed up to do something more useful with your new powers."

The big man smiled. "That's great news! It's been ages since I've been able to enjoy some good old burglaries! I can't tell you how much I miss treasure hunting through other people's stuff."

Favin started shuffling through the items on his desk and then pulled out a piece of paper. He said, "Don't forget this list. All of the homes and shops on this list are off limits. We need to be careful, and make sure our people don't hit any of these places.

"Yes, we know! The list's posted in like ten different places around the house!" Skoots rolled her eyes and repositioned the pillows to sit up with her back against the wall. She asked, "Are all those the places listed as off-limits by the Shrouded?"

Kimly smiled to herself. She had made the list to make sure that she wasn't training people to rob from her home, or the homes and businesses of her friends.

He nodded, "Yes, mostly. I've added some as well, including the merchants that we're protecting." He waited to see if anyone was going to comment further, and then he asked, "Skoots, what else are you hearing on the streets?"

"Last night I heard whispers of an imperial agent showing up in the city. Sounds like he's a Magi hunter."

The room got quiet, and Kimly felt her heart jump to her throat. The last time imperial Magi hunters arrived in a city with Kimly, she ended up getting captured. She wasn't about to let that happen again.

Rath said, "They won't come after the Shrouded, will they?"

Favin and Skoots both started talking at the same time. Skoots didn't stop, "Of course they will! In their eyes all who use magic are Magi. They don't care that we can't shoot fireballs or turn people into lizards."

When she finished, Favin said, "She is right. We're in as much danger as the Magi. We might be in more danger, because if any of the rival guilds suspect that some of our people can use magic they will turn us in immediately."

The one person in the room who hadn't spoken yet, a little man called Viper, said quietly, "What should we do about this agent?"

Kimly was happy to hear Viper speak up. He was the closest thing that Favin's group had to an assassin. Favin recently told her that he'd known Viper since they were children, but the little man left the city years ago. When Viper returned to the city a few days ago, Favin quickly offered him a position within his growing guild. She agreed that a quick and clean assassination was exactly what they needed to solve the imperial agent problem before things got out of hand.

Favin shook his head, "No, Viper. I don't think we'll be needing your skills in this case. Hopefully the agent is passing through and this will all blow over quickly. I've heard nothing about the Magi being active here, so there is really no reason for the agent to be here long. We shouldn't act, at least not right now."

Kimly stood up. She was very close to running into the room and demanding that the guild assassinate the agent right away. She took a deep breath and let it out quietly. It wouldn't help Favin's status within his guild to be bossed around in front of his people, and it wouldn't help Kimly at all to have these thieves knowing who she was. It also wouldn't help to start making demands of Favin in the name of a secret organization that didn't really exist and one that she promised him wouldn't tell him what to do. So, she stood there and tried to breathe calmly and figure out what to do.

She stopped paying attention to the things happening below her, as she considered her various options. After a while she noticed that the people below were starting to leave, and before long Favin was alone at his desk. She waited several minutes and then walked down from the balcony. When she got to his desk, she dropped the shroud spell.

He was looking down at his papers and didn't notice her at first. After a few moments he glanced up, and shouted, "Zortha's diddies!" He stood up quickly, while stepping backwards, and almost tripped over his chair. When he saw who was standing in front of him, he calmed noticeably and slid his daggers back in their sheath. "By the gods, Kimly! You shouldn't scare me like that!"

"Do you kiss your lovers with that foul mouth?"

"I'm sure the goddess of war doesn't mind if I reference her bosom in times of surprise."

"Alright, but if you're smote by a vengeful goddess with divine diddies, I'm going to laugh at your funeral."

"Fair enough, how long have you been here?"

"Long enough. Favin, we can't ignore this Magi hunter. We've seen this in other cities. None of us are safe as long as he's here. This ain't an order from the Shrouded, it's just advice from a friend. If you care about Floppy, Skoots, and the others then you'll do something about that hunter."

"Duly noted. I'm going to have a chat with the chancellor, maybe he can give me an idea how long this hunter is going to be here."

Kimly was more than a little surprised. "You're buddies with the chancellor now?"

He gave her a mischievous smile, and shrugged innocently. "Let's just say that he was extremely grateful to have his daughter returned unharmed. I've enjoyed dinner with him a couple of times, and for a small cut of our profits the chancellor will quietly keep the sentinels from hounding us much. Provided, of course, that we don't hit any Aristocrat homes."

She grinned at him, "Very nice! I'm impressed!"

"Thank you for your warning. I hope this hunter is just passing through."

"On a different topic, I have a task for you. If you're interested. We would like some information about a merchant named Cletis Watters."

He raised an eyebrow in surprise. "Cletis Watters, the Dreg broker? Why is the Shrouded interested in a broker?"

Kimly reached out and grabbed onto his desk to steady herself. She was so shocked that it almost took her breath away. Her husband was so sweet and caring; it was a huge shock to hear him called a broker.

He looked at her with concern on his face, "Are you alright? You look like you swallowed a marmot."

She shook her head, "I'm fine. The monthly cramps hit me hard sometimes. Cletis Watters the merchant is a broker?"

"It's not common knowledge, of course. Potential clients go through several layers, and pay outrageous fees, before they ever get a meeting with him. However, I hear that he is the best broker along the south coast of the empire, if you can afford him. I ain't dealt with him myself, but I know people that have worked for him."

Her head was spinning. Cletis had told her that they both had secrets, but never in her wildest dreams would she have guessed that her sweet husband could be a broker. She didn't even really know exactly what a Dreg broker did, she only knew of the rumors that swirl about. The most common rumor about a broker was that a client could hire him to arrange for a certain target to get framed for some kind of crime and get sentenced as a Dreg. The broker would then ensure that the client was able to buy the target. Kimly had heard many stories of wealthy Gentry seeing a pretty Denizen on the street or in a market and a few days later, with the help of a broker, the Gentry would own the woman.

When she was young, her mother frequently warned her not to make eye contact with the Gentry men or she'd end up getting brokered to one of them.

Favin said, "Kimly?"

She looked at him and realized that he'd still been talking to her. She had zoned him out as she thought about the implications of her husband being a broker.

She said, "Yes, I hear you."

"What do you want to know about him? The Shrouded should tread lightly if they're going after him. He is powerful, well-connected, rich, and ruthless. I know that I'm happy sitting this one out. I don't want to attract his attention."

She didn't have the heart to tell him that Cletis was already paying attention to him, because of her. She said, "I'll send them the information that Watters is a broker, that might be all they want to know."

- = - = -

Cletis was sitting behind a large fancy desk in a large room. There was also a small cabinet near the desk and a comfortable looking chair sitting in front of the desk. The walls of the room were covered with shelves, and a variety of statuettes and other expensive baubles sat on those shelves. Other than that the large room was empty. Even though Cletis' desk was large, the size of the room made it seem small.

Kimly squatted down next to a small skylight window looking down into the large room below. The window was one of many skylights in the room's roof, and she positioned herself carefully so that she couldn't be easily seen from the ground and so that she did not cast shadows into the room.

For almost two hours she sat in her uncomfortable position, listening into the room, bored out of her mind. She wanted to go and do something fun, or at least mildly entertaining. However, she had gone to great lengths to follow her husband to one of his warehouses, and then to another building, and finally to this location using multiple different carriages and drivers along the way. She'd struggled at several points to keep from losing him, but in the end she was successful. If one could consider being bored out of one's mind while squatting uncomfortably on a hot roof as being successful.

She perked up when she saw him look up from his writings at the desk. Two soldiers walked into the room, leading a blindfolded man. They led the man to the comfortable chair and sat him down, and then removed his blindfold.

The man was large and unattractive. He was mostly bald, but what little hair he had was greasy, dirty, and disheveled. She'd dealt with too many people like this when she lived in Sorgo. The man was clearly a dirtbag low-life, and Kimly already hated him.

The dirtbag said, "Were you able to find my niece? I miss her dearly." The man's words were innocent, but the lecherous sneer on his face and the inflections in his voice told her that the man was not looking for a niece.

Cletis nodded, "We found the girl you are looking for. She is a Dreg owned by a small Gentry family in Tharrin, the family is quite fond of her and they are reluctant to sell her."

"The girl's my kin, I got every right to buy her!" He slammed a fist down on the table.

Calmly Cletis replied, "You, sir, are a liar. You are Albes of Orgrak, the new owner of two of the raunchiest brothels south of Clornoss. You aren't looking for your niece; you're looking for a comely lass to add to your stable of working Dregs."

Albes laughed in a fully-belly laugh for a while, and then finally he said, "You're very well informed. I am Albes."

"What made you choose this girl? The owners don't want to part with her."

"Like you said, she's a sexy little minx. I've got my scouts all over the southern cities looking for the finest looking Dregs out there. If you get me what I want, you'll get a great deal of repeat business."

Cletis shook his head, "No, I'm sorry. Your contract specifically asked if you were a pimp or brothel owner. I rarely do business with their ilk, and if you can't be honest with me from the beginning then we have nothing further to discuss. You lied and our business here is now concluded. Good day, Mr. Albes."

"Now, don't answer too quickly. Surely you cannot blame me for being creative. I will pay whatever fees you demand and I'll add a little something on there for your troubles."

Cletis was quiet for a time, then he said, "Good day, Mr. Albes."

The door opened and two guards walked back into the room. They blindfolded the man and took him from the room.

As he was escorted out of the room, the man shouted, "I will have that Dreg!"

Kimly stretched a leg, and tried to get feeling back into her toes. She was relieved that her husband was not willing to sell the girl into what would surely be a dreadful existence. She had seen what could happen to Dreg women who get sold into that life. She was impressed that her husband was a shrewd businessman who didn't need to lower himself to the level of the scumbag who was just taken from his office.

"Hey, what are you doing there?"

She looked up in surprise, and saw two guards on a landing overlooking the roof. They started walking towards her. She swore softly.

"Keep your hands where I can see them, scurvy thief!"

She stood up slowly. The pitch of the roof, and the numbness of her legs, made it difficult to stand at all. She slowly pulled back the cowl of her cape.

One of the guards gasped in surprise, and he lowered his sword. He said, "Mrs. Watters? What are you doing up here?"

"Take me to my husband!" She tried to sound like she was in command, even though she was extremely nervous. There was obviously a side of her husband that she'd not yet seen, and she hoped that being caught spying on him would not bring it out.

The guards escorted her from the roof and through a maze of halls and rooms. Finally they opened the door to the large room where she found Cletis sitting at his desk.

He sighed as the guards brought her into the room. He said, "Bring my wife a chair."

When the guards returned with a lavish chair, Cletis directed them to place it behind the desk near him. He said, "Send in the next client whenever he is prepared."

She wanted to say something, but no words would come. So, she sat in the chair quietly.

Soon the door opened again, and a very handsome young man entered the room blindfolded. Kimly was not normally the type of woman to ogle a pretty man, but even she was not immune to the man's charm. He was dressed like a tradesman, and he still had the work grime on his hands as testimony to that fact.

Cletis smiled at the man. "Viktur, I am happy to see you again. I'm told that you were able to raise enough money to afford my services."

"It took me almost four years, saving every copper falcon and silver dove I could get my hands on."

"And in a few short years you saved a platinum raptor and now you can afford to find your brother. I've already tracked him down, and we've been keeping an eye on him for you."

"You've found him already? Where is he?"

"It was a bit of a challenge to find him. He was sold in the Khardifar bazaar on a Dreg Day six years ago to a farmer outside of Khardifar. That farmer sold him to a rancher's widow south of Rinamek City. Once you've taken care of our financial agreement, my people will tell you where to find him. The current owner does sound agreeable to letting you visit briefly."

"Visit him? I thought I was paying you to rescue him. ...to free him?"

"Don't try to change the arrangement now. You were very clear that you wanted to see your brother alive. You never once said anything about freedom or rescues. I'm afraid those services are much more costly. You've simply paid for the opportunity to visit your brother one time, to catch up on old times. I recommend that you make the most of it."

After a moment the man lowered his gaze, and his shoulders drooped slightly. He said, "I am grateful for the chance to speak with him, and to know that he is alive. Good day." The man stood up.

The guards entered the room, blind folded him, and led him away.

When he was gone, Kimly asked, "How much did it cost you to find out where the man is at?"

Cletis shrugged. "My people made a few inquiries. It cost us very little. Jobs like that are usually extremely profitable."

She smiled at him seductively, "I find that wildly exciting."

He reached over and pulled her to him for a long passionate kiss. When he finally released her, she wanted him more than she ever had before. They had enjoyed many sexual playtimes together, but they had usually been something she did for him because she knew he wanted it. Now, she wanted it for her own enjoyment. She reached down to rub her hand along his upper leg.

Cletis placed his hand over hers. With a frown he said, "Sadly, dearest, I have one more client to see before we can have our fun. It would probably be best if you let me handle this one privately."

She moaned her disappointment. Surely the next client could wait a while, so she could enjoy some time with her husband? She tried to continue her hand's journey up his leg, but his hand held hers firm. With a pouty face, she said, "It's fine. I'll stay and watch."

"I understand your curiosity, and I am trying to be forgiving even when my men found you spying on my business dealings. But there are some things you shouldn't see. I'll not have my wife thinking less of me because she is squeamish about the realities of the world and the place I've built within it."

She didn't entirely understand what he was trying to say, partly because she was distracted and thinking about naughty games that she wanted to play, and partly because he wasn't speaking openly. She said, "I'm not squeamish."

He didn't reply and soon the door opened and the guard brought in a blindfolded woman. She was in her middle years, but Kimly thought she was still quite pretty. Her hair was light blond and her skin was sun-darkened.

When the guards removed the woman's blindfold, Kimly could almost see the desperation in the woman's eyes. The woman was very nervous and anxious about something.

In a very calm and soothing voice, Cletis said, "Well met, Mrs. Sauthers. My condolences for your loss. Losing your husband and having your daughter become a Dreg within the same fortnight must have been very difficult."

The woman looked down at her hands. "Can you help my daughter, or not?"

"Mrs. Sauthers, there are truly very few things that are beyond my abilities. It is just a question of whether you can afford to pay the costs involved. Freeing a Dreg is dangerous, and expensive. My information tells me that you are a woman of limited resources. Are you able to afford my services?"

She nodded, "It was difficult. It took all of my savings, and handouts from almost everyone that I know. But I was able to pay your people what they demanded."

Kimly glanced at her husband and saw that he looked genuinely sad.

He said, "Mrs. Sauthers, my people should have made it clear. The money you've paid thus far was paid to them to arrange this meeting. You've paid me nothing, and I assure you the cost to free your daughter will be significantly higher than the trifling fees needed to visit with me today."

"But I've got no more money! I've already paid it to you! You've gotta help me, my daughter is innocent!" The woman broke down and began to cry.

Kimly was beginning to get annoyed. She'd seen this ploy used so many times that it made her ill. Every time she saw someone trying to use tears to get their way, it made her sick to her stomach. She hoped that her husband did not fall for the manipulative woman's games.

He said, "If the girl is innocent, surely the magistrates will listen." He sat and watched the woman for some time. After a bit, he said, "Am I to assume that you killed your husband, and your daughter is now a Dreg for life because of your crime?"

The woman sobbed and nodded in the affirmative.

"As I figured. If you confess what really happened, they will likely let you take her place as a Dreg to pay for the crime."

The woman sobbed more heavily. After a bit she took a deep breath to calm herself. With some effort, she said, "I can't! I couldn't live as a Dreg, I'd rather die!"

Kimly wanted to throw something at the selfish woman. She couldn't understand how any woman could allow her daughter to be made a Dreg to pay for their own crime? It was the kind of awful thing her mother would have done, and there was a special place in Khalius waiting for her.

When the woman quieted down, Cletis said, "What skills do you have, that you could use to pay off your debt to me if I were to agree to free your daughter?"

"I'm a porter, it's really the only skill I've got."

He was quiet for a moment, looking at her. "Surely you have other skills, perhaps physical skills that you save for your lovers?"

Her eyes went wide and she sat up straighter. "You want me to work as a common chippie to pay your fees?" The woman practically spat the words. The disgust on her face was plain.

He laughed gently, "Don't be foolish, Mrs. Sauthers. I wouldn't ask you to work as a common prostitute, because you're much too old to make enough money that way to afford me."

Kimly struggled to suppress a laugh, and the woman crossed her arms over her chest and glared at him in indignation.

He continued, "However, you are in luck. One of my business associates is hosting a gathering in a few days and he's looking for ladies to provide some special entertainment. Of course, I don't know any of the details, but I'm told that his guests have some very unorthodox interests. If you can be away from your job for a few days to work as one of the entertainers for my associate's gathering, I'm sure that will go a long way towards paying my fees. And, I might add, it will get you one step closer to freeing your daughter."

The woman looked like she might scream, or start crying again. Finally she said, "If I agree, how much will I be paid?"

"You will be paid nothing. The real question is how much will I be paid, and that all depends on what they ask you to do and how satisfied they are with your performance."

The woman stood up and placed her fists on her hips. She said, "This is an outrage! How dare you ask me to give myself to these freaks without even a promise that you won't make me do even worse when that's done! I oughta turn you in to the magistrates!"

Cletis calmly motioned for the woman to sit down. When she did, he said, "Mrs. Sauthers, how old is your daughter?"

"She just passed twenty summers."

"Is she pretty?"

"Yes, she is a beautiful girl."

He sighed and shook his head slowly, "That is truly unfortunate. I frequently have the scum of the earth sitting across from my desk looking to buy the most beautiful Dregs, to make them work in their despicable houses of debauchery. They won't get them from me, but there are plenty of brokers who deal with that sort of request. If you don't find a way to free your daughter soon, it is likely that she'll end up spending the next decade enduring far worse than the unorthodox oddities that this group is likely to expect of you for only a few days."

The woman lowered her eyes and didn't respond.

He continued, "Let us get one thing straight. I am not making you do anything. You came to me asking for my help, and then you have the gall to complain when I provide a method for you to repay me for my services? Quite frankly, Mrs. Sauthers, I couldn't possibly care any less what you do. Leave and never return, find an alternate way to raise the money for my fees, or provide entertainment at my associate's gathering. It's all the same to me."

She looked up with venom in her eyes, "If you were a decent human being you'd free her and not charge me anything!"

Cletis smiled, "Mrs. Sauthers, I am a businessman. It is by our very nature that we're not decent human beings. But you killed your own husband and allowed your daughter to take the punishment for your actions. I believe you take home the award for worst person in this room."

Kimly saw him discreetly pull a lever below his desk. When he did, the two guards entered the room.

Cletis said, "One more thing, Mrs. Sauthers. I do not take kindly to threats. My men will be watching you. I strongly advise that you avoid magistrates. You'll now be taken to someone who can give you more details about the gathering, if you are thus inclined to proceed."

The guards blindfolded the woman and took her from the room.

Before the door was closed, a different guard looked in and said, "Sir, there is one more person waiting to see you."

"Who is it? I thought the Sauthers woman was the last client of the day?"

The guard raised both hands, indicating that he didn't know. He said,

"Another new client. They should be bringing the paperwork up soon."

"Fine. One more thing. Arrange to have the Sauthers daughter bought and moved to one of my factories. She can work there until we get things worked out with her mother. I don't want her gobbled up by Albes or someone like him."

The guard nodded, "Yes sir." He closed the door behind him as he walked out.

Cletis looked to Kimly, and said, "I hope you weren't too traumatized by the realities of my work. It's rarely pleasant."

She leaned over and kissed him deeply, while turning to him and tossing one leg over his lap. She hugged him to her tightly as they kissed. She kept her eyes closed for a moment as she pulled away. Sitting there on his lap, straddling him, she caressed the side of his face. She said, "You are humiliating and punishing a truly wicked woman, you'll be saving an innocent young lady from a dreadful life, and you're going to make a disgusting amount of profit from it." She leaned forward and looked into his eyes. Finally she said, "I've never wanted someone so badly in my entire life!"

CHAPTER 24

Jessa

The wench was whining once again. "We've been here for a fortnight now, when can we burn this place down and go home? I hate it here."

Jalinox exhaled audibly and sat a candle down on the altar harder than needed. He looked up at the wench, and said, "Ezmorelda, dear, this place is practically a king's palace compared to some places I've stayed. There is a little hamlet just south of Thudo called Aberton's Roost with only one inn. Gods forbid that you ever find yourself in Aberton's Roost needing a place to stay for a single night. You'd be better off sleeping in a cattle pasture outside of town; it would certainly smell better that's for sure."

Jenna smiled at him as he finished his story. She barely listened to these stores when he told them, but she found that he seemed pleased if she gave the impression that she cared about them.

The wench hadn't learned that yet, and she rolled her eyes and began fidgeting with the fabric of her dress.

He turned his attention back to arranging the items on the altar. When he had things the way he wanted them, he said, "Fear not, my dear Ezmorelda. We've found wondrous tomes and learned far more than I thought we might. I have a few more things I want to accomplish here, but very soon you'll get your wish. We'll raze this place to ashes when it's time to leave."

They were in the sanctuary of a temple, and the three necromancers formed the three points of an equilateral triangle about the altar. Nine tall candelabras, three on each side and each with three lit candles, formed the sides of the triangle.

He said, "We will be attempting to summon a spectre from the depths of Khalius to serve me. If we're successful in bringing it here, it will take a few moments to bring it under my control. Remember what we talked about. You must maintain your position at the point of the triangle and join me in the ritual until it's completed."

The wench said, "What's a spectre?"

Jessa rolled her eyes; apparently the woman had paid no attention at all to Jalinox's discussions and lectures over the past few days. She said, "A wicked spirit pulled from Khalius to our lands."

Jessa started running through the words of the ritual chant in her head. Once she was confident that she was ready, she looked over to the wench. The woman looked around the sanctuary like she was bored out of her mind.

The sanctuary was large, with a high vaulted ceiling and large stained-glass windows along the two side walls. A large mural of the goddess of magic, Nalria, dominated the front of the room. However, the mural had been smeared with rabbit blood soon after the necromancers took over the Stronghold.

The three remaining idiots stood guard at the two exits. She suppressed a laugh when she looked over at the Crater-Face Idiot, who was still bandaged in several places after being mauled by a bear. Jessa had been astonished when Jalinox allowed him and the wench to live after they failed to capture a single Magi and they failed to recover the body of the woman Magi that Baeldin had practically gift-wrapped for them.

That got Jessa thinking about the traitorous Magi, Baeldin. Jalinox had been shocked, and quite skeptical, when the large Magi approached the Stronghold and offered to make a deal. He offered to deliver the Grand Shadow of the Magi Society, in exchange for one day of access to the Magi Library. Jalinox had agreed to the deal, but Jessa was certain that he had no intention of letting Baeldin leave the Stronghold alive. Not that it mattered, they didn't capture the Grand Shadow and Baeldin disappeared into the hills. Jalinox had sent a couple of the idiots to find him, but they failed.

Jalinox began to chant the ritual prayer, which brought Jessa's thoughts back to the present. She joined him in the chant, and she could hear the wench chanting with them.

The three of them repeated the chant over and over. It was an ancient phrase in a long dead language, one that she had never heard. The one word that she recognized was Wirmyntas. Wirmyntas, she knew, was one of the long dead ancient gods.

She counted his seventh and eight repetitions of the phrase. As she chanted the phrase that Jalinox had painstakingly taught them, she realized that she was chanting a prayer to the ancient god Wirmyntas.

The wench, and the idiots, had probably never even heard of Wirmyntas. Jessa knew that people had long ago stopped worshiping the ancients, including Wirmyntas, and these days only the Pantheon of Nine held temples in most cities. If they were praying to Wirmyntas, then Jalinox had found some extremely old tomes.

Jalinox reached out and placed both hands on a skull resting on the altar. He picked up the skull and held it into the air.

For the ninth time they repeated the phrase. Then Jalinox said, "Oh great and powerful Wirmyntas, the Warden of Khalius and greatest among all deities, hear my prayer! I beckon the spirit that once lived within this skull! Send forth this spectre!"

Jessa didn't hold much hope that the long-dead ancient deity would answer his prayer. It was one thing to animate the physical corpses of the dead, but calling a spirit back from the depths of Khalius was quite different.

A shiver went down her spine. It started at the base of her neck and quickly shot down her body. At the same time she noticed that the flames of the candles begin to flicker.

She felt a growing sense of uneasiness and fear as the smell of sulfur grew heavy in the room.

A disembodied scream echoed through the room, piercing through her head like a knife. She felt terror like she'd never experienced, and she was vaguely aware of warmth running down her legs. Standing before her near the altar, in the middle of their triangle, was the mostly transparent form of a spectre.

The spectre looked at Jessa and screamed again. The piercing scream was excruciatingly painful, and she wanted to flee the place more than she had ever wanted anything in her entire life. She focused on her ritual and she struggled to keep her arms held out to the sides as she mumbled her ritual phrase over and over.

The transparent form before her was human shaped, and looked like an extremely old woman who was dressed in tattered rags. The woman's hair and tattered clothing flowed wildly about as though she was standing in extreme wind blowing chaotically from all directions. The woman's mouth was agape and her eyes were wide open. Jessa feared the spectre could see through to her own spirit.

Jalinox's voice became strained as he chanted the ritual phrase over and over, his volume and intensity increased with each repetition.

Suddenly the ghostly woman turned and rushed at the wench. The woman didn't even have the courage to look it in the eyes for a moment. She turned and ran towards the doorway, screeching as loudly as possible as she fled.

The candles nearest to the wench's corner of the triangle blew out as she fled from her spot.

That was the opening that the evil spectre needed. It flew out of the ritual triangle and chased after the wench. It easily caught her before she even got halfway to the door. When it got close, it wrapped both hands around the wench's head as she ran. The wench stopped running and reached up as if trying to pull its hands from her head. The screaming continued from both the spectre and the wench, and Jessa couldn't look away from the two.

Jalinox cursed and threw Khalius Fire at it, but the purple magic sphere passed right through the spectre and slammed into the wench instead. The spectre was completely unaffected by the necromancer's magic, but the Dark Apostle screamed in pain as the purple flame flickered upon her clothes.

Within moments the struggle was over. The wench collapsed to the floor, and Jessa was certain that the annoying woman was dead.

The spectre turned her attention to the two idiots who guarded the nearest door. Both men had their swords drawn, but it didn't seem worried about the weapons. It flew at the nearest idiot and grabbed his face with its hand. Both warriors slashed wildly at the spectre with their swords, but the weapons passed through the spirit like there was nothing there.

The idiot in the spectre's grip screamed with rage and helplessness. The spirit gazed into his eyes and screamed back at him as it held his head tightly. The man tried to turn and flee out the door, but his head was held solidly by the incorporeal entity.

Jessa had to grudgingly give the Bald-Head Idiot credit. As it held Crater-Face Idiot in place and drained his life, Bald-Head Idiot did not flee. He stayed at his friend's side, hacking desperately with his sword trying to save his friend. Unfortunately for Crater-Face, those strikes did more damage to the wall and Crater-Face than they did to the spectre.

She thought about trying to use Khalius Fire against it, but she was certain that her attempts would be no more effective than Jalinox's, and she was likely to hurt the idiot more than the evil spirit.

Finally Crater-Face Idiot stopped screaming, and slumped to the floor. Jessa almost felt bad for the idiot. She'd wanted him dead for a long time, but this death seemed even more awful than the idiot deserved.

Jalinox muttered, "By the gods."

She turned to look at what he saw, and he pointed towards the wench's body. When she looked at it, she saw a spirit rise from the ground over the body. The spirit was mostly transparent and slightly luminous like the spectre, but the face was clearly that of the wench. It wore tattered remains of the robes that the wench had been wearing.

Ezmorelda's spectre turned to Jessa and screeched.

From her left, she saw a series of Khalius Fire orbs zip past her from Jalinox, and each one passed completely through the newly formed spectre.

Jessa started launching orbs of purple Khalius Fire at the approaching spectre, but they all just passed harmlessly through it as well. She changed tactics and began throwing elemental orbs of Magi magic at the spectre. These had a little impact, and the creature continued towards her. Jessa retreated closer to Jalinox as it slowly advanced towards her.

Jalinox shouted, "Here!" He swiped his hand from the left to the right, and a large wall of purple Khalius Fire erupted across the room forming a magical barrier of fire across the entire room. The necromantic fire didn't even slow the spectre.

As she hurried closer to Jalinox, Jessa saw him fumble with something in one of his pockets. With shaky hands, he pulled a talisman from a pocket. It was made of sticks, beads, feathers, and wax. He dropped to the ground and shoved the short bone spike into the floor, and it sunk down through the stone. A moment later the beads began to glow softly and the wax melted and flowed around the talisman and onto the ground.

The spectre was almost upon them as Jalinox reached up and grabbed Jessa's hand.

She blinked her eyes, and suddenly everything changed. She was no longer in a temple; she was outside in a courtyard of some kind. In front of her was a massive manor house, and all around her was an impeccably maintained yard. There was an elaborate gazebo to her right, and a large fountain with an imposing stone statue in the middle of it to her left.

Jalinox let go of her hand, and pulled the backpack from his shoulders. He looked inside and smiled. "Fear not, my dear. We got what we went there for. It was a successful adventure!"

Before she could respond, a woman rushed out of the manor. She was dressed in servants clothing and when she got closer, Jessa saw the Dreg tattoo on her wrist.

The Dreg hurried over to Jalinox and said, "My Lord, thank the gods you're back. The emperor has summoned for you several times. He wants you right away."

He sighed, "Yes, yes. Have a carriage brought around, I'll be along shortly."

CHAPTER 25

Konrad

Alin shrugged, "I don't know. I haven't heard either. I hope it's soon, we've been here at the ranch for a fortnight now. I'm ready to attack the Stronghold and get it over with. Mostly, I want to get back together with Keta and get to Khazror so we can start rebuilding our Coterie."

Konrad nodded and said, "Me too!"

Really Konrad didn't care at all about the Khazror Coterie. However, Alin was the closest thing that he had to a friend within the Magi. They had endured the boat ride to the Dinbera Isles together, and had spent a lot of time together over the last fortnight at the Magi ranch. In his occupation, it was unusual for Konrad to build any real friendships. However, Alin was a rare exception to that. He genuinely liked the man. He hoped that he wouldn't have to kill him when things eventually got ugly.

Alin stood up. He asked, "Do you want to practice some weapon fighting, before we call it a night?"

"Absolutely!" Konrad stood up and moved away from the crate he had been sitting upon. Waiting around at the Magi ranch for so long had been frustrating, but the combat lessons made it worthwhile. The combat instructor, an old Fighter's Guild Master named Thon, taught combat skills daily and all able-bodied Magi were required to attend every day. Konrad had been fighting hand-to-hand and with various weapons since he was old enough to walk, so at first he expected Thon's lessons to be worthless. However, the old man taught weapon fighting mixed with magic use and Konrad looked forward to every lesson. Over the past fortnight he'd learned a great many tricks for integrating magic use into his already impressive combat skills, and he was eager to absorb as much as the old man could teach him while there was still time.

His practice sessions with Alin gave him a chance to perfect the things he learned from Thon earlier in the day. Konrad liked to practice with a variety of different weapons. Sometimes he used a sword, and occasionally he used a club or a staff. Tonight he was wearing two daggers, and he had been looking forward to some practice with them.

Alin almost always fought with a sword. Konrad had been impressed with the Magi's sword skills when they first started working together. Over the past fortnight, Alin's skills had grown considerably. The man was a quick learner, and his lessons with Thon and practice with Konrad had paid off quite well. Konrad considered Alin to be at least as skilled as any imperial sentinel that he'd seen, and, with magic, Konrad was sure that Alin could easily best most sword fighters in the known world.

Konrad said, "Tonight, let's practice with me doing only defense."

Alin nodded his acknowledgement, and drew his sword. It was common for them to do matches where one or the other could only defend. That was a tool that Thon advocated, and one that Konrad had grown to enjoy. It gave the attacker the freedom to attack without having to worry about counters, to force the other partner to really improve their defensive skills. As Thon so often said, offense wins the battle but defense keeps you alive long enough to enjoy the win.

Drawing two daggers, Konrad squared-off against Alin. Using two little blades against a sword put him at a disadvantage. Only being able to fight defensively put him at an even greater disadvantage. The main reason to use two daggers was to use speed to quickly end a battle. In a prolonged confrontation using daggers against an opponent with a sword, defeat (usually meaning death) was always just one tiny mistake away.

That was exactly why he wanted to practice it. As Thon said many times, don't be embarrassed to make mistakes in practice. Learn from them so they don't happen when it counts. That was a new and radical concept for Konrad. All his life he'd trained with masters and senior students who gloated with every practice victory. It created a training atmosphere where he never wanted to try new things because every training exercise was about winning at all costs. It wasn't until he trained with Thon that he discovered that losing in practice might be even more beneficial than winning in practice because it revealed areas for improvement.

That's where having Alin as a training partner had been such a benefit. The man seemed to have no ego what-so-ever. They had sparred dozens of times, and Konrad never felt like the man needed to one-up him. It was much easier to try new things, and accept a training defeat, when the partner didn't brag about it.

Without warning, Alin attacked with a flurry of sword strikes. They were both using live blades, and clearly Alin was attacking with every intention of landing the blows. By now they knew each other well enough to know that neither of them wanted their partner to play it safe. They were both confident that any killing blows would be pulled back at the last moment if they weren't blocked properly.

Konrad moved smoothly, responding to each of Alin's cuts with practiced grace. At this point he wasn't even using the daggers to block, he simply watched Alin's body movement and arm movement, and anticipated the sword strike before it even happened which allowed him to smoothly evade each attack without needing to block.

After a few dozen attacks in rapid succession, Alin threw in his first tricky movement. He stepped forward and raised the sword above his head for a downward vertical strike. Konrad read the strike properly and moved to his left to evade it. However, halfway through the strike Alin redirected the blow into a horizontal cut, coming straight at Konrad's neck.

He had no time to move out of the way because his current movement to avoid what he expected to be a vertical cut made it almost impossible to properly duck to avoid the horizontal attack. So, he was forced to throw out his first magic trick. He quickly summoned a small amount of magic and threw a magical shield out in front of him. The sword slammed into the invisible shield, and completely stopped Alin's attack. The sword stopped instantly, as if it had just hit a stone wall.

Alin staggered back a step, and re-centered the sword between them. If Konrad wasn't fighting fully defensively, he would have used the disruption to launch a counter attack.

The magic shield was a magical defense with almost no finesse, and Konrad didn't like using it. There were so many other tricks he could have used, and many of them would have been preferable. However, most of them were offensive in nature so he tried to avoid them in this training exercise. Besides, he needed to get better with the magic shield because it could save his skin in dire situations.

For another ten minutes the two men sparred. Konrad tried out a few other tricks that he'd learned recently. Alin threw in several magic tricks as well, and for the most part Konrad was content working on his footwork and reaction skills while Alin practiced incorporating magic with the sword work.

All too soon, Alin said it was time to stop. He wanted to get to bed early so that he could go fishing in the morning.

Konrad was disappointed to end the training already. He'd never enjoyed fishing all that much. He preferred to leave the fishing and food preparations to others.

Alin said, "Pleasant rest. Keep your tent sealed, I heard some of the other Magi waking up with snakes in the tent with them!"

Konrad laughed. "Snakes fear me."

The two men laughed together for a moment, and then Alin walked off towards his tent.

Konrad sat back down on the crate he'd been sitting on earlier, and watched Alin walk off. Once the Magi got to his tent, he turned his attention to the rest of the ranch.

Off to his left was a large barn, where all of the Order Magi slept. He hadn't been inside the barn, but he assumed that the seven Order Magi probably had much nicer accommodations than the twenty Society Magi who slept in tents outside of the barn.

He knew that those twenty Society Magi were made up of the four members of Khazror Coterie which was led by Keta and included himself. Then there were the nine Society Magi from the Sorgo Coterie which was led by Thon.

There were two Society Magi from the barbarian lands, but he hadn't talked to either of them.

That left the five Society Magi from the Libur Coterie which was led by some woman named Eleyne. Those Magi had arrived shortly after he did, and their arrival was met with some drama, because six of their Society Magi had been killed by imperial agents the day before Eleyne brought her Coterie to the ranch. Of the five remaining Society Magi in the Libur Coterie, one of them stood out to Konrad as suspicious. She was a woman named Jewli. He had tried to get to know her, to see if she was also an agent of the emperor, but he had yet found an opportunity to talk to her alone. For some reason she had been absent from the ranch for two full days recently.

If Jewli wasn't an agent of the emperor, then he figured it was an agent working from outside of the Society who lead the ambush on the Libur Magi. Whoever it was, that person was Konrad's rival and someone he needed to watch. While he was embedded within the Magi other imperial agents were making progress and stealing his glory. Even though he had led the raid in Sorgo last year, and even though he had earned a great deal of status and coin from those achievements, he still had much to lose. The emperor wasn't one to let his agents rest on old accomplishments, and if Konrad wanted to stay on the emperor's good side he would need to do something impressive very soon.

Movement to the east brought his attention back to the Magi ranch. The tents gathered near the barn weren't the only place where the Society Magi gathered. Off to the east was a large home, owned by one of the Magi named Uli. There were another dozen Society Magi who slept in that house, but they were all elderly Magi who didn't participate in the daily training and wouldn't be going to help conquer the Stronghold. He didn't know any of them, but it was said that they were all old Magi from the barbarian lands.

All together that made well over three dozen Magi just at this ranch. He had no idea how many others were out there throughout the known-lands who hadn't yet come to the ranch. Clearly the Magi Society was much more organized and expansive than the emperor realized. That was not information that Konrad was willing to take to the emperor, at least not without including a high body-count of dead Magi to keep the emperor from lashing out unexpectedly. He wasn't known for his patience.

Once again he thought about sneaking out of the camp and getting back to his contacts. He could lead an army to wipe out the Magi once and for all, and he would be welcomed into Clornoss has a hero. He'd be rich and more famous than he could imagine. It was an option that tempted him on a daily basis.

The one thing keeping him from going through with it was the unknown knowledge and potential powers he might gain once the Magi take over the Stronghold. If the rumors were to be believed, the Stronghold housed spell books and artifacts of unimaginable power. If he could just wait until after the Magi captured the Stronghold, there was no telling what spells he might learn, or what powers he could gain. Personal power was so much more appealing than personal wealth.

For now, that thirst for power kept him loyal to the Magi.

He watched as the last sliver of the sun dropped below the horizon. With the low clouds in the west, the western sky took on a nice orange glow. For several minutes he enjoyed watching the cloud shapes as they slowly slid across the darkening sky.

Then he noticed someone coming out of the barn and his heart skipped a beat. He knew instantly that it was Keta, heading out for her evening walk. Once again he wondered whether the woman had cast some kind of spell on him, because she captivated him.

He jumped down from the crate and stepped between two tents, and dropped a *Shadow Shroud* spell on himself. He followed her, far enough back that she couldn't hear him. Not that she would notice, he had followed her many times during her nighttime walks, and she rarely turned around or paid much attention as she walked.

Each night when she walked she took a different route. He didn't know if she was scouting the surrounding lands, or if she just liked walking a varied path. Tonight was no different.

He followed her for over an hour and eventually she walked into a large grove of trees. He followed her into the trees and after a bit she walked to the shore of a large pond. She leaned against a large rock near the water and took off her boots.

Konrad settled in behind a fallen tree and got comfortable.

When she had her boots off, she started pulling off other clothes. First to come off was her tunic followed by her breeches. She folded them both carefully and placed them on the rock beside her.

He watched with growing interest as she began removing her small clothes and placing them neatly on top of the other garments. Before long she stood naked in the moonlight, and then she walked slowly to the water. With one foot she tested it.

He wanted nothing more than to join her in the lake. He had been with many women, but there was something alluring and enchanting about this Magi woman.

As she walked slowly into the water, it took all of his control to resist the desire to join her. The animal within screamed at him that the water would make the perfect place for the games that he wanted to play with her.

The self-preservation side of him forced him to maintain his control and leave her alone. She was not like other women and if she said 'no', she would actually have power to enforce 'no'. Since she was one of the Order of Champions Magi, he didn't know the extent of her magical abilities. However, he was certain that she had access to a great deal of magic power than he did not possess. He hadn't seen her fight yet, and he certainly didn't want to learn the extent of her abilities first hand.

That power made her all the more enthralling to him. He struggled to resist his urges as he watched her fully submerge herself in the pond, leaving only her head and shoulders above the water.

The longer he watched her the less control he felt, and he stood up to move over to the pond. As he stepped towards her he heard the unmistakable sound of a horse and rider somewhere nearby. He cursed viciously, but silently, as he turned to his left to see who was coming to ruin his fun.

Off in the distance, near the edge of the wooded grove, he saw a man on horseback. The rider couldn't see him, because he still had his shroud spell around him. However, the rider was looking for something.

Curiosity won out over lust, and he moved towards the horseman to see who was invading the grove. He thought that perhaps he could kill the rider quickly, and still get back to Keta before the mood was ruined.

He assumed the rider was a local farmer or rancher, possibly even the barbarian who thought he owned this grove. Konrad didn't mind killing a barbarian. It'd been too long since he'd killed a man anyway, he was afraid he was starting to get too soft by living with the Magi for so long.

As he got closer he saw the imperial soldier's tabard, and his heart sank. He recognized the armor and horse tack of a scout when he saw it.

This far into the barbarian lands, there was only one reason to see an imperial scout. Someone had already alerted the imperials to the Magi gathering at the ranch. His suspicions jumped first to the Magi from Libur Coterie, Jewli. He couldn't help but wonder if her two day absence had been to make contact with imperials to report the location of the Magi ranch.

If there was a scout then somewhere nearby there had to be a large army, and it was only a matter of time before they descended on the Magi at the ranch.

All thoughts of Keta and lewd fun were gone. He had missed his opportunity. Jewli or some other agent knew about the location of the Magi, and had claimed the prize for him or herself. Konrad had waited too long, and someone else was about to get all of the glory.

He cursed silently again. His mind was reeling, and he didn't know what to do. He could fight alongside the Magi, and help them defeat the imperials. Then his rivals would be killed or humiliated, leaving Konrad to claim the glory for himself later.

On the other hand, he could fight on the side of the imperials, and try to kill as many of the Magi as he could. There was still some glory to be had that way, and if he killed enough Magi he might still gain some favor with the emperor.

However, if he chose the losing side it would cost him everything. It became obvious that his best option was to bide his time. When it became clear which side was going to win, he'd swoop in and aid that side.

Konrad was a winner, and it was imperative that he come out on the winning side in the upcoming battle. Much of the future would be decided from events that were quickly unfolding.

The scout moved further into the grove, and Konrad moved to stay out of his way.

CHAPTER 26

Rissyl

Ayris walked into the room carrying a cup of warm milk.

"You're up late, shouldn't you be sleeping? You're a growing girl, you need your rest."

The girl stuck her tongue out at Rissyl as she walked past him. She walked over to the bed and handed Sarasa the cup. She said, "Randol wants you to drink this. It's a different herb mixture; it might help with the pain."

Rissyl mussed her hair. "Thanks kiddo, now off to bed. It's really late."

"Is Cynia coming back tonight?"

He shook his head, "No, not tonight. She's getting the Magi ready. She'll be sleeping at the ranch tonight."

Ayris grumbled as she trudged out of the room.

He looked over to Sarasa. She was laying on a bed in one of the many rooms in the basement of Randol's house. It has been a fortnight and a half since he'd brought her here. The teleportation was traumatic for both of them and, if Randol was to be believed, Rissyl and Sarasa almost both died that day. Rissyl had no memories from the first six or seven days after teleporting with Sarasa from the Stronghold.

Over the last fortnight, he had completely recovered and he felt fine. Sarasa's recovery had been much slower.

She was getting stronger, and the two of them had even gone for a few short walks recently. Even that amount of exertion seemed to drain her quickly, but the woman was remarkably strong and he was pleased to see her finally looking like she might recover fully in time.

He felt responsible for her injuries, since he had agreed to her plan to rush off to the Stronghold practically alone. It was a decision that he made against his better judgment, and completely ignoring his intuitions and better sense. He vowed not to let that happen again.

He had spent the majority of his time sitting beside her bed since he recovered. Each night he slept on the floor next to her bed, so he was there if she woke up in the middle of the night and needed assistance.

Ayris had been a huge help as well. The girl was constantly coming to check on them both, usually at Randol's direction.

When Randol and Ayris weren't sitting with them, it was typically just Rissyl and Sarasa sitting together day after day during her recovery. At first he spent many hours reading books to her from Randol's library. However, recently she'd been feeling strong enough to read the books on her own, so he silently sat at her side.

Dalen and Bran had visited frequently, and those visits gave Rissyl a chance to travel to the ranch and check the progress of preparations there for the assault on the Stronghold, as well as the inevitable conflicts with the empire, not to mention the possible conflicts with the Rolimi.

For the most part Cynia was in charge of preparations at the ranch, and Rissyl was extremely grateful for all of her work there. Dalen had been working on crafting wands with the wood received from the tribal elves on the Isles. Rissyl was happy to see progress in that aspect of their plans.

Cynia had been dividing her time between the ranch, Randol's house, and their home. She wasn't able to spend nearly as much time with their son as they'd like, and they'd even talked about bringing Chardy to Randol's house so that Rissyl could spend more time with him. In the end they decided that he was probably better off in the care of Cynia's grandparents and the nursemaid Gwen.

Rissyl knew that he couldn't ask for a more amazing partner. Most women would have been very jealous of the care and attention that he'd been giving to Sarasa, especially given the history between the three of them. Cynia had not shown a hint of jealousy. Sometimes she slept on the floor next to Rissyl near Sarasa's bed, but most of the time she slept at home or at the ranch. He hadn't told her how much he appreciated her trust and support, but he was confident that she knew.

Sarasa finished drinking the milk that Ayris had brought her.

Rissyl took the cup and placed it on the dresser. He said, "Are you about ready for bed? You're still looking pretty ragged; you're going to need all the beauty-sleep that you can get."

She teasingly flashed him a rude gesture. She asked, "What have I missed? Have there been any more attacks from the emperor's troops?"

He didn't want to trouble her with bad news, but he wasn't willing to lie to her. "There have been rumors of imperial troops doing raids in many of the cities. Some say that innocent people have been accused of using magic, and troops show up and pull them from their homes. Those who aren't killed are dragged away and made Dregs."

She sighed. "That happened during the times of the Betrayal too. It's bound to get worse before it gets better. Our emperor's grandfather, Ryal I, slaughtered countless innocents that way."

Rissyl nodded, "I remember the stories you've told. Let us hope that Emperor Ryal III is more sane than his grandfather."

She nodded as she sat up in her bed and slowly moved her feet to the floor. She asked, "Would you hand me the chamber pot please?"

He grabbed the chamber pot from under the dresser. He handed it to her and walked out of the room to give her some privacy as she relieved herself.

When she finished, she called him back in. He carried the simple metal pot to the other side of the room and placed it on the floor near the door so that Ayris could empty it and wash it out in the morning.

When he sat back down on the floor next to her bed, she reached out and grabbed his hand. She squeezed it and then she tucked her hand under her chin. "Good night, Riz. Thanks for taking care of me." At first he thought she was going to say more, but after a moment she closed her eyes and he could hear her quickly drifting off to sleep.

He settled into his blankets next to her bed. He loved her, and he was starting to come to grips with his feelings. The part that surprised him was that he no longer felt conflicting desires between Sarasa and Cynia. Over the past fortnight his feelings for Sarasa had changed noticeably. His love and affection for her had grown, but it had transformed somehow. He didn't look at her as an object of his desires; his love for her had grown beyond that. Perhaps it was that he had grown as a man, and he was no longer blinded by lust and desires that he didn't understand.

He knew that he and Sarasa would never be a couple, and he was at peace with that.

He loved Cynia as a man should love his wife, and she was the one he wanted in that way. His feelings for Sarasa were strong, but they were different. For a while he thought that it might be best described like the love of a sister or child. However, that wasn't quite right. It was more like the deep affection that a person felt towards a treasured friend and companion.

He closed his eyes and let his thoughts wonder to Cynia. It'd been too long since the two of them had enjoyed any quality time together. He promised himself that the next time Dalen came to visit Sarasa that he was going to find a way to sneak away with Cynia for a few hours.

Suddenly the door slammed open and Ayris rushed in and threw herself to her knees next to Rissyl. She grabbed him with both hands and started shaking him, like she was trying to wake him up. She was crying hysterically, and trying to talk at the same time.

He couldn't understand anything she was saying. He placed his hand on her shoulder as he sat up. He said, "Calm down. What are you trying to say?"

She took a deep breath, and then said, "The armies are going to attack! The Magi are going to die!" She started crying and breathing heavily again.

He smiled and caressed her hair. "It's ok, Ayris. It was only a dream. Try to calm down and get back to sleep."

She shoved his hand away. "No! It's not just a dream! You're not listening 'cause I'm little! Cynia is in danger! The armies are coming for her, and all of the Magi! They gotta flee!"

Rissyl was starting to get a little alarmed, because the girl hadn't acted that way before, but he was still convinced that she was dreaming. He smiled slightly, to reassure her that things would be fine.

She poked him in the chest, hard. She said, "Dammit Rissyl, listen to me! This happened before, the night before my parents died. I dreamed it would happen." She looked away from him. "And I dreamed about you and Cynia that night before I'd ever met you."

He felt a cold chill run down his spine. She was little, but she'd already shown several times that she possessed magical abilities that they didn't understand. After a moment he said, "Go tell Randol that I'm bringing the Magi here."

He dressed quickly and then he summoned his cloak and staff.

In a groggy voice, Sarasa asked, "What's wrong, Riz? Was Ayris in here?"

"Yes, I think she had some sort of vision. She thinks that the emperor is sending his men to attack the ranch. I'm going to bring them here, now."

She grabbed his hand and held it for a moment. She said, "Be careful."

He kissed her forehead. "Of course!"

He stood there for a moment, and then said, "*Kur'Gezbar*."

The vertigo hit him immediately, like it always did when he teleported, and he reached out for a wall of the barn to help steady his shaking knees.

The barn interior was dark. There were a few light orbs stuck to walls and bunks as some of the Magi studied spell books, but for the most part the barn was quiet.

He walked quietly to Cynia's bunk, and found her asleep with her nose buried in one of his old tunics. He bent down and kissed her cheek softly. He said, "Cynia, wake up."

She woke with a start, and sat up. "Riz! What are you doing here, is something wrong?"

"Ayris woke from a vision of some sort; she thinks the emperor is sending his troops to attack the ranch." She looked skeptical, and he added, "She said she had a vision like this the night before her parents were killed."

Cynia stood up. She said, "Dalen is here too." She tossed his shirt, which she had been snuggling, on her bunk as they walked away from it.

He raised his eyebrow.

She shrugged. "It smells like you. It comforts me."

"I'm sorry, Cynia. Things will be back to normal soon, I promise."

"There's no such thing as normal, not for us."

He didn't respond and they walked to the far side of the barn where the men had their bunks setup.

She added, "But Dalen's gonna need to take a turn sleeping next to Sarasa, or she is going to find out just how needy your woman really is."

She gave him a playful grin, and he hugged her close as they walked up to Dalen's bunk.

He looked up from his spell book as they walked in through his curtains. He said, "You two look like you're up to something. What's up?"

Rissyl let go of Cynia. He said, "She's being dirty again. But that's not why we're here."

Dalen closed his spell book. He said, "I would hope not, you weirdo!"

Rissyl told him about Ayris' vision.

When Rissyl finished explaining it, Dalen stood up and slipped on his traveling clothes. He summoned his cloak and both swords, and then he said, "I think we've waited long enough. If we wait too long, the emperor is going to catch up with us and ruin our chances to take the Stronghold. It's time to act."

Cynia asked, "Do we have enough wands already?"

Dalen nodded, "I've crafted six of them, that will have to be enough."

Rissyl thought for a moment. Then he asked, "Are we all in agreement? We launch the attack on the Stronghold, tonight?"

They both nodded.

He looked at Cynia, "Okay, you and I will spread the word with the Magi who will be going with us." He then looked to Dalen, "Would you spread the word to the others who are staying behind? They should evacuate to Randol's as soon as the rest of us have ported to the Stronghold."

Dalen nodded.

Rissyl looked back to Cynia, "Make sure everyone knows that we're leaving immediately. They should leave the tents and camps setup here. They'll need a backpack, and only the most vital things that they need to carry into combat. We'll worry about food and provisions when the fighting is over."

CHAPTER 27

Ferth

This was complete chaos, and there was very little that Ferth hated more than chaos. There were just four things, actually, that Ferth hated more than chaos. While boats had been recently added as item number nine on his Sarding Grubby Chippies list, bumping the other items on the list down one place, chaos had been at number five since he was a young man. He enjoyed order and routine, and chaos made his head want to explode.

They'd been training for many days, but when the time to attack the Stronghold finally arrived, most of the Society Magi acted like they were headless chickens.

It had been nearly an hour since the Magi had started porting to the Stronghold, and the chaos had started almost immediately. It didn't help that the command to attack came in the middle of the night while most of the Magi were sleeping. It also didn't help that the order to attack came with warnings of an imminent ambush by the imperial army, so everyone rushed around in a half-asleep daze trying to gather everything they'd need for battle.

Only four Magi could use the portal stone at a time, and since no planning or practice had been done to organize the teleporting, the actual act of teleporting was not nearly as smooth as it could have been. Once everyone had ported to the Stronghold portal stone, Rissyl had divided the Magi into three units.

Unit one was led by Rissyl and it consisted of Thon, the nine Society Magi in his Sorgo Coterie, and some new guy named Bran. That unit would be attacking up the center directly at the main gates of the Stronghold.

Unit two was led by Dalen. It consisted of Eleyne and the five remaining Society Magi in her Libur Coterie as well as Zahr, Aruk, and the two Society Magi who made up what was being called the Free Cities Coterie. That unit would be attacking on the west flank.

Unit three was led by Cynia. Ferth was a part of this unit with the three Society Magi from his Maethral Coterie: Asha, Bull, and Peke. Also in their unit were Keta and her Khazror Coterie which was made up of four Society

Magi, including Konrad and Alin. A Free Cities Order of Evokers Magi named Firana was also a part of their unit. They were moving to the east to take position on the right of the others so they could attack on that flank when Rissyl gave the signal.

Even though things had been chaotic, Ferth was impressed that three of the principle officers of the society were personally leading the attack.

All together there were thirty-four Magi preparing to attack the Stronghold, with eleven or twelve in each unit. All of the rest of the Magi from the ranch, all of those too old to fight, were evacuating to Randol's home. He wasn't sure how many old Magi were at the ranch because many of them spent most of their time in the large house and didn't spend much time at the barn or within the tent area where the other Magi had lived. He guessed there were a dozen or more.

Ferth stepped in a small hole and promptly fell to the ground as his unit moved to their position in the darkness. He cursed quietly as Keta reached down to help him up. His pride hurt more than anything as he let her help him to his feet. He tested his right leg and his knee felt fine, but his ankle was going to be sore.

His first few steps were tentative, as he tested his ankle. Luckily it just seemed like a minor twisting, and each step felt a little better than the last as the group continued its march without pausing.

After a few steps he pulled his arm away from Keta. He wanted to ask her where she had been. When the initial command went through the camp, Keta was nowhere to be found. Neither was one of her Society Magi, a man named Konrad. The two of them returned to camp sometime after the command to assemble went through camp, but before everyone had ported to the Stronghold.

He wanted to trust Keta, because she seemed like a nice woman and she was the leader of a Coterie. However, ever since the word of an imperial ambush on the ranch had started circulating, everyone had been whispering that they must have a traitor in their ranks. How else could the emperor have known where the Magi were located?

He had to at least consider that Keta and Konrad were the most suspicious at this point. Perhaps they had just wandered off for a roll in the hay, but he was not ready to cross them off the list of potential traitors just yet.

To make matters worse, before porting to the Stronghold, Rissyl had warned the group that a Society Magi named Baeldin had gone rogue and had killed Uli and tried to get Sarasa killed right here at the Stronghold almost a month ago. No one knew where Baeldin had gone, what his motivations were, or whether he would try to hamper the Magi as they tried to retake the Stronghold.

To make matters even worse than that, they had absolutely no idea how many necromancers to expect. Rissyl had said that Sarasa warned that the necromancers had learned new spells and have some new type of Awakened in their control. However, there was no telling what other threats they faced from the necromancers during this attack.

They had all slowed their pace a bit after Ferth tripped in the hole. The moon and stars gave a little light to the evening, but the field was still extremely dark and no one wanted to be the person to be taken out of the battle by blowing out a knee because of a rabbit hole.

Ferth looked to the others in the unit with some alarm as he heard several quiet curses and exclamations of surprise. He saw a large dark shape in the middle of their unit, and his heart skipped a beat until he realized that the large panther with them was actually Cynia. Ferth had heard stories that Diviners could shape-change, but this was the first time he'd seen it in person.

As they walked in the darkness, he kept glancing over at the panther who was Cynia. He was happy with his choice to become an Evoker, but part of him was a bit jealous of the Diviners. The power to teleport at will was nice, and a strong command over primal elements was great. However, he did feel some disappointment that he'd never know what it was like to prowl through the grass as a great cat or soar through the air as a bird of prey.

Ferth tried to focus on the problems at hand. He looked to the other people in his unit. He was confident that the people from his Coterie were not traitors, he was also confident that Cynia could be trusted. He didn't know much about Firana, and as far as he was concerned the entire Khazror Coterie was suspect at this point.

He noticed Firana cast a quick spell and summoned a small bear to her side. Ferth decided he should probably summon a companion now before the battle got underway. As an Evoker he couldn't shape-change, but he could summon an animal to aid him in battle. The animal that he was currently tied to for his summoning was a large Oodasian Tiger.

He formed the spell quickly and whispered, "Krol'Zi Taldium." A moment later he saw the tiger appear next to him. The animal seemed slightly disoriented at first, but it saw him walking and it quickly fell into step next to him. Ferth wondered what the animal had been doing before being summoned to his side. He hoped he didn't catch the tiger at a bad time. It seemed a silly thing to wonder about, but he hoped that the large cat wasn't about to catch his dinner or get wild and crazy with a mate.

After a bit, the panther stopped walking. The others stopped and looked to Ferth. They were in the general area where they were supposed to wait for Rissyl's signal to attack. He sat down on the ground and worked out his sore ankle.

As he sat there waiting for the signal, he thought about the other concern that was on everyone's mind, although no one was talking about it. The Rolimi. No one knew if the Rolimi were going to attack, and having to fight them along with whatever else they faced to capture the Stronghold would be phenomenally bad. He felt a chill crawl up his spine as he considered how quickly everything could fall apart.

The tiger grumbled a low growl, and plopped onto the ground next to him. He casually scratched the cat's head, next to its ear, as they sat there.

He looked to the north and off in the distance he could see the darkness that must be the Stronghold. He couldn't make out any features, but the various shapes were probably buildings. They were too far away to see if anyone was standing on any of the walls or other defenses.

Bull and Peke sat down next to him quietly.

After a few moments, Bull said, "It's a nice night out."

Ferth looked over at the large man and gave him a dirty look.

Bull looked hurt. "What? The breeze feels good."

"Some of us aren't going to live to see the Stronghold controlled by the Magi. You realize that, right?"

Bull nodded, "Many of us will live to see the Stronghold controlled by the Magi! I'm confident of that, and it fills me with excitement. Just imagine all of the things we'll learn, the power we will have, once we control it."

Peke nodded his agreement.

Ferth usually found Bull's positive attitude to be a bit annoying. However, with a major battle looming, he had to admit that his friend's optimism was a helpful spark.

He said, "Fine, we'll go with that. Just keep yourselves alive so we can enjoy the spoils of victory together."

Before either man could reply, the sky to the west lit up brightly as a large fireball launched towards the Stronghold. He could hear shouts and battle cries from the west as the first unit began the attack.

He saw the panther streak off quickly towards the Stronghold. He stood up and shouted, "Let's go!"

Ten Magi, a tiger, and a small bear rushed after Cynia the panther. In the excitement and nervousness immediately preceding the battle, several of the Magi shouted out battle cries as they rushed towards the enemy.

Ferth murmured a quick prayer to whichever god happened to be listening, asking for courage and protection. He wasn't really a religious man, but in the face of battle it couldn't hurt to have a little divine assistance.

The outer wall of the Stronghold grew close quickly as they rushed towards it. Soon he could see a line of people standing outside of the walls motionless. Their forms became clearer as he got closer to them, and the green glow of their eyes drew his attention. It looked eerie in the darkness. Then he was able to see that most of the forms standing outside of the wall were at least partially skeletal. Some of them were just skeletons with no muscle or skin coverings at all, but most of them had as least some muscle and skin left.

The sight was almost enough to turn his stomach. He stopped running and lowered his staff to launch a fire orb at one of the closest horrific creatures. The orb shot out from the tip of his staff and slammed into the stomach of the creature. The tattered remains of clothing and skin caught fire, but the green-glowing eyed Awakened didn't even seem to notice the flames.

The panther reached the creatures first. Ferth saw her pounce into one of the Awakened and slammed it against the wall. The tiger and the bear both engaged the creatures a fraction of a second after she did.

As Ferth pointed his staff to launch another fire orb, he saw that several of the Society Magi had moved into melee combat range with the skeletal Awakened creatures. He changed targets to keep from hitting one of his own people. As soon as Magi got close to them, the skeletal Awakened began attacking with surprising quickness.

Even though they had spells which they could use against the creatures, the Society Magi needed to rely primarily on their melee weapon skills. The magewels of the brown and white cloaked Society Magi were generally smaller than those of the Order Magi, and the Society Magi's spells consumed the magical essence within their magewels more quickly. That was the reason for the focus on making sure the Society Magi knew how to fight with standard weapons. They could use their magic to aid their standard combat, without draining their magewel too quickly.

Ferth lobbed several fire orbs at some of the creatures, and he watched the progress of the Magi spread out before him. Slightly to his right he saw a brown and white cloaked Magi stagger backwards and fall to one knee. The Society Magi dropped his weapon as he fell, and Ferth saw him raise a hand to cast a spell. The skeletal Awakened hacked recklessly with its sword over and over, quickly overpowering the kneeling Magi.

Further to his right he saw Firana. She was also standing away from the fighting. Like Ferth, she launched fire orbs at the creatures one after another.

The battle was not starting out well. With easily a dozen creatures in their immediate area, and more moving over from the left and right, the Magi had made no progress. Already a Magi was motionless in the grass, and not a single Awakened creature had been killed.

The three animals, including Cynia, seemed to make progress. They tore flesh from the bones and scattered bones across the battlefield. However, as quickly as they ripped opponents apart, those Awakened spontaneously rebuilt themselves.

It was the creepiest thing Ferth had ever seen. All around the battlefield in front of him, bones were flying through the air. As the battles scattered skeletal bones away from the creatures, the bones simply few back and reassembled the creatures a few moments later.

Ferth decided to change elements, and lowered his staff at a skeletal Awakened joining the battle from his left. He summoned a bolt of lightning from the gem of the staff, which raced at the creature causing a thunder clap to echo around him. The lightning slammed into the creature, tossing it into the wall. After a moment, the creature turned and rushed at Ferth.

He stepped back a step, and launched more lightning at the Awakened creature. Each time the creature staggered back a step, but its relentless run towards him could not be stopped.

As the creature got almost close enough to engage in melee combat, Ferth spun his staff in a wide circle in front of him, then he redirected the motion into a circle above his head and then around his back. The constant spinning of the staff continued to increase the speed and power of the whirling weapon. As the staff crossed behind his back, and once again into his right hand, he caused the spinning to redirect into an additional spin over his head. He kept the momentum going as he stepped forward and leveled the staff into a horizontal strike towards the skeletal Awakened's head. At the last moment, just as the deadly spin brought the end of the staff directly at the creature's head, Ferth summoned a small amount of magic and shoved the staff with a little bit of magic force to deliver even more momentum to the weapon.

The weapon slammed into the creature's exposed skull with amazing speed and power. The creature's skull exploded into thousands of tiny pieces, and the rest of the creature fell to the ground.

Ferth struggled to gracefully bring the staff's momentum to a halt. The creature's skull gave almost no resistance to the deadly spinning weapon, and the staff almost went spinning from his hands as it passed through the creature's skull. He breathed heavily as he brought the weapon back to a guard position in front of him, preparing for when the Awakened skeleton reassembled.

His heart was pounding heavily in his chest, as he took a few steps backwards. He continued to watch the undead creature, but it did not stand up. The bones were scattered in a heap before him, and none of them were reassembling.

He shouted in triumph. As he looked around he realized that another Magi had gone down, and his tiger looked like it wasn't going to last much longer. He scanned the battlefield before him until he found Bull, Asha, and Peke all alive and seemingly unharmed. However, all of them were locked in deadly battles against relentless magical foes.

Ferth ran towards them. As he ran, he shouted, "You have to crush their skulls! They'll die if you break their head!"

The knowledge of how to kill the skeletal Awakened quickly turned the tide of the battle, and before long the Magi had defeated all of the creatures in their immediate area. Ferth and Firana both joined in the melee battles against the creatures, using their long staffs as deadly skull-smashing tools of death.

From the corner of his eye Ferth saw Keta smash the skull of one of the partially skeletal Awakened, as her heavy sword cleaved right through it. The creature collapsed immediately in a heap of rotting flesh and bone.

More skeletal Awakened continued to approach from the left and right, but they were dealt with quickly as they arrived.

Cynia placed her hand on his shoulder from behind, and he almost jumped out of his skin. He didn't see her change her shape back to her human form, but she stood next to him as her normal self. She was holding her staff and wearing her green and white cloak.

She said, "Let's start making our way to the west, to meet up with Riz and his unit. We need to make sure they know how to kill these things."

He nodded, "Agreed."

Cynia rushed past him, shouting, "Everyone to the west! Keta, see to our wounded."

CHAPTER 28

Rissyl

Small shards of bone pelted Rissyl in the face as he smashed his staff down onto the head of another Awakened creature. The grounds in front of the Stronghold gate were thick with the green glowing-eyed horrors. He didn't have time to guess how many there were because as soon as he smashed the skull of one, there were four others trying to surround him.

The battle started out poorly, and they quickly lost three or four Magi to the swarm of undead creatures. Once they figured out how to kill the monsters, things had gotten better.

It had become a dance. He stepped to the left, spun his staff around his head once and then leveled it into a horizontal smash to kill one of the Awakened to his left. As soon as that one was dead he stepped to his right, spun his staff around his head and leveled it into a horizontal strike to kill another. Sometimes he turned to his rear, spun the staff vertically and let the end smash directly down onto the top of the Awakened creature's skull. Other times he pressed forward and engaged an enemy before him to his left or right.

All around him, his fellow Magi fought hard. Off to his left was Thon in his blue and white cloak of the Order of Champions. The old fighter killed two or three monsters for everyone one that Rissyl managed to kill. The remaining Society Magi were also making excellent progress against the swarms of undead.

He kept looking towards the tops of the Stronghold walls, and scanning around the battlefield looking for the necromancers who must be controlling these creatures. As far as he knew, a single necromancer could only control a dozen or so Awakened. At that rate, that would mean that there were dozens if not a hundred or more necromancers somewhere nearby. However, he had not seen a single streak of purple necromancer fire since the battle began.

A loud low scraping sound from his right caught his attention, and between attacks Rissyl looked to his right. He saw the main gate to the Stronghold open slightly and a large malformed creature walked from within the Stronghold. He recognized it immediately as a Motlite. The magic-absorbing abominations had been almost unbeatable last year, but this time the Magi were prepared. The Dinberian oak wand should be able to kill the creatures, if the information in the book Sarasa found was accurate.

The Motlite shoved its way through swarms of Awakened skeletons to get at the nearest Magi. As it pushed its way away from the gate, two more Motlites walked from within the Stronghold. A smaller human soldier walked out with them, brandishing a sword and screaming obscenities.

Rissyl and Thon both had Dinberian oak wands, the other four wands were with the other two units. He tried to reach down to his belt to grab his wand, but each time he did another Awakened skeleton attacked and he had to use his staff to block the attack or bash the creature in the head.

He started moving back away from the gate, to keep distance between himself and the Motlites until he could afford a moment to grab his wand. He blocked the sword attack of a nearby skeletal Awakened, and quickly redirected the staff's momentum to cave-in the creature's skull. It dropped at his feet, and he backed up carefully. The ground was completely littered with random bones and body parts, and he had to move his feet carefully to avoid slipping and falling.

From his left he heard a sharp buzzing sound zipping past him. He looked up to see a reddish orange light streaking past him. It slammed into the nearest Motlite and the creature screamed in agony. The sharp buzzing sound repeated time and again as Rissyl fell back into block-and-attack dances with swarming skeletons. Each reddish orange streak was immediately followed by the anguished screeches of the Motlite.

When he glanced up he saw that the large creature had stumbled to a knee, but still Thon launched volley after volley of attacks from the Dinberian oak wand. When the first Motlite fell to the ground, Thon changed targets to the next closest Motlite.

Rissyl finally moved far enough away from the mass of Awakened to draw his own wand. He added to the sharp buzzing sounds with reddish orange magical streaks of his own. The simultaneous screams of terror from the three dying Motlites were almost enough to make Rissyl risk covering his own ears.

The battle became a blur after that point. He fell back into his rhythm of striking, blocking, moving and wherever he stepped another skeletal Awakened dropped. His trusty staff felt good in his arms, and even though it seemed he'd been battling for hours he didn't feel drained.

242

He risked a quick look towards to the door to see what the one human that emerged with the Motlites was up to. He found the man locked in a losing battle against two Society Magi. As Rissyl watched, the one human combatant that they'd faced thus far was vanquished without fanfare.

Rissyl was pretty sure that he had a number of wounds all around his body, but he was confident that none of them were serious yet.

As he looked around to see how the others were doing he only counted four Society Magi still standing. Thon was very near the gate and it seemed like he was uninjured. The Motlites were all dead, and the swarm of Awakened skeletons was even starting to look noticeably thinner.

Rissyl noticed movement from the east, and he saw Cynia and other people from the third unit making their way towards the gate. He breathed a sigh of relief seeing her upright and fighting. Off to the west, Dalen and much of his unit was making their way towards the gate as well.

The sight filled him with joy and a renewed vigor to finish the battle once and for all.

Several minutes later the battle was over. Rissyl's arms felt like they had lead weights tied to his wrists. He rested the bottom of the staff on the ground, and fell into Cynia's outstretched arms. She hugged him tightly, and he took a deep breath of her hair and neck. She smelled like sweat and blood, mixed with a lot of decomposing skin from the creatures she had fought, with just a hint of the herbs she used when she washed her hair. It was vile, and he savored it as he held her close.

When he released her, he saw several Magi move over to the wall and lean against it. No one wanted to sit on the ground because it was covered in bones and decomposing tissue, but everyone was exhausted.

Rissyl figured that all of these corpses that they'd been fighting were probably the corpses that had been laying outside of the Stronghold the very first time they visited over a year ago, when the Rolimi guardian demanded the signet ring. Somehow the necromancers learned how to turn them into Awakened even if they didn't have a heart any longer.

The thought made him look around the area once again. He couldn't understand why they hadn't fought any necromancers. Finally he said, "Have any of you seen a single necromancer tonight?"

All of the Magi either answered in the negative, or shook their head.

Something wasn't right, and Rissyl felt on-edge wondering what traps the necromancers still had waiting for them.

"We need to be careful. When we walk into the Stronghold, we might be ambushed by an army of necromancers, and who knows what kind of Awakened they'll have with them."

Dalen said, "That's true, Riz. But first we need to catch our breath. It's been a long battle, and this might have been the easy part."

Several Magi groaned, and Cynia gave him a dirty look.

She said, "Gee, thanks for that."

As Rissyl debated whether or not to make a comment, he noticed Firana walk over to Dalen and she fell into his arms. He knew the two had grown closer, but it seemed that they were even closer than he originally realized. He put his arm around Cynia and pulled her to him.

He looked around the group to assess their casualties. First he looked to each of his Order Magi, and he was relieved to see that each of them were alive and seemed mostly unharmed. Then he turned his attention to Society Magi.

His unit still had four of its original nine Society Magi that seemed fairly unharmed. The unit suffered two fatalities, and three injuries which Rissyl hoped were too severe.

Dalen's unit looked almost completely unharmed. They were missing one Society Magi, and Rissyl assumed that one had been killed. Sarasa would be relieved to see that Bran had returned.

He turned to the final unit, which Cynia had been leading; they were missing one Society Magi.

Rissyl said, "I see Keta walking with someone, that leaves one Magi from your group unaccounted for, Cynia."

She nodded, "Yes, we had two Magi go down with wounds. Keta, how is the other wounded Magi?"

The blue and white cloaked woman stopped and let the man she was helping step away from her. She helped him lean against the wall. Keta shook her head, "Malya was dead, but I was able to bandage Vindle."

Rissyl looked around the gathered Magi. He said, "So, unit one had two killed and three wounded. Unit two had one killed and none seriously wounded, and unit three had one killed and one seriously wounded." He paused for a moment, trying to decide how to say what he wanted to say, without coming across callous.

After a long pause, he said, "Four dead out of thirty-four is better than I feared for this battle. There will be time to mourn the dead when our work is done. We still need to take control of our Stronghold, and the battle is probably not over yet."

Several Magi moved closer, anticipating his order. Rissyl said, "We have four wounded pretty badly. A couple of you need to take them back to Randol's so they can recuperate. The rest of us need to press on."

Keta said, "Konrad and I will take the wounded back to Randol's and care for them."

Rissyl looked over to Konrad and saw the man's face grow dark and angry. The Society Magi took a step away from Keta.

Konrad didn't respond right away. After a moment, he said, "With all due respect, there may be more battling here. It would be best if I stayed here to fight, if needed."

Keta shook her head, "No, you will come with me."

Rissyl could tell that she was angry, and Konrad was clearly angry as well. For a brief moment, he wasn't sure if the man was going to do as he was told.

Finally the man nodded, "As you wish."

There was more going on here that what he had seen on the surface, and he wished he had time to get to the bottom of things. It was obvious that there was a spy within their midst, otherwise the emperor wouldn't have known about Uli's ranch. So, of course, treachery was the first place his mind went to explain the odd exchange between the two Magi.

He watched as Keta and Konrad led the four wounded Magi towards the portal stone. She urged Konrad to walk in front of her, and that further fueled his suspicions that something odd was happening. However, that was a mystery for another day.

When the wounded had been escorted away, he said, "Let's get in there!" He led the way into the Stronghold.

It was still dark in the very early morning hours of the day; he guessed that there was probably at least an hour before the sun peeked over the horizon in the east. However, he was still in awe as he walked into the Stronghold. There were so many buildings within the walls of the Stronghold, and many of them held untold treasures and magical artifacts.

He smiled to himself as he thought about what fantastic items they might find or what spells they might learn.

He was completely ripped from his daydream when an unholy and extremely haunting screaming sound tore through the night. The frightening sound stopped him in his tracks, and he heard several gasps from the Magi behind him.

Rissyl looked around to find the source of the frightening scream, but he didn't see anything. After waiting a few moments, he started walking again.

Behind him and to his right he heard someone say, "By the gods, what is that?"

Dalen said, "What is that sarding thing?"

Rissyl looked that way and was shocked to see what could only be described as a ghost, floating quickly towards them. It was a large, semi-transparent, partially glowing, and extremely terrifying ghost. It looked like an extremely old woman who was dressed in tattered rags. The woman's hair and clothing whipped about wildly about as though she was standing in strong wind. The woman's mouth was agape and her eyes were wide open, and it screamed again.

The sound ripped through Rissyl's head and hurt terribly.

From behind him, other Magi gasped and exclaimed, as other horrible screams ripped through the night but these were coming from the other direction.

When he turned to look in that direction, he saw three more ghostly creatures. The first appeared to be a young woman who might even be pretty if it wasn't for the fact that she was dead and lacking a real body, the other two were the ghostly forms of young men in tattered armor.

Several of the Magi sprang into action, and started summoning small fire orbs and throwing them at the spirits.

Rissyl turned to Cynia and said, "Can this be happening? Are we being attacked by ghosts?"

One of the Society Magi from Ferth's Coterie answered him. Rissyl was pretty sure the man was named Peke. Peke said, "Actually, I believe they are spectres. I've read about them some, and if I remember right they're much more dangerous than simple ghosts."

"Oh, that makes me feel better. How do we kill them?"

The old looking spectre was almost on top of some of the Magi to the right. One of the Society Magi pulled out his sword and stepped forward to attack the incorporeal foe.

Peke said, "Regular weapons will have no effect on it."

Rissyl felt his anger building. "Our spells don't seem to be doing much either!" He lowered the gem of his staff and summoned a series of fire orbs at the closest spectre. The orbs struck the creature and passed through it, striking the ground behind it.

"I am pretty sure they hate sunlight! We should be safe from them once the sun comes up."

"That doesn't help us at all, now."

The old woman spectre reached out and grabbed the face of the nearest Magi. Rissyl threw more fire orbs at it, but the spells barely affected the ghostly creature.

The Magi in the spectre's grip screamed in terror but it held his head tightly. It gazed into his eyes and screamed. Rissyl took a step forward as it held the Magi's head, but it was too late. After a brief moment the Magi went limp and the spectre dropped the lifeless body to the ground.

Rissyl cursed loudly. All around him Magi scurried around, trying to help the fallen Magi, and trying to avoid the spectres at the same time. Magic orbs of every element shot from the hands and staffs of the gathered Magi, but none of them seemed to hinder the ghostly creatures much.

The three younger-looking spectres flew at a Society Magi. Aruk grabbed the man and yanked him back. They turned to Aruk and one of them grabbed him by the head. The Evoker tried to grab the creature, but his hands passed through it. With his hands still inside the transparent creature, Aruk screamed, "Krol'Tu Nari!"

Suddenly a large pillar of fire shot down from the sky. The swirling fire engulfed the three spectres and Aruk, as several other Magi dove away from the deadly flaming pillar. The awful death screams echoed briefly from the nearby buildings, and Rissyl stepped back and shielded his face from the intense heat.

Cynia screamed, "No!" It was drowned by a chorus of gasps and exclamations which rang out from the Magi.

When the fire disappeared, Aruk and all three spectres were gone. Nothing was left of any of them, but Aruk's ashes.

Rissyl felt like he had been punched in the stomach, by a gorilla. He and Aruk had spent so many hours together, travelling around the Free Cities. He tried to take a breath, but it wouldn't come. He wanted to scream or lash out at something. Aruk was his friend, and he didn't deserve to have his life cut short. The man would never see his goal of settling down as a farmer.

Peke tapped insistently against Rissyl's arm. He said, "Rissyl look!"

"Dammit! Leave me alone!" He pushed Peke away.

Cynia grabbed him and pointed. She said, "Riz..."

In his grief, he had forgotten about the first spectre. He turned back that way to see what everyone wanted him to see. It was flying towards one of the Magi, Vannis from Eleyne's coterie, who was sprinting away for his life.

Now that he knew the things could be killed, he started in the direction of the first spectre to find a way to kill it when he noticed what the others had been pointing at. A new one was coming into existence, out of the body of the Magi who had been killed by the first spectre.

"By the gods!"

The old looking spectre captured Vannis. His screams were almost more than Rissyl could stand. He realized that they had to escape or they'll all be turned into spectres. At the very least he needed to get the other Magi out of the area.

He shouted, "Retreat! Now! All of you!"

Cynia said, "I'm not leaving you! I won't let you sacrifice yourself like Aruk did! We need you! Your son needs you!"

"I won't sacrifice myself, but I need you to get out of here!"

She paused only a second and then she started shouting at the other Magi to retreat. He breathed a sigh of relief as he watched her lead their Magi to safety.

Dalen stepped over by him and Rissyl shook his head. "Go, my friend. This is Evoker work. Keep her safe!"

Without a word, Dalen took off running and caught up with Cynia and the others as they fled towards the gates.

The old looking spectre screamed and looked around when it finished draining the life from Vannis. The other spectre, who had been one of the Society Magi until moments ago, looked around. It looked slightly disoriented, and Rissyl hoped that it would take a while to gain its full power.

He jumped when Firana placed her hand on his back. He didn't realize anyone else was still in the area. He said, "Get out of here Firana, I will fight them!"

She punched him in the arm, hard. "There's no sarding way that I'm fleeing! Aruk was my friend to, and you just said this is Evoker work. I'm an Evoker too!"

He sighed and didn't reply to her. Both spectres had turned their attention to the Evokers and were flying towards them.

He said, "I've got the old one."

He gathered a large portion of the magical essence that he had remaining in his magewel, and formed it into the *Flaming Pillar* spell. He quickly shaped the spell in his mind, careful to form it properly.

From beside him, he heard Firana shout, "Krol'Tu Nari!"

The heat hit his face almost instantly as the large flaming pillar landed on the new spectre. He completed his spell formation and shouted the vocal component of the spell. "Krol'Tu Nari!"

He let himself smile as the warmth of his pillar added to the waning warmth from the pillar that Firana had summoned. The blinding brightness of the two pillars of fire quickly died, and left him momentarily unable to see in the darkness of the morning.

As his vision returned to normal he looked around. He was greatly relieved to see that both spectres were gone. He turned to Firana to congratulate her on a great casting, and saw that she had collapsed. She had been casting spells throughout the battle and clearly the *Flaming Pillar* drained her magewel to a dangerously low level.

He reached down and checked her blood-pulse. She was alive, but weak. He mentally kicked himself for letting her stay, even as he admitted to himself that he would probably be dead if she hadn't. His magewel was almost drained as well. It would not be possible for him to cast another Flaming Pillar spell. The young woman had saved his life, and now he needed to make sure that she recovered.

Movement beyond the burnt ground before him caught his attention. It was the body of Vannis. Yet another spectre was born, and he knew that he didn't have enough magical essence left to kill it. He looked down at Firana, and decided to carry her to safety. They'd have to find some other way to kill it.

He heard footsteps running up. As he looked in that direction he heard Ferth shout, "Krol'Tu Nari!"

The welcome heat from the Magi's pillar of fire warmed Rissyl's back. He put his hand on the Magi's shoulder, and said, "Good job, Ferth. Help me with Firana."

The other Magi were running back to them, as he picked her up. Dalen was the first to him and he took Firana from Rissyl's arms.

Cynia was the second Magi back, and she pulled him into a strong embrace as soon as Dalen had hold of the small Evoker. She hugged Rissyl tightly for a long time.

By the time he let her go, the others were gathered round and several Magi patted him on the shoulder.

There was a pit in his stomach as he looked over to where Aruk gave his life. He couldn't help but think that maybe there had been more he could have done, or that he could have reacted faster to save more lives.

Cynia squeezed his hand. She said, "Come on, let's go and look at the spoils of our battle. Aruk and others lost their lives to give us this reward."

He squeezed her hand back and kissed the top of her head. "It's been a long time coming."

Dalen said, "I'm going to take Firana back to Randol's. She needs to recuperate with the others."

The young Evoker opened her eyes and shook her head no. She said, "Did we kill them? Did we win?"

"Yes, you did fantastic." Dalen smiled at her.

She said, "I'm not going back to Randol's. I'm fine. I wanna see the secrets of the Stronghold!"

CHAPTER 29

Kimly

As she had been doing frequently over the past fortnight, Kimly was sitting on the balcony looking down on Favin and his four agents of the Shrouded. They met every few days to discuss business, and she tried to be there when she could to quietly oversee the meetings.

The longer she kept up the charade, the more she started to believe that she could actually turn the Shrouded into a real thing with actual power. She would need to travel to other cities, and setup a base of operations like she'd created with Favin and his group. None of them would need to know that there was no authority higher than her, they would all just think of her as their contact within a much larger, secretive organization.

The more she considered the possibilities, the more she liked the plan. If she could recruit a handful of rogues and sneak-thieves in nearby towns, all of whom would need a magewel so she could teach them a tiny bit of magic, then she could build a network of people working for her. The thought of being the queen of her own empire of rogues made her extremely excited. The possibilities were endless and they made her gooey on the inside.

She had been observing Favin's meeting for well over an hour, but she really didn't have any idea what they were discussing. She'd been lost in her own thoughts the entire time.

Kimly decided that she would travel to Tharrin first, and see if she could get the seeds planted there for another group of Shrouded.

She was abruptly pulled from her day-dreaming when Favin stood up, and the other four people in the room stood up with him. She heard some kind of commotion happening outside of the room.

Before she could come down from the balcony, she heard the door to the room below crash open. That was quickly followed by a great deal of shouting and the savage growling of a large dog.

Looking down, she saw the dog and it turned out to be a huge wolf. The terrifying creature bounded across the room and knocked Favin to the ground. The wolf didn't even seem to be savagely attacking him. It was simply holding the man pinned on the ground. However, Favin looked and sounded like he was being killed.

She had seen Favin suffer intense punishment, and she knew him to have a remarkable tolerance for pain. Yet, he was on the ground under the wolf writhing in pain, and screaming in agony. The wolf snarled and nipped at his arms, but the minor bites couldn't have been causing all of the pain.

Soldiers stormed into the room and begin trying to capture Favin's people.

The self-preservation side of Kimly screamed at herself to stay quiet and keep hidden on the balcony. There was a good chance the soldiers would kill or capture Favin and his people and not even look on the balcony.

That, however, would completely wreck everything she was hoping to build. Going and building a group in Tharrin didn't sound nearly as fun if she was completely starting over.

She moved closer to the balcony and formed a part of her magic essence to summon a fire orb. She needed to get the wolf off Favin. She launched the fire orb at the wolf, and it hit the large beast square in the back. The wolf didn't even seem to notice the attack, because the orb dissipated as soon as it hit the wolf. Somehow the creature was immune to magical attacks just like the Motlites.

The room below was a flurry of movement. As Favin screamed in pain under the wolf, his four agents battled for their lives against imperial soldiers.

One of the soldiers pointed at her, and shouted, "Magi on the balcony! It attacked the Garrolwolf!"

She cursed to herself. She could already hear at least one person running, probably headed for the stairs to the balcony.

Hearing the soldier refer to the wolf as a Garrolwolf confirmed her suspicion that the creature was some new construct of Jalinox, just like the Motlites before. Knowing that, she knew that none of her magic spells would work against it.

Fortunately, thanks to Jalinox, she didn't have to rely completely on magic spells. She also commanded the necromantic gifts of Viator, the god of death.

With a quick prayer to Viator, she whispered a vengeful curse and a genuine hope for ill will towards all of the soldiers below. She completed her prayer and felt the taint of Viator flowing in her veins. She quickly launched a series of purple orbs of necromancer magic, commonly called Khalius Fire, at the wolf below.

The huge creature yelped and jumped away as the first orb of Khalius Fire hit it. The next two orbs slammed into the creature before it could get away. She tracked the beast and continued the onslaught of purple fire until it slumped to the ground, lifeless.

Without a pause she turned her attention to the soldier who had just climbed the steps to the balcony. She launched a stream of five deadly Khalius Fire orbs at the soldier, and he was dead before the fourth struck him. The lifeless corpse fell backwards down the stairs.

When she looked back down to the room below, three corpses were at the feet of Viper. Skoots had moved over to protect Favin, and the others were locked in fierce battles with soldiers.

As she was about to jump down from the balcony, she saw the Magi hunter move further into the room. She knew that this was the imperial agent, because she had followed him on a couple of occasions. The man was large and dangerous looking.

He moved into the center of the room, and he was dragging Floppy along with him. The imperial agent held the large rogue in a choke-hold, and was using him as a shield between himself and Kimly. There was a large dagger held against Floppy's throat.

The imperial agent looked at her and said, "Come down the stairs very slowly, and don't try anything stupid, or your friend here dies!"

In one fluid motion she grabbed a dagger from her belt and flipped it at the imperial agent. As she flipped the dagger she summoned much more magic than she needed to speed the dagger towards its target.

The dagger streaked into a blur of motion as it picked up speed to a nearly-impossible rate, and it slammed into the face of the imperial agent before he could even consider moving a muscle. The force of the dagger hitting the man caused his entire head to burst like a watermelon dropped from a window.

Skoots' jaw dropped open as she exclaimed, "By all the sarding gods!"

Kimly rushed to the stairs, and dropped a Shadow Shroud spell on herself as she ran. When she got down to the main room, there were only three soldiers left and two of them were locked in combat with Viper. The third moved towards Favin and Skoots.

She drew her other dagger and quietly bounded up behind the man. She jumped up onto the soldier's back, and ran her blade across the soldier's throat before he could react to her pouncing onto him.

As the man fell to the ground, she landed gracefully to stand over his dead body. She looked around the room and saw that the rest of the soldiers were dead. Then she noticed that all eyes in the room were on her. Kimly wiped the blood from her dagger and slid it back into its sheath.

She looked at Skoots and said, "Skoots, would you grab my other dagger?

I think it landed over there." She pointed to the far side of the room, where large parts of the imperial agent's head had landed.

Skoots didn't move and didn't take her eyes from Kimly.

To her left, Viper said quietly, "Who are you?"

Favin sat up slowly, and moved slightly to lean against his desk. He said, "This is Kimly, she is my contact and a high-level agent within the Shrouded."

CHAPTER 30

Sarasa

"I'm scared for Rissyl and Cynia. Are they going to get dead like my parents?" Ayris sat down on the edge of Sarasa's bed.

Sarasa mustered more confidence than she felt. She said, "No, kiddo. They'll be fine."

She reached out and gently pulled on the girl's shoulder. Ayris snuggled up in front of her, as Sarasa repositioned the blankets to cover the little girl.

Sarasa put her arm around the girl and the two of them rested quietly for a long time. She wasn't sure if she was comforting the child, or if the child was comforting her. Whatever the case, both of them dozed off before too long.

"Get up! Everyone up, we're under attack!"

Sarasa woke up suddenly, and for a moment she wasn't sure where she was or what was happening.

Outside of her room, she could hear chaos. There was a great deal of shouting and the banging of large objects being hit or slid into other large objects.

"Come on, kiddo. Time to get up!" Sarasa gently shook the little girl beside her.

"What's wrong?" She could tell that Ayris was as sleepy and disoriented as she had been.

"You've got to go hide in the woods. Imperial troops found us, get up!"

The girl sat up and said, "No, if there are bad guys here, I wanna help!"

Sarasa winced in pain as she sat up. Her wounds were healing, but they had a long way to go before she would be able to run around without pain. She gave a little push to encourage the girl to get out of bed. "Yes, of course. You'll help by going to the woods and helping the old and injured Magi who will be there with you. You can help keep them safe."

Ayris nodded.

She called a small amount of magic to summon her cloak and daggers from the plane of magic. It was the first time she'd used magic since being rescued from the Stronghold. Her magewel was full so if she could get her body to cooperate she might actually live through this.

Sarasa pushed the girl towards the door, and opened it. She didn't know what to expect, but so far she didn't see any sign of imperial troops. Up and down the hall there were Magi running this way and that.

One of the elderly Magi from the Free Cities hurried past her. Sarasa grabbed the old man's shoulder as he pushed past.

She said, "Are you going out the back to take shelter in the woods? Take the girl with you. Keep her safe!"

The old Magi looked like he was going to pull away and continue down the hall. After a brief pause he reached down and grabbed Ayris by the shoulder. He said, "Keep up, kid! If you slow me down I'm leaving you."

Ayris cried out to Sarasa. "No! Please don't leave me!"

Sarasa turned and started making her way towards the front stairs. She dropped an *Invisibility* spell on herself as she walked.

When she got to the steps she was already tired. She stepped aside as two injured Magi hobbled up the stairs.

She rested against the wall for a moment. Her old wounds were starting to hurt worse, and she was not looking forward to the long walk up all of those stairs.

From up the stairs she could hear the sounds of battle. If she couldn't even walk the stairs she knew it was stupid to try to engage in combat with seasoned warriors. She had plenty of magic to maintain her invisibility for several hours. She could easily hide in the woods with Ayris and the elderly Magi, and she knew that Rissyl, Cynia, and Dalen would all advise her to take that path.

Sarasa would rather die fighting than live with the shame of having cowered in safety while others battled for her. She started walking up the stairs. As she walked, she amended her previous thought. She'd rather die a thousand deaths in a thousand unique and horrible manners, instead of cowering in fear while others fought her battles.

When she was almost at the top of the steps a young Magi staggered into Randol's home. The man was grievously wounded and he could barely walk. Hanging onto the wall, the man hurried to the stairs. She moved out of his way, since she was invisible and he didn't know she was there. The man tried to hurry down the stairs, but from the sudden screams and the rapid succession of thumps and thuds she could tell that the man ended up falling down most of the stairs.

She didn't stop to help him. Through the open door she could see the battle raging outside.

As she stepped outside, she found herself in the heart of the chaos. There were at least a dozen Magi just outside the door; one of them was Randol in his green and black Grand Diviner cloak. He had his staff firing a steady stream of fire orbs at the troops before him. Most of the Magi were the elderly from the Free Cities.

The imperial troops formed a large mass spreading out for a hundred yards or more. She quickly guessed that there were a thousand or more troops pushing forward, all of them trying to be the ones to take down the first Magi.

Immediately in front of the Magi was a line of imperial soldiers that seemed to be fighting to keep the Magi safe. It was surreal to see the imperials fighting each other, and at first she was confused. Then she saw one of the troops break through the lines and rush at Randol. The Grand Diviner held out his hand towards the advancing soldier and the man suddenly stopped, turned, and started attacking other imperial soldiers. Sarasa smiled as she saw that Randol was using mind control to force some of the soldiers to help the Magi.

For a bit, Sarasa was impressed at how well the Magi were doing. The dozen or so Magi near the house continued to attack the troops with elemental orbs and the magical attacks were proving quite effective. The ground near the protective line formed by the mind-controlled troops was littered with the bodies of fallen imperial troops, some killed by their own companions and others killed by the relentless volley of magical attacks.

She knew it was only a matter of time before the Magi began to empty their magewels and then things would get ugly quickly.

Off to her right she saw a soldier slip through the lines and rush at Randol. The Grand Diviner didn't seem to see the advancing warrior, so Sarasa rushed over to his side.

The warrior raised his sword and hurried in for a sneaky and devastating attack against the unsuspecting Magi. Sarasa got there first, and while still invisible, she lunged forward and drove one of her magic daggers deep into the chest of the soldier. The force of the man rushing forward, combined with the force of Sarasa's lunge forward, drove the dagger all of the way to the hilt into the man's chest. Her skillful maneuvering guided the blade directly into the man's heart, killing him instantly.

The attack caused her to lose focus on her invisibility spell, and suddenly she was in the thick of things. Two of the mind-controlled soldiers to Randol's far right were finally defeated by the other soldiers, creating a break in the defensive barrier that had been partially protecting the group of Magi. Several soldiers advanced together.

Sarasa met them head-on and skillfully evaded and redirected the soldiers' attacks with her daggers. Her body quickly fell into muscle memory mode as years of combat training took over her actions. She let go of conscious thought and simply fought on instinct.

She was vaguely aware of magical orbs of various different elements slamming into enemies all around her. The magical attacks helped to distract her foes as she finished them off one at a time.

For a short time she was able to push aside the pain and fatigue of her previous injuries.

She heard a vicious growl and several screams from behind her. Glancing back quickly, she saw a massive wolf push through the line of soldiers. It slammed into Randol and shoved him up against the house.

She turned to help the old Magi and suddenly her head exploded in pain. Something had slammed into the back of her head and for the briefest moment she tried to turn back to her attacker. The world went black as she felt herself falling to the ground.

Darkness.

- = - = -

Sarasa felt like she was caught in a bad dream and couldn't wake up. She had no idea where she was or how long she had been out. She vaguely remembered a battle, and Randol being attacked by a wolf.

She could hear voices and shouts all around her, but they were subdued as if she was wearing ear muffs. She moaned and tried to open her eyes, but she didn't have enough energy to even open her eyes and look around. Her body still hadn't healed from her previous injuries, and fighting alongside the other Magi had been a stupid idea. The throbbing in the back of her head hinted that the battle had brought even more damage to her still-healing body.

"This one is still alive!"

Settling on just one eye, she peeked one open to assess her surroundings. The battle seemed to be winding down, and the Magi had lost. There were imperial soldiers all around. She was relatively sure that she was still near Randol's house where she had fallen. There were several young soldiers nearby, and one of them was walking towards her.

"Woah, boys! What have we here? I ain't never seen a prettier Magi."

She heard other Soldiers approach her and then she felt two very strong hands pick her up. He held her in an upright position. If she had the strength to stand she felt like she could straighten her legs and she would be standing. Her head felt very heavy and everything was spinning as she was roughly handled, but she opened her eyes a crack to see what the man was doing.

The soldier held her at arm's length like he was examining a bag of grain. He slowly turned her from side to side.

Several soldiers had gathered around her, and one of them said, "Oh Royni, it'd be a shame for a pretty little Magi like this to hang from the gallows without giving us a little fun time first!"

She felt the soldier pulling her to him. He placed her against his body like he was going to hug her, and wrapped his arms around her back. He said, "Let's take her over to the woods while we still have some time."

The man started walking, carrying her along with him. She felt her fury grow as a red-hot fire deep within. She felt no fear or dread, just a white hot anger at the retched wickedness of these soldiers. With every ounce of strength that she could muster, and reinforced with some magical force, she drove her knee up into the abdomen of her attacker. She felt her knee sink deep into the man's stomach, above his groin armor and below most of his chainmail shirt.

The soldier tried to scream, but all of the wind was forced out of him as Sarasa's brutal knee strike drove home with unbelievable force. The man dropped her as he fell to the ground.

By the aid of some miracle, Sarasa remained on her feet. Her head still spun wildly, and her legs felt like they would collapse at any moment, but she was fueled by a burning fury and she refused to go out without a fight.

The surprise of having their victim turn into their opponent gave Sarasa a second to launch a series of fire orbs at the nearest soldiers. In the blink of an eye she cast three burning spheres at the three nearest attackers, and all three men went down screaming.

One soldier thrust his sword at her from her right. She didn't see the attack until it was too late, and her weak and weary muscles dulled her normally quick reflexes. The deadly blow was coming straight towards her. She was able to move slightly and swat the blade away with her bare right hand. The block saved her life, but she felt the sword cut deep into her unprotected hand.

The man squared off with her, and held his sword between them. She tried to form a somewhat decent defensive combat stance, but her legs were about to fail her. The bright red blood flowing freely from her severely damaged right hand caught her eye and momentarily distracted her.

Suddenly, from behind, she felt at least two men grab her and restrain her. That was followed quickly by a loud thudding sound against the back of her head and a bright explosion of pain in her skull.

Darkness.

- = - = -

"Sarasa!"

She groaned to herself. She didn't understand why the nightmare wouldn't end. Her body felt broken everywhere and all of the different pains competed to see which could be the most awful.

Again she heard the voice calling her name. It wasn't the rough and taunting voices of the soldiers, it was the sweet voice of a small girl. For a moment she thought that perhaps it was the voice of an angel coming to take her to the eternal paradise and finally put an end to all of the pain.

"Sarasa! Wake up!"

It was not an angel. In a weak voice she said, "Oh gods, how much must I endure?"

The voice got closer to her face, and Sarasa felt herself being jostled. It said, "Please wake up! We've gotta hide before more come!"

She dreaded the thought of opening her eyes again. Everything was a haze and she could barely think. She was afraid to move because moving brought pain. Finally, she clinched her teeth and opened her eyes.

The men were no longer there, it was only Ayris. Sarasa tried to smile at the girl, but it hurt too much.

The girl held out her hand. She said, "Come on! We've got to hide!"

With all of her strength, Sarasa forced herself to sit up. Pain reverberated throughout her body, and she wanted to scream.

When the pain subsided enough for her to see again, she looked around. She was sitting on the ground just inside the woodlands near Randol's house. Off in the distance she could see his house, and countless soldiers were swarming around the house and were scattered about the meadow between the woods and the house.

She looked down and found several bodies of imperial soldiers all around her.

Ayris stood next to her. The girl had some sort of shimmering bubble all around her body. She held out her hand.

Sarasa took the girl's hand and, with great effort, she stood up slowly. As she stood she saw the shimmering bubble expand and soon they were both within the bubble.

They walked slowly, deeper into the woods. Behind them she could hear the sounds of battle and the shouts of soldiers.

The pain was almost too much to bare, and she quickly found herself living from step to step. Each one became a monumental accomplishment in her mind. When she thought she could go no further, the girl stopped pulling her forward.

She said, "Can you get on there?"

Sarasa sat carefully onto the large fallen tree. She let herself collapse onto it and she thanked the gods for making the walking stop. For a long time she was content to stay motionless and enjoy a time where the pain level was only partially unbearable.

Time dragged on slowly, and she wanted to turn and look towards Randol's to see if the imperial army was looking for them. She knew that they were deep in the woods and she wouldn't be able to see the meadow from this deep in the woods. Besides, moving meant fierce pain, and she wasn't sure she could handle it. The pain in her side and leg told her that she had managed to reinjure the wounds she received at the Stronghold.

She tried to clinch her fists, but she had no feeling or movement in her right hand at all. She glanced at it and saw that it was covered in blood and was still bleeding badly. The hand was destroyed; it was cut almost completely in half right through the middle of her palm.

Ayris said, "We could use your cloak to bandage your hand. I think that's the worst injury."

She closed her eyes as the pain became too great, and she let the girl try to bandage her wounded hand.

CHAPTER 31

Konrad

The four Magi who had been injured during the battle at the Stronghold placed their hands on the portal stone. Konrad watched as they activated the stone's magic and teleported back to Randol's place. He stepped up to the stone and placed his hands upon it.

Keta stepped up also, but she didn't place her hands on the stone. She said, "Why did you follow me to the wooded lake back at the ranch?"

Konrad could hear the anger and accusation in Keta's voice, and it bothered him. There was something so very captivating about the woman and he was making no progress with her. He didn't have a good answer to her question, so he decided to try to redirect her instead. "Shouldn't we follow the others? They might need help getting to Randol's house? It's already been a very long and slow walk just to get to the portal stone from the ranch."

She looked at him with an angry glare for a long while. Then she said, "If you meant to get me alone to get in my breeches, you're going to be disappointed."

He couldn't help but smile at her anger. "We're alone now. If that was my wish, we'd already be naked getting busy with the bugs in the tall grass. I highly doubt that I'd be disappointed."

Keta reached out and grabbed the portal stone with both hands. She said, "I don't trust you."

He nodded, "I wouldn't trust me either."

They activated the portal stone together.

Konrad braced himself for the normal vertigo from teleporting. He held tight to the stone pillar so he wouldn't topple over from the sudden dizziness. Regardless, as soon as he arrived at his destination, he ended up on the ground.

He blinked in confusion. In addition to the expected dizziness, he had a tremendous pain in his right side, and his ears were flooded with noise. With the disorientation from the teleporting, it took him a moment to realize that he was under attack.

A large wolf was on top of him, and it had him pinned to the ground. It snarled at him and he could feel the magic draining from his body. He reached down to his belt and grabbed his dagger. In one quick motion he drew the dagger and drove it deep into the creature's abdomen. He jerked the dagger up towards the wolf's chest.

The beast let out a surprised yelp, which was cut short. The massive wolf fell to the ground dead, and Konrad pushed it away from him. He looked up to find two swords pointed at his head.

As he stood, he saw two imperial soldiers holding Keta with her arms behind her back. The other two leveled their swords at Konrad. He raised his hands in surrender.

Konrad was impressed. Whoever tipped off the emperor knew about both Randol's house and Uli's ranch, and the emperor sent troops to ambush the Magi at both locations almost simultaneously. It was genius, and he was jealous that he hadn't orchestrated it.

The soldiers began to check the Magi for weapons. Konrad saw Keta send her cloak and weapon to the plane of magic. He had already sent his cloak to the magic plane during their walk from the Stronghold to the portal stone.

One of the soldiers said, "Where'd her cloak go?"

Keta asked, "What cloak?"

One soldier took Konrad's sword and both daggers.

The other said, "Shut up, Magi, or you'll end up like your friends."

The soldiers led them from the portal stone, and Konrad saw the bodies of all four of the Magi who had been injured in the fighting at the Stronghold. It looked like they had been killed shortly after they arrived at Randol's.

The two Magi were led towards Randol's house and Konrad decided that the situation was hopeless. There were soldiers, horses, and wagons as far as he could see. The emperor sent an entire regiment to the Magi's home, and they were in the process of ransacking the place.

There were bodies everywhere. The motionless bodies of several Magi lay near the house, but he wasn't surprised to see that the vast majority of the corpses were those of imperial soldiers.

Eventually the soldiers led Konrad and Keta to the heart of the imperial camp. Konrad could feel the point of at least one sword pressed against his spine as they walked.

The soldiers stopped walking next to a large covered wagon. One of the soldiers said, "Commander, we have prisoners."

Two men stepped out of the wagon. Konrad recognized one of the men as General Belvador, the commander of Raptor Regiment. He recognized the other man as Imperial Agent Salamin, one of the agents who had been sent to Khazror.

Keta hissed, "You! I thought you were dead?"

Salamin laughed.

"I trusted you! You were a spy?"

"You were far too naïve, Keta."

Konrad saw a blur of moment as Keta spun to her left and summoned her sword as she spun. In a quick movement she slid her magically enhanced sword across the face of one of her captors. The runes up her blade glowed brightly.

A series of shouts erupted from soldiers all around them, and General Belvador shouted orders for his men to kill her.

She stepped to the side as her first captor fell, and just as quickly she dispatched her other captor with a feint and then a strong thrust straight at his chest. Keta left her blade in the man's torso as he fell to the ground. She turned to look at the man next to the general.

Even as several soldiers rushed at her, she reached to her belt and summoned another magic weapon. This one was a small dagger. She stepped forward as she drew and threw the weapon at Salamin. The runes on the weapon glowed and sparked with electricity as it spun through the air. Konrad didn't even know that she had such a weapon, but he was impressed.

Salamin lunged to the side to avoid the attack, and he crashed into the general. The weapon still found Salamin's shoulder. As soon as it hit, the blade exploded with magical lightning that surged through the man's body.

The thunder clapped loudly, drowning out the agent's death screams as he spasmed on the ground. The lightning continued to surge until the body stopped moving.

Konrad saw the smoke rising gently from the corpse, and for a brief moment everyone paused. The general continued to shout for his men to kill the Magi. She stood like a panther waiting for the first soldier to attack her.

None of the soldiers wanted to be the next one to be electrocuted.

Once again, Konrad was faced with a decision. As much as he wanted to learn more secrets of the Magi, he knew that he just might end up in a cold dungeon or worse if he didn't cast aside the Konrad the Magi guise and reaffirm his place among the emperor's loyal troops.

He launched himself at Keta, and his sudden attack took her by surprise. He tackled her and tried to pin her to the ground. She recovered quickly and started punching and kneeing him wildly, as she squirmed and struggled to get out from beneath him. The actions quickly awoke a primal excitement deep within him, but he struggled to keep that side hidden away. He had long dreamed of getting her into a position like this, but in those dreams they weren't surrounded by an entire regiment of the emperor's soldiers.

He delivered punches and elbows, while trying to avoid Keta's attacks and trying to keep her from wriggling away.

He screamed as she summoned an orb of fire that erupted his ribs on his left side. It burned briefly, with intense heat. He tried to ignore the pain as he slammed his elbow down into the Magi's face over and over. The woman was much more resilient than he expected. She managed to move and block several of his elbow strikes as she kept alternating her quick hands between protecting her face, and punching him relentlessly. The attacks she couldn't avoid or block, were stopped with a solid but invisible magical shield around her face.

"Dammit!" He screamed again, as once again she summoned a fire orb which burst against his right arm, burning him severely and causing intense pain.

The two Magi wrestled on the ground, moving through the grass as both combatants struggled to gain better position. As they wrestled around, something smacked against the back of Konrad's head and he looked to see that it was the handle of Keta's sword which was still stuck in the dead soldier's chest.

He raised his body from Keta's slightly. He punched at her face with several attacks in quick succession, to keep her attention away from the sword. When she moved to full defense to protect her face, he reached over quickly and yanked the sword from the soldier's body. He raised it, and quickly drove the blade down through her chest. He felt a magical shield form around her chest as she desperately tried to defend against the attack, but it was too late.

He let out a scream as he felt the blade pause against her ribs and then sink clear through her body and impale in the ground beneath her. His battle lust turned to disappointment as he realized that he would never know what pleasures the woman could have given him had things been different.

Several soldiers seized him at once and dragged him over to the general.

Konrad did his best to stand with his head held high, like he was the man in charge. He was covered in dirt, blood, sweat, and his skin and clothes were burned in several places from Keta's fire orb attacks. His tattered clothes were dirty and torn from over-use and a number of recent battles. He didn't look like an imperial agent.

The general said, "Who are you? If you think that killing your friend will gain you favor in my eyes, you're wrong."

He stood up straighter, and said, "I am Imperial Agent Luigey, and I demand to be unhanded at once!"

General Belvador looked at him closely. "Agent Luigey, is that you? I barely recognize you!"

"Yes, general. I am deep undercover. I've infiltrated the Magi and I've been orchestrating Agent Salamin's actions for months now."

The general made a gesture at his soldiers and they released Konrad. Belvador said, "Salamin didn't mention anything about working with another agent. I got the impression that he'd been working alone."

The agent had been working alone, but it was time for Konrad to bolster his own reputation a bit. Salamin was dead, and it would be a shame for all of his hard work to die without getting someone some glory and coin. He shrugged, "You know how agents are, general. None of us like to share the credit. But I've been leading the mission against the Magi in Khazror since I led the mission against those Magi in Sorgo last year."

The general laughed. "It's a pleasure to work with you, Agent Luigey. It looks like things are just about wrapped up here. My men will be burning the place to the ground, and then we'll make our way to Clornoss to earn our place as heroes to the empire. Let's have a drink!"

Konrad followed the general into his large wagon.

CHAPTER 32

Sarge

In all his life, Sarge had never felt so good. His sleeping had returned to normal as soon as he reached the isles, and things improved quickly after that.

For reasons that he still didn't understand, he was chosen by Kelegar to be the Azure Paladin. During his time with the Kelegarian monks he had been sanctified and reborn in an elaborate ceremony. Most of the details were a blur in his mind, but he would never forget the feeling of rightness, or the revelations that were made known to him, on that day.

He had no idea how long he had been with the monks. It might have been days, but he was pretty sure it was closer to a month. The monks hadn't been exaggerating when they told him that fourteen wives were awaiting him, and that he'd be expected to sire a child with each one. During the ride to the islands he was afraid he would be expected to breed with several unwilling women, but that wasn't the case at all. Each of his new wives was eager to conceive and take their place among the legends of their peoples. The prettiest of his many wives was also the last to conceive, a problem which brought him great joy for many days.

Sarge had no idea how the wives knew they had conceived, as far as he understood about those woman-things it took months to know that for sure. However, the herb-woman of the tribe checked the wives each morning and announced which ones had conceived.

Once his spiritual and reproductive duties had been attended to it became time to return to the empire to serve Kelegar.

He was back in the city of Khardifar, and shortly after arriving he found a tavern where he could enjoy a warm ale and a relaxing game of Goblin Squares. The last time he was here he had been hating life, and had no idea where he was going or what he was supposed to do. Now he was well-rested, felt great, and he had a new sense of purpose in his life.

"Brown wolf rider to H5." He reached out and moved the wolf rider figurine forward to the H5 square. It had been a very long time since he'd been able to enjoy a nice relaxing game of Goblin Squares.

His opponent wasted no time making his move.

"Blue archer to F6." The burly man pushed the blue-headed archer figurine towards Sarge, and then sat back with a smug grin. The man had the look and build of a warrior, but he had suffered some sort of injury to his right arm. The arm was tied to the man's body, and his right hand flopped around flaccidly as the man moved.

The game wasn't going well, and the dice had been against him all night. However, Sarge was never one to take the safe path. He went on the offensive. "Shaman to B3."

Several people had gathered around their table to watch the game, and they all started murmuring and whispering to each other at his bold move. It left his king exposed and vulnerable, but if he survived he'd have a chance to win the game on the next move.

Sarge was wearing armor given to him by the monks. It was plate and chain mail armor, with Kelegar's symbol on the chest. The armor was highly polished, and it had a slight blue tint to it. The helmet, which was resting under his chair, had small wings on the sides and it was open face so his vision wasn't hampered.

As he waited for his opponent to make his move, a blinding light appeared in the seat diagonal to him. Sarge had experienced this several times during his time with the monks. He pushed his chair back and lowered himself to the floor, knees bent under him, hands out before him, and his head lowered far enough to almost touch the floor.

Once again the divine-sire, Kelegar, father of five of the gods in the pantheon of nine, had come to him. Sarge didn't need to look up and see the ancient god to know that he was there. The familiar aura of extreme reverence and adoration filled his soul, and he knew that he was in the presence of a being much greater than himself.

He tried to open his eyes slightly, but the blinding light forced him to keep them shut.

In his mind, he heard the deep bass voice of Kelegar declared, "Paladin, the time for merriment must be put aside for now. Your companion Sarasa Dodisen is badly injured and is in need of healing, she is in the woods near your Grand Diviner's cottage."

Sarge's first instinct was to stand up to rush to the aid of his friend, but he still felt the presence of his deity and he didn't need to open his eyes to detect that the blinding light was still there. If the image of Kelegar was still present, then the god had more to say. Sarge remained in his deep bow awaiting further instructions.

A vision appeared in his mind, the face of a young lady with long blond hair that was pulled back into a pony tail. She had a distinctive looking, little, up-pointed nose and big light-blue eyes. The young lady was crying.

The deep booming voice of Kelegar spoke in Sarge's mind once more. "This is the face of she who will become my first cleric in this epoch. Find her in this city, and take her with you to heal your companion. Hurry, you have not much time."

Just as suddenly as it appeared, the blinding light vanished.

Sarge stood up slowly, and looked around at the gathered crowd. They had moved back and had been shielding their eyes from the blinding light.

Someone said, "What in Khalius was that?"

With that, all of the gathered onlookers began talking at once, and the entire room was filled with voices as everyone talked louder to be heard over the others.

Sarge looked down at the game board on the table and sighed. He would have liked to have completed his game, but now he had more important business to attend to. He pulled a gold cardinal coin from his pouch and set it on the table in front of his opponent. He said, "I'm sorry, Bub, I must be leaving. I concede. Here are your winnings."

The man just stared at him in disbelief and Sarge turned to find the barmaid. He saw her staring at their table like so many other people in the room. He stepped over and handed her a coin for his drinks.

As he took his first step towards the door, he stopped and looked back at his Goblin Squares opponent. He wondered what had happened to the man to cause so much injury to his arm and hand. If he was going to find this girl, and save Sarasa, he was going to need to hurry but he knew that a lame warrior was a man who might end up going hungry or turning to crime.

He walked back over to the man and placed his hands upon the man's right shoulder. He said, "Blessed Kelegar, I ask you to heal this man. Restore his arm and remove his pain. You are the sire of gods and the one true creator of life. If it is your will, grant me this prayer."

The man clinched a fist with his right hand, and then began to move his right arm around in its bindings. He exclaimed, "It's a miracle! My arm is whole again! Praise the gods!" He stood up, ripped the bindings from his arm, and embraced Sarge in a strong hug.

Sarge said, "Praise be to Kelegar, the divine-sire!"

The man worked his arm around in circles and then slammed his right fist down onto the table. He let out a loud shout, and then said, "Thank you, stranger! You have restored my life on this day!"

Sarge grabbed his helm from under the table and placed it on his head. He said, "Not me, Bub. It was Kelegar."

As he walked out of the tavern, the volume of talking escalated quickly as the gathered spectators all began speaking at once. Several people called out to him for healing, and some even walked up to get in his path.

He pushed one man to the side gently, side-stepping him as he continued to walk. He said, "Make way, people! Make way! I've places to go, I can't screw around here all day!"

One more man tried to step into his path, pleading with him to listen. Sarge placed a stiff arm against the man's shoulder, preventing him from stepping into his path. As he walked past the man, Sarge said, "Dammit! Are you dim? Stay out of my sarding way!"

When he was finally outside, Sarge breathed a sigh of relief. Several people came out of the tavern and watched him walk down the street, but to his relief they didn't follow him.

He didn't know where the girl lived, but he trusted the divine-sire to lead him where he needed to be, so he just started walking through the city.

For well over an hour he walked. He wasn't lost, he just hadn't yet found the girl from his vision. However, he didn't doubt the vision. He just needed to continue to look until he found the right place.

Eventually he heard cries for help, coming from a house to his right, and he was certain they came from the girl he needed to find. He hurried forward and rushed through the door. He didn't know what he would find there, he was just certain that he was in the right place.

The first room he entered was empty. He looked into the kitchen area, and that was empty as well.

"Oh gods please, someone help me!" The voice came from upstairs.

He rushed up the stairs and found the girl from his vision sitting next to the bed. On the bed was a motionless woman who was naked from the waist down. Her legs were spread and a lifeless blood-covered baby was on the bed between her legs. The baby was still attached by the cord to her mother.

The girl beside the bed gasped when Sarge walked in. She said, "Help us please! My baby sister is stillborn and I think my mom has lost too much blood. I tried to help deliver the baby, but it's all going wrong! By the gods, help us!"

He moved to the other side of the bed. He said, "Not all the gods, just the divine-sire, Kelegar."

Sarge placed his hands on either side of the woman's head. She was still warm to the touch, and he could feel a faint blood-pulse on her neck. He began to pray, "Blessed Kelegar, I ask you to heal this woman. Restore her strength and mend her body. You are all-knowing and flawless, the sire of gods and the one true creator of life. If it is your will, grant me this prayer!"

The woman opened her eyes and looked around. When she saw her stillborn child she picked it up and started wailing in despair, hugging it to her bosom.

The girl beside the bed grabbed the woman's arm. Her eyes lit up with hope, and she said, "Mother! Are you truly alright? How do you feel?"

The woman ignored the girl and cried as she rocked the baby in her arms.

Sarge walked around to the other side of the bed.

The girl looked to him, "How did you do that? Was it a miracle?"

He nodded. "Would you like to know how to do that?"

She nodded back at him.

Sarge placed one hand on her head gently and said a silent prayer, asking Kelegar to share the light of his wisdom and power with the girl.

After a moment she opened her eyes and gasped. She looked at Sarge and said, "What have you shown me? Could it be real? The ancient divine-sire has not abandoned us?"

"We abandoned him. He is willing to take us back, if we give ourselves over to him."

She didn't respond. Her mother's sobs were loud and disruptive.

Sarge asked, "Would you like to heal the baby?"

The girl nodded slowly, as she grasped the momentous nature of what he was asking her to do. "I don't have the power to do that!"

He shook his head. "No, you don't. Kelegar does. Pray to him as I did. If it is his will, it will be done."

The girl placed her hands on the baby, as she had seen Sarge do to her mother. She said, "Blessed Kelegar, I ask you to heal my baby sister. Please make her heart beat again. You are the sire of gods and the one true creator of life. If it is your will, please grant me this prayer!"

The mother sat breathless, waiting to see what would happen. Suddenly the baby started to scream and wiggle. The mother squealed in delight and the girl reached over and hugged Sarge.

He said, "I didn't do it. That was all you, and Kelegar."

The three of them watched the baby for some time.

Finally the mother said, "I don't even know your name, how can I ever

271

repay you for what you've done?"

Sarge looked at her and said, "I am the Azure Paladin, the servant of Kelegar, and there are two things that I demand in payment."

The woman swept her hand across the room. She said, "Take what you will."

He shook his head. "First, spread the word of Kelegar for all of your remaining days. Tell of his glory to all who will hear."

"Of course! Blessed be Kelegar!"

Then he looked to the girl, "And second, the girl must come with me."

The mother reached out and grabbed the girl's arm. "What? Why? She's not leaving home, I need her!"

Sarge placed his hand on the girl's shoulder. He said, "It is the will of the divine-sire that the girl be made a cleric of his temple. If she is willing, it is her destiny to save countless lives and to spread word of the one true creator of life throughout the known-lands."

"She's but fourteen! She is too young!"

He shrugged, "It is Kelegar's will."

"I'll not have her roaming the countryside on her own at her tender age."

"She won't be alone, she'll be with me."

"That don't make me feel better."

The girl pulled away from her mother, and looked up at Sarge. She said, "I'll go get some things."

Her mother said, "Madalyn Morissa Chardwil! You think to defy your own mother about this?"

Madalyn placed her hand on her mother's hand, and then leaned over and kissed her on the cheek. "The healing powers of Kelegar saved you, and the baby. Would you really have me defy his wishes?"

The mother looked like she would object once again.

Madalyn leaned over and kissed her on the cheek again. She said, "It will be alright. Let me help you with the cord and we'll get the baby cleaned, and then I must go."

Sarge nodded to the girl, and then moved to the door.

She said, "When I am done here I will meet you outside."

Before too long she came from the house. She was wearing plain brown dress that extended to her ankles. A floppy blue hat rested on her head. She was small, barely as tall as his shoulders, and on her small shoulders she carried a backpack.

As she walked up to him, Sarge started to wonder if he was making a mistake. When he saw her in his vision he had no idea how young she was, he was simply thinking about finding the girl who would become the first Kelegarian cleric. Now that he saw her in person, he feared that she might yet be too young. War was fast approaching, and the battlefield was no place for a young lady.

She said, "Where to?"

He pursed his lips. He had to have faith that the divine-sire had a plan. He had been given a vision of the girl, and now the girl was by his side. The next part of the divine-sire's message was less pleasant. Sarasa was at Randol's home and she needed his help. He said, "We're headed to the house of my friend, far away near a city called Sorgo."

"How long will it take to get there?"

"Not as long as you'd think, because we'll be taking..." He stopped in mid-sentence. If the girl didn't have a magewel, she wouldn't be able to travel by portal stones. That would make life much more complicated. He grabbed her by the upper arm and pulled her close to him.

She winced in pain, and he regretted being rougher than he needed to be. She didn't resist and she didn't pull away from him.

He looked into her eyes and opened his magesight. At first he did not see any magewel and he started to get nervous. After a bit of looking, he discovered that it was really small but it was there.

He breathed a sigh of relief, released her arm, and continued walking.

She hurried to keep up.

He said, "Not far, we're going to take a magical portal."

She gave him a skeptical look, but she didn't respond.

They walked through the city without talking. Once they passed through the city gates, she said, "I've never been outside of the city before."

He was shocked. He'd been traveling the lands of the Free Cities since he was much younger than her, and he couldn't imagine staying in the same place for very long.

"Stick with me, kid, and you'll see much more of the known-world than you really care to see."

They walked in silence after that, and he let his thoughts wander. He was starting to get a bad feeling in the pit of his stomach about what they'd find when they got to Randol's. He picked up the pace until the girl was practically running to keep up.

When they reached the spot of the portal stone, the girl squealed in excitement as he summoned the magic and caused the obelisk to rise from the ground. He quickly explained to her how to use what little magic she possessed, and how the portal stones worked.

After several minutes the girl indicated that she was ready to try. They both placed their hands on the stone, and activated it.

The scenery changed instantly, and when he looked to Madalyn he saw that she was about to fall down even while holding onto the stone. He reached over and grabbed her by the waist. He held her up and she leaned against him.

Madalyn gasped, and then dropped to her knees and started vomiting.

He looked around and figured that it probably wasn't the teleporting that caused the girl to begin retching. He steadied himself against the portal stone as he looked out towards Randol's house.

There were several bodies on the ground between them and the remains of the house. Within a few feet of them were the badly damaged remains of four brown and white cloaked Magi.

Randol's house had been burned completely to the ground, and it was still smoldering and smoking terribly. He had felt a sense of foreboding about this for some time, but he didn't expect it to affect him so much.

He reached out his hand towards the girl, without looking at her.

She took his hand, and said, "I'm sorry. I'll try to be stronger."

He squeezed her little hand, "Don't worry about it kid, it's no easier for old people. Puke if you need to puke, just don't get it on me."

They were walking through the scene of a massive battle. He estimated at least a hundred dead imperial soldiers, scattered across the battlefield outside of the still-smoldering remains of Randol's house. He also noticed the twisted and broken remains of several large wolves. Intermixed with the other bodies were a few dead Magi as well.

He assumed most of the Magi who died were inside of Randol's house. The extensive basement complex probably held the remains of scores of additional imperial soldier corpses as well.

As they got closer to the charred remains of the house, Madalyn asked, "Is everyone dead?"

"No, my friend is here and she is hurt."

"How do you know?"

"Kelegar told me."

They walked quietly for a few steps and then she asked, "Did he show you all of this death? The burned down home?"

He shook his head, "Nope. We need to hurry."

They both started jogging past the burnt down home and towards the woods beyond it. As they neared the trees, a young girl walked out of the woodlands.

Sarge didn't know her.

Madalyn took a step back and gave the girl a dirty look, but didn't say anything. Sarge was surprised to see the young cleric react negatively to a little girl that they'd just met.

The little girl said, "It's about time you got here! Sarasa is dying, hurry up!"

They followed the girl deeper into the woods, and finally they found Sarasa resting on a large fallen log. She opened her eyes slightly and then closed them again.

Sarge put his hand on Madalyn's back and urged her forward. He said, "Time to save a life, young cleric."

The girl walked over to Sarasa and gently placed her hands on either side of her face. She said, "Blessed Kelegar, I ask you to heal this woman. Heal her wounds and repair her broken body. You are the sire of gods and the one true creator of life. If it is your will, please grant me this prayer!"

Sarasa opened her eyes. She moved her hand and then her whole arm. She sat up and looked down at her hands as she opened and closed them.

Suddenly she jumped from the log and stretched her arms wide. She exclaimed, "By all the gods! I am healed? How is this possible?"

Madalyn said, "Not all the gods, just Kelegar the divine-sire."

Sarge grinned widely, and mussed Madalyn's hair. "You learn quickly, kid. You're going to do just fine."

Sarasa hugged the girl tightly. Then she looked at Sarge and gave a tiny smiled. She said, "Sarge, you are a gift from the gods. How can I be completely healed, it must be some kind of miracle?"

He motioned towards Madalyn, "This is Madalyn, she is to become the first Kelegarian cleric. The divine-sire grants the power of true healing to his followers."

Sarasa hugged the girl once again. She said, "I can't thank you enough."

Madalyn smiled and stepped back.

Sarasa looked back at Sarge, and asked, "What's with the blue armor?"

He gave her a long hug. Then he said, "I'm a paladin of Kelegar. It's a long story. What happened here?"

"It's a long story, one that I won't forget, and one that the emperor is going to pay for." She paused for a moment and then added, "Let's see if anyone here is still alive. Then we need to find Rissyl and the others. Last I heard, he was leading an assault on the Stronghold, and I have no idea how that turned out."

Sarge followed, and the others fell in behind him. He said, "It doesn't look very likely that anyone else survived. We'll check quickly and then we should get to the Stronghold and see if they need our help. Can the girl use the stones?"

Sarasa said, "Her name is Ayris. She is going to be a powerful Magi someday." She walked quietly for several steps, and then she added, "She's already a powerful Magi, she saved my life today."

CHAPTER 33

Rissyl

He couldn't believe that it had already been two days since the battle for the Stronghold. Rissyl had been busy getting things organized, recovering bodies, securing supplies, and just trying to regain some semblance of normalcy. In the middle of all of the things that needed accomplished, they needed to take a moment to lay to rest their fallen friends.

Rissyl hadn't been looking forward to it, but it was needed.

He said, "We are gathered to pay respects, and say our final goodbyes, to the fellow Magi who lost their lives in the battle for this Stronghold and in the imperial attack on the home of the Exalted Grand Diviner of the Grand Coterie of Sovereign Magi of Menelia."

Rissyl paused and looked to Sarge, motioning for him to rise. He continued, "Champion Sarge, the Azure Paladin of Kelegar, please lead us in prayer."

He sat down and watched Sarge walk up to the podium. His young cleric companion, Madalyn, walked beside him and stood to his left. Sarge had requested a chance to lead a prayer at the memorial service, and Rissyl felt obligated to let him. The middle-aged Magi walked with a new confidence and purpose. Rissyl hadn't had a chance to talk to him about what happened while he was away, but whatever it was had brought a significant transformation.

They were gathered in a huge meeting hall, similar to the one in Randol's house but this one was much bigger. The floor was made of marble and the walls were adorned with banners representing the Sovereign Magi Society and each of the four orders of the society.

When they first found the hall it had been ransacked, like most of the other places within the Stronghold. However, the majority of furniture and adornments of the room were salvageable, albeit damaged to one degree or another. They had straightened the room quickly and it had become the regular gathering place.

All of the remaining Magi of the society fit within the huge room and left the vast majority of the seats unused. Rissyl thought that was a fitting reminder of how much work still stood before them.

Sarge cleared his throat and said, "Everyone please rise and bring both fists to your heart for the proper attitude of prayer." He and Madalyn both assumed that posture.

Rissyl stood and looked around as the others slowly stood up as well. Like most people that he knew, Rissyl had never been a very religious man. In his family, like in most families, prayer was something done in the temples or in times of great distress and he had never seen it done like this. He was, however, open to anything that would help them in their cause against the empire. If that meant praying to a deity whom everyone thought was long dead, so be it.

"Wise and omniscient Kelegar, divine-sire and the one true creator of life, we humbly call upon you. Great and powerful Nalria, divine-daughter and goddess of magic, hear our prayer. Lift up our fallen, bless them and accept them into your realm of eternal rest and peace. Grant serenity and tranquility to the Magi gathered here. Our fight is just beginning, as you well know, great and wise ones. We ask for strength, power, and tenacity to face the trials before us. We ask you both to move the hearts of those people throughout the known-lands whom you've blessed with the gift of magic, and call them to seek us out that the numbers of our Magi might swell to better enable us to meet the challenges that face us! You've warned us of dark days ahead. Those dark days are upon us! Grant us this prayer as we prepare for the trials before us. In the names of Kelegar the divine-sire and Nalria the divine-daughter we pray. Amen."

Led by Madalyn, many of the gathered Magi replied with, "Amen."

Over the next hour, several Magi stood up one after the other to talk about the fallen members of their society. Rissyl was so caught-up in his own thoughts that he didn't even listen to the heart-felt words. A year ago the task before them seemed impossible. He'd hoped that after a year of struggles and sacrifice that he'd feel like they had made progress, but if anything they were worse off than before. They had finally captured the Stronghold, and that was a major accomplishment, but at what price?

In the past three days they'd seen roughly half of all Magi killed. Almost two dozen Magi were killed in the ambush at Randol's, including Randol and Keta. Granted, many of those were elderly Magi from the lands of the Free Cities, but they were Magi none-the-less and it was a staggering loss.

The necromancers had clearly gained powerful new spells during their time within the walls of the Stronghold, and there was no telling what awful surprises still awaited them from that ruthless enemy.

The troubling reports of citizens being pulled from their homes and accused of magic use were a sign that the emperor was getting more desperate to wipe out the Magi. Rissyl feared that these attacks on the people would escalate quickly.

If all of that wasn't enough, he still had no idea what the Rolimi decided. As far as he knew the race of magical creatures could show up at any moment to bring war and destroy any hope the Magi had of stopping the awful events that were unfolding throughout the known-lands.

He thought back to the prayer that Sarge gave. If a group of people ever needed divine assistance, this was it.

Cynia squeezed his hand, and he gave her a little smile. She looked almost as stressed as he felt. Asleep on her lap was their son, Chardy. After the attack on Randol's, they decided not to risk another ambush and Rissyl brought him to the Stronghold.

Next to them, Dalen sat with his arm around Firana.

On the other side of Rissyl and Cynia was Sarasa. Next to her on one side was Ayris, who had her head rested against Sarasa shoulder. On the other side of her was Brandam, who sat holding one of her hands in both of his.

Cynia elbowed him and he realized that the last speaker was finished and they were waiting for him to speak.

He stood up and looked around the room. Out before him were all of the Magi of the society. Each one wore the same look of nervousness and determination that Rissyl assumed was impressed on his face. The events of the past few days were a sobering blow to all of the Magi, and he worried that darker days were still ahead.

He said, "A few days ago, imperial troops descended on a single home near the woods south of Sorgo. Nearly one thousand trained warriors slaughtered two dozen Magi, mainly our elderly and severely wounded. They will be avenged!"

A cheer sounded throughout the hall, and before long all of the gathered Magi were on their feet shouting and waving their fists in the air.

He let them vocalize their frustrations for a while and then he held up his hands for silence. The Magi before him quieted, but did not sit down. He continued, "At long last, the Stronghold is ours!"

Once again the gathered Magi burst out in cheers.

He held his hands for silence once again. "From this day forward, the Stronghold will be known as Fort Randol, to honor our fallen friend and mentor."

The shouting, cheers, and raucous applause let him know that his impromptu idea to name the Stronghold after his murdered friend was a popular idea.

When the cheering finally subsided he said, "Our next mission is to scour the Stronghold for every spell, artifact, and weapon that we can use to our advantage! Additionally, we'll be travelling to all of the cities throughout the known-lands to rebuilding our numbers. May the gods grant our Azure Paladin's request and move the hearts of hundreds of gifted to come with us to Fort Randol and join us in our fight! The challenges before us are great, but together we will overcome!"

EPILOGUE

Kimly

As she entered Favin's office, she was disappointed to see that he wasn't alone. Kimly had been out of town for several months and she was excited to tell him about the progress she'd made in expanding the Shrouded in Libur and Tharrin.

Favin stood as she entered the room.

The two people sitting in front of his desk stood and faced her as well.

Skoots looked surprised. "By all the sarding gods, where have you been?"

"I've been traveling, what's new?"

"Come on over and we'll fill you in. Viper, grab her a chair?" Favin sat back down.

The little man hurried over to the side of the room, grabbed a crate, and pushed it near Favin's desk for her.

She nimbly climbed onto the crate, pulled both knees up to her chest, hugged her legs, and rested her chin on her knees waiting for Favin to begin talking.

"As the guild has grown more generous in our 'donations' to the chancellor, he has become increasingly supportive of us. Of course he doesn't openly support our guild, but I do have the opportunity to dine with him frequently. He has been vocal with me about his frustrations with the emperor and the increasing persecution of Khardifar citizens in the imperial hunt for Magi. I'm sure he would never openly defy the emperor and risk open rebellion, but he wants to send a message to Clornoss."

Favin took a long drink from his tankard, and then continued, "The chancellor arranged for a 'scheduling snafu' with the sentinels guarding the sleeping quarters of an imperial agent and several officers of the imperial army who were in Khardifar to hunt Magi. This little window gave Viper a chance to sneak in and capture one of the imperial officers in his sleep."

Kimly let her feet drop to the floor. She placed both hands on the crate and leaned forward, her mouth agape. She couldn't believe what she'd just heard. When she set these things in motion she just wanted to have some fun, and maybe make a few more coins. She certainly hadn't planned to abduct imperial army officers. After a long pause, she said softly, "You've abducted an officer in the imperial army?"

"Yes, but with the chancellor's support and blessings. Sort of. Well, not in a way where he'd ever admit it of course, but I know he wanted us to!"

She scooted forward, letting her feet dangle over the edge, so that only her butt was on the crate. She sat up straight, crossed her arms at her chest, and gave him the most annoyed expression she could muster. "You've abducted a sarding imperial army officer?" Kimly felt like her head might explode. She rubbed her temples with both hands, trying to keep her head from exploding, and giving herself a moment to think. A thousand thoughts raced through her head, and most of them ended with her hanging from the gallows. She let her hands fall down to her knees, and said, "You've got to kill him, you realize that right? If you release him, he'll lead the entire sarding army to your door and we'll all hang, or worse."

Favin gave her a mischievous grin and said, "I haven't told you the most interesting part yet."

She closed her eyes and groaned. Without opening her eyes she beckoned with one hand for him to keep talking.

"We've had the officer locked in a supply room at the bottom of the compound for almost a fortnight. Viper has been..." He let the sentence pause for a moment, and then continued, "...'encouraging' the officer to give us information about the Magi hunting and what the imperials are doing. The other day the man made an intriguing statement. He claims that the imperials have a Magi defector who has given them detailed information on how to reach some Magi hideout called the Stronghold. The officer claims that at least four regiments are being mobilized to march to this place and crush the Magi once and for all."

Kimly steadied herself with one hand on either side of the crate. This was catastrophic news for her former companions. She had left the Magi because she had no desire to live under their rules, and to avoid being hunted by the emperor, but she didn't want to see those people slaughtered by the imperial army. The Magi had rescued her from Jalinox, and some of them had even treated her like a friend. She couldn't imagine any Magi turning against the others and assisting an emperor who obviously wants all magic users dead. She looked at Favin, and asked, "Did he say the name of the Magi defector?"

Favin looked to Viper.

The man thought for a moment, and replied, "Beldin? Something like that."

Favin shrugged, "It's not someone I've ever heard of."

"Me either." Kimly was certain she'd never met a Magi named Beldin, so she was relieved that at least the traitor wasn't someone she knew.

After another long drink from his tankard, Favin said, "I think the Magi would pay a fortune for this information. They might even want the captured imperial officer so they can 'interview' him themselves? We could really profit from this, and we might gain a strong ally. Do your superiors in the Shrouded know how to contact someone important within the Magi Society? Could the Shrouded help us broker a deal with the Magi?"

She nodded slowly. The last thing she wanted was to openly oppose the emperor and get involved with the Magi once again, but she knew that she couldn't sit on information like this and let the imperial army take her former companions by surprise. She said, "Let me talk to my people, and I'll get back to you."

Kimly hopped down from her crate and walked towards the door. She had to decide how she wanted to contact the Magi. Next she needed to come up with some creative way to explain how she came across this information without revealing the existence of the Shrouded and her involvement with them.

It would be best if they didn't know that she was involved at all. She was certain that they wouldn't approve of her teaching some magic to people.

As she thought about it, she remembered that perhaps she had taken an oath promising not to teach magic to people outside of the Magi Society.

She sighed to herself. Just as things were getting fun, they were about to get complicated and annoying once again.

The End.

Society Inciting
The Sovereign Magi Society trilogy – Book 3

Having secured the Magi Stronghold, a small group of dedicated but still relatively inexperienced magic users have achieved their first major goal. With the capture of the legendary fortress comes the promise of powerful new magical weapons, artifacts, spellbooks, and much more.

However, the struggle to rebuild the Sovereign Magi Society is far from over. The emperor's agents have been hard at work, and the Magi are about to discover that betrayal from within is as much of a threat now as it was a century ago when it led to the downfall of the original Magi Society.

Even the threat of the entire imperial army storming the gates of the Stronghold pales in comparison to the ever-growing threat posed by the necromancers. The potent new rituals and curses gained during the necromancers' brief control of the Stronghold could very well sway the balance of power firmly in favor of the evil clerics led by the ruthless Lord Jalinox.

The people poised to suffer the most are the innocent folks throughout the lands who are viewed as pawns to be used and exploited by two sides of a three sided war.